DEAD PEOPLE

DEAD PEOPLE

Ewart Hutton

WINDSOR
PARAGON

First published 2013
by Blue Door
This Large Print edition published 2013
by AudioGO Ltd
by arrangement with
HarperCollinsPublishers Ltd

Hardcover   ISBN: 978 1 4713 5785 5
Softcover   ISBN: 978 1 4713 5786 2

British Library Cataloguing in Publication Data available

Printed and bound in Great Britain by TJ International Limited

For Jean and the two Georges,
who left too early

Boy had my life turned glamorous since my ejection from Cardiff. Not too many cops get to start off their day trying to chase down a character who is castrating ram lambs, and end it in the company of a mutilated corpse. At that precise moment, however, I was still at the crappy midpoint of that day. And lost.

It didn't help that I knew exactly where I was lost. Pinpoint stuff. The satnav was telling me that I was deep smack bang in the middle of a conifer forest in Mid Wales. I could almost smell the resin coming off the satnav screen. The problem was that I was on a logging trail that didn't exist. It didn't surprise me. I had had enough experience of forestry tracks by now to know that they were a constantly shape-shifting and mutating phenomenon.

'Sergeant, someone's nicked a bulldozer.'

I had taken the call in a moment of reckless altruism. Helping out my local colleagues. And, admittedly, to take a break from my sheep-molesting case, which was going nowhere, and giving me the blues. A Forestry Commission operative had called in to report that they had had some plant stolen. Chainsaws, I figured, protective clothing, brush-cutters, a generator at most.

I hadn't thought big enough.

I met the guy in a large clearing where the logging tracks forked off and wound up the hill. We were both working on a Sunday, although he looked less happy about it than I was. It was voluntary on my part. I had found even the routine drudgery of updating my investigation reports preferable to the stretched-out grey static numbness that constituted the Sabbath in these parts. The prospect of chasing down a lost bulldozer had seemed positively radiant for a while.

From where we stood, I could see that rain and trucks had turned the surface into a superfine slurry of light-grey mud. Stripped branches from fir trees were strewn along the side of the tracks, as if a religious procession had suddenly taken fright and bolted off, leaving their devotional foliage behind.

'Is this where it was taken from?' I asked, making a professional show of casing the surroundings.

'No, it was further up. On a spur. We were using it to clear a new trail.'

'When did you last see it?'

'Friday.'

No one had reported a bulldozer ripping up the streets of any of the neighbouring villages. 'Are you sure it isn't still up there?' I asked.

He gave me a hurt look.

'Okay,' I relented, 'I'll go up and check it out.'

He gave me directions. 'Don't you want a description?' he shouted after me as I headed for my car.

I didn't need one. I knew it would be yellow and big, with shiny stainless-steel hydraulic shafts, and that it would smell of diesel and rust and that grim, grey, heavy clay that had never been meant to be turned over into the light of day. I also knew, in my heart of hearts, as I started my engine, that I would get lost. I always did in these places. It was the same, I reckoned, with the bulldozer. It hadn't been stolen. It had just got lost. It had succumbed to the weirdness that were forestry tracks.

I got out of the car now. The drizzle was as fine as a mist. The silence was total. No birds. I looked out into the thick, dark, matted mass of Sitka Spruce, or whatever the fuck kind of trees they were. The perspectives were tight and mesmeric. Strange and creepy. I wasn't cut out for this. Lost in Pig Wales. A real country policeman wouldn't get lost. He would find missing bulldozers, deliver lambs, and have his own pet collie. Me, I still needed buildings and corners, streetlights, signs that announced where I was.

I kicked a stone out over the edge of the track and incanted a curse on DCS Jack Galbraith. It worked to break the spell. I heard the sound of an engine approaching.

It was the Forestry Commission guy in his crew-cab pickup. 'Where the hell did you get to?' he shouted, leaning out of his window. 'I've been waiting for you for half an hour.'

'I must have missed the turning,' I confessed.

'Your people have been trying to get in touch with you.'

He let me try his radio. But the weirdness had got to it too. An earful of feedback and static.

'It could be important. I'm going to have to go down the hill to call in,' I told him, climbing back into my car.

'What about my bulldozer?' he shouted after me.

'I'll be back,' I lied. It was time to cut altruism adrift.

Perhaps, I prayed as I drove, they were calling in to say that they had nailed my man. So that I could forget about him and the veterinary equivalent of pincer pliers that he was using to crimp the *vasa*

3

deferentia of Badger Face Welsh Mountain tup lambs. The bastard was selective. Just that one breed, no others. And he could get close to them. He obviously knew his way around sheep, and how to handle them. I was supposed to be the good guy and they ran away from me.

I pulled off the road as soon as the signal bars on my mobile phone showed a flicker of life. I looked at the skyline. Clouds thickening and greying-up in the south-west. I never used to do this in the city. There, weather was something that trailed on in, after the television news. Out here, I had discovered that it was useful to know what degree of wetness to expect.

I called in: 'DS Glyn Capaldi. Someone's been trying to reach me.'

'Sergeant Capaldi . . .' the dispatcher gasped. But it wasn't hero-worship, as I was soon to learn. It was excitement. She was making her first real dead-corpse transmission. 'Detective Chief Inspector Jones wanted us to get a message through to you.' She took in a deep, savouring breath. 'There's a possibility that human remains have been discovered. He would like you to get to the site as soon as possible, and he will call you there. I'll inform him that you are on your way now, shall I, sir?'

'Whoa, whoa, whoa,' I said, trying to rein her in before she cut me off in her eagerness to get back to Bryn Jones. 'You'd better tell me where I'm supposed to be going.'

'Sorry, sir. It's Cwm Cesty Nant—'

'Sweetheart,' I cut in over her big moment, as gently as I could, 'could you just give me the coordinates, my satnav system doesn't speak Welsh

4

yet.'

*   *   *

It was the construction site for a wind farm. Not that far from Dinas. I turned off the main road into a small, level-bottomed valley, with the ubiquitous tufts of forestry plantation on the surrounding hills looking like a fungal disease. The river was shallow and wide, and looked grander than it was. The fields were peppered with moraine boulders, and the occasional sprawl of waste from old lead workings.

The track ran up a narrow cwm that curved round on itself, cutting off my view of the valley. It was of recent construction, crushed stone, professionally laid and rolled, with proper culverts and drainage. Around another bend the cwm widened and levelled out onto a small, marshy plateau below the main ridge. I had arrived at the construction site. Temporary buildings on jacks, parked cars, a couple of crew-carrier pickups with the company logo, and diggers, rollers and earthmovers standing idle. For a whimsical moment, I wondered whether my lost bulldozer could have run away from home to take up with this circus.

I drove up slowly, aiming for the knot of people and the marked police car parked above the site huts. I assessed as I got closer. Earth and stone pushed into low mounds from where they were excavating for roadways and turbine bases. Piles of fresh stone and drainage pipes waiting to go down. A lot of mud and a lot of dirty water, standing and running.

5

The two uniform cops were talking to a couple of civilians beside the roughly rectangular outline of one of the base excavations. One of the civilians, I noted, trying not to be surprised, was unmistakeably female. The remainder of the onlookers, all site workers by the look of them, were congregated on my side of the police car.

The big uniform with the bolt-on Stalin moustache, Emrys Hughes, was the local sergeant, an old-school up-country cop, who resented what he had taken to be my intrusion onto his parish. The fact that I had never had any choice in the matter hadn't cut any ice. I recognized his sidekick, a young constable, but couldn't put a name on him.

Emrys turned away from the two civilians and made a show of watching my approach. Not quite tapping his feet, but definitely playing a man whose patience was being stretched. He bent his head and whispered something to his partner. Both then made a point of staring at me and grinning.

They shouldn't have. Now I was going to have to overcompensate.

I got out of the car and looked slowly around, not focusing on anything. Letting the message sink in that I was not coming to Emrys. He shrugged wearily for the sake of his audience, and sauntered over with his sidekick. 'You took your time.'

I ignored the barb. 'Why haven't you taped the site off?'

He pulled a quizzical face and half spun around, as if to make sure that I was really addressing him. He spread his hands expansively. 'Where does the site end and the mud pile begin? You tell me.'

He had a point. The excavators had been hard at work; the entire area was a mess of churned soil and broken stone.

But this was political now. 'You . . .?' I pointed at his sidekick.

It took him a moment to realize it was a question. 'Constable Friel, Sarge,' he answered, looking at Hughes for support, some of the humour draining.

'Go and get the incident tape.' I turned to Emrys. 'And you, Sergeant Hughes, are going to show me what we've got here.'

He stared me out for a moment. Technically, we ranked equal, but we both knew that I was the one who had been called in to do the thinking. He shrugged and led off towards the civilian couple. I approached them with my warrant card held out. 'Detective Sergeant Capaldi,' I introduced myself. The man took a pace forward. I held up my hand to stop him speaking. 'Sorry, sir, I just need a moment on this.'

I wanted to read it myself. Before anyone else's viewpoint and opinions impinged. It took me a couple of beats to focus on it, create an outline, trying to distinguish it from its surroundings. The bones were a nasty grey-green colour, the chest cavity full of earth, gravel and root filaments, the unexcavated legs still under their cover of damp soil and course grass.

For a moment it looked more like the thorax of a giant crayfish than anything human. Then I realized why. The head was missing. No skull. That's what had thrown me. I knelt down to get closer. No trace of the smell of putrefaction, but I hadn't expected it, skeletonization was too far advanced. The body was slightly twisted, the arm that was uncovered was minus a hand. I scanned around carefully.

To the side was a pile of material the digger had excavated. The skull and the missing hand had probably been scooped-up with that. I took some close-up photographs with my digital camera.

I stood up and smiled at the man now, nodding, giving him his cue.

'I'm Jeff Talbot. I'm the site engineer.' He had a South Wales accent, and looked vaguely familiar. He was medium height, skinny, with an angular face and a worried expression that was accentuated by the high forehead and receding hairline. He was wearing a dark-blue quilted jacket, and, like the rest of the site crew, a yellow high-visibility tabard over it.

I stole a glance at the woman. She was prettier than I had first thought, and smiled when my eyes caught hers. She was also tall, but carried herself slightly stooped, as if to avoid drawing attention. I registered blonde hair, full cheeks, and that she was built in such a way that the duffel coat couldn't quite hide the curves. She didn't look at all shaken or disturbed to be standing beside a headless corpse.

'Has anyone touched it?' I asked him.

He shook his head gravely. 'Only to brush the surface debris off. To confirm what it was. Then we stopped everything and called you people.'

'Can I speak to the digger driver?'

'That was me. I was excavating this base.' He reacted to my surprise. 'We're short-handed, we were working on a Sunday to try to keep up to schedule.' He looked sheepish. I expect he was breaking some sort of local by-law or clause in the planning permission. I decided not to arrest him.

'Did you see the skull?'

8

'No. But I might have picked that up in the cut before.' He nodded at the pile of excavated material. 'It could be in there. We didn't think we should touch anything.'

I nodded my appreciation. 'It was the right decision. And you did well not to do any more damage.'

'It was luck. The light was right for me, I just managed to see it before I crushed it.'

I looked around carefully, but it was useless, the entire periphery resembled an opencast mine. 'Tell me something. I know it's difficult, but I want you to think back to just before you uncovered this section. Was there anything on the surface? Mounding? A depression? Any kind of marker?'

He thought hard, his face tight with concentration. When he eventually shook his head it was like a small spring being released. 'No. I'm sorry. If there was anything out of the ordinary, I didn't notice it,' he said apologetically.

'You said you stopped when you realized what it was.'

'That's right.'

I looked down at the remains again. I was still getting a huge insect's carapace. 'It's hard to tell.'

He looked puzzled. Wondering what I was getting at.

'That it's human,' I clarified.

'I just saw bones at first. I wasn't sure whether they were animal or human, but I knew they would have to be checked out. Tessa confirmed that they were human.'

I looked at the woman. She smiled, amused at my expression of surprise.

'Oh, I'm sorry,' Jeff said, flustered, 'I should

9

have introduced you. This is Dr MacLean.'

'Doctor.' I nodded at her, trying to pull back my composure.

She grinned. 'Don't get too excited, Sergeant. I'm not a medical doctor. I won't be able to help you out on any forensic technicalities.' She was Scottish, a touch of east-coast inflexion in the accent.

'Dr MacLean's an archaeologist,' Jeff explained, 'she's working on a dig farther up on the ridge of the hill. I asked her to come down. In case this was in any way connected to what she's working on.'

'We've discovered a medieval grave site,' she elaborated. 'Jeff wondered whether this body could have anything to do with ours.'

'Does it?' I asked. 'Can you tell whether this is medieval?'

She hunkered down close to the remains. I dropped down beside her, our splayed-out knees almost touching. She took out a pen and used it as a pointer. 'Can you see that?' she asked, directing my eyes down to a point close to the elbow of the one uncovered arm.

I caught it. A scrap of something with a dirty-brown sheen to it, damp, a surface-texture like kelp. 'What is it?'

She turned her face to mine. 'Whatever variation on polyethylene sheet it turns out to be, Sergeant, I don't think they were making it six hundred years ago.'

'Could it have got here independently?'

'I'm not the detective, but the material does appear to be under the remains.' She smiled again, sympathetically, I thought, but before I could confirm it, she stood up. I joined her and heard

10

Emrys Hughes smother a snort of laughter. He wouldn't have known polyethylene if it turned up on his breakfast plate, but he obviously thought that I had just had my nose caught in a hinge.

'So the plastic could have been used as a wrapping?' I asked.

She shrugged. It wasn't her business. It didn't matter. I was airing the questions for my own benefit. 'Or as a carrier? Something to stop the fluids leaking?' I turned to Jeff. 'What was here before you started your operation?'

'Nothing. Just open hill.'

'No track?'

'A pretty rudimentary one.' He pointed out a track that was little more than twin wheel ruts that ran up to the shoulder of the hill. 'That's a continuation of it. It goes up to Tessa's . . . Dr MacLean's dig.'

'So you could have got a vehicle up here?'

'It would have to have been a four-wheel drive.'

The wind gusted. I felt it cold in my face. 'It's going to rain. Have you got a tarpaulin we can use to cover the body and the excavated material?'

'Sure. Are we going to be able to carry on and work round you while you do what you have to do?'

So that's why he was looking so worried. 'Not immediately, I'm afraid,' I said sympathetically, 'and then it's going to depend on what we find before we can release the site back to you.'

'Jeff . . .'

We all looked round at the man at the open door of one of the site huts who had just shouted. 'There's a call come in for the cops.'

I looked at Jeff quizzically. 'There's no cellular reception up here,' he explained, 'we had to put our

11

own landline in.'

'Jeff . . .' Tessa put a hand on his arm. 'I'm going to go back up the hill now. I'll catch you soon.'

'I'll come over.' He smiled wryly. 'It looks like I'm going to have time on my hands.'

She bobbed her head at me. ''Bye, Sergeant.'

'Goodbye, doctor,' I replied, feeling the formal distance. I felt an irrational twinge of loneliness and wished that I was playing in the same movie as she and Jeff.

*   *   *

They left me to take the call in a partitioned-off area of the hut, with topographical-survey plans on the walls. The long table was home to a cluster of tannin-lined mugs and a bottle of tomato ketchup with a crust around the top like a botched circumcision. On the wall above it, an ironical placement if there ever was one, a calendar promoting drill bits featured a heavy-breasted, naked woman with rosy nipples and a blue hard hat.

DCI Bryn Jones's steady deep voice came down the line. 'Glyn, can you tell us what you've got there?'

I described it, sticking purely to the observational facts. The line emitted soft static. He had put his hand over the receiver. I knew exactly who he was relaying my information to.

'Glyn, take an educated guess,' he said, coming back to me. 'How historic is this?'

'It's gone to full skeleton,' I said, and started laying out my reasoning path for his benefit. 'The ground is pretty compacted, and looks like it

12

hadn't been disturbed for a long time before the excavators arrived. No sign of any clothing, so it's either been in the ground for long enough for it to have decomposed, or it was buried naked. There's what looks like plastic sheeting present, so I would say that we're not talking ancient, but not too recent either.'

'So it's unlikely that, as we speak, we'll have the villain's footprints scorching the mountain dust as he makes his escape?'

'Highly unlikely, sir.' I smiled; that wasn't Bryn Jones-speak, it had to be a Jack Galbraith line that he had just recited.

'And the clues are not withering on the vine?'

'This particular vine resembles an opencast mine, sir.'

'Not exactly a productive evidence farm then?'

'No, sir.' I knew where he was trying to lead me, but that was going to have to be their decision.

'Capaldi . . .' DCS Jack Galbraith's heavy Scottish brogue boomed in. 'We've got a SOCO team, the forensic pathologist and the forensic anthropologist all lined up. And I want to keep them as a happy and productive bunch. So is anything going to be served by them having to work under arc lights through a shitty night at the arse end of the known universe?'

'I don't know, sir.'

'I do not have a young, ripe, virgin girl in a communion dress in that hole?'

'No, sir.'

'I do not have a vast array of female relatives rending their garments and keening over the body?'

'No, sir.'

'So, Capaldi?'

'I don't think I should make that decision, sir.' I braced myself.

'It's your fucking corpse, Capaldi, you're the finder. You're supposed to be a professional, you make the call.'

'I would think it could all wait until the morning, sir.'

'Wise move, son.' He chuckled, but even that managed to contain a threat in it.

Wise move indeed. I had just saved them from a night of rain and bleak wide-open spaces. I just hoped it would be remembered and appreciated. But, knowing Jack Galbraith, I doubted it.

*   *   *

By the time I came out of the hut, we were losing light, and the rain was sweeping in. Some strange vortex effect in the cwm bringing it up the hill at us. But Jeff's men had managed to rig a tarpaulin over the crucial areas, the half-exposed skeleton and the mound of excavated material, and Hughes and Friel had taped off the rectangle I had prescribed for them.

Vehicles were leaving, a procession heading down the access road. Jeff had obviously released his men. Mine were attempting their own escape, Emrys keeping his head down to avoid eye contact as he got into the passenger's side of the patrol car. Which had been turned around and was now facing downhill, I noticed.

'*Sergeant!*' I yelled.

He froze in his crouch, half inside the car. He wanted to ignore me, but a conditioned reflex had kicked in at my shout.

14

'Where do you think you're going?' I asked, approaching, as he unravelled himself. Inside the car, I could see Friel in the driver's seat, craning past him to watch me.

'We're going back down to take up our normal duties,' Emrys stated challengingly.

'You're supposed to assist me here until I release you.'

His eyes narrowed meanly as he tried to remember when that one had popped up on the order book. 'I thought your people were taking over.'

'They are, but the SOCO team aren't starting the investigation until tomorrow. Which means that we need to secure the site.'

'It is secure. We've taped it off, the workmen have covered it.'

'I need a watch kept.'

He looked at me disgustedly, realizing now where this thing was going. 'Isn't that your responsibility?'

I smiled at him. 'That's right, and that's why I'm delegating it to you. I have other things to do to get this investigation started.'

He almost shook his head in defiance. Instead, he thought better of it and smiled slyly. 'Sorry, no can do.' He tapped on the roof of the car. 'We've just taken an urgent call requesting assistance. Haven't we, Constable?'

On cue, Friel leaned over. 'That's right. Extreme urgency, they said.'

I took Hughes's elbow. He resisted for a moment, then let me steer him away from the car. 'Do you want me to write this one up,' I asked him softly, 'or are you going to be a good plod and do

15

what I've instructed you to do?'

He bristled. 'Write what up?' he asked, a sneaky streak of doubt cutting through the belligerence.

'That you've spun me a fucking lie to evade your duty.' I held my hand up in front of his face to hush his protest. 'That landline I was on is the only communications tool available here. No radio, no phone signal.' I made a show of gazing up at the heavens wonderingly. 'And I don't see any sign of Pegasus, or Mercury the Winged Fucking Messenger, having delivered your urgent summons.'

He glared at me. I wondered whether I had taken him just too far. He had a short fuse, and had laid into me once before. Was he balancing the prospect of a reprimand against the instant gratification of realigning the side of my face? He snorted, and turned back to the car. 'Get out of there, Friel,' he snapped.

I drove down the hill thinking that this was the investigative equivalent of the Phoney War. I hoped that the body we had uncovered didn't mind—whoever and whatever they were—that the start for the search for justice was on hold for a brighter new morning.

But I could feel the buzz starting. Much as my sympathy went out to all those poor tup lambs I had been seeing in their pens, huddled, stiff and ball-busted, this was a real case. Jack Galbraith had to let me in on it. It was what he had exiled me out here for. Like it or not, this was my country now, and I was his man in it.

I stopped at the nearest farm entrance. COGFRYN FARM neatly inscribed on a slate panel. It looked tidy. I made a note of it. I would start there

16

tomorrow. Then work outwards. Build up a picture of the neighbourhood. The people whose doors I would soon be knocking on. The difference around here, from what I had been used to in Cardiff, was that instead of shuffling onto the next doorstep or garden gate when you were making enquiries, the move could involve a couple of miles, a 500-foot climb, and a stretch of mud that required an embedded team of sappers.

I turned onto the main road. The headlights swept the direction sign: DINAS. I smiled wryly to myself. Whoever would have thought that that would ever have meant going home?

2

If Dinas had been allowed to remain as an opportunistic collection of shacks on a dubious ford on a secondary river, it would never have known disappointment. But it hadn't, it grew, and it got prosperity. Twice. Lead and sheep. And lost it both times.

And then it got me.

I didn't have a choice about it. Dinas was prescribed for me. The day that Detective Chief Superintendent Jack Galbraith, obviously repaying my former superiors some deep Masonic favour, rescued me from disgrace in Cardiff, tucked me briefly under his wing, and then booted me out of the nest and into the boondocks. I was to be his piggy in the middle. His catch-all detective in the empty heartland. In which capacity, I was kept busy chasing down missing livestock, stalking stolen

17

quad bikes and tractors, observing first-hand how the full moon fucked people up, and generally trying to avoid confrontations with the local cops.

Don't get me wrong, Dinas is not a bad place; it can even be quite quaint in certain lights. It also helps if you have somewhere else to keep on going to when you get to the far end. I didn't, so I headed for the next best thing, the Fleece Hotel.

I took a stool at the rear bar and nodded cursory greetings to the few men in the room. They were all regulars, so I was able to do that on automatic, a nod more to the zone than the person.

David Williams, my best buddy in Dinas, and not just because he owned the pub, was busy serving at the crowded front bar. He saw me and smiled happily when he turned to the cash register.

'Quite a crowd,' I commented.

He nodded contentedly. 'They've all come down from the wind-farm site.'

Then I realized that this was where I had seen Jeff Talbot, the site engineer, before. In the front bar. A figure glimpsed occasionally, drinking with his men.

David finished up and came over and started pulling a pint for me.

'So, what's the verdict on the body?' I asked, knowing that the Dinas rumour mill would already have digested, analysed and spat out its own theory.

He winced. It was a warning, but it arrived too late. I turned in the direction of his almost imperceptible nod. A middle-aged couple in rain-slicked coats were standing in the archway between the two bars, staring at me. Their smiles were clamped into a rictus. I didn't recognize them, but I did recognize anxiety.

18

'Mr and Mrs Salmon,' David introduced them.

They flowed forward towards me like penitents released into a sanctuary. It was hard to put a precise age to them as the rain had smoothed and darkened their hair, and freshened their skin.

'We heard about the discovery, Sergeant.' Mrs Salmon spoke, her eyes glistening, scorching mine, already afraid of what they might find there. Her look was accusing, as if I was attempting to hide something from her.

'Up at the wind-farm site,' her husband clarified. He gestured his head towards the front bar. 'We've been talking to the workmen, but they say they don't know anything. They said that you were the one to talk to. That you're in charge.'

Even stressed, they both had the lazy vowels of Estuary English. Essex or Kent.

'Can we go up there?' Her voice was pure raw entreaty. I glanced down at her hands, already knowing that they would be tightly clenched.

'Helen . . .' Her husband checked her, as if she had just broken an agreement they had made.

'Please . . .?' she implored, ignoring him.

'There's nothing to see up there, Mrs Salmon,' I said soothingly, stalling, trying to fathom what strange event field she was trying to drag me into.

'It's our daughter, Sergeant,' Mr Salmon explained. I waited for him to elaborate. 'We need to know what you've found up there.'

'Who! *Who* you've found up there,' she corrected him in a hoarse whisper, the tension arcing between them.

'Tell me about your daughter,' I said quietly to Mrs Salmon.

'Evie. She left home. This is Evie . . .' Her voice

a fast stutter. She thrust a photograph under my nose. It showed a young girl astride a fat pony, blonde hair in bunches under a riding hat, a cautious smile, bright-blue eyes, and a spatter of freckles on her upper cheeks. She lowered the photograph and looked up at me beseechingly. 'We have to know if it's her that's been found up there.'

I placed another piece into the jigsaw. I turned to Mr Salmon, hoping that he was less sparked. 'Your daughter's gone missing?'

'Why won't you tell us?' she wailed, riding close to her breaking point.

'What age is she? When did she leave?' I persisted, trying to gently ignore her, needing facts, not hysterics.

'She'll be twenty-three now,' Mr Salmon explained, throwing his wife a worried look, 'and she left close to two years ago.'

It was hard to put an age to the kid in that photograph. One thing I would be willing to bet on was that the 23-year-old version was no longer looking like that.

'We need to know . . .' She couldn't contain it; the tears and the snot finally erupted. Her husband tried to comfort her, but she shrugged him off.

I pictured it again. The dirty carapace choked with grass and heather roots. Two years in that ground could have turned a body to a skeleton. But that one had been in there longer. Hunch and experience convinced me. That wasn't their daughter.

I turned to face her. In the last few minutes, her face had puffed up and welled out, into a frantic mask that had abandoned any sense of caring about appearance. I spoke slowly and carefully. 'It's too

20

early yet. We don't know who we have up there, Mrs Salmon, but I think we can be fairly sure that it isn't your daughter.'

Miraculously, she dried up. 'How sure?' she challenged me, turning, in that instant, from pure mush to interrogator.

'Totally,' I lied. But it didn't worry me—I had inner certainty. Boy was I going to regret it.

*   *   *

David and I watched him lead her off. Back out into the rain. Turning themselves out of the inn. Their misery had rooted deep.

'Another runaway kid?' I asked.

David dried a glass absently, and nodded. 'He's an ex-fireman from Kent. Took early retirement. They bought a run-down smallholding up at the head of a crappy valley. They expected a teenage daughter to swap Bromley for the dream of the good life.'

I could empathize. 'Mud and chicken shit.'

'Broken generators and no phone signal.'

'Still, she lasted it out until she was twenty-one,' I observed.

'On and off,' he corrected me, 'there was a time when they had to keep fetching her back. This time she must have found somewhere better to hide.'

'Glyn, you *are* here . . .'

I turned round. Sandra Williams had come through from the kitchen. She looked tired and had wicked half-circles under her eyes. She was carrying a cordless phone, her hand over the mouthpiece. She proffered it. 'I didn't think you were, but I said I would look.'

21

I took the phone. 'Hello?' I said, hoping that I was not going to hear the sadly familiar sound of bleating lambs in the background.

'DS Capaldi?' The voice was brusque and authoritative, with a North Wales accent. And familiar.

'Yes,' I answered warily, desperately trying to recall the voice. 'Who am I speaking to, please?'

'Inspector Morgan.'

Oh, shit . . . Emrys Hughes's boss. A scowling red-faced man with a widow's peak. He considered Jack Galbraith the Antichrist. And, as his perceived little helper, I also qualified for the rite of exorcism. 'How can I help you, sir?' I asked, pitching for amicable.

'Who gave you the right to commandeer my men, Sergeant?'

'I required their assistance to help secure a probable crime scene, sir.'

'And subject them to exposure?'

'There is shelter available, sir.' I had an image of Hughes and Friel safely ensconced in the site hut, drinking coffee and choosing their favourite nipples from the drill-bit calendar.

'That's beside the point. What you have asked my men to do is totally unnecessary. You don't understand the terrain. We don't have the same problems that you do in the city. We don't have the ghouls and the vandals, and an intrusive, prurient press. Tell me—' I could hear the scorn building in his voice—'who do you think is going to turn out on a filthy night like this, in that wilderness, to dig up a pile of old bones?'

'The person who put them there?' I suggested.

That silenced him for a moment. 'Don't be a

smart alec, Sergeant. That site has its own security. Sergeant Hughes has informed me that there is a watchman.'

'Yes, but with respect, sir, he is only responsible for the security of the construction site, not for a crime scene.'

He leaped over that one as well. 'And, in the meantime, while my men are suffering the vagaries of the elements, I find you well-ensconced in a public house.' The reprimand came from deep within his soul and his faith.

I looked over at David Williams. My local informant. 'I am currently in active pursuit of the preliminary aspects of the investigation, sir.'

'I am pulling my men out of there. And I am going to complain formally to Detective Chief Superintendent Galbraith.'

'Yes, sir,' I replied meekly.

'You should have stayed in Cardiff where you belong, Sergeant Capaldi.'

'I know, sir,' I agreed wholeheartedly.

'We don't want or need your kind around here.'

'No, sir.'

David looked at me speculatively as I went back to the bar. 'Trouble?'

'I've just upset the local mullah.'

I took a drink of my beer. Should I go back up to the site and make my own night vigil? No. Morgan had been right. Different rules applied here. And all I had ever really been doing was punishing Hughes and Friel.

And I didn't regret it.

* * *

I did make a concession, though. I got myself up early in the morning, while it was still dark. There was no moon, the night was anvil black, the sound of the river kept up its own incessant dynamic, and an owl hooted, flitting from location to location like a trickster.

I drove over the wooden-plank bridge out of Hen Felin Caravan Park. Jack Galbraith had forced me to live in Dinas, and I had chosen to stay in a caravan. Unit 13, to be precise. I needed the sense of impermanence, putting up with the cold, the mould spores and the intermittent electrical and water supplies, the very discomfort comforting me with the knowledge that this surely couldn't last.

This time, even in the dark, driving up the valley to the wind-farm site, I felt that I knew it better. Last night, when I had got home from The Fleece, I had studied the OS map and the electoral register. I had a loose fix on where people lived. There weren't that many of them.

It had been cold at the caravan, but it was even colder at the construction site. Higher, and more exposed to the raw wind that was whipping in from the northwest, but keeping the clouds moving too fast to rain. For the moment.

The morning was showing itself as a weak aura against the ridge above the site. But the watchman was on the ball. He was out of his caravan with a torch before I had shut the car door behind me.

'Detective Sergeant Capaldi,' I introduced myself.

He checked my warrant card under his torch beam before he looked up. 'Hi, I'm Donnie Raikes, I take care of security here.' He shook my hand firmly. He was shorter than me, but built better,

24

and the light from the hut's open door caught the gleam of two ring piercings in his right eyebrow.

'All quiet?'

'Nothing's fucking happened here since the glaciers melted,' he replied with a yawn. A Northern accent, Yorkshire, I thought.

'We've got a dead body,' I reminded him.

'I saw it. It looks like something the glacier dumped.'

'It's probably a bit more recent than that.'

He shrugged. 'It'll be a long-lost hiker, then. Nothing more dramatic. Take my word for it, mysterious shit doesn't happen in places like this.'

I nodded, acknowledging his wisdom, and looked round. Objects were beginning to take form. Machines, huts and the folds of the hills. 'Where's Jeff Talbot?' I asked.

'Asleep in his caravan.'

'Alone?'

Donnie grinned. 'Don't worry, we haven't gone native yet, we haven't resorted to the sheep.'

I smiled dutifully at the tired old stereotype. I knew it was irrational, but the information soothed me. That Jeff wasn't with Tessa MacLean.

I waited it out in the site hut, drinking strong tea dotted with atolls of powdered milk, until the SOCO team arrived. The light was establishing itself now, but it was still early, and from the way they bitched about the cold as we backed ourselves into the wind to don our sterile suits I knew that they were letting me know that they had had an even earlier start than me.

They looked even more miserable when I showed them the site.

'Is it any better preserved under there?' the

25

leader asked me, bobbing her head at the tarpaulin.

I shook my head.

'Where are we supposed to start?' she asked despairingly. 'There's no surface left.'

I sidled away from her anguish, leaving them to unroll the tarpaulin and start erecting the tented canopy, while I went to greet a new car that had just driven up.

Bill Atkins, the forensic pathologist, was a dour old guy in his late fifties, who I had worked with before in Cardiff. His eyes flickered in recognition, but he made no comment. The forensic anthropologist, who introduced herself as Sheila Goddard, was younger and carried herself around in a bubble of enthusiasm, which even encompassed the wildness of the countryside. I could see, as we walked up the hill, that Bill Atkins was not sharing this.

I hovered behind them while they crouched over the remains. Whispering to each other. Exchanging observations.

Bill was the first to turn round to me. 'I hope you're not expecting anything too dramatic from the *in-situ* inspection.'

'What will you be able to tell us?'

'Bugger all.' He shook his head and turned back to the remains. 'Nothing on cause, or duration of interment, until we get it dug up and back to the lab. Unless we get lucky and find a bullet, or a knife, or an obvious trauma event.'

'What about age and gender?' I prompted.

He looked at Sheila, who shrugged happily. 'Maybe,' he answered for both of them. 'We wait to see what's uncovered, but the age is only going to be broad-spectrum.'

I thought of Evie. 'Could this be a young woman? Buried two years ago?'

'I think the pelvic structure's male,' Sheila offered.

Bill pursed his lips. 'This soil could prove to be extremely corrosive, advance the deterioration. But . . .' He tapped the ribcage with a stainless-steel spatula. 'The patina and the pitting would make me think it has been in the ground for a lot longer.'

I wafted off a silent thanks to the angel who looked after my hunch skills. 'It's a possibility that the skull and the missing hand were accidentally dislodged by the excavator,' I offered.

Sheila shook her head. 'No,' she said cheerfully, beckoning me down beside her, 'not possible. See here . . .?' She used her own spatula to indicate the points where the skull and the hand were missing. 'There are definite indications of mechanical severance in both cases. And notice that the wounds have exactly the same surface encrustation and patination as the surrounding bone. If the separation had been recent I would expect to see a cleaner bone surface at the junction.'

I should have noticed that. The rocks that had been touched by the digger had shown brighter scores where they had been scraped. The same thing would have happened to bone, the surface crud would have been removed.

'So their removal was contemporary with the interment?' I asked.

'Or before.'

Which meant that we were probably not going to find a hand on the end of the other arm that was currently under the skeleton.

So why remove them? The obvious answer was

27

to eliminate the means of identification. The skull, if the teeth were intact, could yield dental records, or even facial reconstruction. But skeletal hands? Whoever had buried the body had not wanted to take the risk that it wouldn't be discovered before decomposition had taken the fingerprints.

I stood up slowly. Black magic? There was also a possible ritual explanation that couldn't be discounted.

I looked around me, screwing my eyes against the wind. Trying to see it. A featureless spot on an empty hill. What gave this place its significance?

*   *   *

Back down in the valley I chose Cogfryn Farm as my first port of call, on the scientific principle that it looked neat, cosy, and the dogs were shut away. It was also not in the Badger Face Welsh Mountain sheep-flock book.

I left the professionals up on the hill painstakingly excavating the skeleton. I had no authorization to start an official investigation, but I reckoned no harm could come from putting out preliminary feelers. Get the taste of local reaction.

Cogfryn was a low, two-storey stone farmhouse, with an attached stone barn, both recently whitewashed.

'Mrs Jones?'

The woman who answered the door didn't seem surprised that I knew her name. She was small, with her hair tied back in a bun, wearing an apron, and was as neat as her house. I showed her my warrant card and introduced myself.

'You'll be here about that body they've found up

Cwm Cesty Nant, I expect?'

'You've heard?'

She looked at me incredulously.

I laughed. 'I'm sorry, I forget how quickly news travels around here.'

'My husband's busy with the lambing, but you're welcome to come in.'

'I'd be grateful.'

She opened the door and stepped back to let me through. 'Watch you don't trip over the suitcase,' she warned as I followed her down the hall and skirted a red and well-travelled case, which looked cosmopolitan and incongruous in this rustic setting. 'It's my son's,' she explained, as if reading my thoughts.

'This is Owen, my son, and his friend Greg Thomas.' She introduced me to the two men who were sitting at the scrubbed pine table in the kitchen with mugs of tea and a depleted plate of chocolate digestive biscuits in front of them.

Owen Jones had a stocky build, close-cropped hair and a bright smile, but what immediately struck me was his deep suntan, which looked so out of place in these parts, especially at this time of the year, when the rest of us had complexions that made us look like we had just crawled out from the under the boulder where we had spent our winter.

I put Greg Thomas in his forties, the same sort of age as Owen. Lean and fit in a sweatshirt and sweatpants. His brown hair was also shorn, and his face was weathered and tight. As I nodded at him I saw how alert and attentive his brown eyes were.

'That's quite a shock for Dinas,' Owen commented when his mother announced the purpose of my visit.

29

'It's a dreadful thing.' Mrs Jones tutted in concurrence.

'Any idea who you've found?' Owen asked. I was aware of Greg watching me closely.

'Not yet, we're working on it.'

'Owen, it's time to make a move,' Greg announced.

Owen laughed. 'Just when things are getting interesting around here for the first time ever.'

'Owen!' his mother rebuked, but there was proud amusement in her tone. I watched the sadness cross her face as her son and Greg got up.

He nodded at me apologetically. 'Don't mean to be rude, Sergeant, but we've got to go. Greg's driving me to Birmingham airport.'

'Going anywhere nice?'

He smiled. 'Not really. Not unless you're into heat, mosquitoes and oil-rig spotting. I'm catching a plane to Lagos from Heathrow. I work in oil-field security,' he elaborated.

I was left in the kitchen on my own as his mother went to see him off. So that explained the suntan. I also realized that his friend Greg Thomas had not said a word to me.

The wait gave me the opportunity to take in the room. It was shabbily immaculate, a space that retained the memory of baked scones and jam-making and damp socks drying. It was an art director's dream of a certain rural package, from the faded Royal Worcester plates on the dresser and the vintage Rayburn cooker, down to the framed photograph of a couple of gawky-looking kids on a crocheted runner on top of a sideboard.

Mrs Jones returned, wiping the tears from her eyes with the bunched-up corner of her apron.

30

It was such a private and homely gesture that it brought a lump to my throat.

'He doesn't talk about it, but I know that he has to protect all those people from some very bad things that can happen out there,' she said, explaining her lapse, and sitting down.

'I'm sure he can take care of himself.'

She nodded absently, her mind still far off in siege and hostage situations.

'Does your daughter live away as well?' I asked, nodding at the photograph, to divert her from her immediate melancholy.

She surfaced again and looked at the photograph, a dim, wry smile forming and crinkling the lines in the corners of her mouth. 'I'm afraid poor Rose is no longer with us.' I winced internally at my gaffe, but she was already moving on. 'It was a long time ago now. Things heal.' And I saw in her expression that gleam that I had seen so often in people caught up in the excitement of terrible events that they had never expected to experience, even on the edge of their quiet lives. She shook her head wonderingly. 'It's a terrible thing that's happened up there, finding that murdered body.' She gave me a piercing look. 'If that's what it really is.'

'What do you mean by that, Mrs Jones?'

She lowered her voice conspiratorially. 'I've heard talk that it could have been the work of the wind-farm protestors. You know, if they could make it look like an ancient burial place, like the other one they've found farther up the hill, they wouldn't be allowed to carry on with the construction.'

I nodded, 'Interesting,' and wrote it down in

my notebook. But it was an unlikely scenario. Wind-farm protestors were, on the whole, middle class, and the closest they got to civil disobedience was shaking their walking poles in the air. And even if Jeff Talbot, a civil engineer by training, had been mistaken about the ground being undisturbed, where would a bunch like that have got hold of an appropriate corpse?

But, for the moment, without anything more concrete to work on, I was happy to entertain crackpot theories.

'You must know everyone in these parts?' I asked.

A slyly humorous smile spread across her face. She was astute. By my reaction to the protesters theory she had concluded that the body we had found was the real thing. 'You want me to tell you who I think might be bad enough to do something like this?'

'I'm always interested in local knowledge.'

'And this is private?' she asked warily, but I could hear the thrill in her voice.

'Strictly between you and me.'

'Gerald Evans, Pentre Fawr. I'll say no more than that.' She sat upright, looking quickly around to make sure that the walls weren't going to betray her. But she wasn't finished. She leaned forward. 'And Mr Gilbert at Cae Rhedyn. The man who messes up the river with his so-called gold mine.'

The Gold Mine Man. I remembered him. That's what Sandra Williams had called him when she pointed him out to me one day in Dinas. On the other side of the road, head down, scurrying, carrying a ragged canvas shopping bag. And dressed in what looked like a grey school blazer

32

with a scorch mark on the left sleeve. It was a cold day, but he was wearing shorts, fat grey socks collapsed around the ankles of his stick legs, his knees protruding like the knob on the end of a shillelagh.

She saw me to the door. I sensed a reluctance to release me. 'Is there anything more?'

'It's what my husband said about it, but I think it's a bit silly.'

'Go on,' I prompted.

'It's about the planes that fly over, the big slow ones, not the small ones that fly too fast and make such an awful noise.'

'The Hercules?'

'Maybe—' she shook her head dismissively, the ability to name planes was boys' stuff—'but they used to say that sometimes they dropped bodies.'

'Why did they say that?'

'They said that they dropped dead bodies to see what happened to them. They were trying to see if there was any safe way that soldiers could jump from planes without parachutes.'

'I'll look into that, Mrs Jones.' I was only partially humouring her. It sounded like one of the half-crazed ideas that Special Forces might actually contemplate. I put 'M' in brackets beside the note. Something Mackay could help me out with later.

Mackay and I went back a long way. We were tenuously related, his family having a connection with the Scottish branch of the Capaldi family. We had shared a reckless adolescence before he joined the army and ended up in the SAS. Our relationship had been troubled after that, and had hit a real low when he took up with my ex-wife, Gina. Since then he too had been dumped by her, and we had now returned to our old close conjunction, but with the former wildness hopefully burned-out.

I left Cogfryn and drove down towards the main road instead of turning back to the wind-farm site. It would be useful to get a feel for the valley in daylight.

Just before the junction I pulled in beside a sign I had missed when I had driven the road in the dark: PEN TWYN BARN GALLERY. The driveway had been newly surfaced in tarmac, and led to a large circular parking area in front of a refurbished and freshly limewashed stone barn. Just up the rise from the barn was the house, also restored, and with a tasteful, contemporary, glazed rear extension. Money had been spent on both the buildings. They were also both equally shut up. I made a note of them. Pen Tywn had not featured in the electoral roll.

*   *   *

On the way back I turned off the road at the signpost for the by-way, an old drove track that wound up to the ridgeway. I had checked it out on the OS map, and was pretty sure that it would lead to Tessa MacLean's dig site.

And discovered a bonus. This particular spot possessed a mobile-phone signal, a rare attribute in these parts. I decided to put that call through to Mackay.

'Glyn, how are you?' The reception was fuzzy. But that was par for the course when calling Mackay. He had retired from the SAS, but the background chatter on his line made you think of wind in a high desert and an old truck's engine being nurtured with an oil can to keep the mobile phone's batteries charged. Perhaps the regiment gave them a filter to put on their phone when they retired, just so they would be forever reminded of the good old days.

'Mac, here's a bizarre one for you.'

'I'm listening.'

'Did you ever come across talk of an experiment that had the military dropping dead bodies from planes at low altitudes to assess if there was a possibility that live soldiers would be able to handle the jump?'

He was silent.

'Mac?'

'Sorry, Glyn, I can't say.'

Can't or won't? I had learned over the years not to press him on these things. 'Okay, let's try another tack. Hypothetically, could such a thing ever have happened in this country?'

'What have you found?'

'A body on a remote hillside. It looks like there's been identity erasure.'

'It's not the military. All detritus would have been cleared up. Mislaid body parts are not good PR.'

'Thanks, Mac.' I closed the phone down. The elimination of an admittedly weirdo theory was, I suppose, progress of sorts.

I took off up the by-way. It was potholed, with grass growing up the middle, but it didn't look too badly rutted. I drove very slowly, ready to make my retreat at the first sign of loss of traction, or drumbeats on the sump. I didn't want to find myself explaining this distraction to Jack Galbraith.

I didn't see the camp until I crested a rise. The dig, I assumed, was under the canvas enclosure that looked a bit like a bird-watching hide rigged up against a heather-topped earth bank. The camp comprised a rickety caravan, a few small tents and an old long-wheelbase Land Rover station wagon with QUEEN'S UNIVERSITY BELFAST on the front door panel. The flash modern intruder was Jeff Talbot's four-wheel-drive crew-cab pickup.

Tessa came out from under the tarpaulin at the sound of my approach. She was wearing a sweatshirt, and dungarees with earth-stained knees, and her hair was pulled back with a red, knotted bandana. She had a tiny gardening fork in her hand, and dirt on her forearms where the sleeves were rolled up. She pushed her hair back with her wrist and a smear of dirt appeared on her forehead. She looked great.

But I was not exactly getting a great big warm smile of welcome.

And, lurching like I was, in my very ordinary car, on a terrain that was better suited to pack mules, it was going to be hard to casually announce that I was just passing and had decided to call in to say hello.

I caught sight of Jeff as I got out of the car. He was approaching from the campsite with a tray loaded with assorted steaming mugs. He, for one, was making himself useful. 'Hi,' he shouted over, 'you should have told me you were coming, I would have driven you up the short way.'

'Thanks, but it's part of a circuit I'm doing. Trying to get an overview.'

'What can we do for you, Sergeant?' Tessa asked.

'So this is the dig?' I retorted enthusiastically, hoping that the way into an archaeologist's grace was through her work.

Jeff raised the tray. 'I'll just take these in for the crew,' he announced, ducking under the enclosure like one of the family.

'I would have thought that you would have been very occupied by now,' she observed.

'This is my occupation, Dr MacLean. Some people call it being nosy.'

She almost smiled properly.

I gestured towards the tarpaulin. 'Has your man in there still got his head and his hands?'

This time the smile broke through. 'Yes, why do you ask?'

'I'm just chasing possibilities. That maybe you had a collection of headless and handless bodies here, and someone had lifted one and dumped it down there.' I nodded towards the wind-farm site, which was just visible.

She shook her head. 'Sorry, but we've only got one here, and he's still intact. I'd invite you in to have a look, but we're pretty crowded at the moment.'

'That's okay,' I said, not too upset about being unable to share close quarters with the ancient dead. 'Do you know what it is that you've got?'

'He's not an "it", he's our Redshanks,' she corrected, mock-affronted.

'Yes?'

She laughed. 'It was a colloquial name that was given to highlanders. From their red legs under the kilt.'

I showed my surprise. 'Your guy's a Scottish highlander?'

37

'We believe so. Some of the stuff we're turning up has a definite Western Isles connection.'

'He's a long way from home.

She nodded. 'And I think that he came an even longer way round. My theory is that he was one of the Gallowglass. Pure happenstance. But it turned out to be wonderful for us when someone found the remains of a brass boss from a Highland targe here.'

'You've lost me.'

'A targe is—'

'A targe is a small shield,' I interrupted, 'I know that, it's the Gallowthingy, that I don't get.'

'Gallowglass. They were mercenaries from the Western Isles of Scotland who hired themselves out into the service of Irish Chiefs. We think this one could possibly have been a McNeil from the Mull of Kintyre.'

I looked around. Scrub grass, gorse and patchy heather, everything bent over like supplicants by the prevailing wind. If anything, this place was even more desolate than the spot where we had found our body.

'What would a Scottish warrior working for an Irish Chieftain be doing dying in a godforsaken spot like this in the middle of Wales?'

She grinned at me. 'Good question.'

An idea drifted in. The timeline spanned six hundred years. But could there be a Celtic connection?

The big, dark Ford saloon, with new mud on the polished bodywork, was parked at the construction site when I got back. Jack Galbraith was here. I got out of my car, checked my reflection in the window for rectifiable flaws, prepared my psyche for tension, and started off up the hill to the small canvas pavilion that they had erected over the grave site.

'Glyn . . .'

DCI Bryn Jones was leaning out of the door of one of the site huts, beckoning me over. I forgot to take a deep breath of good clean air before I entered. They were both heavy smokers. They had already created the effect of a full-blown chip-pan fire.

'Preening yourself, Capaldi?' Jack Galbraith asked with a sardonic grin. I glanced out the window. My car was in full view. He looked pointedly at his watch. 'Is this dereliction of duty?'

'I was here earlier, sir. I left the experts to it. I've been out getting the feel of the locality.'

He picked up a sheet of paper and flapped it in front of me. It had the effect of diverting the smoke from both their cigarettes into my face. 'Inspector Morgan has been bitching about you.'

'Inspector Morgan doesn't think I should be here, sir.'

'Inspector Morgan doesn't like the competition? Wants all the prettiest sheep for himself, does he?'

I tried not to smile. 'I wouldn't know about that, sir.'

He chuckled, pleased with himself, screwed the paper into a ball and aimed it in the general direction of a waste-paper basket, not caring where it landed. 'Sit yourself down, Capaldi.'

Bryn had already taken the seat next to him, forcing me to sit opposite them, like the suspect under interrogation. They had an open laptop in front of them, connected to the SOCO camera.

They were both big men, but the spread of their bodies moved in different directions. Bryn Jones dark, squat and powerful, Jack Galbraith taller, his face more angular, the big head of swept-back hair betraying his underlying vanity.

'Have the forensics people been able to tell us anything more, sir?' I asked Bryn.

'They think it's male, and they think it's middle-aged, and they're not even going to attempt to tell us how long it's been up here until they get it back to the lab.'

I nodded, keeping my pleasure at Evie Salmon's continued existence to myself. I made a mental note to call her parents to confirm it for them.

'And we're the poor bastards who have to attempt to identify him,' Jack Galbraith stated cheerfully.

'The other hand was missing?' I asked.

Bryn nodded. 'And no trace or residue of any clothing. Every possible identifier has been removed. Only that plastic sheeting, which, after all this time, is next to useless.'

'But at least we can discount suicide.' Jack Galbraith chuckled facetiously.

'Ritual killing?' I offered.

Jack Galbraith snorted and shook his head contemptuously. 'It's a fucking hit. This place is just a dumping ground.'

I wasn't quite sure whether he was referring to the actual grave or the entire locality he had assigned to me. 'Will you be setting up an incident room, sir?'

Jack Galbraith grinned at Bryn. 'I think Capaldi's looking for some action.'

'It's going to be desktop to start with,' Bryn explained. 'Marry up all the stuff SOCO and forensics can give us and try to come up with an identity. Work the missing-persons route at the same time.'

'You look crestfallen, Capaldi,' Jack Galbraith commented.

'It's a crime scene, sir.'

Bryn leaned forward, but kept his tone sympathetic. 'I know, but there's nothing left here to investigate. Too much time has elapsed and the site has been devastated.' He shrugged. 'A place like this, if there were locals unaccounted for, we'd have known about it long ago.'

'It's a hit, Capaldi. As I've already said, this is just the rubbish dump.' Jack Galbraith made a pistol using his thumb and forefinger and pointed it at me. 'Dope? Gang related? Someone got caught fucking the wrong man's wife? Who knows? I just know there's nothing here.' He clicked his thumb, mimicking a firing pin striking. 'Kerpow . . . It's a vanished legend. All those years ago someone drove out of somewhere, dumped a body in the boondocks, and then drove back to that place where things happen. The only thing that happens here is the fucking weather.'

'You put me here, sir.'

He shot a smile at Bryn. 'Is this a complaint?' he

asked me.

'You put me here for this eventuality. To be in place when bad things happened.' He was wrong. The tingle was telling me that there was a local connection here.

He gave me a wise, mock-patient look. 'But I've just explained, the bad things didn't happen here.' He scrunched his eyes shut and took in a deep breath. 'Okay,' he said, resigned to it, 'play my devil's advocate. And don't *sir* me every time. It gets tedious.'

I took in my own deep breath and almost choked on the smoke. 'Why here?'

'It's remote, hard to get to,' he came back at me quickly. 'A fucking good place to hide a body. Until the Save the Planet Brigade decide to construct a wind farm.'

'As you said, it's hard to get to.'

'Meaning?'

'You would have to know it. And we're talking about what was only a rough hill track in those days. I can't see a hard man from Salford or wherever driving up it with a naked, dismembered corpse in the boot, just in the hope that he might arrive at somewhere convenient to dispose of a body. And he would have needed to be in a four-wheel-drive vehicle. And why travel so far out of the place where things happen?'

He glanced at Bryn. 'Underline your point,' he commanded.

'They knew about this location. They had researched this. Or they were living here.'

'Which makes them still around, does it?'

'It's a possibility.'

He looked over at Bryn again, who shrugged.

42

He thought hard for a moment. 'I suppose it works on a PR level. We're seen to be doing something tangible. Okay, Capaldi, go and ask your questions. But I still say you're wrong.' He grinned. 'And don't step too hard on Inspector Morgan's toes,' he added.

'Thank you, sir,' I said gratefully. Mentally I had already hit the ground running.

*   *   *

PRIVATE—GOLDMINE—KEEP OUT

The sign had been daubed on the sheet-metal gate with red paint that had dripped and run below the letters like fake theatrical blood. It was written in English only, which seemed to me to be a bit imperialistic. It was also a bit daft if you valued your security and privacy, to advertise the fact that you were sitting on top of a goldmine. Literally.

Mrs Jones at Cogfryn had intrigued me. Nice Welsh farmers' wives don't generally finger their neighbours as potential killers. So what had these two done that had placed them beyond the pale?

Gerald Evans was in another valley, so I decided to start with Bruno Gilbert, the Gold Mine Man. And it was a goldmine. Deep boyhood mythologies kicking in from a time of innocence, before big holes in the ground, putatively awash with treasure, had accumulated sexual baggage.

I had remembered more of what Sandra Williams had told me about him that day in Dinas. He was a recluse. No one was quite sure whether he had been a schoolteacher or a civil servant, or whether he had taken early retirement or suffered

43

a breakdown. He came into town for his shopping, scurried about with his head down, and ordered his goods by pointing.

He may have been pretty inept socially, but he had managed to construct a solid pair of gates. Which, despite repeated hammering and calling out, he wasn't opening. Perhaps he just couldn't hear me. Maybe he was mining a vein, or crushing ore, doing whatever it was that made the place qualify as a goldmine in his book.

I was conscious of time passing. Jack Galbraith could change his mind and haul me off this at any moment.

I studied the gate again. Three obstacles to progress: the gate, the barbed wire on top of it and the fact that I hadn't been invited.

I got over the height issue by standing on the roof of the car. The coiled barbed wire on top was old, rusting and laced with cobwebs that had trapped leaves and thistledown. One good push would send it down like an uncoiling slinky.

On the other side of the gate, the track, flanked by a pair of rusted Morris 1000 Travellers, turned round a sharp bend out of sight. The hidden side of a sharp bend was always tantalizing.

This was where an invitation would have been useful. Technically what I was contemplating was illegal entry seasoned with criminal damage. But fuck it, I reasoned, a man who wasn't even capable of asking a shopkeeper for his favourite cheese was hardly likely to have me dragged up in front of the High Sheriff.

I dislodged the barbed wire and jumped down, landing heavily, my heels kicking up two little geysers of dust. Everything about this side of the gate—the air, the vegetation—felt more desiccated. I wouldn't have been surprised to see a bird sporting fluff instead of feathers.

I called out Gilbert's name again. No reply. No sounds of any activity. I walked round the bend in the track. Ahead of me, across a yard of massed junk, was a green timber shack, with a rusted corrugated-iron roof, which was in the process of deconstructing itself. The paint was peeling down to rotting boards, the roof was slumping, and a couple of the windows were falling out.

'Go away!'

The voice made me jump. I hadn't seen him. I turned to find him squatting in a niche in a bramble cluster that I discovered later had overwhelmed an old tractor. He had his head down and his fingers pressed to the sides of his brow.

'Mr Gilbert?' I asked.

He shook his head.

I bent my knees to lower myself to his level, my warrant card out. 'Mr Gilbert, my name is Glyn Capaldi, I'm a police officer, I'd like to ask you some questions.'

He shook his head again.

He was an old man. Dressed in his usual shorts and a faded khaki shirt, both tattered, his arms and legs deeply tanned, but knucklebone thin. I couldn't see his face, but his hair was grey and closely cropped in irregular patches as if it was growing out after a scalp infection. Then I realized that it was probably because he cut it himself, the angle of the mirror, and the way he had to crank the scissors, distorting things.

By not looking at me he was holding on to the pretence that I wasn't really there.

45

I stood up briskly. 'Well, if you don't mind, I'll have a look around. A setup like this must be fascinating,' I declared chirpily.

'No!' He leaped up with almost alacrity. A definite crackle. A creaky old elf unfurling. His eyes were blue and scared. His face was lean and fissured, with a sparse dirty-white billy-goat beard accentuating the length of his chin. His expression was a definition of anguish. 'You can't! No one's allowed in here.'

I took a couple of steps back to reassure him. 'It's all right, Mr Gilbert. I promise, I'll stay back here, I won't go any farther. But I do need to talk to you.'

'I've done nothing wrong.'

'I know, it's just a routine enquiry, I'm talking to everyone in the valley.'

He shook his head. 'I don't have anything to do with the rest of the valley. I can't tell you anything.'

'Have you heard that we've discovered a body at the site of the new wind farm?' I watched him carefully.

'I don't care. That has got nothing to do with me.'

He wasn't even curious. As far as he was concerned it was news from a dead planet. He just wanted to be left alone to live the life internal that he had constructed around his tumbledown Shangri-La.

He looked at me defiantly. 'She sent you here, didn't she?'

'She?'

He nodded in the direction of Cogfryn. 'The one at the farm.'

'Why would she do that?'

A smile almost broke through. 'I used to have to chase her children off my land. They came trespassing, poking their noses into things.'

'That must have been a long time ago.'

He nodded sagely. 'It was, but none of them have ever forgotten.'

I thought about it as I drove back. Okay, no butchered and trimmed cadavers strung up on meat hooks, but the visit had been useful in a couple of respects. Now, having met him and seen his reaction, I was fairly certain that Bruno Gilbert had had nothing to do with the body we had found. And I now knew that Mrs Jones's finking had been personal.

So what, I was now even more interested to know, was the grudge that she held against Gerald Evans, a man who was not even a neighbour?

*   *   *

I was twitching to brace Gerald Evans, but had to spend the next day frustratingly back up at the construction site to babysit the SOCO team, and oversee the removal of the body, which was now ready to be trucked back to the lab. I did manage to call the Salmons to give them the good news.

When I eventually got to The Fleece that evening I found that David Williams was no longer a happy man. His bounty had decamped. The wind-farm construction workers had been discharged and sent home or relocated until they were required again.

'How long is this going to take your people to sort out?' he grumbled as he pulled my beer.

'No idea,' I replied, slightly irked that I didn't

seem to be included among the people who were capable of sorting it out. I waved reflexively to the group of regulars at the far end of the bar.

Seeing them gave me an idea. 'Who among that lot would know about the wind-farm site?' I asked David.

He looked at them appraisingly. 'Blackie Collins might. He used to work at Pentre Isaf. It's way over on the other side of the hill, though.'

I had heard the story. Blackie had worked man and boy as a labourer and shepherd for the Haymer family at Pentre Isaf farm. The sons who had inherited the place had decided that life had to be about more than sheep ticks, deflated livestock prices and splashing around in organophosphate dips, and had sold it off as a riding school. Not surprisingly the new owners hadn't seen Blackie as an asset that would work in harmony with prepubescent girls fixated on horses. So Blackie was now living with his sister in Dinas.

I walked down to the far end of the bar. 'Blackie, can I buy you a beer? Can I buy all you boys a beer?' I offered expansively. There were only three of them, so it wasn't going to break the bank.

They looked startled. I had obviously crossed a line. It was okay to throw a greeting over, but intruding into home space was something different.

I moved Blackie off to the side. He had lank grey hair, watery brown eyes, and hadn't shaved for days. There was a light brown staining on the whiskers at the corners of his mouth. He didn't smoke, so I hoped that it was only tea.

He looked at me mutely. He knew I was a cop. He was wondering if a new and incomprehensible change in the rules of life had caught up with him.

'You've heard about the body that was found over at the place where they're building the new wind farm?'

He nodded cagily. 'Cwm Cesty Nant. But I don't know anything about a body.' It came out as a croaked whisper.

'I know you don't. I just want the benefit of your local knowledge.'

He digested that warily. 'We were only over there when we were taking the sheep off the hill.'

'There was nothing unusual about that place? Nothing that makes it stick in your mind? Nothing to do with it that you've ever heard people talking about?'

He shook his head. He was staring at me, his eyes round, more confident now that I hadn't arrested him, or turned him into a frog. 'You don't know who it is?' he asked tremulously.

'It would have been a while ago. You don't remember hearing anything about anyone disappearing?'

'I wouldn't be the person to ask.'

'Who would?'

He looked around furtively. His voice dropped. 'Gerald Evans.'

I smiled inwardly. It was always a good feeling to sense the spheres sliding into conjunction. A couple of them anyway. 'What makes you mention him?'

He leaned forward. 'He used to steal our ewes,' he whispered, 'take them off the hill and change the marks to his own.'

A rustler? Is that why the Joneses at Cogfryn had it in for him?

'And he's filthy,' he added quickly, picking up on the downshift in my interest.

49

'Can you explain what you mean by filthy?'

'There was a bit of snow on the ground a few years back. The postman couldn't get up to Pentre Fawr, so he left a parcel for him with us. This was before he got married. From Holland, it said on the front. I don't know how it managed to get opened, but . . .' He shook his head. 'It was terrible stuff, Sergeant. And poor Mrs Haymer seeing it and all.'

I suppressed my smile. Dutch pornography. Nosiness rewarded. I had an image of the huddled bunch of them, sheepdogs included, all agog and aghast, the world of dildos, butt plugs and bondage gear having just been revealed to them.

He took a deep breath. 'But that's not the worst.'

'Go on,' I prompted

'He shot my dog.'

I pulled an appropriate face, grunted sympathetic noises and retreated to my end of the bar. 'What do you know about Gerald Evans from Pentre Fawr?' I asked David as I climbed onto a stool.

'I've barred him from here.'

I looked at him with surprise. 'Why?'

'He shot Blackie's dog.' He shrugged. 'I've got to show solidarity with my regulars.'

I was almost taken in. 'Come on, David,' I protested, 'that's too altruistic for you.'

'The bastard cheated me once. He sold me a Land Rover that had sawdust in the sump to stop it knocking.'

'Couldn't you take it back?'

'I couldn't afford the stress of the ensuing vendetta.'

'He's like that?'

'He's a mean fucker, Glyn, amoral and totally

50

ruthless.'

'Sergeant . . .'

We both looked round. Jeff Talbot was standing in the archway between the two bars with Tessa MacLean.

How long had they been in here? An irrational surge of social panic gripped me. Had they seen me hunkered over there with Blackie? Thinking that he was my buddy? Maybe even my only buddy?

Jeff held up his mobile phone. He looked wearily grim. 'Sergeant, I don't know whether this is going to involve you, but I've just had a call from Donnie at the site. He's scared someone off who was messing around with our machinery.'

'Any damage?' I asked.

'He's still checking, but it looks like they've managed to screw-up the hydraulics on one of the diggers.'

I thought quickly. It could be saboteurs. The wind-farm protestors that Mrs Jones had mentioned. Or it could be something richer. I pushed my beer away virtually untouched. 'I'll follow you up there.'

I caught David smiling at me as I got into my coat. 'My hero,' he pouted mockingly.

I shot him the finger, and followed Jeff and Tessa to the door. Then I realized why them thinking that I might be associated with Blackie had stung so much. I was jealous. And it was only partially sexual. The rest of it was to do with the company they had found with one another. They were outsiders in Dinas, they had bonded together to share a common experience. But I was an outsider here too, and it rankled that they hadn't thought to include me in the party.

51

They hadn't recognized my kindred spark. It was more than depressing, it was a shock to my system. Was I now beginning to be mistaken for a local in the eyes of the outside world?

*   *   *

It was going to be a cold night. The light cloud cover was fragmenting, there was already a light dusting of stars, Venus low and bright in the west, and the fluorescent promise, behind a far ridge, of a rising moon.

The construction site was lit up. As we drove closer I saw that it was one of the company pickups, its headlights full-on, illuminating a parked row of assorted earth-moving machinery.

I parked behind Jeff. Tessa didn't get out. I followed Jeff to the pickup. Donnie Raikes got out as we approached.

'What happened?' Jeff asked.

'Someone's had a go at one of the diggers.' Donnie led us towards the line of machinery.

'What kind of a go?' I asked.

'Watch your feet there,' Donnie said, taking my arm as we stopped beside a mechanical digger, nodding at the ground. A thick, viscous liquid that, in the dark, looked like treacle, was pooling in a rut in the mud. 'Hydraulic fluid. Someone's cut the hoses,' he explained.

Jeff bent down to inspect the damage.

'Did you see anyone?' I asked Donnie.

'I heard him, that's what brought me out of the hut. I think he must have accidentally banged the side of the machine. By the time I was outside he was storming off down the gully.'

'Him?' I asked.

He smiled indulgently. 'It's usually blokes.'

'You've checked the rest of the plant?' Jeff asked.

'Yes. It looked like he was starting with this one, but got careless.'

'Has it happened before?' I asked them.

'Not here,' Jeff said.

'And it's not usually damage,' Donnie explained, 'it's usually shunted onto a low-loader and then off on a long haul to Romania or other such points.'

'Could this be the work of protestors?' I asked.

They exchanged glances. Donnie shrugged. 'I don't know,' Jeff said, 'but why bother, the site's already shut down.'

'Is the damage fixable?' I asked.

'New hydraulic hoses. It's a question of waiting for parts and a fitter. Which will not be a company priority up here at the moment,' Jeff said, smiling wryly.

I turned to Donnie. 'Can you show me which way he ran off?'

He looked surprised. 'It's night, Sergeant.'

'Humour me.'

We walked to the edge of the light-spill and Donnie pointed out the direction the figure had taken. He had kept off the track, knowing that a vehicle could have outrun him, and instead used the gully that the stream ran down.

I walked forward slowly, shining my torch ahead. It was rough, shelving terrain with irregular banks and terraces.

'You looking for footprints?' Donnie shouted after me.

'No, the shape of the ground. You say he just

kept on running?'

'Yes, as much as I could see.'

The guy had known what he was doing. Keeping up a pace in the dark over rough terrain like this. He knew this place, exactly where he was, and how to get out.

I felt it then. A prickle at the back of my neck. Someone watching?

I turned around and quartered the side of the hill slowly. But it was useless. Too many vast patches of dense shadow. He went down the hill, I reminded myself. No one could be watching me from up there.

Unless there was more than one of them?

Jeff banged on the side of the pickup to catch our attention. 'I'm going to take Tessa back up the hill now,' he shouted.

'Wait for me, I'm coming with you,' I called up. I saw him flash a look at Tessa, still inside the car.

'I'm just taking Dr MacLean back to her camp,' he explained as I approached, not doing too much to disguise his annoyance. 'I'll be back soon.'

'Good, I'll tag along for the ride.' I grabbed my binoculars from my car, and got into the back seat of the crew cab before he could launch another objection.

'It's dark, Sergeant, you won't be able to see anything.' Tessa spoke from the front seat without turning round. I wondered if I had just imagined a touch of intentional ambiguity in her voice.

'It's the company I crave, Dr MacLean,' I announced cheerfully.

I was conscious of her eyes on me in the rear-view mirror. I was probably not making the best impression. The rumpled creep on the back seat. Outside, by contrast, we heard Jeff, manly and incisive, instructing Donnie to jury-rig a set of lights over the earth-moving machinery.

He got into the pickup, and we set off. Lurching and swaying on the rough track. No one speaking. One of those ramrod silences. I watched the track unrolling in the headlights, waiting for the moment to break it.

I saw the ground rise ahead and leaned forward into the gap between the front seats. 'After we go over that rise we'll be out of sight of your camp.'

'So?' he asked, puzzled.

'When you've gone over the top, slow right down, as if you're negotiating a deep puddle or something, but don't stop.'

'Why?'

'I don't want them to know that I'm getting out.'

'What the hell do you want to get out for?' Jeff protested.

'Who's "them", Sergeant?' Tessa asked, picking up on the important question.

'I don't know, Doctor, it's just a hunch that I want to run with.'

'This is crazy.' Jeff shook his head despairingly.

'Be careful,' Tessa said, turning round. This time, as she looked at me, I hoped that she was seeing a little bit of the Apache in my soul.

4

I paused, crouched down, with the door open to get the feel for the car's motion, and then tumbled myself out of the cab, and rolled a couple of times with the momentum. And stayed down, flat on the ground, still and quiet. Which was not Apache training, but more to do with the fact that I had winded myself.

I sucked in air, and watched Jeff's brake lights flicker like an overworked Aldis lamp as he continued up the track. If there were anyone out there watching, hopefully they would assume that I was still in the car.

Or was I just being crazy? Allowing a spook impulse to drive me to mad and essentially pointless acts? I suppressed the thought. Just as I had already buried the one that told me I was showing off for Tessa's benefit.

I kept low and worked myself up along the hidden side of the rise to the top of the saddle. At that point I dropped to the ground and crawled over, keeping my head below the skyline, until I could see down into the construction camp.

Donnie was working on setting up the lighting. Standing on top of the machines, moving over them like stepping stones, stringing lamps onto an invisible wire. As I adjusted to the soft swish of the wind and the backdrop of the night, I started to hear the sounds of the generator and a radio playing rock music coming up from the camp.

I started to get really cold. The chill in the wind pressing in on my head, the damp cold clutch of the bare ground working its way in through my clothes. Instinct told me to move, to jump-start my circulation, but I knew that if I really wanted to find out if there was anyone else out there, I was going to have to stay totally still.

I heard the sound of the engine announcing Jeff's return. I smiled childishly to myself. He

56

hadn't stayed very long. It didn't look like an invitation for coffee and comfort had been forthcoming.

The sound drew closer. Donnie had almost finished setting up the line of lights, and nothing else moved down on the site. It looked like I had been wrong. Then Jeff's engine note changed. Out of gear. He had stopped.

The sound of his horn was an auditory shock that broke the night up.

And it confused me. I only realized that it was a signal when I saw Donnie jump down off the top of the last earthmover in the line and trot towards a parked pickup. What had Jeff found? I tried the binoculars on him, but he was too deep in shadow.

I was about to stand up and run down the hillside to find out when I saw him. A fragmentary movement in my peripheral vision. I swung the binoculars, and when I managed to focus I picked out a dark, crouched figure slipping in and out of the shadows formed by the lights over the line of machines. Unseen by Donnie, who had now left the camp, and was driving towards Jeff's pickup.

I got up and started running down the hill, keeping low, hoping that the figure would be too intent on his purpose to look my way. I measured out the imaginary parabola in front of me that would intersect with the line of machines.

I was back to being Geronimo until something hard, at ankle level, took my feet out from under me. I was catapulted into sudden bad momentum on a steep, stone-pocked hillside.

Which reached terminal velocity with my face in a puddle, and my mouth chewing on gravel, while I tried to pinpoint what, precisely, was wrong with

57

my head.

I stood up. The dizziness flared up behind my eyes like the collision instant in a particle accelerator. The pain localized and seared, as if a hot poker was being thrust into my ear. I buckled, drooped onto my knees, and tensed against a spasm of nausea.

This Apache needed help.

Everything had shifted into a fuzzy state. But I could still make out Jeff and Donnie's headlights off to the side and below me. I stood up again, slowly and carefully this time, intending to call out and attract their attention. But I soon realized that that process involved too many complex actions. Instead, I decided to keep it simple and utilize gravity. I stumbled down the slope in a series of wide, wandering lurches.

They were changing the front wheel on Jeff's truck. I staggered into their light, feeling like a demented old hermit who has just spent the last forty days fasting on locusts and thorns.

'There's someone in the camp . . .' I gasped, my tongue working like an unfamiliar reptile.

They leaped into Donnie's truck and drove off with the rear cab door flapping open. It was only later that I discovered that I had been expected to get into it. Some hope.

I was still sitting on the running board of Jeff's truck, my head in my hands, waiting for my world to come back into some sort of order, when they returned for me. 'Are you all right?' Jeff asked, and I heard the concern in his voice. 'What happened?'

I knew better than to shake my head. 'I don't know.' Did I have a memory of something that had suddenly appeared out of the darkness to run for a moment beside me? Or had that happened in a parallel universe? 'I think I tripped. But I might have been nobbled.'

I heard his breath draw in. 'God, you look terrible . . .'

'What's happened with the machinery?'

'Don't worry about that now. I'm going to get you into the truck. I'm going to get you to a hospital.'

*   *   *

I didn't argue. I saved that for the duty nurse at the Dinas Cottage Hospital who confronted us. 'I'm sorry, but I'm afraid we don't have an A & E department here.'

'He's had an accident,' Jeff protested.

'Which is why you'll need to carry on to either Newtown or Aberystwyth, where they have the proper facilities.'

I didn't want to go to Newtown or Aberystwyth. They were too far away. I could wake up there to find an officer who outranked me telling me that I was off this case and back on the trail of mutilated sheep.

'I want to stay here,' I said feebly, letting go of Jeff and grabbing at one of the tubular metal wheelchairs that were lined up by the entrance desk.

'You can't,' she stated officiously, trying to block me.

'I can,' I returned defiantly, wriggling into possession of the chair.

'You can't use that,' she squealed, 'those are for the use of our patients.' She appealed to Jeff.

'You'll have to take him out of here, or I'll have to call the police.'

'I am the fucking police!' I yelled at her, holding my warrant card out in front of me like a silver cross against a vampire. 'I have been injured in the line of duty, and I expect some care in my fucking community.'

They got their own back in the amount of hair they shaved off above my right temple to clean the abrasions. Also in the scrubbing brush they used, which looked more suited to removing heavy-duty stains on the urinals than to the healing arts. But I took it all without complaint. I was their damaged goods now, and I had no intention of going anywhere else tonight.

I had been treated for superficial cuts and abrasions, and was under observation for possible concussion. They also found and treated a nasty contusion on my left ankle. Consistent, they reassured me, with having run into an exposed tree root in the dark. Fine, I didn't argue, it kept them happy to keep cause and effect in cosmic balance. But I had no recollection of seeing any trees on that sector of the hill.

Jeff came back in to see me after they'd patched me up. 'You can tell me what happened up there now,' I said.

'How much of it did you miss?'

'Your puncture? Was it rigged?'

'A piece of two by four on the track studded with nails. I thought one of the crew had got careless.' He shook his head. 'I wasn't thinking. That's why I called Donnie over. Leaving the camp open. We were even taking the time to change the tyre, for Christ's sake,' he remonstrated against himself.

60

'What did he get?'

'The hydraulic lines on the other diggers.'

The drugs they had given me kicked in. Jeff went into soft focus. I tried to blink him back, but I had forgotten what went where, gave up, and joined the undead.

I came to in the muzzy, grey, artificial twilight that passed for darkness in the ward. Jeff had gone and my head hurt.

I forced myself not to drift off again. I tried to concentrate on taking myself back to that moment before I had found myself launched off the hillside. Had someone turned up beside me? Or could it have been a tree? But my memory didn't want to play.

Because there was something else nagging.

I shifted tack. I brought back the picture of Donnie rigging up his lights. What was wrong with that image? What jarred with the information that Jeff had given me?

The hydraulic lines on the other diggers . . .

That line of machinery had not been task dedicated. The diggers had been mixed in at random with bulldozers, self-propelled rollers and dumper trucks of assorted sizes. So why had he been selective? His time must have been scary and limited. If you were just trying to screw with the system why not go down the line taking stuff out as you come to it?

Why complicate it by just targeting the diggers?

Because the diggers were important.

Get back to basics. What do mechanical diggers do?

Diggers dig.

I felt the tickle in my kidneys, and my stomach

lurching southwards.

They wanted to stop us digging up something else on that site.

*   *   *

Six o'clock in the morning. I groped in the bedside drawer. Keys, coins and wallet, but no mobile phone. Then I had a vague memory now of Jeff taking it from me when we had driven here. Why had he taken it? Why hadn't he given it back?

I dressed quietly. It was a bit ironic, I reflected—I had bullied and wheedled to get to stay here, and now I was doing a runner. The porter on the front desk eyed me curiously as I approached down the corridor.

'Have you been discharged?' he asked.

I flashed my warrant card. 'I'm discharging myself.'

'Suit yourself.' He shrugged and heaved himself up reluctantly to unlock the front door.

'How do I get some transport around here?'

He looked at me like I had just awakened from a coma. 'Do you know what time it is?'

'Isn't there an ambulance?'

He grinned maliciously. 'If you're discharging yourself you must be better. You don't need an ambulance.'

'Ambulances take cured people home too,' I countered.

His grin widened, and he shook his head. 'Not at this time in the morning.'

It was frustrating. There was no one around to appreciate the urgency of the situation. There was no one around, period. I was a cop on a mission, but the place was dead, there wasn't even a milk float to commandeer. And it was cold. It was that grey, miserable hour of the morning that you know you were never meant to belong in.

And what was I going to do when I eventually got up there? All the diggers had been put out of commission. But that was the least of my worries. I was deliberately ignoring the fact that I was soon going to have to stare at a whole fucking hillside, with no idea where to begin searching.

The hospital was way outside of town. A drear, dark-stone Victorian building that had once been a refuge for fallen women. I started walking. It was too early to wake David Williams up, but I had already figured that I could hot-wire the old Land Rover that he kept parked and unlocked in the rear yard of The Fleece.

It kept churning over in my mind. What else were we going to find? Could the missing head and hands be buried elsewhere on the site? I was so wrapped up in speculation that I almost didn't hear the approaching vehicle.

And it was a big one. I stepped out into the road with my warrant card in my outstretched arm, waving him down.

'Have you escaped?' the driver asked, pulling up, a short cheery guy with red hair and a thick forearm perched on the open-window ledge.

It took me a moment to realize that he'd made the link between the dressing on my head and the hospital. 'No,' I said reassuringly, 'I'm a policeman, I desperately need to get somewhere where I can organize some transport.'

He looked slightly disappointed that I wasn't an injured loony on the lam. 'So where to?' he asked, shifting noisily into gear as I climbed up into the cab.

I explained about the wind-farm site, but said that I would be happy to be dropped off in the centre of Dinas.

'No worries, I'll take you up there,' he said chirpily, introducing himself as Jim. 'We can pretend it's a car chase,' he added with a grin.

He explained that he worked for the local animal-feed mill and delivered to all the farms in the area.

'Anything unusual about the farms down the wind-farm valley?' I asked.

'You're looking for someone for that body you've found up there, aren't you?' he conjectured happily, jumping slightly out of his seat to notch the truck into a recalcitrant gear.

'Background only. My own interest.'

He thought about it for a moment. 'There's not that many left that are still farms. Pen Tywn has been turned into some kind of fancy shop that's hardly ever open. Then Fron Heulog Farm, which is now the activity centre.'

'What kind of activity?' I asked.

'A bunch of Brummies bought the place. They take in gang members from the city. It's supposed to help them see the error of their ways. They get to come out here on a break from thieving cars. Using our tax money to give them a holiday because the deprived bastards have never seen a sheep.'

I made a mental note of Fron Heulog. It contained the elements of Jack Galbraith's suggested city connection.

'It's Cae Rhedyn after that?' I prompted.

'That's right. Crazy Bruno with his so-called gold

64

mine.'

'I've been there.'

He glanced over to see if I was going to expand on Crazy Bruno before he continued. 'Then there's the Joneses at Cogfryn.'

'I've been there too.'

'Tidy farmers. Up from them there's The Waen. Old Ivor Richards, who's let most of his land out to the Joneses and the Pritchards, who farm Tan-yr-Allt at the head of the valley.' He nodded to himself, working his way up an imaginary map.

'Who around here, in your opinion, isn't a tidy farmer?'

'Ivor Richards, but it's the poor old bugger's age. He's lost it.'

'What about farmers outside the valley?'

He glanced over at me, a shrewd look on his face. After a moment he nodded. 'You want me to tell you about Gerald Evans, don't you?'

'Why would I want you to do that?'

He smiled knowingly. 'Because he's the bastard that everyone around here would like to see toasted.'

'Does he deserve it?'

'They say he tried to buy in infected sheep during the foot-and-mouth. To get the compensation.'

'I've heard that rumour about a lot of farmers.'

'Yes, but he's the sort of bastard who would have really done it.'

Gerald Evans was getting more and more interesting.

We turned off the main road into the valley. As we passed the Pen Tywn Barn Gallery I thought I caught a glimpse of a yellow car parked up by the house. 'When does the gallery open?' I asked Jim.

65

'God knows. They're not like a regular shop, it's all posh and expensive, nothing in there for any local to buy. They seem to turn up when it suits them.'

'They?'

'Two women. They say they're from Cheshire. Somewhere posh anyway.'

Cheshire worked as a generic location for people who were rich enough to escape from Manchester or Liverpool. I craned round to get a last look at the place. My quick reconnoitre yesterday had told me that they had spent money on it. But why the hell would anyone with any sort of business acumen open an up-market joint in a place like this? A dead-end valley from which even the glacier had packed up and left.

I glanced down the drive to Cogfryn Farm as we went past. Fantasizing the sort of breakfast Mrs Jones could probably conjure up.

'Stop here!' I yelled to Jim, as the image I had just seen resolved itself onto my consciousness, erasing the vision of bacon.

I walked up the driveway to the farm. The dogs started barking, bringing a man out of the lambing shed. He was tough-skinny, weathered, and wore an old flat cap at an angle that had probably never changed over the last thirty-five years.

'Mr Jones?' I called out as I approached.

He nodded warily, taking in the dressing on my head, but making an adjustment in his expression for the fact that I knew his name.

I held out my warrant card. 'Detective Sergeant Glyn Capaldi, I met your wife yesterday.'

He held up his forearms, showing me the uterine gloop and iodine on them to let me know that we wouldn't be shaking hands. 'She mentioned it. So what can we do for you this early in the morning?'

'I'd like to borrow that, if I could,' I said, nodding in its direction.

He looked puzzled. 'Borrow what?'

'That.' I pointed this time. 'The tractor.'

He flashed me an anxious look.

'It's for official business,' I explained reassuringly.

'That's an old bugger, we just use it as a yard scraper. We can spare you a newer one if you need a tractor.'

We walked up to the tractor. It was old and grey and had a metal seat covered with dusty sacking. But it was the hydraulic attachment with the wide bucket at the front that had caught my attention.

'This is exactly what I need,' I said, tapping the bucket with my foot.

He looked at me dubiously. 'Would you know how to use that?'

'No.' I smiled at him. 'But I think I know a man who would.'

*　　　*　　　*

Driving the tractor was like perching on top of a giant crab with a grudge. It buckled and scuttled and slewed up the track, while I bounced up and down on the metal seat that acted on my backside like a solid trampoline.

And it made a big, unhappy noise. So much so, that by the time I rounded the last bend, Jeff and Donnie were outside the huts watching anxiously for whatever was coming their way. And their faces didn't exactly break out into great big smiles of

67

relief when they saw that it was only me.

'What the fuck is that?' Donnie yelled.

I killed the engine. It protested with smoke, and fluttered out. 'It's a digger,' I informed him.

Jeff shook his head sagely. 'No, it's not.'

'How far have you come on this?' Donnie asked.

'Only up from the valley.'

They shared a glance, and then, in unison, turned to look up at me with overelaborate smiles. 'You should have called,' Jeff said soothingly, 'I would have come and collected you.'

'I didn't have a phone, Jeff. You took it with you.'

He looked at me, puzzled. 'You asked me to. Said that you wouldn't be able to use it in hospital and asked me to look after it for you. It's up there in the office.' He looked at me appraisingly. 'Are you sure they said it was okay to leave?'

The memory lapse was worrying. But now I understood Jeff and Donnie's reaction. Imagining the picture I presented, with a big dressing stuck on one side of my head, and lurching up the hill on an old tractor that I evidently couldn't control. They probably thought that my mental faculties were still back there in the hospital, sedated and resting in a locker.

'Jeff, honestly, I'm okay, but I do need your help.' I explained my theory. That the diggers had been sabotaged to prevent us from using them to uncover the missing skull and hands.

It was Donnie who saw the obvious flaw. 'The site's been closed down, so why go to the bother?'

'Because Jeff here might just take it on himself to sneak in a bit more work while we're not looking.'

Jeff flushed guiltily. 'But what do they get out of the spoiling tactics? At best it's only a temporary respite.'

I had already thought this one through. 'Desperate measures probably, but they might be hoping for an opportunity to get in here and recover them. Remember, they know where they're buried, they just need a pickaxe and shovel.'

Jeff looked up at the line of stationary plant. 'We haven't got a digger, and we don't know where to look.'

'I've just brought you one.'

He laughed, but I noticed him looking at the tractor again. As I had hoped, the engineer in him was rolling up its sleeves, and nudging the sceptic out of the light.

'I suppose . . .' He walked round to the front of the tractor, dropped to his knees and squinted. 'It's a bit crude, but it could work in a fairly primitive way. As long as we didn't encounter rock.' He looked up at me, something new crossing his mind. 'Is this official?'

I looked back at him for a moment. Gauging. How stuck on rules was Jeff? 'What else have you got to do?'

He laughed. It was the answer I wanted. He faced the hill. 'But where the hell do we start?'

I followed his gaze. The hillside, still mostly in shade, rolled up massively in front of us. This was the nightmare I had avoided envisaging back at the hospital. But now I had had a little more time to think it through. 'You start where you would have if you were carrying on with the job.'

'The roadway?'

'We have to be close. Something rattled them

into action.'

He shook his head. 'The shale level's rising that way.'

'Is that bad?'

'No, it's good. Good for us,' he corrected himself. 'It means that we can get a firm base down without having to go too deep. But it's bad for you.'

By which he meant that it was not ripe grave-digging strata.

'What about over there?' I pointed to where a large rectangle had been pegged out where the ground sloped away from us. It was dotted with tussocks. The grass, reed and heather cover was charred. There had been a fire over this area. 'Is that deeper soil?'

He nodded cautiously. 'Probably. That's the next turbine base to be excavated. But it doesn't fit in with your theory.'

'How?'

'The roadway access to this turbine goes round the top.' He described an arc in the air with his finger.

His deflation was catching. I felt my energy levels sag. Then I looked down at the pegged-out area again without a civil-engineer's hat on. 'They wouldn't know that.'

'Wouldn't know what?'

'That you wouldn't excavate until you had the roadway in above it.'

I ran down to walk the perimeter of the base while Jeff brought the tractor over. I looked at it again, trying to see it the way a guy who was already pissed off with digging would see it. A guy with a bag over his shoulder, the hefted weight of a human head and a pair of hands in it.

I looked behind me and got a fix on the tent that covered the grave. Taking a straight-line bearing on it I walked slowly away. I stopped when the ground began to rise. I tried to get into the guy's mind. You've already dug one big hole, you're weary, so does your mind work some sort of psychological delusion on you? If you started going up a slope, does it tell you that the hole you're going to dig would have to be deeper?

I waved Jeff over. 'Start here,' I yelled.

I watched the blade of the bucket slide in easily. The ground was soft. Jeff started to carefully peel the top layer off. I waved for him to stop.

'What's the problem?' he shouted.

'We haven't got the time for precision. We may have a lot of ground to cover. Just scoop the stuff up and dump it for me to go through with the spade. Hopefully, if there is something in there it'll come up clean in the bucket.'

'Aren't you meant to do this systematically and scientifically?' he asked, looking concerned.

'I'll take the risk,' I said.

After all, I thought, as I sifted through the second pile of spoil that Jeff had dumped beside me, if you accidentally break a couple of fingers off, or crack a skull, there's bound to be systems in place for rectifying things. The vital thing was to locate them. Weld in another link.

I had my back to the tractor. It took me a beat to realize that something had changed.

Silence.

I turned around. The front attachment of the tractor was raised. Poised in front of me. There, minus its head, minus its hands, minus its legs, perched upright in the tractor's bucket, like it was

71

sitting on a designer fucking sofa, was a rotting, naked torso.

5

The stink hit us with the olfactory equivalent of a water canon. Jeff vomited over the side of the tractor. I cupped my hand over my mouth and nose, checked my gagging reaction, and forced myself to look, distracting myself from the ghastliness by trying to remember the stages of decomposition a forensic scientist I had once dated had taught me.

Autolysis had caused skin slippage on the chest. The green tint of putrefaction was present, but the worst of the bloat had gone, the gas and fluid accumulations already purged out. Insects were crawling or dropping out of the huge wound the tractor's bucket had made. But no adipocere yet. I tried to remember. How long for the soapy deposits of adipocere to form?

Her breasts had collapsed into triangular flaps on the slumped chest skin. But they were still recognisable as breasts. This was a she. This one was fresh.

I sent out a silent prayer to the angel who watched over my hunches. *Don't do this to me. Don't let this be Evie.*

Evie left two years ago. This one still had skin. Skeletonization would have occurred if she had been in the ground for two years. It came back to me. Those gruesome pillowcase lectures I had had with my forensic scientist. Adipocere formation takes from several weeks to months to form. There was no adipocere formation yet.

And Evie had been gone for two years. I clutched at that.

I found the legs. Down on my hands and knees with a trowel, an old T-shirt of Jeff's soaked in aftershave and wrapped around my lower face, keeping the worst of the stench at bay. I had left Jeff with Donnie at the site huts, still in shock. I had called this one in from down there before I had come back up with my jury-rigged face mask.

I knew I should have left this bit to the experts, but it was personal. I felt that I had desecrated her. She had been chopped in half as a result of my instructions. I had to do the best I could to make her at least symbolically whole again.

The bastard had left her shoes on. It turned her back to human, and I felt my stomach churn again. Raised heels, thin strap at the back, wickedly pointed, and still recognizably red.

One had been partially dislodged by the swelling that accompanied decomposition. I took a photograph of it and the leg *in situ* with my digital camera. For the forensic record. Then I grasped the heel, closed my eyes, and pulled it away. I took another photograph of the shoe, zooming in so that the grotesque dead foot was not in the shot. If I was going to have to show this picture around I wanted to keep it as trauma-free as possible.

I stood back and looked down at the legs, still lying where I had uncovered them. We hadn't scooped them up from the deep. This was a shallow grave. Much more so than the other one. And, given the condition of the body, it had to be much more recent.

Why? The illogicality of it had started to crowd

in on me. Why bury something on a construction site just before the work has started?

Because, in other respects, they had been clever. By setting fire to the surrounding vegetation they had disguised the freshness of the excavation. Just another one of the many burned or blighted patches that scabbed the hillside. And they would probably have had to bury her in daylight as the torched heather would have shone like a beacon in the night. Or wouldn't that matter around here? Was that why this place had had been chosen? Because even God had His blind spots?

*   *   *

Jack Galbraith and Bryn Jones turned up shortly after the SOCO team and Bill Atkins. We were now all wearing white gauze respiratory masks and white sterile suits, which gave us the look and the fuzzy sound of the survivors of an alien virus.

They both stared at the dressing on the side of my head. 'Husband came home unexpectedly, eh? Had to close her legs a bit too quickly, did she, Capaldi?' Jack Galbraith quipped, deadpan.

I assumed that I wasn't meant to answer that.

He made a big deal of taking in the whole scene and groaned theatrically. 'How do you manage it? Didn't I say it, Bryn? On the way back to Carmarthen the last time we were here. "Just you watch," I said. "Just you watch Capaldi fuck up the serenity. Watch him turn a nice, cold, total cul-de-sac case into a fucking Hollywood spectacular." He looked around him with unfeigned disgust. 'In Indian fucking territory.'

Bryn was taking in the remains. 'Looks like this

74

one's coming off the desktop.' He glanced at me as he said it. I couldn't tell whether it had contained a smile or a frown.

'Where's your big black box and your saw, Capaldi?' Jack Galbraith asked eventually, breaking the silence that had accompanied his ruminations over the corpse, which was still sitting in the tractor's bucket.

'Sir?' I asked, wondering what was coming at me.

'Your amateur magician's kit. Saw the lady in half. Missed the rest of the lesson, did you? The bit where they showed you how to put her back together again?'

'I'm sorry, sir.'

He turned to Bryn Jones. 'I'm getting a very bad feeling about this.'

Bryn nodded his concurrence morosely.

Jack Galbraith came back at me. 'Tell us about it, Capaldi. What brainstorm made you decide to start mashing around this spot with that mechanical deathtrap?'

'It was a lucky guess, sir.'

He winced. He didn't think it was lucky. He could now see part of his future stretching out in front of him with an accompaniment of mud, drizzle and Inspector Morgan. 'The doc reckons she's been in the ground for anything between four and eight weeks,' he reflected.

'Only a guess at this stage,' Bryn cautioned.

'Close enough to start running a working hypothesis. When did the work start here?'

'Just under five weeks ago, sir,' I said. I had already asked Donnie.

'So, he just managed to dump her in time,' he mused.

75

'If he was local he'd have known about the prospect of the wind farm for a long time, sir,' I said.

He shook his head dismissively. 'He's not local. Give me the stats on the first one again, Bryn.'

'Forensics are saying about six to eight years in the ground,' he replied without consulting his notes. 'Male, broad-spectrum middle-age. Zero identifying marks or indicators as to cause of death.'

Jack Galbraith spread his arms, an index finger pointing at each of the gravesites. 'Six years . . . Six weeks . . . What the fuck is going on here?'

Bryn and I stayed quiet, we both knew that the question was rhetorical.

'Head and hands gone in both cases,' Jack Galbraith ruminated aloud, 'both bodies naked. It's too soon for a copycat, and there hasn't been any publicity. We have to assume it's the same workman.'

'Different genders,' Bryn observed, 'and this latest one looks young, which would make different age ranges.'

'So, no nice, tight victim pattern to work with. This guy is not particular. And why the time spread?' Jack Galbraith looked at me when he said it. 'Why six years between them?'

'We don't know that this is it, sir. The final victim count,' I ventured.

'You win the coconut, Sergeant Capaldi, for providing the answer we did not want to hear.'

'There's something strange, sir.' I had to share the illogicality that had started screaming at me as soon as I had got over my first visceral response to the sight of the body.

'Something strange . . .?' he said sarcastically, raising his eyebrows, and letting me see his glance over at the corpse in the tractor's bucket.

'They must have known about the wind farm. I thought that was why they were trying to sabotage the diggers. To get the evidence out before we could get to it. But why bury another one here just before they started the site work?'

'He's not local,' Jack Galbraith said with conviction, 'this is a dumping ground, I'm sure of it. So he may not have known about the wind farm.'

'The site would still have been advertised, sir. Even if he had managed to get the body up here before the work started he must have seen that they were going to be pulling the hill apart to build the wind farm.'

He frowned. 'I'm changing my mind on this one. I don't think these are professional hits. I think we've got a nut job. I think we're going to find more. I think this is his dumping ground, his squirrel's nest.'

'Why bury a fresh one, sir,' I persisted, 'if he knows it's going to be discovered?'

'You may be right, Capaldi. Either he hadn't been keeping up with the news, or that's what he wants. The thrill of exposure. His craftsmanship coming out into the light. So much so that he decides to welcome us here with fresh meat.'

I had a sudden bad feeling, which I was not about to share with my superiors. Could the sabotage of the diggers have been a double bluff? Was my reaction the one they had been manoeuvring for? Had I been led here to find this body? Had I been played for a patsy?

'That's when they fuck up, isn't it, Bryn?' Jack

Galbraith continued, happily mining his new vein. 'When they start to think they can play around with us.'

'I'd be happier if he'd left us with more identifiers,' Bryn replied morosely.

Jack Galbraith pointed at the torso in the tractor's bucket. 'That thing there has to be DNA soup.'

'We're working on getting a mitochondrial DNA profile off the skeleton, too. But where do we start the match process?'

'Got any missing girls in your patch, Capaldi?' Jack Galbraith asked with a smirk. 'That aren't covered in wool and say, "Baa"?'

'I've got one that went astray two years ago.'

He frowned, he hadn't expected that answer. 'This one hasn't been in the ground for two years.'

'I know that, sir. But the parents will hear about this and I'd like to try and reassure them.'

He nodded towards the torso. 'The sight of that is not going to reassure anyone.'

I showed him the image of the red shoe on my digital camera. 'I can ask them if their daughter ever wore anything like that.'

'If she's been gone for two years, what's to say she didn't buy the shoes in the interim?' Bryn asked.

'It would be an elimination, sir,' I pushed. 'We can then start moving the ripple outwards.'

Jack Galbraith shook his head. 'She's not local. I expect the poor cow was a tart from somewhere. But not here.'

Bryn shrugged. 'We've got to start somewhere. May as well clear the local field before we spread.'

David Williams had said that the Salmons' smallholding was at the head of a crappy valley. In my book a valley was a piece of level ground where the hills had come down to rest. There was nothing level about this place. It was all on a slant. The tilt in the land affected everything, the runty trees, the stone field walls, even the weeds looked tired with trying to find the true vertical.

I walked the last fifty metres rather than risk my car's suspension on the deeply rutted track. It was a low stone house with a patched slate roof, the rendered walls painted sky blue, which, with the wind chimes, marked the owners as outsiders. An old-model Isuzu Trooper was parked beside the grass-choked hulk of a Ford Sierra, which had probably died pining for the asphalt of Bromley.

Mr Salmon was in a field behind the house, bouncing on the seat of an open-topped tractor, dragging what looked like a rusty iron bedstead behind to scarify the grass. He waved, and cut across at an angle towards me, the tractor taking on the universal list of this place.

Mrs Salmon came round from the back of the house at the same time as he arrived. He cut the engine. They were both wearing blue overalls, and looked earnest and worried, as if they had been expecting a visit from the foreclosure man. Or perhaps it was the dressing over my injury, damaged cops being a not-too-reassuring sight.

'Hello, Sergeant,' Mr Salmon called out warily. His wife stayed tight-lipped.

'Hello,' I called back cheerily, 'I thought I'd call by to allay any worries you might have.'

'Worries about what?' Mrs Salmon asked.

Oh, shit . . . I swore inwardly. The rumour-mill had stalled. The news hadn't reached them yet. 'We've found another body, I'm afraid.' I found myself in the weird position of trying to project casual reassurance into that announcement.

They both blanched. Her hand went to her mouth. He tried to put an arm around her shoulder, but she shrugged him off.

'It's a girl . . .?' Mrs Salmon croaked.

I nodded. 'Yes.'

'We showed you a photograph of Evie,' Mr Salmon reminded me anxiously.

'We can't go on visual evidence, I'm afraid,' I said, trying to make it sound procedural, hoping that they wouldn't ask me to elaborate.

'Have they done something horrible to her?' Her voice quaked.

'I'm sorry, but I can't go into details.'

'Does she fit Evie's description?' Mr Salmon asked shakily.

'You told me Evie left two years ago?'

'Yes.'

'And no one has reported having seen her since?'

They shared a glance. 'No.' Mr Salmon spoke for both of them.

'I can't be precise at this stage, but I can tell you that the time frame doesn't appear to match Evie's leaving. So you may be able to help us to eliminate her from the enquiry.'

'How do we do that?' Mr Salmon asked.

'By telling me if she ever possessed a pair of shoes like this?' I passed the photograph.

Mrs Salmon grabbed it. She stared at it for a moment, and then shook her head slowly, an expression of palpable relief forming. 'No. Definitely not. She would never have been allowed anything as tarty as that.'

I glanced at her husband, who was looking over her shoulder. If anything his pallor had got worse.

'Mr Salmon?'

He pulled a weak smile and shook his head. 'Don't ask me, I'm not an expert on the ladies' shoe front.' His voice was hoarse and soft. His way of expressing relief, I thought.

'Poor girl.' She handed back the photograph. She beamed at me. This one was someone else's problem. Her world had clicked back into its safe and comfortable groove. 'Will you stay and have a cup of tea?'

'No, thanks.'

'I'll walk you down to your car,' Mr Salmon offered.

I felt the bad vibe as soon as we started walking. 'Are you all right, Mr Salmon?' I asked.

'Don't turn round. Please don't let her see you turn round. Just keep on walking.' He still had the hoarse voice, but now he let me realize that it wasn't relief. This was a man of ash and lye, an absolute inversion of joy.

'What's the matter?'

'Those were Evie's forbidden shoes.'

'But your wife . . .'

'She never knew,' he interrupted. He took a breath, which rattled in his throat. 'I caught Evie in those shoes one night in Dinas when I arrived early to collect her from a party. She hadn't had time to change back into the sensible ones. They were meant to be a secret, she'd saved up her earnings to buy them. I promised not to tell her mother.'

81

I kept on walking and waited for a reaction. But I didn't feel the trapdoor drop beneath me. Just a wave of sadness. No shock, no surprise, no horror. Had I instinctively realized that it was Evie as soon as I had seen those devastated breasts and the piteous red shoes?

Poor Evie. I allowed her a short, silent benediction, and prepared to concentrate on her father. He was in the pre-grief stage, he was on his way to hell, he had started the flight, but didn't know the destination yet. He was open and numb, and the state was as good as any truth drug.

He took a deep, shaky breath, and let the cry out from the heart. 'We brought her here to be safe!'

'When did she start running away?' I probed gently.

'It wasn't running away to begin with. It started with not coming home on the school bus. Hanging around in Dinas. Then she started hitchhiking without telling us. Newtown at first, then Hereford or Aberystwyth. She would only call us to pick her up when she ran out of money to feed herself.'

'Do you think she could have ended up living in any of those places?'

He shook his head, beginning to catch a glimpse of the abyss. 'We don't know. We've been visiting them all regularly since she went away, walking around, just hoping we might catch a sight of her.'

'Did she have any close friends here? Boyfriends?'

'She wouldn't talk to us about anything like that. She would never bring kids she knew from school back here.'

'You said she saved up her earnings to buy those shoes? Where did she work?'

'Babysitting, mainly. And she helped the ladies at the Barn Gallery at Pen Twyn when it was open. And she used to help Mrs Evans over at Pentre Fawr with her horses.' He smiled wanly at the memory. 'She would help her with hers, but she had no interest in our animals.'

I felt the spark. 'Would that be Mrs Gerald Evans?' I asked, forcing myself to keep it flat. Pornographer, dog killer, rustler and cheat. And now?

He nodded disinterestedly. His flight path was tilting. He looked at me mutely. Despairingly. I knew that he wanted me to make it right again.

I forced a smile. 'You said it yourself, you're not an expert on ladies' shoes. Nothing's definite yet.' I inserted a sensitive pause. 'But just to make the elimination certain, someone is going to have to come out to see you.'

He looked at me dully.

'To take DNA samples. And if it will help, we can put you in touch with counselling?'

He nodded slackly, and then put his hand out to stop me. 'I'm going back up to the house. I'm going to have to tell her.'

I watched him walk back up the track towards her. She stood on tiptoe and gave me a last cheery wave.

I pretended that I hadn't seen it. I couldn't wave back. I was the one who had promised her that it wouldn't be Evie.

*   *   *

To David Williams's delight we were setting up the incident room in the defunct ballroom of The

83

Fleece. I had had no part in the decision, but, for the prospect of his future generosity, I didn't see the need to enlighten him of that.

The equipment was being delivered and assembled when I got back to Dinas. The SOCO team had been increased and were busy up at the construction site searching for more bodies. I had gone back to see if I could help, but they had made it very apparent that I wasn't on the guest list.

Jack Galbraith had returned to Carmarthen to organize the command structures at that end. The bad news was that Bryn Jones was not going to be acting as his Chief Apostle as he had been called down to deal with a gypsy arson case near Fishguard. We would have to wait for the whole team to assemble tomorrow morning before we would know who was replacing him.

In the meantime I logged in the information I had got on Evie Salmon, and started the process for the collection of the DNA samples. I found a note from Bryn Jones informing me that Jack Galbraith had agreed to include me on the investigative team. I tried not to show my pleasure in the midst of other people's pain and anguish, but it was hard to keep the self-satisfied smile off my face. It was a sad fact that the prospect of dealing with death and mutilation felt like a return to the nest.

To compensate I floated out a silent promise to Evie. *We're going to get him for you.* Him? Her? I recalled last night's spooked hunch on the hillside, the phantom tree root. Them?

I was helping the technicians assemble desks in the ballroom when David Williams stuck his head round the door. 'I couldn't find you. I've just taken a call from Dr MacLean.'

84

'What did she want?'

'She asked if you'd call her back. She sounded a bit upset.'

I started to dial the number he had given me. I looked up at the clerestory window. We still had light.

I borrowed David's Land Rover to handle the by-way. When I reached Tessa's camp I was surprised to see a SOCO vehicle parked by the dig. Tessa came out from under the canopy as I parked. She watched me with a hand shading her brow from the setting sun.

'I heard about the accident,' she said, as I got closer.

I touched the dressing instinctively. 'It's nothing serious.'

She squinted at my face. 'It makes you look a bit lopsided.' She softened the judgement with a grin.

'I got your message.'

'You didn't have to come all this way.'

'That's okay.'

She nodded. She suddenly looked preoccupied. 'I heard that you'd discovered another body. Jeff isn't up to talking. I tried to go over, but it's all cordoned off.'

'We're trying to keep the press out.'

'Is it another skeleton?'

'I can't divulge that information, I'm afraid.'

'Please, Sergeant?' She didn't try to play it coy. It wasn't a plea. She was just making it plain that this was important to her.

'In strictest confidence?'

She nodded once.

'We've found the recently interred body of a young woman.' I didn't bother informing her that

85

she had arrived in two halves.

'Oh my God . . .' Her face drained. A tremor ran through her. 'What's happening . . .?' She stared at me. The question was involuntary.

'That's what we're trying to investigate.'

'I'm sorry.' She forced a smile.

I smiled back. But I was really wondering what had caused this reaction. She had been so composed with that first corpse. So what had upset her so much about this one?

She read my mind. 'I'm used to skeletons. It's the archaeologist in me. Fresh graves disturb me. We have to sleep up here at night, remember?' This time the smile broke through to let me know that she wasn't entirely serious. 'Thank you. It is actually better to know.'

'You're welcome. And I'm only ever a phone call away.'

She nodded gratefully, and then gestured behind her to the dig canopy. 'I'd show you mine if it weren't so crowded in there.'

'Who's here?' I asked, nodding at the SOCO vehicle.

'Your forensic anthropologist. She's come to make sure that I haven't been duped,' she explained, more amused than annoyed. 'At least mine was here first. And has an excuse for being here.'

'I thought you didn't know that?'

'This is an ancient ridgeway, so we're working on the assumption that he probably died in transit and was buried by his travelling companions.'

'Fellow Gallowglass?'

She shrugged and smiled wistfully. 'It's an intriguing and romantic notion. We're playing

86

with a loose theory that they could have been military emissaries from the Irish going to offer their services to the Princes of Maelienydd against Henry II.'

'The Scots, Irish and Welsh against the English?' She smiled. 'Sound familiar?'

We were distracted by the flap on the dig-enclosure opening. The forensic anthropologist emerging, followed by two SOCO people. She nodded, surprised to see me.

'Satisfied?' Tessa asked.

'Yes, what a beauty,' she enthused. The two women beamed at each other, in joint communion over a corpse.

'You can discount this one?' I asked the FA.

'Definitely. How come he's so well preserved?' she asked Tessa.

'I've had a soil analysis done. There's a lot of galena present, which could explain it.'

'Right . . .' The FA nodded, digesting this. 'Fascinating.'

'Phew, in the clear . . .' Tessa exclaimed, mock-dramatically, making a show of wiping her brow, as we watched the SOCO vehicle drive off.

'What's galena?' I asked.

'It's a lead ore. It could have acted as a sterilizing agent. Killed off the microflora and stopped total decomposition.'

'Right.' I nodded sagely.

'Want to meet him?' Tessa asked.

I didn't really, but I didn't want to lose Tessa's grace either. 'Yes, please,' I said enthusiastically.

The light inside the enclosure was muted. There was a soft hum of machinery. A dehumidifier, Tessa explained, attached to the polythene bubble that protected and isolated Redshanks from what had turned out to be his future. Two young assistants, with their tiny trowels poised, looked up patiently from the excavation that surrounded him, waiting for yet another interruption to pass them by.

It wasn't a skeleton, the body was covered with desiccated skin, the colour and texture of tea-stained parchment, and there were even some scraps and wisps of what must have been cloth, and the odd shard of leather that looked like dried and twisted cat turds.

I scoured my repertoire and came up with noises appropriate to the admiration of a long-dead and deeply dehydrated Scotsman.

Tessa nudged me, and nodded towards the entrance. 'Well?' she asked, when we hit the outside air again.

'He looks like I feel.'

She let out a short laugh. Then suddenly she was looking at me with concern. 'Does it hurt?'

I realized that I hadn't looked in a mirror for hours. 'What colour is my face?'

She cocked her head and studied me for a moment. 'It's quite a rainbow around the dressing. Yellow through purple with magenta highlights?' She qualified it with a grin.

'I should have telephoned.'

She shook her head and briefly touched my wrist. 'No, the visit was appreciated.'

It was a start.

6

Weirdly, I was wakened by silence. There had been an owl flitting around outside, but now it had gone. There was still the sound of the river, but that was a constant. Apart from that, the night acoustic was flat and empty. Too empty.

It was two o'clock in the morning and it was cold out of bed. I pulled a sweatshirt on over the T-shirt I slept in, and walked through to the living area to put my anxiety to sleep so that I could get back there myself. As I approached the large rear window that overlooked the river the clouds pulled back and the moon swathed the opposite bank with a pale opalescent light.

The figure standing on the other side of the river outlined by the strange light startled me.

A chill emanated from my brainstem and ran straight through me. I started to look beyond time and reason for an explanation before I forced myself back into the now. Concentrate, I told myself. This is a man. He's here because he knows you.

I went back to my bedroom and pulled on a pair of jeans and shoes. I half expected him to be gone by the time I got round to the riverbank. A big part of me hoped that he'd be gone.

He hadn't moved.

His head was in the shadow of a tree. It was those pale heron-thin legs under the shorts that gave him away. 'Mr Gilbert,' I called out across the river, 'what are you doing here?'

'I remembered something,' he called back, his

voice just strong enough to be heard over the sound of the river.

'Come round,' I said, gesturing at the bridge, 'we can talk in my caravan.'

'I can't cross the river at night.'

I should probably have realized then where this was going. 'Stay over there, I'll come to you.'

By the time I had run round he was waiting for me on the other side of the bridge. He surprised me by holding up a hand like a cop halting traffic as I approached my side of the bridge. I stopped.

'Walk across backwards,' he instructed.

'Why?'

'Then you can see which ones are trying to follow you.'

I didn't argue, I just humoured him. I didn't bother checking for the ones who might be following me, though. I was too busy keeping an eye on my feet. It was tricky walking backwards in the gloom on the shaky planks and with gaps in the deck of the wooden bridge.

'Couldn't you have come over to me that way?' I asked when I reached him.

He shook his head, his face deadpan. 'No. Mine have learned the tricks.'

I saw a whole new minefield opening up there, so I didn't pursue it. 'What did you remember?' I asked instead.

He stared at me intently. His eyes were very pale and he was blinking. Probably myopic. The combined effect, with his thin hair and the wispy beard, was of a goat on the verge of distress.

'I remembered the lights.'

'At the wind-farm site?'

He nodded.

90

'How long ago?' I asked carefully.

He shook his head. 'Time doesn't matter to them. They're beyond that construct. They wouldn't be able to get here otherwise.'

I wised up then. 'Mr Gilbert, are you talking about UFOs?'

His sad pale face lit up for a moment. 'Have you seen them too?'

'Not for a long time. They're gone now.'

He dipped his head sadly. 'They must have completed their mission.'

'Moved on,' I concurred. 'But thank you for coming to tell me.'

He nodded gratefully. My heart went out to the poor old bastard. He had sought me out. Had that last talk of ours sparked something in him? A realization that he could still commune with another human being?

'Mr Gilbert, have you ever had any dealings with a Mr Gerald Evans?' It was a long shot, but if I'd managed to open a communication window I might as well try to take advantage of it. 'From Pentre Fawr Farm.' I gestured off in the vague direction of where I thought Evans's place lay.

He just stared at me expectantly, as if he was still waiting for the question. I decided to bring it closer to home. 'Do people still trespass on your land?'

This one got through. 'Not since I put the fence up,' he answered. 'That stopped them talking about taking my land back from me.' He chuckled.

'Who was that?'

'The son and the daughter and the other one. When the girl was still alive.'

I assumed that the son and the daughter were the Cogfryn children: Owen and Rose, the dead

91

daughter. 'The other one?' I asked.

'The one who was meant to marry her.'

'But she died?' I prompted.

He nodded.

'When?'

He shrugged. 'I don't know, I wasn't there.' The subject didn't interest him. He stared at me. Even in the gloom I could see that his expression had turned hopeful. 'Do you think they'll come back?'

'Who is that, Mr Gilbert?'

'The lights.'

I patted him gently on the shoulder. 'I'm sure they will.'

I didn't bother to walk backwards over the bridge after I left him. Perhaps, in hindsight, that was a mistake. It would have saved a lot of grief if I could have seen who was trying to follow me then, before it all went shitty.

*   *   *

The ballroom at The Fleece had been built in the twenties, and had since functioned as a cinema, a bingo parlour and, once, to the local population's total mystification, as a Hatha Yoga centre. It had a high, water-stained ceiling, clerestory windows that let in a drab dusty light, and pine floorboards, the lacquered surface brittle and peeling like old nail polish. It felt like the sort of place that could have been commandeered to act as a temporary mortuary for train-wreck victims.

The circus had got into town early. When I arrived everyone was busy eating the breakfast that David and Sandra had provided. Proper filter coffee, croissants and fruit. I wondered how long this would last.

Alison Weir, a DC from headquarters, who was to act as collator, waved at me from behind her computer terminal. There were two other male DCs from Carmarthen who were on wary, sideways-nodding terms with me. Emrys Hughes shot me a glance that would have burst a child's balloon. Beside him three uniformed PCs hovered in their own territorial space, new to this, not yet knowing what was expected of them.

'Have I got a title?' I asked Alison quietly.

'Yes,' she said, without having to check the roster. 'Local Liaison Officer. Impressive, eh?'

'It just means I know how to tell the different ends of a sheep apart.'

Luckily we had a front lobby door that creaked. So that when Jack Galbraith made his entrance we were all on our feet. I was glad that I was the only one in the room not having to brush crumbs off themselves. I wasn't glad to see the man standing beside him. Kevin Fletcher. I caught Alison's sidelong glance at me. She was gauging my reaction. She obviously knew that Kevin and I had a History.

Jack Galbraith stood by the door and took in the room. His smile was meant to be easy, but we all knew we were under inspection. He nodded towards the table with the breakfast trays. 'I'm glad to see they're treating you well.' We all chuckled dutifully, and felt immediately guilty.

He moved into the room and took up his stand in front of the display board. Fletcher followed him. 'Right, as you all know, I am the senior investigating officer. This is Detective Chief Inspector Kevin Fletcher, who has been seconded to us from Metro, and is going to act as my field officer. DCI Fletcher will be in charge of the incident room, and the day-to-day running of the operation.'

I winced inwardly. The bastard had had yet another promotion. The last I had heard, Fletcher had been a detective inspector. And it was almost as if he had been fitted with a receptor that picked up on my anguish. 'Glyn . . .' he announced loudly, striding over to me with his hand out, '. . . Glyn Capaldi, it's been a long time. How are you doing?' He could have stayed where he was to acknowledge me. By coming across he was making a statement, reminding the others of the height that I had dropped from, unmasking the leper.

'I'm fine, Kevin,' I said, shaking his hand unenthusiastically.

'It looks painful,' he commented, drawing everyone's attention to the fresh dressing on the side of my head that we had all been trying to ignore.

He left me and worked the field, shaking hands all round, and ended up back beside Jack Galbraith. In the old days, I remembered, he would have looked smug, now it looked like he had been taking lessons in benign authority.

Jack Galbraith gave us the overview on the two bodies. No identification was as yet possible on the skeletal victim. Following my tentative identification they were now waiting for DNA confirmation that the recent body was Evie Salmon. Apart from the red shoes there were no remains or traces of clothing in either of the graves, so it had to be surmised that they both had been naked when they had been interred. Also, so far, there were no

94

indications as to the cause of death in either case.

Galbraith held a silence for a moment, reeling in our attention. 'These people were killed unlawfully. There are a lot of theories that will fit, so let me give you mine, before Kevin sends you to sleep with the forensic evidence.' We chuckled on cue. He held up two fingers. 'Two bodies. We are working on the possibility that there are more up there. But, at the moment, there is no pattern, there is no clear and shining path pointing the way ahead. So my hunch is that this is a dumping ground, and that these people were killed at a far remove. Someone tell me what's wrong with that?' he asked, looking straight at me.

I obliged. 'If the young woman is Evie Salmon, she was local. She also disappeared over two years ago.'

'Correct, Evie is the spoiler. But forget the emotive word "disappeared" and stick with the facts. She left home two years ago. She never disappeared, she has existed somewhere. Statistically that somewhere is probably a city. And that is probably where our man found his other victim.'

'It's too coincidental, though, sir,' I protested, 'to think that Evie met her killer in a city, and he just happens to use her particular back yard as a burial ground.'

Jack Galbraith beamed. I was unintentionally playing his foil. 'It's not coincidence, it's our connection. Our killer has an association with Dinas. Which is how he and Evie came into conjunction. That's our starting point. Evie met our man. Now, was this man from Dinas, or visiting Dinas?' He paused and gave us his goshawk stare.

95

'Someone ask me something pertinent?'

Kevin Fletcher complied. 'Why the time lag?'

Jack Galbraith nodded. It was the question he wanted, which made me wonder if they were working a double act. 'Six to eight years. We may have to rethink this if we find anything more on the hill. But let's stick with that timeline. It's a big gap between psychotic urges. So maybe he'd been able to sublimate them on less-extreme outlets. Then Evie comes along. Still no outburst. They manage nearly two years together. Then something flips. He regresses. But what's worrying is that there is now a new element of showmanship. As far as we can tell the first body's burial was meant to be permanent. Evie was there to be dug up and put on display. He even left her shoes on for us.'

'Is he changing, sir?' one of the DCs asked.

He shook his head. 'I don't know, I can't answer that yet. But, people, if he has rediscovered the taste, we had better get to him before he starts indulging again.'

An audible emotional whir ran through the room.

'Should we be warning the locals, sir?' I asked.

He smiled at me indulgently. 'We should be warning the tarts and the homeless and the junkies in the city this bastard is operating out of. Although we do not yet know where that is, do we, Sergeant?'

'No, sir.' I recognized my shut-up cue.

*   *   *

Kevin Fletcher presented the forensic evidence. It was sparse, nothing I hadn't already heard, except that we had managed to identify the polyethylene sheeting as a grade used to wrap and protect rolls of carpet.

One of the DCs put up his hand. Fletcher nodded. 'What about the young woman, sir? Is it possible to tell if there was a sexual element to this?'

Fletcher smiled grimly. 'We can't say yet. The lab people are doing their best, but unfortunately the well-intentioned excavators managed to turn her gynaecology into a ragout.' A collective groan went through the room, and all eyes turned on me. So that one was obviously doing the rounds in Carmarthen. Had the question been a plant? Or was I just being paranoid?

Fletcher uncovered the display board. There were mortuary and site photographs of both the bodies, and a plan showing the locations where they had been found. He jabbed his finger over them. 'This is an out of the way spot. It's a long way off the road, and it can't be seen from the valley. So we're working on the assumption that whoever dug these graves knew the territory.' His eyes caught mine for a moment, as if challenging me to reclaim my theory.

'We have had one big break, though. We have found a pair of bootprints that were missed at first because they had been covered by running water. We think these were made when he was running away from the site security guard. We've managed to get a cast, and the boffins have been hard at work trying to build up a composite of the man.'

He turned to the table, produced another photograph, and pinned it to the board. 'Our putative killer's bootprints. And now . . .' He picked up another, larger piece of paper, holding its blank side towards us, and shaking it tantalizingly. 'Our composite,' he announced triumphantly, turning it over.

Even Jack Galbraith laughed at our reaction to the anticlimax. I had to give Fletcher credit, he was working his audience well.

The composite was little more than a caricature. A pure extrapolation of the weight and proportions of the body based on the size and depth of the bootprint. All science, no art.

Fletcher started nodding in anticipatory sympathy. 'I know it's not great. But I'm afraid it's all we have for now. So you officers at the coalface will have to work with it.'

A low, collective groan rose up from the uniform corner, orchestrated by Emrys Hughes. You couldn't blame them. They were going to be knocking on doors trying to jog people's memories with a cartoon.

Jack Galbraith stepped forward. 'Let me step out of character for once and play the wicked old stepfather.' A dutiful laugh rippled through the room. He raised the composite and held it out to face the room. 'Another spoiler. Because this, of course, may not be our man. He may be wearing an entirely different label.' He clicked his fingers at Alison Weir.

'And what label is that, sir?' she came back crisply.

'I am a wind-farm saboteur. I am an annoying, malicious and destructive bastard, but I am not a killer. I want you to keep that in the back of your minds. This may be a false trail.' He scrutinized us all for a moment, and then nodded. 'Okay, Kevin, back to you.'

A copy of the composite was passed along the line to me. I stopped listening to Fletcher's pep talk and studied it. There was only one fact, which was the size of his boots. His weight, his size and his posture were all conjecture. How many of these variables would fit Gerald Evans?

I checked myself. I had never met Evans, so why was I getting so obsessed with him? Why did I want him to turn out to be a monster? I knew the answer. I wanted a local villain to give my life here some meaning. I didn't want Jack Galbraith to be right. I didn't want this place to be merely a dumping ground. I wanted us to have consequence. I didn't want to be left as merely the caretaker of a charnel house.

I put my hand up tentatively.

'Glyn?' Fletcher gave me the stage.

'We keep talking about "him", but I think there could be a possibility that there's more than one person involved.' I saw Jack Galbraith glare at me, but I wanted this out in the open. Just in case there was anyone else in the audience who was having the same doubts. No hand shot up.

'What evidence have you got to back that up, Glyn?' Kevin asked in the pleasant voice of a patronizing bastard of an uncle.

I touched the dressing on the side of my head involuntarily, beginning to wonder if I was about to wedge myself into a big mistake. 'It's a hunch, Kevin.'

'Serial killers don't work in pairs, it screws up their agenda,' Jack Galbraith announced gruffly.

'Yes, sir.' I didn't think it was politic to point out that, with only two bodies, it was a bit presumptuous to be talking about a serial killer.

I saw Emrys Hughes's hand go up in the uniform sector. It surprised me. Could it be possible that he was about to support me?

Fletcher nodded at him. 'Yes, Emrys?' He had done his team-recognition homework.

'Hearth and home, sir,' he bellowed, misjudging the room's acoustic.

Fletcher and Jack Galbraith shared a quick glance. Reassuring each other in the company of hayseeds. 'I don't quite get you, Emrys,' Fletcher said, smiling patiently.

'I know the people around here, sir. They know me, they trust me.'

'I'm sure they do, Sergeant.'

'No disrespect to Sergeant Capaldi, but they're not going to want an outsider coming into their houses to ask them delicate questions.'

The realization flashed. The bastard . . . Emrys was trying to hijack the case.

'What are you suggesting, Emrys?' Fletcher asked, Jack Galbraith glowering impatiently beside him.

'That we work with the locals. Sergeant Capaldi can do the incomers. There's plenty enough of them around, and he probably speaks their language better.' He flashed a grin at his men.

Fletcher nodded sagely, digesting this. 'Glyn?' he asked.

What could I do? The bastard had sideswiped me. I could smell Inspector Morgan behind this. But the awkward thing was that he had a point. I had come across people here who wouldn't give you the time of day unless you could prove that your forebears had served as retainers with Llewelyn the Last Prince of Wales. And he wasn't down on

100

record as having hired any Italians.

'It's a fair point,' I said, stalling, thinking hard for some way to block him. Emrys was looking over at me, a triumphant gloat lurking underneath the open and honest smile. I wanted to ram something flat and heavy into his face. I didn't give a shit for all the tosspot farmers whose company I was going to be deprived of, but I did not want to miss my chance at Gerald Evans. 'But I'm not sure whether his men have got the requisite interviewing skills.'

'You're going to be using us anyway,' Emrys whined. 'Whichever way we work it, we're still going to be knocking on doors for you. You set the questions if that's what's worrying you.'

Jack Galbraith's mobile phone rang. The digitalized strains of 'Scotland the Brave' surprised us all. He answered it, turning his back to us. Kevin Fletcher looked suddenly abandoned. He shot us a discomfited smile, like an actor who had just lost touch with his prompter.

Jack Galbraith turned back round and held up his hand. He needn't have bothered, he already had total silence. 'That's SOCO. They've just found another one. Skeletonized. Early stage investigations showing broad similarities with the first corpse. Although the forensic anthropologist reckons that this one is female.' He passed his phone to Fletcher. 'Take the details, Kevin.'

We were all stunned by the news. How many more were we going to find? It looked like Jack Galbraith was going to earn his serial-killer tagline.

He turned his attention back to Emrys Hughes. 'Are there really that many people who have moved up here?' he asked, sounding surprised and appalled.

101

'Oh, yes, sir,' Emrys replied.

He looked over at me. 'You talk to them, Capaldi. There has to be some real weirdness among that bunch.' He shook his head. I knew what he was thinking. The same thoughts still visited me from time to time. The fact that people would voluntarily leave a city to take up residence in the boondocks placed them in a seriously disturbed category.

*   *   *

'Hold on . . .' Fletcher's muffled voice responded to the knock I had just given on his door in The Fleece. He opened it and looked surprised to see me. Behind him, on a faded green bedspread, I saw his suitcase and the small piles of clothes waiting to be allocated drawer space.

'I'm sorry to disturb you, Kevin. I know you're trying to settle in, but . . .'

He held up a hand to quiet me. 'Boss or skip?'

'Sorry?' I wondered if I had missed a connection.

'Boss or skip? What's it to be?'

I smiled tentatively. 'Are you serious?'

'Fixing the demarcation lines, Glyn. It'll be good coming from you. Set an example for the others.'

He was serious. And just when I'd begun to think that perhaps I'd been a bit too hard on him, here he was, turning into an even bigger arsehole than he'd been before. He watched me expectantly.

I held out the folder I had been carrying. 'I thought you might want to see this.' He waited. I forced it out. 'Boss.'

He nodded, satisfied. 'What is it?'

'Some pre-investigation notes I've made.'

102

'Give them to Alison in the morning.'

'I thought you might want to be up to speed with them first.'

He thought about it, and gave me a clipped nod. 'Okay, summarize them.'

I glanced up and down the corridor meaningfully. He took the hint and stood aside to let me into the room. The furnishings were heavy and mismatched pieces of French-polished walnut and mahogany, and the air was thick with a synthesized distillation of lavender or gardenia. The net curtains in the bay window had random specks of bluebottle and crane-fly legs caught in the weave. Sandra had given him the best room in the house. 'Nice room,' I observed, nodding appreciatively, trying to make him feel special.

'No, it's fucking not,' he replied, closing the door behind me, 'it's a place where furniture comes to die, and it smells like an overworked hooker's crotch.'

'Is DCS Galbraith not staying?'

'No, rank has its benefits.' He clicked his fingers impatiently. 'Come on, Glyn, I'm tired, I've got to attempt to get the suicide vibes out of this room, so just give me what you've got.'

'It's a very brief profile of the people who live in the valley. All the nearest neighbours to the crime scene.'

He looked unimpressed. 'And surprise me. Not one Son of Satan among them.'

'Not in the valley.'

He opened the door for me. 'I know we go back, Glyn, but no special favours here, I'm afraid. In future let's just process everything through the official channel.'

103

I didn't move.

He stared me out for a moment, and then closed the door again. 'I thought there had to be more.' He groaned. 'Spit it out,' he commanded, sitting heavily on the bed.

'Emrys Hughes.'

He winced, demonstrating the weary burden of leadership. 'The man's got a point. This is a close-knit community. They know him. But don't worry about it, it's not as if we're going to get anywhere talking to the rednecks.'

'What about a redneck with a penchant for pornography and criminal behaviour, and who's a known associate of Evie Salmon?'

He frowned. 'Why is this the first time I'm hearing about this?'

'Because I haven't talked to him yet. I want him, boss. I want first chance at him.'

'You think Hughes will fuck up?'

'I know he will. He has obsequious genes. The guy's a serial forelock-tugger.'

He looked away for a moment, collecting his thoughts. 'Feed me more,' he instructed.

'Gerald Evans is a farmer. He steals other people's sheep, he shoots dogs,' I pressed down on the exaggeration pedal, 'and he imports heavy-duty porno from Holland. He also has direct cross-country access to the burial site from his land. He lives here, he knows the place. He's the only one in the locality that fits under the umbrella.'

'Motive?' Fletcher snapped the question at me.

I shrugged. 'I can't say without talking to him.'

'How does Evie Salmon fit into it?'

'She helped his wife out. He had to know her. Maybe they got as far as blow jobs in the hayloft.

104

Then she moves. But they keep in touch. Who knows, maybe he even set her up in a fuck-pad somewhere. Evie was living away, no one could connect them any more, and that's when she became safe to be a victim.'

'DCS Galbraith is convinced it's an outside agency.'

'This makes more sense, boss.'

He pondered. 'If he's such a bad bastard, why haven't we had him already?'

'Because he's careful. He does what he does on his own land.'

'Okay,' he came to the decision, 'tomorrow morning, you go and talk to him.'

'Thanks, boss.'

'And I go with you.'

My grateful face didn't flutter.

I walked back down the corridor, trying to see the similarities between this pompous bastard and the Kevin Fletcher I had originally known. I had been a raw DC in Cardiff myself at the time, working the deadbeat stuff that the older guys tipped out of their ashtrays for me to pick up: the council-estate break-ins, the foreign-sailor muggings and the over-the-hill hookers who were reduced to knee-tremblers against lock-up garage walls.

He came in through the graduate-recruitment route and I was assigned to him as a minder. We got on well then. He was intelligent and we discovered that we both read books, and liked films and music that bypassed the mainstream. The sort of thing that could have fucked him if he'd ended up with the wrong partner. I hadn't been quite so lucky, I had been landed with the derogatory nickname 'Pablo' after making the mistake of trying to turn one of my colleagues onto an album track called 'Pablo Picasso' by an American indie band called the Modern Lovers.

I showed him the ropes as best I could. I drove him round the streets, pointing out the hot and the cold spots, introduced him to my small but developing team of snitches, and I put myself out there to watch his back. He learned the shortcuts and the cynicism quickly, how to spot and drop the no-hope cases, but, more importantly, how to nail the bad bastards who had either fallen out of grace with their protection, or had never had any to begin with.

I had thought we had the makings of a duo, a proper crime-fighting team. Until the day I walked into the pub that was our unofficial squad room and saw him nested there with the big boys. I knew it was over when he grinned at me and called out across the crowded bar, 'What are you drinking, *Pablo*?'

Kevin Fletcher had started his ascendancy.

And me? I'd like to think that I retained most of my integrity. Which was probably why he was now able to treat me as his fucking slave.

7

There was an air of charged suspense in the incident room when I arrived the next morning. It had the quiet concentrated intensity of the control deck of a submarine during a depth-charge attack.

'What's happened?' I asked Alison, a whisper

seeming appropriate.

She inclined her head towards the room that Fletcher had commandeered. 'Nothing's been announced, but he's been on the phone a lot. And DCS Galbraith is on his way back.'

'So?'

'He was meant to be staying in Carmarthen for a couple of days dealing with politics and getting the proper resources allocated. He's just been on the phone and he's not in a good mood.'

So, Galbraith descending in grumpy mode. That explained the studied sense of doom in here. I smiled cockily. 'Shame I won't be around to share the greetings.' I nodded at Fletcher's closed door. 'The Young Pretender and I have got a prior appointment.'

She flipped me a finger. I knocked on Fletcher's door, opened it and stuck my head round. 'Ready, boss?'

He looked up at me from behind his desk, surprised and distracted. He had a shaving rash and shadows around his eyes. He looked like the victim of a sleep-deprivation curse that he had begun to believe in.

'We're supposed to be going out to interview Gerald Evans,' I reminded him.

The memory came back. He frowned. Hesitated for a moment. And decided that misery preferred company. He waved me in. 'Shut the door behind you,' he instructed.

I sat down in front of him and waited him out.

'We've found another one,' he said eventually. 'Under arc lights. I was summoned up that hill at three o'clock this morning.'

'Number four?'

He nodded morosely. 'DCS Galbraith wants to see it *in situ* before we make any kind of announcement.'

I took that as a warning that any leaks would be traced. 'Fresh or skeleton?'

'Skeleton. Similar condition to the previous two. No head, no hands. Looks like its been in the ground for at least as long as the others. And Evie Salmon's been verified by DNA.'

We both went quiet. So Evie was official. And the toll of the anonymous ones was now three. And rising?

'Have you ever come across one like this before?' It was an unguarded moment. He was actually looking for solace.

'We had that guy a few years back, who was killing schoolgirls up the Valleys,' I reminded him. It had been a case that we had both worked on. Still equally ranked then, I remembered ruefully.

He shook his head. 'That was different. We could identify the kids.'

'We've got Evie now.'

'She doesn't help with the spread. The others are three big blanks. We can get a mitochondrial DNA profile on them, but where do we go from there?' He groaned in frustration. 'It's a classic catch-22. To get a match we need to find a close relative. To find a close relative we need to know who the fuck the victim is.'

Boy did he have a big case of the morning blues. Or responsibility fugue. I didn't care, I was excited about the forthcoming confrontation. 'Or we discover Gerald Evans stirring up heads in his acid bath?' I offered, reminding him of our current mission.

He shook his head. 'We're not going.' He looked up at me. 'How the fuck can I leave here with all this shit coming down on us? And DCS Galbraith arriving at any moment.'

I made a big show of disappointment. 'So I'm going to have to do this myself then, boss?' I asked, starting to get up.

'No.' He flagged me back down. 'I had a talk with DCS Galbraith about it. He doesn't want you disturbing the locals.'

The deflation felt like a kick in the stomach. 'You told him what we had on the guy?'

He flashed me an irritated look. 'I thought that over. There's really nothing that solid there. We agreed that Emrys Hughes can handle the initial interview, and, if he picks up any bad waves, we'll take over.'

The bastard had copped out. 'But the guy's ripe for it, boss,' I pleaded.

He shook his head resolutely. 'You're not getting Evans. DCS Galbraith wants you to interview someone else. A man Inspector Morgan has been bending his ear about. Some incomer weirdo.' He searched his desk and found the relevant piece of paper. 'A crackpot called Bruno Gilbert.'

'Gilbert's harmless,' I protested, wondering when Morgan had joined the anti-Bruno crusade. I dropped the frustration from my tone. 'I've already spoken to him, boss. I've been out to see him. He's a fruitcake, but he's an inhabitant of Planet Docile.'

'That may well be the case, but DCS Galbraith wants an official report to that effect. We don't want the local plods usurping the game and finding the perp for us. Because that's one we wouldn't be able to live down.'

109

I got up. I now felt fucked over and narky. Kevin Fletcher had successfully managed to share his morning malaise. Now, instead of interviewing a hot suspect, I was on my way back to the ruined kingdom.

*   *   *

Bruno Gilbert was still not opening his gates. And he had re-attached the barbed wire. I got back up on the roof of the car, pushed it down again, feeling less charitable this time, and made my entry. I had almost considered faking it, basing my report on my previous visit and Bruno's tale of UFO sightings last night. Nothing would have changed. But Jack Galbraith had an unfortunate knack for sniffing out shortcuts.

I had the same sense of suffusion this side of the gate as before, as if the air here operated at a different density, tamping down sound. Even the noise of a large bird I had disturbed, a wood pigeon or a crow, crashing up through a tree's foliage, had a muted quality to it.

I called out as I walked down the drive, warning him of my arrival. There was no response from his previous niche, and he didn't appear at the door of the shack. Perhaps he was working in his gold mine. That prospect lifted me slightly. Maybe this time I would get a glimpse of the operation.

'Mr Gilbert, are you in there?' I rapped on the shack's rickety plank door, and cocked my head to listen for sounds off. Nothing came back to me. There was no lock. I clicked the old-fashioned thumb-latch and pushed the door open.

Even without the sight of him I would have

recognized that particular combination of smells above all the others. Blood and shotgun-discharge. Over the mildew, excrement, whisky and bottled gas. It was probably only a trace odour by now, something that wouldn't have registered on most people's senses. But it was a smell that was imprinted on my psyche. I would probably even react to homeopathic levels. The smell of my Cardiff demise. The Farmer and the Pimp.

I stayed in the doorway, partly to calm myself down, partly for the overview. Trying to read the room, keeping my eyes darting, staying away from the body, before it loomed too large and obliterated all other perceptions.

Squalor. A one-room shack with a curtained-off cubicle containing the galvanized bucket that he had used for a toilet. The only window obscured by galaxies of cobwebs.

Generations of dust had mutated to take on the mass and heft of dirt on the floor. Wooden plank walls that had once been painted were streaked with rot, except in the tiny cooking area, where grease had acted as a preservative. A camp bed with stains on the covers that at first glance looked like a deliberate pattern. A matching wardrobe and chest of drawers, both with damp-blown veneer.

And the kitchen table.

He had used the surface to balance the double-barrelled shotgun. The force of the blast had blown his chair back, smashing it and him partly through the rotten rear wall, so that they had come to a rest propped back at an angle. It was through this gap in the wall that most of the light was now entering the room.

It was too early in the year for a major fly strike,

111

but a large bird, probably a crow, had crapped on his chest from its perch on his shoulder, where it had been gorging on carpaccio of cerebellum. Both eyes were also gone. Probably the *amuse-bouche*. Had it been the bird I had disturbed?

I started back to the gate to get to the car's radio and call in the cavalry. I stopped at the niche in the brambles where I had last seen Bruno Gilbert crouched, and looked back at the shack.

Nothing was going anywhere. Whenever this had happened the vermin had since had time to come calling. There were no hot clues cooling down.

I had the scene to myself until I decided it was time to sound the klaxon.

I returned to the shack and stood in the doorway, taking a couple of plastic supermarket bags out of my pockets, not taking my eyes off the scene as I stooped down to put them over my shoes.

I held myself there. It was time to stop being purely reactive. *Read what it says*, I instructed myself.

Bruno Gilbert had committed suicide.

It was so obvious. So why was I balking? Because it was so obvious? Because I had only recently met him? He was still fresh in my memory. Definitely a troubled man. But from our two meetings I had come away with a distinct sense that he had managed to come to some sort of accommodation with his demons. And he had his gold mine.

So why do this? And why now?

I went back into the shack, taking care to stay on the path that daily use had worn through the dirt. I scanned for footprints, but there were nothing but scuffed marks. I bent down to take in the soles of Bruno's shoes, which were angled up due to the tilt

112

of the body. The tread pattern didn't match the cast that we had found at the wind-farm site. And his shoes were too small.

From my crouch I saw a bottle of whisky and a glass that had fallen from the table. Neither had broken. The whisky bottle had obviously been not quite empty, the spilled residue having cut a short, winding gulch through the dry caked dust.

I made a cursory analysis of the wound. From the damage, it looked like he had managed to fire both barrels simultaneously. There was massive trauma to the right and rear of the head extending from the neck to virtually the top of the cranium, and as far as the right ear, which was hanging by a small flap of tissue. It was also compounded by the post-mortem damage caused by rodents and birds.

How loud would it have been? The noise of a gun is principally down to the sudden and massive expansion of gasses. His mouth would effectively have acted as a crude silencer, and the shack itself would have had a baffle effect. Factor in the remoteness, the trees, and the chances were that no one would have heard it.

I backed away. A glimpse of something white on the floor, an alien colour in this midden. I bent down and shone my torch on it. At first I thought it was a small piece of bone. But it was too clean, no blood or gristle adhering. Then I realized that it was a tooth. More precisely a fragment of a tooth.

In front of where Bruno had last been sitting. Whereas every other piece of bio-debris had been propelled to the rear or the side by the blast. I took a photograph of it and left it *in situ*. I wasn't about to tell the SOCO people how to do their jobs, but I was going to make sure that this was brought to their attention.

*   *   *

I found a pair of bolt cutters in a tool shed and used them to cut through the chain securing the front gate. The circumstances sanctioned it. This was shortly about to become a high-activity zone, and the assorted participants were not going to be too happy if they had to vault a barred gate to attend to their specialities. Especially the poor bastards who were going to have to carry Bruno out of there.

I got patched through to Fletcher on my car radio. He emitted a prolonged moan, like the sky had just caved in on him. When he'd finished swearing he told me that he'd get a scratch team together and be over as soon as possible. In the meantime he instructed me to secure the site and stay put.

I had no intention of going anywhere. Because I was a big kid who had just been left in charge of a gold mine.

Except I had to find it first.

And it wasn't all whimsy. This was more than the Pig Wales version of *The Treasure of the Sierra Madre*. I was getting a distinctly bad feeling in my kidneys about this. Could the gold mine have anything to do with it? Could the poor loopy old bastard actually have discovered the wonder seam, the mother lode? And had someone else found out? Was this whole thing simply coincidence, and entirely unconnected to the other deaths?

To keep Fletcher happy I tied some crime-scene tape in front of the open gate before I went off exploring.

I followed a well-worn path behind the shack and found the sluice trays. But no sign of a classic timber-propped hole in the face of the hillside. No sign of anything resembling the entrance to a mine. The sluice trays were like big barbecue troughs, supported on trestle legs on a raised wooden deck. Bruno had connected a length of alkathene pipe higher up the adjacent brook, using the water to sieve the ore. But where was the ore coming from?

Bruno was an old guy. From what I understood about this process it involved washing crushed stone through graded sieves. Someone his age would not be able to carry buckets of rock too far. So it had to be close to here somewhere.

The tap on the end of the alkathene pipe dripped. It had formed its own miniature watercourse that ran down to the edge of the raised wooden deck. But no puddle? Why wasn't the water ponding against the edge of the deck?

I knelt down to look closer and saw the hinges set into the top surface of the deck. Part of it obviously lifted. But how? I looked up and scanned the trees. It took me a while to see it. It was clever. The horizontal arm of a davit, folded back into the foliage, camouflaging it. I swung it out through the branches. There was a pulley at the top of the arm, and a block and tackle lashed against the raking spar.

I found the lifting bracket in the sluice tray. Disguised to look like a simple tool that would be used to rake the ore. It took me a couple of attempts but I managed to slot it into its housing on the deck, connected the block and tackle, and started hauling. The free part of the deck in front of the sluice trays started to lift smoothly, hinged with a counterweight like a bascule bridge.

It was impressive. It was elaborate. It was a lot of time and trouble to go to, to hide a hole in the ground. But then time was what Bruno had had lots of.

I climbed down using the metal rungs that had been fixed to the side. It bottomed out about three metres down. There was a collection of buckets, a small sled with metal runners, and a stumpy but solid little hand-operated machine with a hopper on top, which I guessed was an ore crusher.

Three tunnels branched off from the bottom of the access shaft, slanting down. The tunnels were low, you would have to crouch to move along them, and they all smelled of damp rock and lichen growth. And rats? The romance was dropping out of the gold-mining world.

I shone my torch into each of them. No light was reflected back. Part of my funk was fear of the unknown. How far in did these shafts go? How safety-conscious had Bruno been?

I didn't have to do this, I reminded myself. I could just wait until Fletcher arrived and slot meekly back into the command chain. That prospect galvanized me into action. I ducked down into the left-side tunnel. Everything was clammy, and the air smelled immediately fetid, my crouched body acting like a plug, keeping the fresh air behind me.

The tunnel was cut through a soft, shale-type rock, and it was propped with timbers whose dank, dead bark peeled back like old parchment. The shaft turned and dipped to avoid obstructions of harder, sedimentary rock embedded with reflective flakes of mica that caught the torch beam.

116

Everywhere beads of water dripped.

It was hard work, even without the claustrophobia. Bruno had constructed the tunnels to accommodate his body, and I was bigger. I began to feel the pressure change. It was imaginary, I knew, but it didn't help to ease the sense of the weight of the hill above me. I had also completely lost all judgement of distance.

Periodically there were side shafts. I worked out that these were where Bruno had been extracting his ore. They were usually shallow enough to dismiss by using the torch as a sounder.

Until I came to the one that absorbed light. Instead of a roughly gouged rock face I was registering black. Total black.

I scuttled closer, half intrigued, half terrified. If it was possible to have an optical illusion in a place where you couldn't actually see anything, this was one. An illusion of absolute darkness that turned out to be wooden and painted black.

Up on the surface, Bruno's shack was in a state of collapse. He didn't paint things. So why had he taken such care with this? I ran the torch round the perimeter. It was a door of sorts, a plywood panel set into a frame. I felt my mouth go dry, and a light quiver of tension shivering the end of my fingers. What was in there that, even this far down, had to be sealed off?

His explosives store?

No one in their right mind would have given Bruno Gilbert access to a sparkler, let alone dynamite, but it was the only answer that explained what I was looking at; that went some way to diluting my fear. Something practical and sensible to do with mining, with no spooky overtones.

But the reassurance didn't last, and I kept coming back to it. Why was it here and why paint it black?

I prised it open with the screwdriver blade of my Swiss Army knife. I imagined a slight hiss, a seal breaking, when it opened. When I shone my torch in I thought the batteries were dying. I couldn't pick out the end or the sides of the shaft. It was only when I stepped inside that I realized that it was because this was such a large chamber. Bruno had scooped a room out of the heart of the hill.

And I couldn't identify the half-familiar odour that was now mixed in with the damp mineral smell of the rock.

My torch beam was useless for an overview in this large space. It had just picked up another optical illusion. A bedside table. I steeled myself for the instant of total darkness and switched the torch off and on again quickly. The beam was still picking up a bedside table.

Bedside tables do not feature in mine shafts. Bedside tables live beside beds.

I moved the torch, and jumped back involuntarily, a stab of panic jolting me like an electric clamp. The bed was occupied. I forced myself to move the torch again. And pieced together long blonde hair and a waxy shine on a pale, pale face. And the sort of stillness you just know has not changed in a long time.

I had a sudden flashback to McGuire and Tucker. Oh, please, not again!

We needed more light. I forced myself not to touch anything. *Disturb nothing*, I chanted the mantra internally. Don't vomit. Don't piss yourself. Don't corrupt the scene in any way.

118

I didn't have to force myself to back away. It was time to slot meekly back into the command chain. Let someone else take this over.

*   *   *

'Fucking hell, Capaldi, the state of you! Where have you been?' Fletcher yelled at me as I approached. 'And I thought I told you to secure the fucking site?'

He was congregated with one of the DCs and a couple of uniforms outside the shack. I assumed the scratch SOCO team he had assembled was inside. With Jack Galbraith?

I pictured how I must look. Soaked through, scuffed and filthy, as if I had just crawled through an active sewer, against the flow.

'I've found another one, boss.'

His authoritarian face cracked, just as I had hoped it would. He looked at me as if I was deliberately strewing dead bodies at his feet for him to trip over. 'What kind of a fucking place is this, Capaldi?' he exclaimed, aghast.

'It's normally pretty peaceful, boss.' I told him what I had seen. A woman's body in a bed.

'Dead?' he snapped.

'She looked so pale she could have been embalmed.'

'But you didn't check?'

I held my temper. 'I promise you, she was way past rescuing. I didn't have enough light, and I didn't want to compromise the scene by going in any farther with just a torch.'

He held me in a reproachful stare for a moment to let me know that he was not happy with today's performance so far. He turned to one of the uniforms. 'Go in and tell the doctor we need him,' he snapped, indicating the door of the shack. 'Get me some overalls from somewhere,' he instructed the other one.

'Is DCS Galbraith inside?'

He blanched. I had rubbed a sore spot. 'He's not here yet. Some idiot accidentally cut the landline to the wind-farm site. I've had to send a man up there to fetch him down.'

'So he doesn't know yet?'

'That we apparently have two more dead fucking people? No, Capaldi, he doesn't know yet.'

I knew from past experience not to push him further. Instead, I suppressed my smile and tucked it away in the little mental bank I reserved for such private rewards.

I led the way back down the shaft. The heavy-duty flashlight they had given me was like a searchlight in the confines of the tunnel. The one that Fletcher was carrying behind me projected a warped version of my shadow on the walls ahead. The doctor Fletcher had commandeered from Dinas, and a couple of members of the SOCO team, were behind him. Somehow everyone but me had managed to acquire protective clothing.

Had I been totally wrong about Bruno?

I tried to see him as a serial killer. But I couldn't get past the problem of his timidity and his isolation. He seemed to be too scared of people to kill them. And how could a man like him have got close enough to someone like Evie Salmon?

I pictured that ghastly wax complexion on the bed, the long blonde hair. Was I about to be proven wrong?

And I had still not identified that odour.

I stopped outside the side shaft and let Fletcher come up beside me to get the sense of the thing. I heard him sniff the air experimentally. 'What's that smell?' he asked.

'I don't know. It's familiar, but I can't figure it out.'

He tensed himself. 'Okay, let's do it.'

I shone my torch on the bed to light the way for him. The same blonde hair, but the complexion, in the light from the high intensity beam, was now an unnatural pink. The body was still pinned down tightly under the sheet and blanket.

Fletcher was using his own torch on the floor to make sure that he wasn't compromising anything as he crossed to the bed.

And then it hit me. The smell. A recall. Unit 13. Mould growth on plastic shower curtains. Underscored with the scent of the kind of talcum powder that old ladies use.

It was too late to warn Fletcher.

As he reached down to pull the bedcovers away I saw that he wasn't looking at the body. His squeamishness was his undoing. If he had looked he would have seen what it was before it leaped into action. But he didn't, and jumped back in shocked reaction as the thing on the bed surged up, released from the confines of the covers.

He looked now. 'You bastard, Capaldi!' he shrieked. 'You fucking set this up!' The body's arms had popped up, and its knees sprung into an arch. It was naked apart from a pair of pants and a loose-fitting bra, and was the pink of denture-plate acrylic. The expression of rage on Fletcher's face was magnified and distorted by the torchlight. 'You

121

are fucking screwed!'

It wasn't dead. It had never been alive. Bruno hadn't killed anyone.

I came closer. Fletcher was trembling. The release from the sheets had skewed the blond wig. The odour was now explained. An inflatable plastic sex doll. Its arms and legs, held open in invitation, made it look like it had just fallen from a tree trunk that it had wrapped itself around.

'I didn't know,' I told him softly.

Behind me the doctor and the SOCO guys were at the entrance of the chamber, their torches playing over the inflatable doll. The relief in the air was palpable. I suddenly realized that if they laughed, Fletcher was going to take it personally. I would be even more fucked.

'Shine your torches over the walls,' I instructed, to distract them from the absurdist comedy.

There was a dressing table against the far wall with a rococo gilt-edged mirror, unguents on the surface, a hairbrush. A padded stool in front of it. The talcum-powder smell explained. A woman's short red dress on a hanger was suspended from the wall beside it. A window painted onto the wall. Blue curtains swagged back from a naively rendered *trompe l'œil* view out over a lawn to a white picket fence.

I turned my torch on the bedside table. A glass of water topped with a film of dust. A romantic novel folded open, which I knew would turn to papier-mâché if I tried to pick it up. On the far side of the bed there was a white WC bowl, and a pedestal washbasin with a mirror over it. There was no drainage system to connect either of them into. Like everything else in the place they were pretend.

122

'What the fuck is this place?' Fletcher asked.

'Isn't it obvious? It's a boudoir.'

'This is sick.'

'No, it's not,' I said reflexively.

'You're not serious?' Fletcher sneered.

'It's sad, but it's not sick. It obviously gave him some sort of comfort.'

Both our eyes swung to the plastic doll. 'Do you think he fucked it?' Fletcher speculated incredulously.

I had a picture of Bruno sitting at the dressing table, the doll a reflection in the mirror. Was he recreating a lost domestic scene, or inventing one? 'I don't know.' I winced at the prospect. 'But I'm not putting my hand up its snatch to find out.'

*   *   *

We left the two SOCO guys in the chamber to start their process and retreated with the doctor, who wanted to get back to work on Bruno.

'What are we going to find down those?' Fletcher asked, indicating the other two tunnels, when we emerged into the relative freshness of the access shaft.

'I don't know.'

'Is that where he's set up his Papa Bear and Baby Bear fuck-pads?' he said meanly.

'We should be glad it wasn't a body.'

He watched the doctor reach the top of the shaft before he turned back to me. 'You set that up deliberately to undermine me,' he hissed accusingly. 'You knew exactly what was lying under those covers.'

'Honestly, Kevin, I didn't—'

'Boss!' he snarled, cutting in over me.

'Fuck that,' I snapped back, 'we're on our own down here, and you'd better believe that I'm not going to revert to cadet-force japes in the middle of a murder investigation on my patch, just to put one over on you.'

He laughed nastily. *My patch!* You're fucking welcome to it, Capaldi. Throwbacks and failed weirdos, just your sort of people.'

'DCI Fletcher.' Jack Galbraith's voice boomed down at us from above.

Looking up, seeing him foreshortened and sky-lined, he really did look like an emissary from a dark power.

Fletcher scrambled up the metal rungs. I took my time. By the time I breasted the surface, Fletcher and Jack Galbraith were ensconced together. Fletcher's right arm was semaphoring to accompany his explanations.

The conversation broke up, Fletcher making his way back to Bruno's shack, Jack Galbraith approaching me. I stiffened expectantly. Behind him I saw Fletcher send me a look compounded of anxiety and malice. It was a warning. He was obviously sensitive to what his boss and I might be discussing behind his back.

'You look like you've just lost the bog-snorkelling championship,' Jack Galbraith observed.

'It's a bit damp down there, sir.'

He looked down into the shaft. 'So this is a gold mine?' He sounded disappointed.

'Do you want to go down there and see what we found?' I asked.

He looked at me incredulously. 'No, Capaldi,

that is what I employ people like you for. So just describe it for me, your take on it.'

He nodded when I had finished. 'DCI Fletcher tells me that you don't think that humping a piece of latex in an underground chamber can be construed as weird behaviour.'

'I didn't say it was normal, sir, just maybe not as deviant as DCI Fletcher obviously found it. Mr Gilbert had a hard time coping with people. So he invents a little corner of his ideal world.'

'And tops people and chops their heads and hands off. Where does that particular sideline fit into this ideal world?'

'I don't know whether he would be capable of that, sir.'

He used his thumb to indicate Bruno's shack over his shoulder. 'So what drove him to the final act?'

'We don't know that it is suicide yet, sir.'

He winced and shook his head. 'Capaldi, Capaldi. Sometimes I despair of you. You've heard of Occam's razor?'

'Yes, sir.'

'Right, so heed it. Stay rooted. Stick with the simplest solution. Don't pull this away into fantasy land. We have a demonstrable warp here. Definite signs of maladjustment. You are too tolerant of strangeness, that's what got you here in the first place.'

'Yes, sir.'

'Get more uniforms in and pull this place apart. This guy had set patterns.'

The observation surprised me. He had done his homework. 'That's right, sir.'

'And it's now looking like killing people might be

125

one of them. So get this place broken down for me, and deliver me Mr Gilbert's sins.'

8

I delegated the search of Bruno's place to Emrys Hughes, who arrived with the additional men. I didn't want to waste my time looking for bodies that I was pretty certain wouldn't exist. He didn't try to hide his smirk. His stance had been vindicated by the example of another crazy incomer fucking up in the game of life.

I didn't bother arguing with him. I wanted to check out the surrounding properties, just in case someone had heard the shot. They might not have identified it as one, but if someone had heard something it could give us a timeframe.

But first I had to get back to Unit 13 to change out of my impromptu speleological outfit and get cleaned up and into something that would make me presentable to the public again.

I stood under the thirteen-and-a-half slow drips of tepid water that constituted my shower and tried to make sense of Bruno's apparent suicide. I corrected myself. His apparent suicide *at this particular point in history*. At any other time it would be tragic. Now, with its juxtaposition, it had the potential to change the focus and direction of our investigation.

I froze. The soap slipped from my hand. I ignored it.

Could that be the intention? Had this been manufactured? Had Bruno just been set up as the

126

fall guy?

Was it possible for someone to be that evil and manipulative?

I slammed my eyes shut and shook my head to clear out the judgemental crap. That was only going to get in the way.

Take it back to the beginning.

Three people had been killed, their heads and hands had been removed, and they had been buried over a period of two years, approximately six to eight years ago. Which should have been the end of the story.

Until the wind farm is announced. Which posits a real danger of discovery. But this is a long-term procedure involving consultations and public enquiries, the slow grind of due process. It leaves plenty of time to remove the bodies.

So why leave them in place? And then compound it by adding a new one?

What does this act say about the status of the original bodies?

I ran into a mental blank wall and went back to Evie. She was the disrupter. She broke the pattern. Young and new. What was she meant to tell us?

I took it back chronologically and broke it down into sequence. The first body is uncovered. The diggers are sabotaged. I dig up Evie.

Oh fuck!

We had been manipulated. They had taken over the controls after we had discovered the first body. The whole business with the sabotaged diggers was to alert us to keep on digging. A way of picking up the reins and steering us in the direction they wanted us to take. We had found the first body, which meant that we were going to find the others, so they speeded up the process to make sure that we found Evie quickly. Complete with her distinctive and identifiable red shoes.

Why?

To stop us concentrating too much on the other three bodies? By ensuring that Evie was the second body unearthed, were they trying to distract us from the collective significance of the other three?

If I was right, Evie's murder had just been a device, a counter-play in the game that the original murderer was controlling.

I closed my eyes at the cold horror of it. She had been murdered to provide the meat. The bastard had used her as a fucking chess piece. He had carved her up to suit his purposes, removing her head and hands to connect her to the other victims. Just in case the location wasn't enough of a clue.

And then he had figuratively chopped Bruno into the mix.

It was a storyboard, designed to make us believe that Bruno Gilbert was a retired serial killer who had reactivated himself. That he had started killing again. But then we were meant to understand that he had felt the ineffable pressure as we closed in on him. No option left but to take his own life.

Oh Jesus! If I was right, this bastard had murdered two innocent people to provide a diversion. To shift us down an investigative path that was going to lead to nowhere. Evie had been used to draw us away from the initial focus and to point us down the line, but Bruno was the one that now switched the points. This part of the strategy was designed to swing us in the direction that he had chosen for us.

The warm water in the tiny tank had drained, the

shower was turning cold. I shivered under it, but the discomfort suited my next grim realization. I had just worked out how he was going to manage to consolidate this. How he was going to complete the arc of the story. I flashed on the underground chamber. Bruno's retreat from the world. The red dress! It was as good as a suicide note. Because I now knew as an absolute certainty that the dress was going to turn out to be Evie's.

I bequeath you the total proof of my guilt.

As I towelled myself dry I realized that no one was going to buy a word of this. Because in the real world that even cops were a part of, the world of small pleasures and disappointments, boredom and television news and the belly laugh after the third beer, it still seemed incomprehensible that a person could take the life of two others, for no other reason than to send an investigative train down a branch line that was going to swallow it up.

Bruno may not have known his killer. But Evie must have. It had to be the person she had left home two years ago to be with. She must have trusted him. Been proud of him. She must have talked to someone about him.

And that's how I was going to get the bastard.

*   *   *

As I had anticipated, the Joneses at Cogfryn Farm had been at full tilt in the lambing shed the previous night and had heard nothing that wasn't associated with that process. The three of them, Mr and Mrs Jones and the labourer they employed, had all been in attendance at the pens.

Fron Heolog, the activity centre, adjoined the

gold-mine site on the other side from Cogfryn Farm. I reread the small file I had prepared on it. A couple called Trevor and Valerie Horne and her brother, Greg Thomas, all from the West Midlands, lived there. It was a registered charity, which they ran as a residential centre as part of a rehabilitation regime for young male offenders, mainly street-gang members.

Greg, the brother, was the guy I had met a few days ago at Cogfryn Farm. The friend of Owen Jones who was driving him to the airport.

According to my notes the place had been semi-derelict when they first took it over, and it had taken about five years of working part-time to refurbish the farmhouse and convert the outbuildings to its current use. So, even though they had only been up and running for about four years, they had had a presence in the valley when the first of the bodies had been buried.

It turned out that the place was also one of Emrys Hughes's bêtes noires. According to him it was a nursery of imported urban malevolence peopled with young marauders who were out to overrun Dinas if they could only free themselves from their electronic tags.

Their sign was a big shiny cartoon sun with a wide smile, dark glasses and a starburst of rays that turned to dreadlocks on the top. Any idea of freedom stopped at the graphics, however. The gates were automatic and locked. I got out and went to the intercom.

'Yes?' A woman's voice, tinny behind the static.

'Detective Sergeant Capaldi.'

'Can you show the camera some identification, please,' the voice asked wearily, not giving me time to state my business. The security camera was mounted on the trunk of a tree. I stretched my hand up to it with my warrant card. The gates gave a little shimmy, and started to open.

The drive was surfaced with fresh tarmac, and lined with new saplings protected by tree guards. I followed the signs for Reception and drove into a courtyard formed by a low, L-shaped, whitewashed stone building. A small group of youths, a mixture of races, watched me cross the yard. Their stares of practised defiance took me back to Cardiff. These kids recognized me as a cop. I went back and locked my car.

'I'm Valerie Horne, I'm the voice on the intercom.' She held the door open. I went in, shook her outstretched hand, and she closed the door behind her. 'Please, sit down.'

She was short, had overemphatic cherubic curves in her face, and unstyled, dense brown curly hair, all of which combined to make her appear chubbier than she was. She looked tired. The room was a converted cowshed, open to the roof, National Trust paintwork, newly bought contemporary office furniture, cheery prints, and a couple of computers banked against the rear wall.

I sat down opposite her at her desk. I did a double take on a framed photograph that was hanging on the wall above her head. I had met both the men in it. At Cogfryn Farm. Owen Jones and Greg Thomas again, but much younger versions, with a young woman sandwiched between them, the camera catching her with her eyes closed and a goofy grin that she must have regretted later. It was a buddy picture. The three of them packed tight together, the men with their arms around the

131

girl's shoulders, she with hers around each of their waists.

Both men in army uniform. A new dimension. Did it make any kind of a difference?

She cleared her throat to bring me back to earth. 'Sorry.' I smiled apologetically.

She scrutinized me for a moment. 'We haven't dealt with you before, have we?'

'No,' I confirmed.

'Well, have you actually caught anyone doing anything, or is it just the usual, blame it on Fron Heulog?' she asked, her smile weary and deliberately false.

'Blame what on Fron Heulog, Mrs Horne?'

She blinked in surprise. 'You're not here . . .?' She caught herself. Something relaxed. She allowed herself a short laugh. 'I'm sorry, I'm so used to us getting the blame for anything that goes wrong out there.'

I understood. Emrys must have been a frequent visitor. Every vandalized bus shelter and unsolved crisp-packet theft. 'You're a convenient dark beacon?' I suggested.

'Tell me about it.' She sighed. 'So what can I do for you?'

'I'm trying to find out whether anyone here might have heard anything unusual coming from the direction of Mr Gilbert's place last night.'

'What sort of unusual?'

'Something that might have sounded like a gunshot?'

She glanced out the window. 'So that explains all the activity over there.' She looked back at me. 'Am I allowed to ask what happened? And has this got anything to do with the bodies they've found at the

132

wind-farm site?'

I smiled apologetically. 'I'd rather keep to what you might have heard, at the moment.'

'The kids keep pestering us about it. It's almost made this place cool for them.' She waited me out for a moment, and then shrugged. 'Well, I personally heard nothing, over and above the normal racket that goes on round here until they all decide to settle down.'

'Could you ask the kids?' I pushed a card with my contact numbers across the table.

'Of course, but they're the ones who are usually making the racket.'

'What about your husband and your brother?'

She shook her head vaguely. 'We were all together until bedtime.' Then she realized my question had been more specific. 'They're not here, I'm afraid. It's a Tuesday. They're down at the river doing things with rope bridges.' She saw me glance at the group of youths out in the courtyard. 'There are always some who claim to be allergic to cold water. But I will ask them when they get back.'

'How do you get on with your neighbour, Mr Gilbert?' I deliberately kept him in the land of the living.

She thought about it for a moment. 'He keeps to himself. We see him walking on the moors above here, but that's about as far as contact goes.'

'He doesn't bother the kids?'

'Not intentionally.' She laughed at my puzzled expression. 'They think he's strange. The way he dresses and scuttles around. Although anyone who would chose to walk in the hills when they could be watching television is weird in their book.'

I produced the new photograph of Evie we had

133

got from her parents. This was more recent. No sweet kid on a pony this time. That had been the memory they wanted to hold on to. This was more real. She was scowling, caught turning away from the camera, not wanting them to take possession of any part of her. Her hair was still blonde, but streaked with pink highlights, and cut to hang straight, with a spiky fringe. Her complexion was blotchy, but there was raw energy in her expression, and she was attractive, in a disconcerting way. 'Did you know her?' I asked. 'Evie Salmon?'

'No.' She replied without hesitating, a glum look crossing her face, realizing who she was seeing.

'Ever heard of her?'

'Only from the rumours that are going around town. That she's one of the victims.'

'She was young, Mrs Horne. She might have been drawn to the boys here.'

She shook her head. 'It may sound harsh, but we don't let them fraternize with the locals. We tried it once and it didn't work. We ended up receiving a torrent of abuse from the so-called good people of Dinas.' She smiled. 'They didn't appreciate their children's newly discovered language skills.'

I made a point of letting her see me looking at the photograph behind her desk. 'Your brother looks much younger there.'

She looked surprised. 'You know him?'

'And Owen Jones. I met them both briefly at Cogfryn Farm.'

She turned her head round to look up at the photograph. Her expression clouded. 'That was poor Rose, Owen's sister.' I hadn't recognized her from the photograph of the child in Mrs Jones's kitchen. This time I was forewarned and let my mouth bunch up into a tight little mark of respect. 'That photograph's up there to keep her in our memory.'

I nodded.

'It was through Owen and Rose that Greg got the opportunity for us all to buy this place,' she explained.

I waited for her to expand on that, but she got up instead, making it clear that she was moving on to more important business. 'Could you ask your husband or your brother to contact me if they have any recollection of her?' I asked as I left.

The group of youths were still outside. They eyed me suspiciously as I approached them. I took out the photograph of Evie and went up to them. 'Have any of you seen this woman around?'

They didn't have a chance to answer. Valerie Horne came out of the office behind me. 'There's no point in showing them that. This lot have only been here for six days.'

I drove off, musing on the photograph of Greg Thomas and Owen and Rose Jones.

Either one of those men, on a dark night, could have been the figure I had seen flitting down the line of earthmoving machines. Could the other one have shape-shifted into a tree root?

Then I remembered that Owen Jones was in Africa helping the oil industry fuck up the planet. I bounced back immediately, with the possibility that Trevor Horne, the brother-in-law, was present, correct and available.

*　　　*　　　*

I drove on down to Pen Tywn Barn Gallery. I had

135

checked the council-tax records. The place was registered as a holiday home and a business. Two ladies named Fenwick paid the bills. They lived at separate addresses in Alderley Edge in Cheshire. Sisters, I assumed. I knew just enough about those parts south of Manchester to appreciate that the location was extremely chichi. And probably full of rarefied Barn Gallerys. So why export one to Pig Wales? It was like trying to make a killing in haute couture in the land of the loincloth.

Pen Tywn was too far down the valley from Bruno's place to have heard anything short of a sonic boom. But, according to her father, Evie had worked here part-time.

My mobile phone rang. I glanced down at the caller display, intending to ignore it. It was Mackay. Perhaps he was coming back to me with an update on how the army disposed of its surplus bodies.

'Hi, Mac, just hold on a moment until I get off the road.' I pulled onto the verge and cut the engine. 'Okay, I can talk now.'

'I've been delegated to remind you that your Aunt Doreen's silver-wedding bash is coming up.'

I groaned inwardly. 'My mother's been pestering you.'

'I don't call it pestering. I like her. And she's invited me too.'

'It'll be grim.'

'She wants you there.'

'I can't promise anything, Mac, I'm working a big case at the moment.'

'You tell her that. I'm only the messenger.'

'I took her out recently,' I protested.

'A cream tea in Monmouth,' he snorted derisively, 'she wants to see you in Cardiff. She

136

wants to show off her big handsome son.'

'I can't go to Cardiff, Mac. I told you before, it's part of the arrangement.'

'That's professionally. They don't want you acting the superhero and arresting all their hoodlums. But they can't stop you visiting your family, for fuck's sake.'

Superhero. Mackay had unintentionally hit the nail on the head. My former bosses had used the PR device of turning me into the heroic survivor of a hostage event, in an attempt to salvage the situation when the farmer I had been minding had gunned down the pimp who had fucked over his son and daughter.

The problem was that my mother had bought into it. She was unaware that she was showcasing a fraud when she paraded me around the relatives.

The Vaughans, my mother's side of the family, were staunch Methodists and solid railway-and-heavy-engineering people. Foreman class, with a deep-rooted sense of their place on the social ladder. There had been general alarm when she had announced that she was going to marry my father. Not so much because he was a foreigner—as a port, Cardiff had always been a tolerant city—but because, being an Italian, he was assumed to be a Catholic. What ended up really screwing their heads was the discovery that he had turned his back on the Church of Rome, and was an avowed atheist with communist tendencies.

My sister and I grew up sandwiched between the Methodist Prayer Book and Marx's *Eighteenth Brumaire of Louis Napoleon.* It's a wonder I didn't end up as a convicted parricide, or at least a practising Buddhist.

And some of the mean-spirited old fuckers in the Vaughan family still held a grudge. One of these days, at one of these gatherings, the pretence that I was a knight in shining armour was going to blow. One or more of them was going to raise the point that, if I was such a big heroic deal, how come I hadn't been promoted, and why had I been moved out to where the street lights don't shine? For my mother's sake I didn't want to be the cause of a schism in her family.

'I'll call her, Mac, I promise,' I said guiltily.

'As I said, she's your mother.'

'And while you're on . . .'

'What now?' he asked guardedly.

'A couple of guys, Greg Thomas and Owen Jones, I think they were in the army together. Any chance of asking around and seeing if anything turns up on them?'

'You're an opportunistic bastard, Capaldi.'

'Thanks, Mac.' I hung up before he could get more inventive with his epithets.

I had glimpsed a yellow car in the drive when I had been driven past the Barn Gallery on my way (unknowingly) to exhume Evie. It was still here, and turned out to be a wild shade of egg yolk, parked out in front like a beacon. An Audi TT roadster, 3.0-litre late model, so at least I didn't have to revise my earlier opinion. There was money here, and it was being flaunted.

The vertical blinds had been pulled aside in the glazed threshing bay, and the double doors stood open. Because of the way the sun was reflecting on the glass, all I could make out was the patch of black slate floor at the threshold.

'Do we have a customer?' The voice was raised,

and there was a cheerful trill to it.

She was coming down from the house. A beige coat open over a short grey–black wool dress, tied to accentuate her waist. A pair of sunglasses was wedged into her ash-blonde hair, which had been expensively cut to look wind-ruffled. The make-up was subtle and minimal and worked to soften her sharp features. Her expansive smile didn't match the careful brown eyes. Her shoes had heels, and threw a twist into her walk, as she took the gravel and stone flags on the path carefully.

'Ms Fenwick?'

Surprise flickered on her face. 'Yes, I'm Gloria Fenwick. And you are . . .?'

'Capaldi. Detective Sergeant Glyn Capaldi.' I showed her my warrant card.

'Ahh, right . . .' She made a big play of enlightenment. 'The mystery up the valley? We've been wondering if we would get a visit. But we aren't going to be able to help you much, I'm afraid. We're not here that often.'

'We would appreciate any help you can give us.'

She tilted her head and regarded me with interest. 'Capaldi . . .' She rolled the syllables. 'Unusual for round here, isn't it?'

'I'm from Cardiff. My father was Italian.'

'No offence to Cardiff, but if I was Italian I think I know where I'd want to be retaining my roots.'

'He came over to work for his uncle. He met my mother and stayed on.'

She took the sunglasses out of her hair and nodded. 'Now that's romantic.' She smiled and tapped her teeth with the end of the glasses. They were very white. 'I think you'd better come and meet Isabel.'

139

I followed her into the barn. It took me a moment to adjust to the dimmer light. Everything was shrouded with dust covers. There were no recognizable shapes under them.

'The birds get in and shit on everything,' Gloria explained cheerily. She raised her voice. 'Isabel, the police are here to talk to us about the stuff that's happened up the valley.'

Isabel rose up into view from behind a large packing case at the far end of the barn. She approached carrying a clipboard. She was smaller than Gloria in every way. Thin, her hair dyed grey and styled short; dark, deep-set eyes, the skin tight on her face as if there was a clip on the back of her head keeping up the tension. She wore a grey cashmere polo-neck over loose camel-coloured trousers, and an African tribe-load of thin silver bands tinkled at both wrists.

'This is Detective Sergeant Capaldi,' Gloria said.

Isabel's smile, which had been flagging impatience, took on a twitch of interest. 'Italian?'

'His father came all the way over from Italy to find a Welsh bride,' Gloria answered for me.

'We buy a lot of our stuff from Italy,' Isabel informed me, striding into a sales pitch before I could warn her she was wasting her time, 'from Milan mainly. This is a piece by Ricardo Spinetti.' She heaved the dust cover off. It was something that was covered in vinyl the green of irradiated pondweed, and it looked as if it was collapsing. Nothing gave a clue to its function.

'I like that,' I grunted sagely.

'This is from Studio Abolition,' she said, pulling another cover off. It was tall, a listing bundle of stainless-steel and wood rods tied precariously together with pink, plastic-coated wire. She looked at me expectantly.

I nodded at the piece. Gloria smiled encouragingly and reached in somewhere and flicked a hidden switch. A tiny glow of intense blue light sparked in the heart of the rods.

'Ah, a lamp,' I declaimed, showing off my style cool.

'An installation,' Isabel corrected me coldly, dismissing me as an Infidel. She turned to Gloria. 'The Max Rocks have arrived from New York at last.'

'I think the sergeant needs to ask us some questions,' Gloria said, telegraphing me a conspiratorial smile.

Isabel turned back to me reluctantly. 'There's nothing we can tell you,' she said, looking at Gloria for confirmation of this.

'She's right, I'm afraid,' Gloria agreed. 'We came down a couple of days ago to find that the valley had apparently turned into a slaughterhouse. Which is why we haven't officially opened up yet,' she explained. 'Out of respect.'

'Evie Salmon used to work for you?'

The two women looked at each other. 'The name's sort of familiar,' Gloria admitted hesitantly.

'You haven't heard?' I asked.

'Heard what?' Isabel retorted.

'Evie Salmon's was one of the bodies we found.'

They winced at each other. They were both genuinely surprised. Gloria shook her head. 'People round here don't talk to us. We didn't know.'

I showed them Evie's picture.

Gloria clicked her fingers, a memory returning.

141

'The little floosie who used to hang around . . .' She checked herself. 'Oh, shit, I'm sorry.' She pulled a contrite face and gave a loose-shouldered, apologetic shrug.

'That's right, I remember her,' Isabel said in surprise, as her own memory refreshed, 'about three years ago, just after we'd opened the gallery.'

'Poor little cow,' Gloria intoned her in memoriam.

'She used to work for you?' I asked.

The two women looked at each other. Isabel shook her head. 'No, if she'd worked for us we would have remembered her when you asked,' Gloria said.

'As Gloria said, she tried to hang around, as if association was going to conjure up style sense and taste,' Isabel explained. 'Although I think she did ask once if there was anything she could do to help out.' She looked at me challengingly, as if responding to a criticism I hadn't voiced. 'As you can see, we're not exactly catering to the mass-retail market. More low-volume, high-value, and I'm afraid she definitely did not fit that profile.'

'We had to gently steer her away and tell her to go and play somewhere else,' Gloria added.

'Thank you for all your help.' I gave them a big, disarming, cuddly cop smile, and then turned to look admiringly at the gallery. 'So you've only been here for three years?'

'Oh, no,' Gloria gushed, 'we've only been running the Barn for that time. We've had this place for holidays for at least thirteen years.' She looked at Isabel for corroboration.

Isabel nodded her head slowly. 'Fourteen in August.' Her smile was clipped, and she gave me an

142

assessing look, trying to work out my angle.

I thanked them for their time. They both made a point of watching me leave.

I watched them in the rear-view mirror. Only Gloria waved. Thirteen years. That installed them firmly in the timeframe. But that wasn't at the forefront of my concerns.

Evie's father had definitely told me that she had *worked* at the Barn Gallery.

Who was lying?

*　　　*　　　*

The incident room was end-of-shift crowded. The buzz from the discoveries at Bruno's place still resonating. Uniform cops at the terminals writing up their reports. Emrys Hughes walked amongst them with a phantom whip, like the overseer on a tobacco farm. He saw me across the room and gave me a cocky wave. He was obviously feeling happy. Incomers were dropping like flies.

I finished writing up my own report and filed it with Alison Weir, who was routing the dailies back to HQ in Carmarthen for processing and assessing. I nodded at Fletcher's closed door. 'What's happening in the War Room?'

'They've called a briefing for tomorrow morning.'

I gave her my best charm-school smile. 'Can you run a couple of background checks for me, please?'

She smiled back, unimpressed. 'Put them in your report.'

'I have.'

'Then they will be done. If DCI Fletcher authorizes them.'

'What if you ran them for me before they actually got to him?'

'It's not procedural.'

'What if someone screwed with the procedure by pulling rank?'

She sighed and raised her hands in mock surrender. I leaned in close. 'Whatever you can get on the people at Fron Heulog Activity Centre.' She tapped the information in. 'And the two women called Fenwick at Pen Twyn and addresses in Alderley Edge, Cheshire.'

She finished typing. 'Okay, I'll get back to you when this stuff comes through.'

I clicked my fingers. An afterthought. 'Can you check out the flights from London to Lagos on Monday? See if a guy called Owen Jones was on any of them.'

She mock-salaamed. 'Your wish is my command.'

'Thanks.' I nodded towards the door that led into The Fleece proper. 'Fancy coming through and having a drink when you're finished here?'

'Thanks for the offer, but I'll be heading for home.'

'Isn't that a long way from here?'

She shrugged. 'Here is a long way from anywhere.'

As if she had to remind me. 'Didn't they give you the option of staying?'

She let me see her glance across at Fletcher's door. 'Home's home, Sarge.'

I went through to the bar and slid my car keys across to David. He stashed them on their usual shelf. 'Bike or taxi?' he asked as he pulled my beer.

'Who knows? Let's wait and see. I might even walk home.'

144

He laughed, it was an old standing joke.

I took my drink and a newspaper and sat down at a small table in a quiet corner. The newspaper was a front. To keep people at bay. I wanted time to reflect. I needed to review my thinking on Bruno and Evie for glaring fault-lines before I pulled it out of the birthing pool tomorrow, in front of a live and probably hostile audience.

'Gottcha . . .' Hands grabbed the back of my shoulders.

The fright almost nailed the top of my spine into my cortex.

Tessa MacLean slipped round in front of me, smiling. 'I'm sorry, I didn't expect quite such a reaction.'

'It's all right, I was miles away.'

'Okay if we join you?' She nodded towards the bar, where Jeff was ordering their drinks.

'Feel free.'

She squinted at my face. I had given up on the dressing. She nodded approvingly. 'Looking better.'

Her hair was down, she was wearing a loose, smoke-blue cotton skirt that came above her knees, with no tights, and a light-grey V-neck sweater with a single strand of bright wooden beads, both of which drew me into her cleavage. Or perhaps it was just a homing instinct. Her hair was shiny and she smelled of soap and ionization.

'You're in here a lot these days,' I observed.

'Sandra lets me use a shower,' she explained, tossing her hair to demonstrate. 'There's a certain whiff you can acquire on a dig that begins to permeate if you're not careful.'

'What about your team?'

'They're all geeks.' She laughed affectionately.

145

'It's a badge of honour to them.'

She sat down, looking at me curiously. 'Are you okay? From that expression it looks as if I've just managed to summon you back from the land of the living dead.'

'I'm fine.'

'I thought you would have been happier.'

'Why's that?'

She leaned forward and lowered her voice. 'I thought the rumour was that you might have wrapped it up.'

I turned round and saw David at the bar. He waved. Tessa grinned at me. 'Okay, but he had been talking to Sergeant Hughes before he told me.'

The grin was infectious. 'Don't be fooled, Emrys Hughes only looks like the Sphinx.'

She laughed and placed her hand over mine briefly. I looked at her for significance, but she turned her head away.

Jeff brought the drinks over. I smiled up at him. If he was upset to see me here he didn't show it. He had had long enough now, I rationalized, to have made his move and know how it was going to be received. Tessa smiled at me, as if reading my thoughts.

Kevin Fletcher came into the bar. He had changed into a blazer, and his hair was damp from the shower. I returned his nod. Tessa glanced round. *Don't invite him over*, I willed her.

She didn't have to. The bastard invited himself. He approached with a wide smile. 'Hello, Glyn, mind if I join you?' He nodded at Jeff, and fixed his offensive on Tessa. 'Detective Chief Inspector Fletcher,' he said, offering his hand, 'but please call

146

me Kevin.'

Tessa introduced herself. The small talk wobbled around archaeological digs and the future prospects of wind energy. But Tessa had picked up on something that was resonating along the invisible wire between Fletcher and me. 'Have you two known each other for long?' she asked.

'We used to work together in Cardiff,' Fletcher explained.

It was the smirk he used that did it. 'How's Linda?' I asked spitefully.

On reflection, the look he returned may not have been pure hate, but rather a thank-you for the opportunity I had just provided. His voice faltered. 'The decree absolute came through three weeks ago. She moved to Manchester with her new partner.' He ignored my surprise and looked directly at Tessa. 'I haven't seen my girls for over six months.'

'You poor man . . .'

Jeff and I exchanged a look of disgust. Smacked in the balls by the feather of melancholia. Fletcher had his wallet out and he and Tessa were poring over snapshots of his kids. And a fucking Cairn terrier, I couldn't help but notice. Jeff and I had to resort to a conversation about engineering.

Fletcher got up to buy more drinks. Tessa mimed helplessness. I shook my head and mimed in turn that it was time for me to go. She placed her hand over mine and leaned in close over the table. 'Don't you dare,' she whispered, 'you brought him over.' I disputed that, but silently, because it was a beautifully intimate moment that I didn't want to spoil. Tasting her breath.

Fletcher caught the tail end and sat down aiming

a scowl at me. Tessa noticed. 'Why don't you two work together any more?'

I froze. Fletcher looked at me curiously, and then back to Tessa, a mean little twitch of a smile starting to work. 'Hasn't Glyn told you?'

'No. You knew him in Cardiff, I thought that perhaps you could tell us.'

'I was in Swansea at the time it happened. I'd had a promotion. But we all heard about it. Didn't we, Glyn?'

I had to look up. I felt sweat in the creases at the side of my nose. 'Yes, Kevin—' I was off duty, he was about to humiliate me, I was fucked if I was going to call him boss—'it was hard to miss, wasn't it?'

Fletcher leaned across the table towards Tessa. 'Glyn had a pimp under surveillance. The man wasn't major-league. What was the most you would have got on him, Glyn? Procurement? Immoral earnings?'

'The guy broke people's lives up, Kevin.'

'Collateral damage. Not strictly our business.'

'Kevin?' Tessa leaned towards him.

He looked at her enquiringly.

'Is this going to be a nice story?'

'I'm sorry?' He smiled, surprised, wanting her to clarify.

'If it's not going to be a nice story, I don't want to hear it.'

'You asked . . .' he said, perplexed.

'I wanted you to tell me a nice story.'

'It isn't a nice story, Tessa,' I said.

She stood up. 'Tell it to me yourself sometime.' It was a command. She bent down and kissed my cheek.

Women . . .! Once again that great big eternal exclamation mark popped up behind my eyes.

'Time to go, Jeff.' Another command. Another boy in thrall. She nodded at Fletcher. 'Nice to meet you, Kevin.'

We both watched her leave. The skirt swaying as her butt cut lovely warped planes out of the world. Then Fletcher and I stared at each other for a moment, hands tight on our glasses. I got up and walked to the bar. David watched me. I leaned across and poured the beer down the sink. He passed me my car keys. I left without looking back at Fletcher, the photographs of his kids and his dog still spread out on the table in front of him. I didn't want to have to feel sorry for him.

9

The background buzz in the incident room shut down. I looked up, I had not slept well. Jack Galbraith and Fletcher had walked in and were setting up at the desk in front of the display board. Fletcher held up an unnecessary hand for hush. Jack Galbraith nodded out at us. Both men looked grimly pleased with themselves.

'Okay,' Jack Galbraith announced, 'let's start with some good news, folks. It looks like the body count at the wind-farm site is going to stop at four. I don't pretend to understand the technical stuff, but it appears that the geology of the ground we haven't yet uncovered will not support grave-digging.'

He let our appreciation of this news run through

the room before he gestured for Fletcher to take over.

He tapped his notes together, a stage gesture. 'As you are all aware by now, the body of Mr Bruno Gilbert was discovered yesterday at his home, and we are working on the strong presumption that his death was self-inflicted. This, together with evidence uncovered, has a direct bearing on the future focus of the investigation.'

I put my hand up. He didn't like it, but shit, I wasn't going to have him skating over evidence, as if we were only the worker bees and didn't need to know where the honey went.

'Sergeant Capaldi?' He nodded at me coldly.

'What evidence is that, boss?'

'The red dress that was found in the mine has been identified as belonging to Evie Salmon. I personally verified that fact with her parents yesterday afternoon. We don't yet know about the underwear that was found on the doll, but we are hoping to get a DNA- or at least a fibre-match.'

A susurrus ran through the room. My premonition had been confirmed. It didn't make me happy. I tried to picture the Salmons when this had been presented to them and wondered how fucking sensitive Fletcher had been.

He read out the relevant details of the autopsy report on Bruno. I was only half listening, I was waiting for the opportunity to make my pitch, and rehearsing it in my head. I wasn't going to dispute the fact that death had been caused by a shotgun turning his head inside out, or that a large amount of alcohol had been found in his system. It turned out that he had also been larded with Prozac, for which he had a valid repeat prescription.

Out of it. Just the way you would expect the self-condemned man to be.

Fletcher went on to say that the other two tunnels had revealed nothing of any significance; likewise the wider search of Bruno's ground.

Jack Galbraith stepped forward. He slowly scrutinized the room, holding us in a rapt silence, before he nodded. 'It's time to meet the late Mr Bruno Gilbert.' He uncovered the display board. Someone had been busy. Photographs of Bruno Gilbert in various stages of his path through life were shown, including a savoury few in the kitchen chair at the end of that path.

Fletcher talked us through that life.

Bruno had lived with his mother in Newport, South Wales. He had been a geologist working in the petrochemical industry, which had necessitated frequent trips abroad. On returning from one of these trips he had found his mother dead in bed. Natural causes, an aneurysm. Because they had been so self-contained, no one had visited. He had come home and gone upstairs calling for his mummy, only to discover that she had turned into a pile of jelly.

He didn't report it. He put her in the airing cupboard to dry out, and lived with her like that, in a big box he'd made out of cardboard, for two years. She was discovered while he was away on one of his field trips, when workmen had to break into the house to investigate a suspected gas leak. As in all the best haunted-house movies, the idiots opened the box. He was eventually cleared of any culpability in her death. But she was taken away from him and buried.

With her gone he went to pieces. He gave up

151

on everything. He was institutionalized to prevent him from starving himself to death. In hospital they slowly worked on pulling some focus into his life and providing him with medication that would enable him to at least cope.

Which is how he ended up in Mid Wales, patiently hewing his way into the core of a mountain.

Jack Galbraith took over. 'A psychologist is building up a more-detailed picture, but I think we can see a drift in what DCI Fletcher has told us.'

Dead Mother Syndrome. Bruno was displaying a motive as big as a billboard. Scrambled synapses voodoo. Scooping out a mountain in order to return to the womb. Installing a Rubber Woman inside that mountain, and outfitting her with a murdered girl's dress. It wasn't a great big leap from there to mass murder and cutting off the victims' heads and hands.

And the investigative joy of it was that we didn't need to look for a proper motive. The poor bastard was crazy, he could set his own rules. We just had to delve back into his past life to see who had disappeared from it, and try to find a match with the bodies we had found on the hill.

A branch line that could loop its way on into fruitless infinity.

I put my hand up gingerly. Jack Galbraith frowned, but he was in a good mood. He nodded. 'Sergeant Capaldi?'

I swallowed the lump in my throat. 'What if all this has been stage-managed to divert us away from the real killer, sir?'

He didn't blink. Jack Galbraith was nothing if not decisive. He just swiped his flat hand across the room in front of him like a stage director announcing a cut. 'I'll talk to you later, Sergeant.' He turned his attention to the corner containing Emrys Hughes and his uniforms. 'I want to thank you and all your men, Sergeant, for the sterling work you've put in.' He broadened the sweep of his attention. 'And that goes for all the rest of you who will be standing down now that we are shifting the focus of the investigation onto Newport.'

*   *   *

To give Jack Galbraith credit, he did actually hear me out. Later, in the privacy of Fletcher's office, just the three of us.

I laid out my hypothesis that Evie's death and burial, and Bruno's suicide, had been staged to manoeuvre the investigation into an endless cul-de-sac. As I unrolled it, I was conscious that the vibes I was picking up were not those of universal amazement and admiration.

When I had finished, Fletcher glanced over at Jack Galbraith, looking for permission to come back at me. He wasn't going to get it. This one was Jack Galbraith's baby.

He gave me a genuinely pained look. 'You always have been a perverse bugger, Capaldi. Why now? Why dispute the fucking obvious?'

'Because I met him, sir. I don't think he was capable of the kind of violence involved here. I don't think he was capable of any kind of violence. The gold mine was his therapy, it was working for him. He managed to cope with the loss of his mother by making the chamber and having the doll there. It was a sort of shrine, it anchored him.'

'It's a strange sort of comfort, symbolically copulating with your mother,' Fletcher observed snidely.

'He wasn't. Forensics haven't found any traces of seminal fluids on the doll, have they?' Fletcher shook his head reluctantly. 'It was his mother's room he was recreating, not his own bedroom, or a fuck pad.'

Jack Galbraith cut me off with a snap of his fingers. 'Sod the psychobabble. Give me something concrete.'

'His feet don't fit the footprints we found.'

He shook his head and smiled slyly. 'I prepared us for that eventuality. Remember? The possibility that the man who screwed with the diggers could turn out to be nothing more than a wind-farm saboteur?'

I had just been softening him up. Now I loaded live ammunition. 'There was a tooth fragment in the hut. It was in front of the body.'

'I'm not surprised. He used both barrels, the poor bugger's head was broadcast over half of fucking Christendom.'

'But not in front of the body, sir. That's my point. That tooth could have been broken prior to the shot, when someone was trying to force the gun barrel into his mouth.'

Jack Galbraith looked at Fletcher.

'Where did the shotgun end up?' Fletcher asked me.

'On the table.'

'In front of him?'

I nodded. He had seen the flaw in my argument.

'The shotgun had a small raised sight on the end of the barrel,' he explained to Jack Galbraith.

154

'When he fired, the force drove him back in his seat, but the gun went the other way. If the sight had caught the tooth, the recoil would have propelled the fragment in the opposite direction from the way that the body was travelling.'

Jack Galbraith took a moment to envisage it. 'Plausible?' he asked me.

I nodded reluctantly, but came back quickly. 'The red shoes and the red dress.'

He frowned. 'And what are you going to magic up for us now?'

'The red shoes had been left on the body so we could identify her as Evie. The red dress was hung up in the mine chamber to connect Bruno Gilbert to her. So that we would assume that he had taken his life because we were about to discover his terrible secret.'

He exchanged a glance with Fletcher. 'So, I can't see your problem. As I said, why dispute the obvious?'

'What's your problem with the dress and the shoes?' Fletcher asked.

'Evie left home two years ago. One of the reasons was to reinvent herself. Get out of Hicksville. Why, when she does turn up again, would she be wearing clothes from the life that she had been trying to leave behind?'

'And your answer is?' Jack Galbraith prompted.

'Because it makes her easily identifiable. Just as her killer wanted. Just as Bruno Gilbert's suicide makes him look guilty. And the red dress seals it.'

He shook his head. 'I don't buy it. It's too tenuous. There are too many good reasons why she could have been wearing those clothes. You're simply manufacturing complications.'

155

Fletcher nodded in agreement.

'How would a man like Bruno Gilbert connect with someone like Evie Salmon, sir?' I asked, trying to ease off the desperation pedal.

'That's what DCI Fletcher is going to be taking the investigation down to Newport to find out. That and the identities of the other bodies. Evie left home two years ago; my hunch is that the Newport–Cardiff metropolitan area was where she went to nest.' He shrugged his big shoulders. 'As you said, how someone like him sucked Evie into this is a fucking mystery.' He stared at me. 'And you're going to try to help us resolve it.'

'Me, sir?'

'Yes, why the fuck do you think I haven't been reaming you out for that interruption in the incident room? Why do you think I've given you this chance to tell your side of it?'

'I don't know, sir,' I replied meekly. Although when I had heard him telling Emrys Hughes that he would be standing down, it had hit me that I might be about to get reacquainted with the castrated-tup-lamb fraternity.

'Because, much as it pains me to admit it, you were right. There was a local connection. We're going to find that most of Bruno Gilbert's misdemeanours took place in Newport. But Evie Salmon was local, and somehow he got her back up here. That's your job now, Capaldi: trace the Evie connection.'

'Thank you, sir.' I looked over at Fletcher and was happy to see that he was not sharing my joy.

*   *   *

156

A reprieve. I was back in the saddle. Okay, I was only meant to be an outrider who had been left behind to try to round up stray facts in the dust of the main operation. But that didn't worry me. As far as I was concerned, I was the one at the sharp end, it was the main operation that was drifting off into the tumbleweed.

And the first thing I had to clear up was Evie's employment record at the Barn Gallery. Because either her father had been mistaken, or someone had been lying. And the timeframe, for that lie involved a crucial stage in her development: the period leading up to her decision to abandon home.

I walked out through the bar. David was restocking the spirit-optics gantry. The sight of it brought me up short. I had made a fundamental oversight. The autopsy had reported that Bruno had a high volume of alcohol in his bloodstream. I hadn't questioned it because I had seen the bottle under the table at the scene. And because it appears to be a well-documented fact that getting plastered smoothes out the path to self-destruction.

But I had been forgetting my premise. If Bruno hadn't committed suicide he wouldn't have drunk that whisky voluntarily.

Did he even drink? Had he been force-fed the stuff to reinforce the myth that was being created?

I had found that tiny tooth fragment, but missed the significance of a huge bottle of Scotch. I scrolled through the photographs on my phone. The bottle was in the background in the photo I had taken of the tooth. I looked up and saw David looking at me strangely. I had been standing there frozen in the middle of the room with my phone in my hand like a texting-addled zombie youth.

'You okay?' He asked.

I pressed the zoom control until I could read the label. 'Bunnahabhain,' I said, looking up at him. 'It's an Islay malt.'

'I know.'

'Does anyone in Dinas sell it?'

He shook his head. 'Too specialist. You'd have to go to a big supermarket or a wine merchant for something like that.'

'Do you know if Bruno Gilbert was a drinker?'

He looked at me with interest, waiting for me to expand.

'Please, David, just answer the question.'

'Not in the pubs in Dinas. Fuck it, Glyn, he would have had to be able to talk to people to do that.'

I ducked back into the incident room. There was a definite sense of the caravan packing up and moving on. I got Alison to retrieve the relevant forensics file. Both the bottle and the glass had been badly smudged, the only clear prints they had lifted were Bruno's. I already knew that this had been the same with the shotgun. And the shotgun had been registered in his name. And he had bought the cartridges. No mileage for me there.

I thought about going back into Fletcher's office to see Jack Galbraith and adding this to my shopping list of Bruno's suicide irregularities. But I knew what he would say. It was never too late to start drinking. And facing up to the prospect that you were about to be the instrument of your own execution could seem like as good a time as any.

But Bunnahabhain?

Okay, the big supermarkets sold it. But round

here it was a pretty exotic taste. I would now be making a point of looking at people's drinks cabinets.

Starting with the Salmons.

Up until now I had just thought of them as victims. But no one could be excluded. And they had the closest connection to Evie. As I drove up the hill I tried to think of a scenario that could make it possible.

Could the three bodies have been unwelcome suitors?

But why kill the beloved daughter?

And if she had disappeared two years ago, and had only just turned up dead, where had they been keeping her all this time? The cellar? The cow shed?

It wasn't totally improbable. Cases of families enslaving their children and forcing sex on them were not as unheard-of as they should be.

I pulled up where I had parked previously, before the track up to the Salmons' house got too rough. The dead Ford Sierra still wallowed sadly in the grass, but the Isuzu was missing. I only hoped that it was Mrs Salmon who was driving it.

I was in luck. Mr Salmon came out of the front door. He watched me approach as if I was the guy they sent round to cart away the plague victims.

He was gaunt. Even in this short time of grieving he had lost visible weight, the lines on his face accentuated, and his eyes looked like they had been sucked out with a stirrup pump, rolled in grit, and then rammed back in.

'I hate to disturb you, Mr Salmon, at this time, but there are a couple of questions I have to ask.'

'She's gone. She says she can't bear to be here

any more,' he announced, his voice hoarse with anguish.

I felt for the guy. First, his daughter and now, his marriage. I gave him a short burst of sympathetic silence and tightened up my morose expression. 'I really am sorry to hear that.' In the light of all this misery, how could I now ask him what his favourite whisky was? 'How long have you lived here?'

For some reason the question seemed to soothe him slightly. 'Eight years. We came here when Evie was fifteen.'

Fuck. They were within the timeframe. They stayed on the list.

'When Evie left, was there any build-up to it? A family argument or something else that triggered it off?'

He shook his head vacantly. 'No, it came completely out of the blue.'

'She just literally walked out?'

'No. It was a Sunday. On Sundays she used to help Mrs Evans out with her horses.'

Gerald Evans again. I felt the connection homing. I kept my voice neutral. 'So she pretended that she was going there?'

'No, I know she went, because I drove her over. But the strange thing is that she stayed and worked for the morning.' He pulled a pained face. 'You'd think if she was planning on getting away, she wouldn't have stayed around there, would you?'

'Maybe she was waiting for a bus?' I suggested.

'There aren't any buses from Dinas on a Sunday. According to Mrs Evans, Evie came to tell her that she wasn't feeling very well, and could she give her a lift down to Dinas. Just before lunch, this was. Mrs Evans offered to drive her home, but she said

160

that she had already called me and I was going to pick her up in Dinas.' He looked at me sadly. 'That was a lie. She hadn't called me. The Evanses dropped her off in Dinas, and that was the last anyone round here saw of her.'

'Was that Mr or Mrs Evans?' I tried to contain the excitement in my voice.

He shook his head morosely. 'I don't know.'

'What about luggage?' I knew that she had taken at least the red shoes and dress.

'It must all have been in the big bag that she always carried. Her mother used to get onto her about it, but she said that she wanted to be prepared for something wonderful that was going to come her way one of these days.'

That thought silenced both of us. 'You told me when we last spoke that Evie had worked for the Fenwick ladies at the Barn Gallery?' I asked eventually, changing the subject.

He looked at me sorrowfully. 'Is that important now?'

'It may well be. Can you give me any more detail?'

He shrugged, treating it as a distraction. 'It was the year it opened. The year before she . . .' He faltered. I nodded sympathetically. He continued, 'I used to drive her over on Saturdays. She told us that she helped to keep the place tidy, and made drinks for the customers.'

'You took her up to the Barn?'

'Oh, no.' He almost managed a smile at the recollection. 'She didn't want them to see my crappy old car. Those were the very words she used. I used to drop her off at the bottom of the drive, and then pick her up at the junction with the main road in the afternoon.'

'You never saw the Fenwicks?' I didn't let him hear importance in the question.

'I wasn't allowed to.' Another memory produced an even fonder smile. 'But they must have thought a lot of her, because they paid her really well. Sixty pounds cash was a good days' wage for a youngster.'

I smiled and nodded my agreement. Because I couldn't tell him that the Fenwicks hadn't been paying her.

Or *said* that they hadn't. And if not them, who had?

And what had she been doing to earn it?

* * *

I went over it as I drove down the hill. It was time to stop thinking about Evie as a runaway kid. She was twenty-one when she left. And she was a liar. I didn't like to malign the dead, but it had to go into the character sketch. For all her bluster and protestations about hating Dinas, she could have gone years ago, and her parents couldn't have stopped her.

Okay, she used to haul off from time to time. Those hitchhiking trips to Hereford and Newtown and Aberystwyth. But she always ended up getting in touch with her parents.

If she hated the place so much, why did she keep coming back?

Because she was scared of the big wide world? Had she been just an insecure little girl at heart? And if so, what had happened to change that? To prompt her decision to leave? And why in secret? She was an adult, why hadn't she wanted her

162

parents or anyone else to know?

The answer I kept coming up with was that she had met someone she felt she could trust. Someone under whose wing she felt secure. A protector. But for some reason that person had to remain anonymous. Because they would have been deemed to be unsuitable?

A married man? An older man? A married woman? A woman?

An announcement on my phone that I had a missed call from Alison Weir interrupted these speculations. I pulled over and called her.

'Hi, Sarge, I was getting back to you on those background checks you asked for.'

I took out my notebook. 'Okay.'

'That flight you wanted me to check is a confirmation. Owen Jones took the Air France flight for Lagos on Monday.'

'Thanks.' I ran a line through that query to cross it out.

'The people at Fron Heulog, Trevor and Valerie Horne and her brother Greg Thomas, all came up on the radar.'

'Crime-syndicate bosses?'

She chuckled. 'Not quite. They all had to have CRB checks because of their work with youngsters.'

'I assume, because they're still running the place, that there were no problems there?'

'No, totally clean. Trevor and Valerie Horne have a long history of fostering in Smethwick. The activity centre is a sort of by-product of that.'

'Who funds it?'

'Local authorities, mainly. A small Home Office grant, plus contributions from a variety of charitable organizations.'

'Where does the brother fit in?'

'The Hornes are the main movers; from what I can gather he comes and goes quite a bit. The house is actually in his name, so he's got a big stake in the operation.'

That reminded me about something his sister had said about it being through Owen and Rose Jones that Greg had got the opportunity to buy the place. I made a mental note to try to check out what she had meant by that.

'No dirty sheets?' I asked.

'Just one minor smear. Which is pretty historic. Greg Thomas got pulled in on a drunk and disorderly, and got let off with a caution. You'll be interested in the arresting officer.'

'Kevin Fletcher?'

She laughed. 'He got off with a caution, remember. No, it was a PC Emrys Hughes. How's that for a small world?'

I made a mental note to talk to Emrys about it. Back when he was a plain constable. That sounded like a long time ago.

'Anything on the Fenwicks?'

'Clive and Derek. They're brothers, they run an import–export business in Manchester.'

So Gloria and Isabel weren't blood-related, they had married brothers. That explained the big difference in looks.

'Any form?'

'No. But they are on the system.' I could tell from her voice that she was teasing me out, leading up to something.

'Cut the suspense, please, Alison.'

'They're in the TA. They've both got firearms certificates.'

164

I felt it resonate in my kidneys. 'Rifles?'

'No, pistols. Target-shooting.'

Was I twitching needlessly? Even if they were in the Territorial Army, to have been granted firearms certificates they would have had to demonstrate that they were solid and upright citizens. The type of people who tithe their salaries to the upkeep of widows and orphans, and bathe the feet of lepers. But guys who were into guns disturbed me.

I also realized that it would be another good reason to remove a head from a body if the preferred method of execution was a bullet in the brain. They wouldn't want the evidence left literally rattling around in the skull.

'Sarge?'

I hadn't heard the question she had just asked me. 'Sorry?'

'Do you want me to pass this on to DCI Fletcher?'

'No. Stick it on the file, but don't highlight it yet, or flag it up for his attention. I'll take responsibility for the decision,' I said before she could argue. I didn't want to give Fletcher an excuse to extend his heavy-handed reach back over into my territory.

Was that decision going to come back to haunt me?

'We're just about to break down the displays, Sarge.'

Alison's voice broke into my distraction again. 'What's that?'

'We're shutting down the incident room. Everything's going to Newport or Carmarthen. I just wondered whether you wanted a last look at anything before it goes?'

Shit. A dilemma. I was on my way to Gerald

Evans's place, but Alison had just pricked my conscience. I had been so obsessed with Evie and Bruno Gilbert that I had neglected the other bodies. They weren't meant to be part of my business. But I wasn't belief-restricted to the Newport–Cardiff victims scenario.

I made up my mind. Gerald Evans had waited this long, he could mature on the hook for a bit longer. 'Thanks, Alison, I'm on my way in. I'd really appreciate it if you could make up a file on what we have on the other bodies for me.'

*   *   *

It wasn't a very thick folder that she handed me when I got back to The Fleece. I wasn't surprised. Not only had we still not established identities, but we also had not been able to determine the causes of death. With no organs or soft tissue remaining, and no stiletto left conveniently wedged between the third and fourth ribs, the pathologists were having a hard time of it. Tessa was probably closer to finding out about her 600-year-old guy than we were any of our victims.

I looked over the summary again. Two males and a female, all minus heads and hands, and all skeletonized. All approximately middle-aged and apparently in reasonable health. They appear to have been buried over a two-year period, with the first one—coincidentally the first one we had found—the first to have been interred approximately eight years ago.

And then there was Evie.

What does her presence say about the status of the original bodies? I posed myself the question I had
166

been unable to answer before. And I kept coming back to it. He would have had time, so why hadn't he removed the original bodies? Why had he added an extra one instead?

I looked up at the map.

Evie was the outsider.

The spoiler. Jesus! I had just remembered the word that Jack Galbraith had used. He had meant that she represented the break from any sort of pattern, made us think that the killer was diversifying. But what if it was manipulation again? The addition of her body changed the perception of the place. She turned it into what we were meant to think of it as. The place that Bruno had supposedly chosen for his dumping ground.

Without Evie, it was . . .? What? It came to me slowly. It was *special*. Somewhere that was important enough for the perpetrator to have taken the risk of keeping the bodies in place. In the hope that, in the end, they might not be discovered. That they could continue resting in some sort of twisted kind of peace.

The bodies were specific to that place. They had a reason for being there.

Had the wind-farm excavations disturbed a shrine? Could they have been some kind of a sick memorial?

To who or what?

And how did the victims relate to it?

My mind raced. Had they known each other? It was the first time this thought had struck me. We had assumed that, because of the time lapses between the burials, they had been random victims. Picked off when the urge to kill got hot and sticky, just unfortunates in the wrong place at the wrong

167

time. But what if they had been connected? What if they had been specifically targeted because they constituted a group?

Would it make a difference?

Yes. Because it would mean that there had been a definite and specific campaign. And, unlike random hits, rational plans could be retraced.

So should I call Kevin Fletcher in Newport to share this observation? No point, he would only treat it as coming from the wrong side of the wisdom tracks.

I looked at the large-scale map of the wind-farm site that Alison had left up on the display board for me. The positions where the bodies had been discovered marked with colour-coded crosses. The originals in a cluster to the east of the site, with Evie way out on her own.

But that was to be expected. She had been thrown into the pile to fuck us up.

Were the others saying anything?

Alison came up beside me. 'I've just checked, Sarge. We've got spares, you can take that one with you, if you want.'

'Thanks.' This was going to look good on my caravan's wall. And I already knew that I was going to lose sleep over it. Trying to trace a pattern. Get into the mind of the guy who had left those poor bastards up there.

Because surely this had to be a guy. So much physicality involved. But I cursed inwardly for letting the doubt enter. Instead of containing this thing, I had just expanded the frontiers.

This was turning into real *Boys' Own* territory. Not only had I made my acquaintance with a gold mine, but now I had my very own treasure map to play with.

I distractedly thought about Tessa again. In *Boys' Own* fiction the girl wasn't even a fixture, never mind a reward.

10

It was a Saturday afternoon, a bad day for finding red-blooded country males at home. But at least the shooting season was over, which narrowed their options down slightly.

I went out into the back courtyard of The Fleece where I had parked, and found myself under a dark and violently oppressive sky that had not been there when I arrived. It was as if God had finally come to His senses, realised what He had created, and rolled out the celestial equivalent of weed suppressant over humanity.

'You might want to borrow the Land Rover.' David had followed me to the door. He used his head to gesture at the sky. 'They're forecasting snow.'

'It's nearly fucking April,' I groaned. 'What kind of country is this?'

He laughed at my innocence. 'It's lambing time in Dinas.'

I looked up at the bruise-blue heavens. 'The little buggers are meant to be gambolling under fluffy white clouds in a bright azure sky.'

He shook his head. 'No, that's the day we call summer.'

I declined the offer of the old Land Rover as I wanted to arrive with some credibility. The

169

road narrowed down to a lane that wound up a small valley running parallel to the one with the wind-farm site. No river here though, just a choppy stream fringed with spiked rushes and small clumps of gorse, silver birches and alders. The pasture covered the floor of the valley and ran partially up the sides, eating into the bracken where the marginal lands had been improved.

I passed the entrance to Pentre Isaf, where Blackie Collins had been dispossessed by the pony-trekking centre, which was already showing the signs of its own failure in the paint peeling off its hoarding, and the horseshoes askew on the gate.

I almost drove past the entrance to Pentre Fawr Farm. It was too tidy. Not what I had been expecting: a new hardwood five-bar gate; the name of the farm incised into a slab of slate on one of the stone pillars, the letters picked out in silver paint; the grass recently trimmed. Around these parts I was used to farm names sloppily daubed onto old milk churns rusted through to the colour and texture of brandy snaps.

The driveway added to my sense of disquiet. It was neatly fenced off, and surfaced with new gravel, which crunched evenly under the tyres. Farm driveways were usually a lurching experience.

The farmhouse was red brick, with yellow-brick detailing around the door and window reveals, and a horizontal stringcourse band. The roof had been replaced with new slate, and the windows recently painted, as had the barns that formed a three-sided courtyard.

It was a nice place. This didn't fit the picture I wanted. Neither did the trim row of stables with shiny horses watching me curiously out of two of them, the motorized horsebox parked in an open barn, and the pro-fox-hunting stickers on the windscreen and front bumper.

The yard was clean. Where were the hens, the clumps of variegated animal shit and the lagoons of leaked sump oil? This wasn't Dinas, this was Surrey. As I walked towards the house I began to get a sinking feeling that perhaps everyone disliked Gerald Evans so much because he was too close to being English.

I rang the doorbell and heard the first sound of a dog. It wasn't reassuring though, it didn't transform the place back into a scruffy working farm. It wasn't a sheepdog going mental and straining at its chain, it was something small, yappy and pampered, yelping from deep in the house.

'Quiet, Tata . . .' the voice came at me through the closed door as it approached. High, and sure of itself, a ripe English accent.

She opened the door and cocked her head at me. A confident smile cramming surprise and enquiry into it. She had thin blonde hair that flicked up at her shoulders, escaping from a loose headscarf tied and draped around her neck over a green, quilted, sleeveless jacket. I put her in her early forties, although her complexion was cracking from either too much dry sherry or too much hacking into the wind. Her eyes were deeply recessed above thin, prominent cheekbones, and her tight lips were still flecked with the residue of a sickly pink lipstick.

Okay, she was wearing patchily, but she was still a far remove from the trailer-trash-slut composite I had built up as Gerald Evans's life-companion.

'Mrs Evans, I'm Detective Sergeant Capaldi. I wonder if I could have a word with your husband, please.'

The mannered smile trotted over into frowning territory. 'Tata, shut up!' She turned and snarled at the dog, before turning back to me. 'It's a dreadful business, and it's very upsetting about poor Evie Salmon, but we've already spoken to Sergeant Hughes. There's nothing more we can tell you.' The tone was disinterest now—she had marked me down as trade—and her body language was preparing me for the door to be shut in my face.

It would pain me, but for the sake of progress I was going to have to eat shit.

'It's your husband's judgement that I'm interested in, Mrs Evans.'

That caught her attention.

'Between you and me,' I continued, 'most local people are too insular, so I was hoping to get the overview of someone with a broader perspective.'

The smile returned. 'I understand, and I'm sure my husband would be only too happy to help, but unfortunately he is salmon fishing in Herefordshire this afternoon.'

'Perhaps you could help?' I suggested, covering my disappointment. 'As Evie did work for you.'

She shrugged magnanimously. 'I can try.'

Tata and I trotted obediently behind her to the sitting room, although, thankfully, she only felt the need to yell at the dog. I took in the house as I walked through, including the glass-fronted drinks cabinet, which was Bunnahabhain-free, as far as I could tell. The place wasn't to my taste, everything was overelaborate, and the rooms too dark, but none of it was cheap.

She allocated me a seat, sat down on a sofa opposite, curled her legs up, and allowed Tata to nestle on her lap. 'You're new in these parts?' she observed.

'Fairly.'

'I'm glad to see that you haven't allowed yourself to be swayed by local tittle-tattle about us.'

'I ignore gossip, Mrs Evans,' I lied priggishly.

'Good for you. It's all down to jealousy, you see. We suffer from all this hostility because people are envious of my husband's farming and business acumen.'

'What businesses are those?'

'He's an entrepreneur.' She threw it into the air and let it fly away, and I knew better than to run after it.

'How did you get on with Evie?'

She made a regal show of thinking about it. 'She was not the world's brightest girl. And she had no real passion for horses. She worked here mainly for the money, I think, and to get away from her parents.' She preened. 'But I like to think that we were friends. With me more in the big-sister role, of course, given the age difference.' She raised her eyebrows, giving me the cue, but I didn't contradict her. There was only so much toadying I could do without puking.

'Did she talk about any other friends?' I asked instead.

She gave me a pause to show that I had disappointed her. 'We shared a healthy scorn for the local populace.'

'But she didn't talk about boyfriends, or special friends?'

'No, but . . .' She went back to the memory. 'On about two or three occasions, when she was having her lunch, a very strange boy with yellow hair

173

appeared.'

'Appeared?' I queried.

'Well, it wasn't magic, I suppose. He came over the hill on one of those off-road motorbikes they use.'

'Did she tell you his name?'

She shook her head. 'Oh, no, we weren't introduced, and I made a point of staying away. After the third time I had to tell her that I didn't want motorbikes around, scaring the horses. And it was fortunate that Gerald was never here.'

'Why is that?'

'The boy looked sort of druggy. Gerald wouldn't have put up with anyone like that on our land.'

'You mentioned that you thought that one of the reasons Evie came here was to get away from her parents?'

She nodded.

'So it didn't surprise you when she left?'

'She was here, you know. She worked here that morning, and then just went up and off in the afternoon.' She watched for my reaction, but I prompted her with silence. 'But did it surprise me? Yes and no, I suppose. She was forever running down her parents, how they didn't understand her, how this place was so awful. But she had been doing it for so long I thought it had just become a ritual.'

'You drove her down to Dinas that afternoon?'

'No, Gerald did.'

I felt the warm tingle in my belly. 'This was lunchtime?' I offered innocently.

'Yes, but Gerald was going to a meeting anyway, so he volunteered.'

'So he didn't come right back?'

174

She frowned. 'No, I've just told you, he was going on to a meeting.'

'How well did Evie get on with your husband?'

She went tight-lipped and hag-faced on me.

'Can I ask when your husband got back?'

'No.' She took her displeasure out on the dog, sweeping it roughly off her lap as she stood up. 'I don't think that that has anything to do with you, Sergeant.'

Which meant that it had been late.

And Gerald, from being possibly the last-known person to see Evie in Dinas, could now turn out be the guy who had whisked her off to Xanadu. To set her up in a pleasure dome?

*   *   *

A yellow-haired boy had now appeared on the scene, and I still had to find out what Evie had been doing on her lost Saturdays, but it was getting too late to carry on today. I drove down the hill from the Evanses' place in the dark, and David's snow had still not materialized.

But I had Gerald Evans in the cross hairs, and I was happy. It had been a long slog of a week, and I felt I deserved a Saturday night.

And I had spoken too soon. A cold rain that was starting to take on the texture of sleet had begun as I drove into Dinas. The town was filling up with other peoples' Saturday-night release. Including Gloria and Isabel Fenwick, by the looks of it (I saw the unmistakeable yellow Audi parked outside The Fleece).

I was only half right.

'Sergeant Capaldi!' Gloria had seen me come

175

through the door and was standing to grab my attention, jiggling up and down, arm high, but not quite waving. She was wearing a tight, roll-necked charcoal-grey wool dress that rode high over black tights, and exaggerated all the contours.

I raised my hand socially, but she wasn't going to be fobbed-off with that. She yelled at David. 'Get him a drink on my tab, and another one for me.'

David tapped the top of the beer pump quizzically. I dropped my voice. 'How many has she had?'

'This is the third large Shiraz,' he said, as he poured it.

I shook my head. 'Apple juice.' So much for Saturday night, I thought, as I took the drinks over. 'Hello, Mrs Fenwick.'

'Gloria . . . And what the hell is that you're drinking?'

'Apple juice. I'm driving.'

'So am . . .' She stopped herself with a big grin. 'Fuck, you're a policeman.'

I put the drinks on the table and sat down opposite her, raising my glass. 'Cheers! No Isabel?'

'Clive's driven down. He flew back into Manchester this afternoon.' She leaned across the table and dropped her voice to a whisper: 'I thought I'd be diplomatic and scarper to give them some privacy.' She gave me a dirty wink. 'You know, they haven't seen each other for a while.'

'Flew in from where?' I asked.

'Kuwait. That's where the Middle Eastern end of the business is based.'

'Import–export?'

She raised her glass and smiled over it slyly. 'You've been doing your homework, Sergeant.'

176

'It's a murder investigation, Gloria, we have to cover every possibility.'

'And are we suspects?'

'Should you be?'

She held my eyes, the glass in front of her distorting her amused expression, and I wondered whether she was playing with me. She took a deep drink and didn't answer.

'The Barn Gallery?' I asked.

She cocked her head, wondering for a moment precisely what I was asking. 'It's Isabel's baby, really. I'm happy to trot alongside. We get to go to Milan and Barcelona and New York and Berlin on big shopping sprees.'

'Have you ever questioned the gallery's location?'

She laughed. 'Isabel is convinced that she's creating a style shrine. That sooner or later our exclusivity is going to bring the customers to us. In the meanwhile, we wait to be discovered.'

'Along the Welsh-tweed-and-crappy-pottery trail?'

She laughed again. 'No, a write-up in a style magazine will do. And we're lucky, the economic truth is that we don't have to worry about it. The other business can cover it.'

'What do you import?'

'Anything that's available to fill the containers we've sent out there. The focus is on the export side.' She leaned across the table again. 'Are you really interested in this, or are you just trying to explore my motives?'

'I'm interested.'

'Meat pies are big; saveloys, faggots.' She smiled at my puzzlement. 'We cater for the expat oil workers in the Gulf, and all those NGOs that have sprouted in Iraq. You have no idea how many people in those deserts have a craving for a good old Cornish pasty.'

'And your husband, Derek, he's still over there?'

She nodded her head slowly. 'He runs that end of the operation.' She made a big show of studying me. 'Are you trying to suggest something?' She let it come out mock shocked.

I ignored her banter, and reached over and picked up her car keys from the table next to her purse. I dangled the Audi badge in front of her. 'The business must do very well?'

A momentary flash of uncertainty sparked in her eyes, and then she nodded. 'It pays for Isabel and me to play.' She reached to take the car keys from me. I folded them into my fist.

'I'm driving home now, Gloria. I'm happy to drop you off, or you could call a taxi later, or you can see if David and Sandra can find you a room here.' I stood up. 'Your choice.'

I half expected anger. Instead, she stood up meekly, shook her head to get her expensive hair back into shape, and smoothed the dress down over her hips. It was a calculated and practised gesture. She let me help her on with her coat.

I waited at the bar as she settled her tab with David. She slipped her arm into mine. I looked round at her, surprised. 'For added stability,' she said cheekily. We walked to the door and stopped to wait as some people entered.

What a terrible planetary fucking conjunction.

Tessa walked in. Tessa and her Little Diggers. Not even Tessa and Jeff.

I saw her taking us in, in stop-motion: me,

178

Gloria, the hand on the arm declaring possession. She gave Gloria a vague smile, and turned a cold, slow one on me. 'Goodnight,' she said, and followed her charges into the bar.

Gloria read my expression: 'Oops . . .'

She picked up on my mood and stayed quiet for the ride home. I turned up the drive to the Barn Gallery and my headlights illuminated a Porsche Cayenne. These people were seriously taking the piss in Dinas, where a Rover wasn't a relic from Britain's manufacturing past, but an aspirational dream.

'That's Derek's,' Gloria explained needlessly. 'Do you want to come in?' she asked quietly, sounding completely sober now.

'No, thanks.' I passed her car keys over.

She opened the car's door. 'I'd like you to. You don't have to worry about Derek and Isabel, they won't be around.'

'You're a happily married woman, Gloria.'

She nodded slowly, kissed the tips of two fingers and placed them on my cheek. 'Slight correction, soldier: I'm not a *happily* married woman.'

Jesus, they were like fucking buses. I hadn't had any kind of a relationship since Sally Paterson, and now two possibilities come along at the same time, with the probability that they would cancel each other out.

And still no snow.

* * *

Saturday night in Unit 13 with a reheated mushroom risotto and the second half of a bottle

179

of Sauvignon that had been bad from birth. I got the malt whisky out for dessert (a simple Glenfiddich—I couldn't run to designer Islay stuff) and settled down in front of the gas fire, with the tumbled sloshing of the river outside and the large-scale map of the wind-farm site taped up on the opposite wall.

I gave up on trying to shape a pattern out of the crosses on the map, put my head back against the big cold window, and tried to review what I had.

Not much.

Either Evie's father or the Fenwicks lying about her employment at the Barn Gallery, Gerald Evans as the last person in Dinas to see her, and the conviction that Bruno Gilbert had not killed himself. But earnest convictions did not earn cash prizes.

I dozed off thinking about a yellow-haired boy.

And woke up abruptly because something had intruded. Some extraneous sound had disturbed the aural background of the river and the hiss of the gas fire. But it had no shape, I hadn't been conscious enough to give it form. I got up stiffly to check outside, reminding myself to be wary. The rain was cold but fine, more of a suspension than individual drops.

I walked round the caravan with my torch, feeling strangely uneasy. It was the same sensation I had had that night at the wind-farm site when I had felt that I was being watched. The same sense that had warned me that Bruno had been outside the caravan waiting for me. I stopped and ignored the rain and stood stock still to let the backdrop settle down. Nothing more than the river and the dark tangle of the alder branches shifting in the damp breeze.

It was probably bad-diet voodoo. Telling me to go to bed.

*   *   *

In the morning I drove over to Fron Heulog under the same dark sky that now seemed to be tethered in place like a corny harbinger in a biblical epic.

Valerie Horne was waiting at the door of the office when I got out of the car. She had registered surprise over the intercom when I had buzzed at the security gates. Groups of youths mooched around looking studiously bored or genuinely disturbed by this stuff called fresh air and wide open spaces.

'Morning, Mrs Horne. I'm sorry to disturb you on a Sunday.'

She gave me the sort of shrug that didn't quite excuse the intrusion. 'I didn't get back to you because no one here knew anything more about the girl.'

'Something else has come up I need to ask you about.'

'Okay.' Despite the drizzle she made no move to lead me into the office.

'You may not have known Evie personally, and I have to admit that we're going back more than a couple of years here, but have you any memory of ever seeing anyone matching her description over at Pen Twyn on Saturday mornings? Or leaving there in the afternoon?' I gestured towards the house and the Barn Gallery that were visible on their rise. 'Or a boy with yellow hair?' I added.

She held up her hand. 'I've got to stop you there.

181

I'm never here on a Saturday. I go on the minibus that takes the boys back to Birmingham, and come back in the evening with the new batch. I spend the day in Smethwick, making sure that my parents are getting on okay. I've done that ever since we moved here.'

'What about your husband and your brother? Could I ask them?'

She shook her head. 'My husband's busy with a group.' She heard herself and relented. She was essentially a nice woman, and not in the business of obstructing people. She sighed. 'I'll take you over to Greg. He's in the barn.'

The barn had been fitted out as a gymnasium. The floor was sprung-boarded, and marked out for various court games. There were bars on one wall, a rope gantry that swung out, and a climbing wall at the far end. Greg Thomas was at a bench, inspecting climbing equipment. I reminded myself that Emrys Hughes had once had a run-in with this guy.

I saw the look of recognition cross his face as we approached. I don't know whether he was conscious of it, but he straightened up and moved away from the bench in a way that made you aware of the power he was holding in reserve. He looked like he could give even Mackay and his former SAS buddies a run for their money.

'Hello again, Mr Thomas,' I said, shaking his hand. I felt his grip testing mine.

He nodded. 'Anything we can do to help. It's a terrible business, it's shocked everyone in the valley. We're not used to things like this.' Like his sister, he hadn't lost the Birmingham accent.

And his proprietorship of the valley surprised

me. 'I know, and I'm afraid it means that you've got to put up with the likes of me asking all these questions.' I smiled jovially. It wouldn't hurt for him to think that I was simpler than I was.

'I thought the word was that it was all down to Mr Gilbert next door?'

'We have to make a case for everything,' I said, non-committal. He didn't press, and I asked him the same questions I had asked Valerie.

He thought about it and shook his head. 'If I had seen her it didn't register. But definitely no yellow-haired boy, that one would have done.'

'I'll ask Trev when I see him,' Valerie offered.

'But don't count on anything,' Greg said. He smiled at his sister. 'When Val goes off on a Saturday it's mayhem here for Trev and me. Getting the place tidied up and organized for the next bunch,' he elaborated.

'Go on . . .' She nudged him affectionately. 'You're welcome to take over mum-and-dad duty any day.'

He raised his arms in mock horror. 'Give me the gang boys any day.'

I had a sudden illumination. *Gang Boys!* An image of Evie and her yellow-haired boy flaunting the rustic mores of Dinas. *Rebels!* Had they both thought of themselves as bandits?

'What do you do about dope?' I asked.

They looked at each other, surprised by the sudden topic-shift.

'You deal with gang members here,' I clarified, 'street kids. A lot of them are going to be users.'

'What's your point?' Valerie retorted briskly, her tone hostile now.

'Do you let them bring it in here with them?'

183

'Of course not,' she snorted.

'We're trying to let them see that there's a possibility of enjoying themselves without using drugs,' Greg explained. 'It's one of the conditions of coming here, they have to be clean. They're searched thoroughly before they leave, and when they get here, they know they're not going to get anything past us.'

I nodded. 'I see, thanks.'

'What's your point?' Valerie demanded again, angrily. 'Are you looking to fit up some of these kids?'

'Not at all, Mrs Horne. The opposite, in fact. I just want to be able to help you.'

'And how is that supposed to work?' Greg asked.

'So that when irate, upstanding local parents find their children's stash and try to blame it on Fron Heulog, I'll be able to tell them, hand on heart, to look again.'

If they didn't buy my motive, they didn't pursue it. They just wanted rid of me now. I was the enemy, I unsettled the kids, I was not good for business.

But I'd got the answer I wanted. The kids had to come in here clean. But a lot of them weren't going to want to stay that way. They were going to need at least a bit of weed, just to tolerate the rural weirdness. I knew these kinds of kids. As well as being tough they were resourceful. And this place had been operating for long enough for them to have set up a system.

Now I was looking for a mark.

I drove out slowly and saw him, positioned in exactly the right place, just where the track started to bend away out of sight of the house. A white youth in an olive-drab army-surplus jacket, with

184

long hair under a crew cap with a red Maoist star, and with him a young black guy in a shiny white sports two-piece with a pale-blue stripe down the arms and legs.

They turned to watch me as I passed. Cool smiles of amused hostility. I palmed a five-pound note and held it up to the window as I cruised by. I stopped down the track, out of sight of the house, and hopefully out of Valerie's security-camera range.

They sauntered up irritatingly slowly. The black youth stopped at the rear of the car and took up the watchman's stance. Experience brought the white kid up to the passenger's side, where the best things to snatch were generally found. It also kept the car between us if, for some reason, negotiations broke down and I decided to come running for him.

He leaned down to the open window and nodded down at the five-pound note I had laid on the passenger's seat. 'If you're looking to suck me off, mister, you're going to have to come up with a lot more than that.' He gave me a grin and stuck his tongue into the side of his cheek.

'Are you soliciting?'

He knew the word. His expression didn't change. 'You're the one doing the buying.'

'I'm looking for information.'

'What kind of information?'

'What's the local weed like?'

He cocked his head back, playing it mock-affronted. 'Whoa! How would I be likely to know that?'

'They stop you bringing your own in.'

'Some gets through.'

'Not enough.'

He looked at me carefully now. 'What's it to

185

you?'

'I'm not after your supplier, I'm just trying to trace a contact of his. I promise you I won't fuck up the score.'

He thought about it. I hoped he was thinking that he didn't have to care too much as he'd be back on home turf in less than a week's time, and any future scarcity wouldn't be his problem. 'It works,' he said eventually.

'What works?'

'The hillbilly skunk.'

'Who do you buy from?'

He sucked air in through his teeth and shook his head. 'That is a difficult question, mister.'

I added a ten-pound note to the five. He continued to shake his head until I had added two more tens to the pile. This was getting painful. I wasn't going to be able to put this down on my expenses sheet. But his head-shaking had hesitated. We had reached the point of balance. It was now my turn to show reluctance and move as if to retrieve the money.

He grinned and reached an arm into the car and scooped the notes up like a practised dice player. 'All we know is that he's called TB. The deal is we leave the money on the shithouse windowsill on a Monday night, the weed is there on the Tuesday.'

I drove away before Valerie caught up with me. I had just spent £35 on what? A pair of initials. But at least it was a confirmation that there was a local dealer.

Now I only had to find him, and hope that amongst his clients, past or present, was a yellow-haired boy.

186

11

But first I had a church to attend.

I had a choice of Methodist, two Baptist chapels—the Zion and the Ebenezer—and the Church in Wales. Having met La Evans, I realized that, out of that lot, only the Anglican community would fit her demographic. And, assuming she was a churchgoer, would her husband accompany her to give thanks to his Maker for His munificence?

I was back in Dinas, it was Sunday morning, I had nothing to lose.

St Peter's, a tidy, simple church in dark local stone, was in the old leafy quarter of Dinas that qualified as pretty. A large and ancient yew tree flanked the path from the lychgate to the entrance porch. The small line of cars parked outside were fairly representative of the overseer class, but I was flying blind as I didn't know what either of the Evanses drove.

I parked in the lee of the wind and rolled my window down. A straggle of hesitant voices, mainly out of tune and trying to keep up with an ambitiously creaky organ, wafted lightly from the building. The hymn was unrecognizable.

I caught the patrol car in my rear-view mirror just as it rounded the corner into the small square in front of the church. It pulled up behind me. I smiled to myself. Was I witnessing a pincer movement?

Hughes's sidekick, Friel, was driving. Emrys got out of the passenger's side and adjusted his cap with a businesslike snap as he stood up. I watched him approach in the wing mirror. He couldn't quite cover the smugness under the grim expression he was preparing. I had seen this one before. It looked like Inspector Morgan had given him permission to kick my balls into touch.

'Capaldi, what do you think you're doing here?' he growled, spreading his bulk in front of my open window.

I inclined my head towards the church and beamed up at him. 'Basking in Grace, Sergeant Hughes.'

'We've had a complaint about you.'

'Have you been told to head me off at the pass?'

He scowled. 'What's that supposed to mean?'

I gestured towards the church again. 'Is Gerald Evans in there? Or am I wasting my time sitting out here?'

'You were told to leave the locals to me. Mr and Mrs Evans had already been interviewed. You turning up there yesterday amounted to harassment.'

'Thanks.'

His scowl turned puzzled. 'For what?'

'For letting me know that he is in there.'

'This isn't a joke, Capaldi, I've been instructed to tell you to leave the Evanses alone. And that especially goes for trying to waylay them outside church.'

So Gerald Evans had a direct line to Inspector Morgan? Probably the Masonic underground. I held Emrys's bull stare for a moment before throwing the acid bath into his face. 'Get in the car!' I snapped.

'What?' His righteousness deflated like a stomped puffball. I caught a fleck of panic in his eyes. This wasn't meant to happen. He was meant to be in control.

'Get in the fucking car now, unless you want your young pal Friel to see you turning into a limp prick before his eyes.'

He shot me a look of wounded anger, but there was enough doubt laced in to let me know that he would comply. I had my phone out before he opened the door.

'What are you trying to play at?' he blustered as he got in, knocking his cap off in his annoyance.

I raised a finger to shut him up, and started tapping numbers into my phone.

'Who are you calling?' he asked suspiciously, unable to conceal an edge of concern.

'I want you to personally tell DCS Galbraith why you're trying to block my investigation.'

His face crashed. 'It's Sunday.'

'That's right. I don't know whether he makes a habit of humping Mrs Galbraith on a Sunday morning, or if you're just going to catch him at the third hole on the golf course. Whatever it is, he isn't going to be happy.'

He looked at me calculatingly. 'You're bluffing.'

I leaned over towards him, a big friendly threatening grin on my face. 'I've been given the job of trying to trace Evie's connections here. All of Evie's connections. And that includes Gerald Evans.' I made a big theatrical show of pressing the call button and held the phone out to him. 'It's all yours.'

He recoiled away from it, both hands out, palms up. 'Okay, okay, turn it off!'

I put the phone to my ear and listened, catching the opening riffs of my answering machine before

189

I cut the connection. I grinned at Emrys. 'Mrs Galbraith gets to stay happy.'

'You're a real bastard, you are,' he moaned sulkily.

'And you were just doing your job.'

'I've already interviewed the Evanses.'

'So why isn't there a report that says that he was the last person to see Evie in Dinas before she left?'

'That was two years ago,' he protested.

'What the fuck did you ask them about?'

He gave me a hurt look. 'If they'd seen Evie Salmon since she left. If they knew anything about the bodies. If they'd seen anything suspicious on the hill.' He smirked meanly. 'You don't really believe that Evans was keeping her at Pentre Fawr all that time?'

'He could have kept her in a honey pot.'

'What's that?'

'A flat in town somewhere. He could have been paying her rent. He could have been her sugar daddy.'

He thought about it and shook his head. But the certainty wasn't total.

'Why is he so unpopular?' I asked.

He used a slow shrug to give him time to calculate how deeply to go into this with me. An outsider. 'He's been known not to keep his word.'

I'd been in these parts for long enough to know that that was considered to be nearly on a par with child molesting. 'Where does he get his money?'

'He married rich. She puts it about that he's a successful businessman, but the word is that it all comes from her.'

That would fit. The hunting, the horses, the tidy

190

farm. Her priorities. What would he have spent his pocket money on?

'You don't really think he had anything to do with those bodies up there do you?' Emrys cut in over my speculation.

I ignored his question. 'Do the initials TB mean anything to you?' I asked instead.

He wasn't used to subterfuge. He went into a great big pantomime process of pretending to think about it before shaking his head too firmly. 'Doesn't ring any bells.'

'Who's the local dope dealer?'

The next performance he trotted out was sanctimony. 'We don't have one. This isn't Cardiff, our kids don't need it, they aren't twisted like that.'

I laughed into his po-faced sincerity. 'Come on, Emrys, there's nothing twisted about smoking a spliff. I'm not talking about bringing the Mexican cartels into town, just recreational dope smoking. Stuff the Boys' Brigade would do behind the club house without thinking they'd broken some code of honour.'

He shook his head grimly. 'Not in Dinas they wouldn't.'

I didn't believe him. He was either in denial, or he didn't want me showboating in his parish. Uncovering a crazed dope monster from within the safe and cosy bosom of his hand-knitted community. It didn't matter. I had a fallback.

He was halfway out of the car when I remembered. 'You once had a run-in with a young soldier. It was a long time ago, I was told.'

He looked at me blankly.

'Greg Thomas. One of the people at Fron Heulog Activity Centre.'

191

He slipped back into the seat. 'What's the problem?'

'Nothing, just background.'

He thought about it. 'You're going back about twelve . . .' He paused and shook his head. 'No, more like fifteen years. It was a fight outside The Fleece. This was before David and Sandra's time. Greg was here for the funeral of his fiancée.'

The one who was meant to marry her. Bruno's words came back to me. 'Was Greg going to marry Owen Jones's sister?' It suddenly made sense. I flashed back on the photograph of the three of them I had seen at the activity centre.

He nodded. 'That's right—Rose. Greg and Owen were friends in the army. He got to know the family when Owen used to bring him back to stay. He and Rose got serious, and then got engaged. They were going to live in Fron Heulog after they were married.'

'But Greg ended up there anyway.'

He nodded.

'Was that because of Owen?' I asked, remembering what Valerie Horne had said about their obligation to both Rose and Owen. Since Rose had died before she and Greg were married I presumed that Owen had become the main benefactor.

'Yes, Fron Heulog was his. His grandfather had left it to him. He wanted Rose and Greg to have it. Even after Rose died he sold it to Greg because he said it's what she would have wanted.'

'They must have been close?'

'Inseparable. Right from when they were tiny, Owen was always looking after her. He was really protective.' I had meant Owen and Greg, but I let

192

him continue. 'He was a quiet kid, but he turned into a terrier if he thought anyone was trying to mess Rose around.' He smiled. 'There was a joke going round that he only went into the army because Rose had told him she wanted to marry a soldier, and he said he'd find one for her.'

I flashed back on the photograph again. It would have been hard to tell who had been holding Rose the tightest.

'So he didn't mind Greg turning up?'

'He didn't turn up, Owen brought him home. After that it was the three of them going around together instead of just Owen and Rose.'

'She must have died young?'

'It was a real tragedy.'

'Illness?' I asked.

'No, a terrible accident. The Joneses and Greg were really cut up about it.'

'The fight?' I prompted, remembering what had started this line of the conversation.

'A bunch of hippies were taunting them about being in uniform. Owen and Greg had had too much to drink and eventually laid into them.' He smiled happily at the recollection. 'Ripped the dirty layabouts apart, they did.'

'And you let them off with a caution?'

He looked at me entreatingly. 'They'd been to a funeral. She was Owen's sister and Greg's fiancée. They were in mourning.'

I nodded my understanding. 'But I'll bet you truly busted those hippies' balls?'

He broke into a big grin. 'Damn right.'

I let him go. And ruminated over the way he had talked about Greg Thomas. Almost as if he had been adopted as a local. Was it of any significance?

*　　　*　　　*

The sound coming from the church after Emrys left was what I took to be the priest engaged in some sort of low incantation. I wasn't that up on the order of service in the Anglican convention, but I assumed that this was a contemplative moment, and they weren't all about to come bursting through the doors with their hands high in the air singing Hallelujah.

I had time to put in a telephone call.

I had first worked with Constable Huw Jones on a case involving a poisoned Montagu's harrier, and, after a spiky start, we had come to like one another. Huw was a sensible cop who kept out of departmental politics, and was happiest up in the hills with something like a golden plover in the eyepiece of his binoculars.

He may have spent half his time in the whin up to his knees in bilberries, but he had more perception of what was going on in the area than a combination of Emrys Hughes, Captain Morgan and a police radio grafted together into a new life form.

'Emrys Hughes tells me that there's no one dealing dope in Dinas.'

I heard his low thoughtful laugh come down the line. 'Sergeant Hughes is a very pious man.'

'Meaning?'

'If he doesn't believe in dope dealers then there aren't any. If he believed in them he would have to face up to having a problem in his community.'

'So he's right, there aren't any?' I teased.

He laughed again. 'Only pagans fucking up other

194

pagans. Not his concern.'

'How about a pagan with the initials TB?'

He was silent for a moment. 'You're not on a crusade, are you?' His voice was serious now.

'No, I just need some information.'

'Good.' Another silence. I hoped he was checking his notes. 'The man you're looking for is called Ryan Shaw.'

'TB?' I queried.

'Tractor Boy. His *nom de guerre*. Our Ryan thinks himself cool and ironic.'

'Address?'

'3 Orchard Close, Maesmore.'

'Thanks, Huw.'

'Do you want back-up?'

'Do I need it?'

'He's got a mean streak. He puts himself up there with the hoodlums in Manchester he scores from. But only when he's not in Manchester, of course.'

'He wouldn't stiff a cop?'

'You're going there as a cop who is overlooking his misdemeanours, remember. That is going to give him a certain sense of empowerment. He might try and screw you.'

'Thanks for the warning.'

Maesmore! I laughed inwardly. Ryan Shaw's ironic streak was catching. It was a village about seven miles from Dinas that had never recovered from the collapse of the lead-mining industry. Shortly after my arrival in the boondocks I had been called out there to help the uniforms at a domestic that had spilled out onto the scrubby patch of grass at the front of some former council houses. A recollection of the good neighbours

195

going at each other with missiles in the shape of abandoned shopping trolleys and springs from burned-out mattresses, with junked shock absorbers commandeered as impromptu cudgels.

I jerked out of my reflections and sat up with a jolt when I saw that people were coming out of the church. I got out of the car quickly and went to the other side of the lychgate. People were milling around the porch, waiting their turn to say goodbye to the vicar. Umbrellas went up as they came out from under the shelter of the porch. In my hurry I had forgotten my coat.

People looked at me curiously as they came past. Some nodded politely. Then I saw Mrs Evans in front of the vicar. The big man beside her in a grey suit had his back to me. He had a trilby in one hand, the other was patting the vicar familiarly on the shoulder. His hair was dark and bushy, and he had the build of a prop forward.

They turned to leave. Mrs Evans saw me as she was putting her umbrella up. She put a hand on her husband's arm to restrain him. He put his hat on, leaned down to hear what she was saying, and then looked at me.

He was built like a man who didn't give a fuck what deals he reneged on. More or less my height, about 1.9 metres, but that's where the resemblance ended. He looked like he was made of dense meat piled onto denser meat. His face was florid, gruffly handsome, with the same meat theme, and a nose that had been broken more than once and had retained no memory of its original shape.

She tried to pull him back towards the vicar, but he shook her hand off and strode down the path towards me. He smiled like a hungry man with new dentures.

'You're a persistent fucker, I'll give you that,' he announced loudly, striding towards me. Behind him I saw his wife blanch as his voice carried back to her and the vicar.

'I need to ask you some questions, Mr Evans,' I said, beginning to wonder if he was going to stop, or just walk straight over me.

He pulled up short. He eyed me up and down, his expression a combination of amusement and contempt. I got the impression that this was his stock look, which he didn't bother varying too much. 'You're getting wet, Sergeant.' He put out a hand the size of an overinflated toad and propelled me backwards under the lychgate. He then quickly raised both hands to forestall any protest. 'Just helping you to get out of the rain.' It was a show of power.

'You knew Evie Salmon, Mr Evans,' I said, ignoring the assault. Complaining would just play to his agenda and give him an excuse to shove me again, to demonstrate that he had only been helping.

'Of course I knew her, she helped my wife out.'

'Did she ever help you out?'

A mischievous grin kicked in. This guy was not dumb, he had picked up on my subtext. He leaned in close. I smelled the sort of aftershave that he wouldn't have picked for himself. 'I don't fuck around on my own doorstep,' he said in a tone that kept it between us.

I smiled innocently. 'So it would make sense to move her to neutral territory?'

He shook his head wonderingly, only now grasping where I was going with this. 'Turn that

197

insinuation into plain English.'

'You drove Evie down from Pentre Fawr on the day she left. You were the last person to see her in Dinas. Or were you more generous than that, Mr Evans? Did you take her somewhere farther?'

He stared at me calmly for a moment before he shook his head. 'Tough shit, Sergeant.'

'I'm sorry?' I didn't like the small gleam that had appeared in his eyes. It looked disturbingly triumphant.

'You're wrong. I wasn't the last person to see Evie.'

I didn't respond. I waited for the bombshell.

He smirked. 'After I dropped her off she walked across the square towards Clive Fenwick.'

It felt like the tendons behind my knees had just been severed. 'You know Clive Fenwick?' I blurted uselessly.

'Not too many Porsche Cayenne's in Dinas.' My surprise and consternation delighted him. He summoned his wife. She took his arm and pointedly ignored me. As they both left, the last look he turned on me was, *Crash and burn, fucker.*

*   *   *

Clive Fenwick!

Evie and the Barn Gallery had come back into conjunction. Or had she never left it?

I fought down the impulse to drive out there. I had just gifted Gerald Evans the opportunity to piss in my face, I didn't want the same thing to happen with Clive Fenwick. I needed more information.

I needed the yellow-haired boy.

Orchard Close in Maesmore was another

198

street of former council houses, but it was an improvement on the one I remembered from the tribal war. Some people here had bought into house-pride. A few tidy gardens, some front doors personalized, one house with a stuck-on stone façade. Saplings had been planted in the communal grass area; some of them had not even been snapped off.

None of this makeover nonsense for number 3, though. A motorbike under a plastic cover on the front lawn, broken milk bottles by the doorstep, and a smashed television set that appeared to have died where it had landed. A pimped purple VW Golf with wide alloy wheels, a rear spoiler and a straight-through exhaust pipe that could have served as an escape tunnel, was parked outside, half on the pavement.

I drove past slowly, making like an ordinary john who was looking for an address. Scanning the sociology as I went past. Realizing that I had been in too much of a hurry. I should have done some background checks here. Because these were semi-detached family houses. There was a real possibility that Ryan still lived with his parents.

And that could have an effect on both of my options: bribery or strongarm.

'Good afternoon. Is Ryan Shaw at home, please?'

'What the fuck's he done now?' She was the Fat and Scary Mum from central casting, and had sussed me as a cop just from the way I had knocked on the door. Everything about her was loose, from the nicotine-blonde hair pulled back into a ponytail, to the cheeks, jowls, chins and breasts, right down to the mauve two-piece leisure outfit.

'I need to talk to him in connection with a murder enquiry.'

'Fucking hell! He's moving up in the world.' She swivelled her head. 'Ryan!' she yelled. 'You're wanted. Wait there,' she instructed me, pointing at the front step. She left me and went into the room opposite that had a television set the size of a garage door on the wall. There was a pram in the hall, and, I noticed, before she pushed the door closed, other baby-care accoutrements on the floor of the television room.

Ryan came down the stairs fast, two at a time. He was a bobbing boy. Couldn't keep still, body popping and sneaking glances at all the reflective surfaces. I couldn't work out whether he was on amphetamines, or just speedy from a video game I had interrupted.

'Who you?' he asked, in a curious tone, but no surprise. He was in his mid-twenties, handsome in an amorphous boy-band way, with styled brown hair that lolled over his eyebrows, and he was obviously fixated on body image. He was wearing a tight sleeveless white singlet that showed off his muscle groups, tucked into baggy black sweat pants cinched tightly at the waist.

'Glyn Capaldi, I'd like to ask you a couple of questions.' I didn't produce my warrant card as I didn't want to make it formal.

'CID?' he asked cockily, proud of knowing the lingo.

I nodded. 'DS.'

His head bobbed in slow acknowledgement. 'Heard of you. You got talked about. You the dude who weirded-out in Cardiff. Word is you topped a pimp.' He made a slow-motion gangsta pistol charade to demonstrate.

'Not quite.' I wondered how this prat went down with the real scary guys he scored from in Manchester.

'What you doing at my crib on a Sunday?'

'I need your help, Ryan.'

His eyes took on a cunning glint. 'What kind of help?'

'Can I come in to talk about this?'

He inhaled audibly and wiggled his fingers in a pantomime of terror. 'It's like a fucking vampire, man. If I let you in then you can do all kinds of shit because I have given you some sort of invitation.'

Okay, so I was going to have to do this on the doorstep like a double-glazing salesman. 'You heard about the mutilated bodies we've found at Dinas?'

He nodded. 'You working on that one?'

'Yes.'

'I'm impressed. That must be some kind of disturbing shit to see.' He didn't sound impressed.

'Evie Salmon was one of the bodies.'

He clucked sympathetically. 'I heard. A bad break. But if that's what you're here for, I can't help you. Our paths never crossed.'

'I need to locate a friend of hers, a yellow-haired boy.'

He made a big show of deliberating. He even held his chin between his thumb and forefinger and gazed off into the middle distance. The bastard was taking the piss.

'This is completely off the record, Ryan.'

He dropped the goofy pose. 'But it isn't, is it? Nothing ever is. I do you this favour, assuming that I'm able to, and I'm admitting to something that perhaps I would be kind of crazy to admit to.'

The guy was sharp. 'You'd be helping with a murder enquiry. All the victims were missing their heads and hands. Evie Salmon was found cut in half,' I elaborated, aiming for his sense of injustice. He didn't need to know that I was the one who had done that last piece of butchering.

'This dude must be some kind of a gruesome fucker.' This time he did sound impressed.

'I personally promise you that it will go no further. This is strictly between you and me. I just need a name and then I walk away, and you and I are good, and I will owe you a favour.'

He leaned his head back, stretching his neck. It snapped forward again. 'Forget about the future, man. Forget about owing favours. Let's just say a straight five hundred here and now.'

He was serious. 'I can't offer you that kind of money.'

'Well that's a real shame, because that's the fucking price.'

We stared each other out. He wasn't going to buckle. He may have been prepared to haggle, but I couldn't get into it, not at that starting price. For information that might turn out to be worthless.

'You don't want me as an enemy, Ryan. I could be bad for business.'

'Oh . . .' he let out a theatrical moan of fear, and then moved in closer to me with a scowl. 'Learn the game around here before you try to put the threat on me. I provide a fucking service. You as an enemy don't scare me, with the friends I've got.'

So he was a snitch. That's why the bastard was so confident. Which also put another possible perspective on why Emrys had denied knowing anything about him. And Huw Davies had intimated that he didn't want me upsetting him. He was protected. Strongarm wouldn't work. And he had set the bar on the bribery too high.

I took a breath to suppress my rising anger. This self-satisfied, puffed-out sleazeball was getting to me. 'That bastard who killed those people is still out there. He could do it again,' I appealed to him, little knowing how soon this was going to appear to be prophetic.

He gave me a look to tell me to catch up on the lunacy of what I had just told him. 'In that case, if it's going to make me a target, I'd be fucking stupid telling you anything, wouldn't I?' He waggled his forearms at me. 'Like how am I going to manage my wanking without any fucking hands?'

He shouldn't have leered at me.

I shoved the door hard. It caught him on the shoulder and toppled his balance. Before he could recover I had crossed the hall and crashed in through the door to the room opposite.

'Is there anyone in this family with a shred of fucking decency?'

The two women on the black leather sofa watching a game show on the enormous television looked round slowly and up at me.

'People have died. Can you tell that heartless man of yours to stop thinking about himself for once?' I addressed the young woman on the sofa, who was also large, with dyed-black hair and matching eyebrows and eyelashes, and was jiggling a chunky baby with a dummy in its mouth.

She shared a glance with Ryan's mother. Neither appeared surprised or upset by my intrusion. Invasion and drama were obviously not strangers in

203

Ryan's life. She handed the baby to Ryan's mother who turned back to the television.

She got up and flashed me an annoyed look. I waited for her to ask me to fill her in on the cause of my outburst. 'Tell me if they win,' she called back to Ryan's mother, and left the room.

I was sucked back to the television. It was mesmeric. Phantasmagorical colours filled the wall. The game-show host had a suntan like a cinnamon bun, and teeth like the polar icecap. Compared to this, my little television in Unit 13 was like one of those gizmos that creates crude pictures from magnetized iron filings.

When she returned, the three of us, baby, Ryan's mother and me, were absorbed in the adventures of a walking, talking yoghurt pot that was going to revolutionize our digestive tracts. I was strangely reluctant to turn away from the screen.

'The name you're looking for is Justin Revel and he hasn't seen him for a long time.' She reached out on automatic and accepted the baby that Ryan's mother passed over the back of the sofa, a thread of drool still connecting them. 'And for your information, he's not my heartless man, he's my waste of space fucking brother.'

Ryan was not in the hall when I left. I warned myself to be prepared for flak from my colleagues, but I was pretty secure in the knowledge that he wouldn't be making a formal complaint about illegal entry.

It's the women, I thought, walking to the car, the mothers and the sisters, who are still looped into the simple thread of common humanity. The warm glow didn't last, though. History caught up with me as I got into my car. I remembered that it was also the women who had cut the genitals off the dead English soldiers after their defeat by Owain Glyndwr at the Battle of Pilleth.

And the snow had started.

*   *   *

Justin Revel.

That name had to belong to an incomer family. I could have routed my enquiry through Alison Weir in Carmarthen, but I was reluctant to make this strand public at this stage, and I reckoned that a name like that should not be hard to trace. So instead, I drove back to my research facility in Dinas.

A mug of coffee and the local telephone directory in front of the wood-burning stove in The Fleece.

There were two Revels listed. Neither of them answered their telephone, but at least the second one had an answering machine. A well-spoken voice with a Home Counties accent said that he was Julian Revel, and asked me to leave a message. I did, saying that I needed to talk to Justin Revel, and if he was related could he get him to contact me. I left my contact numbers and hung up.

I then basked in front of the warm stove and indulged myself, watching the snow coming down against the street light outside the window, the flakes bigger now, the ground starting to take cover, the night transformed by the reflective luminescence and the muffling effect of the snow. It was too beautiful at that point to worry about what a pain it was going to be to get around tomorrow.

My phone rang.

'DS Capaldi.'

'Glyn.'

'Tessa!' My surprise hit the register on a number of different levels. I had been expecting Justin Revel or his father.

'This may be nothing, but I think we've just had a prowler up here.'

That bastard who killed those people is still out there. He could do it again.

Oh, fuck! Had I invoked something by saying that to Ryan Shaw?

'Is everyone okay?' I asked.

'Yes. And I'm not sure whether this isn't just a big false alarm,' she suggested apologetically.

'Let me decide that. I'm on my way now.'

'It's snowing quite hard up here.'

'I'll make it.'

The Apache in my soul was flexing his arms again.

12

I borrowed David's old Land Rover. It was late-season snow—heavy, wet and unstable—and the magic went out of it as soon as it was stepped on and turned the colour and consistency of wallpaper paste. And it was hard to drive in, even with four-wheel drive, each tyre trying to slither off in its own preferred direction.

And Tessa had been right, it was snowing harder the higher I drove up the by-way. I had to drive on dipped headlights, the snow setting up too much of a dazzling reflective wall with main beams on.

Tessa had seen my lights approaching, and opened the door of her caravan as soon as I got out of the Land Rover's cab.

'Thanks for coming up,' she said, letting me in and closing the door on the weather. 'I only hope I haven't dragged you up here under false pretences.'

I wiped wet snow off my eyebrows and nodded at the other young woman in the caravan, who I recognized as one of Tessa's helpers. Tessa's caravan was smaller and older than mine, so why, I wondered abstractedly, did it seem more homely and comfortable?

'This is Gemma,' Tessa said. 'Tell Sergeant Capaldi what you saw.'

'I came out of the toilet tent—' she gestured in the general direction—'and I saw someone peering in through Tessa's window. I thought it might have been one of us at first, playing a joke, so I shouted. They turned round, and when they saw me they ran off.'

'You managed to see in *this*?' I asked, trying not to sound too sceptical.

'It wasn't snowing so hard then,' Tessa answered for her.

'When was this?'

'The two women exchanged glances. 'About three-quarters of an hour ago?' Tessa ventured. 'We had a quick look round outside, but couldn't see anything. Then I thought I'd better call you, given what's gone on down at Jeff's site.'

'Can you describe who you saw?' I asked Gemma.

'I think it was a man. I can't be certain, though, because they were wearing a long parka-type thing with the hood up. But it was the way they ran off, it

207

looked like more the way a man would run.'

I checked my phone. If I ran into trouble out there, I wanted to be able to call in the cavalry. There was a signal here.

'It's not very stable,' Tessa said, reading my thoughts, 'you'll lose it if you drop too far off the ridge.'

'I'm going to check outside.'

'Do you want me to hold a torch for you or something?' Tessa volunteered.

'Thanks, but the fewer of us out there the better. And don't worry if I don't appear for a bit.'

'Didn't Captain Oates say something like that and never come back?'

'Thanks, Tessa.'

She smiled warmly. 'Be careful. I'll have the hot chocolate ready.'

Tessa and her helpers had trampled the snow around the caravan into slush. I checked the big rear window. There was a large enough chink in the curtains to see inside. But why? What had Tessa got to do with this? Unless the guy was a voyeur. Some creep up from Dinas. But on a night like this?

I didn't like the feeling this was giving me.

The snow was still coming down hard. I walked slowly out in the direction Gemma had indicated. I walked in a slow zigzag pattern until I cut across footprints that displayed the long stride of someone running. They were now partially filled, but with the slush imprint from the wet snow they were still distinct enough to follow.

The running stride continued at full stretch for about fifty metres then started to slow down, until the prints reached a point where their owner had obviously stopped and turned round to look back. To check if he was being followed? After this the stride-pattern shortened as he reverted to walking. I was actually tracking this guy, reading the signals. I was proud of myself, even though following footprints in this wet snow was as easy as following an airfield's flare path.

It hadn't occurred to me then that he might have wanted me to follow him.

The one thing I didn't have was natural light. No horizon. Just a constantly shifting swirl of snowflakes ahead. The torch beam was fine when it was directed onto the ground, where there was contrast, picking out the prints, but when I raised it, all sense of distance and perspective vanished into a dance of interference. Nothing seemed real, there was no sense of substance, just an eerie blurring, like life inside a ghost signal. The guy could have stopped in front of me and I wouldn't have known it until I walked into him. That thought slowed me down.

The tracks were keeping just to the wind-farm side of the crest of the ridge. He was using a sheep track to keep out of the heather and avoid the danger of tripping. Which was either very fortuitous, or he knew that this particular track was going to take him in the direction he wanted to go.

I decided that this guy knew the hill. You don't just go traipsing off into a blizzard choosing random sheep tracks and hoping for the best.

Now that the first flush of excitement was over I was feeling the chill factor in the wind. I had a good waterproof jacket on, but my trousers were now soaked through from the knees down to my boots. But at least my feet were dry. I was aware of the dangers of hypothermia if I got too wet.

The trail was leading me farther and farther away from the road, deeper onto the moors. But the chances were good that he was still out there somewhere ahead of me. Still on the hill.

It gave me an idea. I dropped into a crouch with my back to the wind, undid my jacket, and pulled out my phone. There was just enough of a signal. I called Headquarters at Carmarthen. I explained quickly to the duty officer what I wanted him to do, and read out the names and numbers. It wasn't exactly science, but it might serve to eliminate a name from the list.

I zipped up again and stood. I shone my torch ahead. The prints were filling in fast now, but at least the sheep track was still distinct through the heather. But this comfort disappeared a couple of hundred metres farther on when the heather gave out and was replaced by snow-covered scrub grass. There was now no defined track, no texture, just featureless white on the ground and flurry in the air.

But at least the footprints were still there, the trail turning back up towards the top of the ridge, where the ground levelled out.

And then I came to the edge of the world.

It was as stark and dramatic as that. The snow suddenly stopping, white becoming total blackness, with no transition.

But the footsteps continued into the black.

The stupid laws of fucking attraction. It was a yawning black void and I had this irrational compulsion to walk straight into it. Because he had obviously gone ahead of me, and how could I not follow? This was mano-a-mano bullshit, even though my sensible side was screaming at me to pause and work out what the fuck was ahead.

My concession was to move forward gingerly. I felt the first seep of the drenching cold on my feet.

The bastard had led me into a dew pond. He had marched straight in here. Had he known that I would be following him? Worse, was he out there somewhere now, watching me trying to pull my feet out of the freezing peaty mud?

I shone my torch full circle, trying to keep any trace of panic out of the motion. I couldn't make out the far edge of the pond. To pick up his trail again I would have to walk its perimeter, scouring the ground for where his footprints emerged. Footprints that were fast filling in. And I didn't know the size of the pond. And, even if I did find them, would my own return trail have vanished by then?

He had led me and left me stuck like an insect on fly paper, all options bar flight shut down.

Now the big question hit me.

Why?

*   *   *

I struggled back to Tessa's caravan cold, wet and worried.

Why had he come out of cover? And why choose Tessa's? Was there something here that had drawn him in? Or had he been deliberately trying to draw me out?

Or was I just being paranoid? Could it have been a lonely shepherd looking to spy on some bra-and-panties action, trying to get his rocks off?

Either way I couldn't take it to Fletcher or Jack

211

Galbraith, as, in their books, with Bruno already dead, I had no business to be up here trailing a killer through a snowstorm.

Tessa opened the door to my knock. Her smile was one of relief. 'I was starting to think about sending out the Saint Bernard.'

I climbed gratefully into the warm space, and realized as I did that it was the smell that was different in here. It was something feminine that cut the odours of propane gas and damp plastic.

'Glyn, you're frozen!' she exclaimed as she caught sight of me in the light. 'You've got to get those wet things off.'

I peeled off my coat, which was starting to drip. She took it from me and handed over a towel. This was softer than anything I owned and had its own fragrance. I understood then how much I was missing the peripheral grace that women added to everyday objects. I rubbed my face dry before I sat down to tackle my boots, only discovering how numb my hands were as I struggled with the laces.

'Here, let me do that,' she commanded, kneeling down in front of me. I winced with pain and relief as she rolled my sodden socks down and reintroduced my blanched and wrinkled feet to the concept of warmth. I glanced down. They looked like something that should have been on their way to the glue factory. They were my feet, but even I was repelled by the sight of them. I flicked a glance to gauge Tessa's reaction.

She wrapped another towel around them, started to massage them dry, and smiled up at me unselfconsciously. 'I don't often say this to the boys on the first date, but you're really going to have to get those trousers off.'

212

There should have been a romantic riposte to that waiting in the wings. More than, 'I can't just sit around here in my underpants,' which was all I managed to come up with.

'Just wait there.'

She left me for a moment and came back with a pair of grey sweatpants. 'They're going to be a tad short, but they'll be a lot warmer than those sodden things.' I took them from her. 'I'll go and make that hot chocolate while you change.'

I peeled my trousers off and towelled my legs dry before I pulled the sweatpants on. The elasticised waist was tight on me, and my ankles were left stranded, but I was more conscious of the fact that my balls were now nestling in a crotch that had been last inhabited by Tessa. I quickly reintroduced cold damp thoughts before an erection came along to spoil this cosy fable.

She carried in the drinks and set them down on a table. 'I had a call from one of your people,' she said as she picked up my trousers and hung them on the back of a chair in front of the gas fire.

'Did they leave a message?'

'Hold on.' She wiped her damp hands on her jeans before picking up a notebook. For some strange reason that gesture made me feel like we were sharing a small, comfortable and continuing domestic intimacy.

She looked at me expectantly. I nodded. She read, 'Evans, no reply. Fenwick, no reply. Valerie Horne did answer, but neither husband nor brother available.' She looked up. 'Make sense?'

I nodded again. So, no eliminations this round. Any one of them could have been on the hill. They were all still in the picture.

'Fenwick?' she queried with a smile I couldn't fathom. 'Isn't that the name of your new girlfriend?' She sat down opposite me on the long banquette under the rear window.

I felt myself colouring. 'Of course not.'

'You looked pretty cosied-up together when I saw you the other night.'

'She'd been drinking. I was driving her home to stop her using her car.'

She cocked her head sceptically.

'She's a married woman, Tessa,' I protested.

She smiled sweetly. 'So why wasn't her husband doing the driving home?'

'He's abroad. In the Middle East.'

'While the cat's away?'

'It's nothing like that.'

She burst out laughing.

'What's so funny?' I asked, nonplussed.

'Your face . . .' She tossed a small cushion at me. 'So serious.'

We stared at each other for a moment. I felt the nervous flutter as I waited for something that might be construed as an invitation to slip onto the banquette beside her. Her expression turned curious. 'Do you want to talk about what Inspector Fletcher was trying to tell me the other night?'

I hid my disappointment under a brave smile. 'Not really.'

'It's the reason you've ended up here?'

I nodded. Her gaze didn't lose its intensity. She wasn't giving up. 'I went soft,' I said reluctantly. 'I made certain judgements that my superiors deemed to be unprofessional. Basically, I allowed myself to be clouded by a sense of injustice. Which I was told was none of my business.'

214

'Was that the official verdict?'

I shook my head. I was far enough removed from it now to be able to display a certain amusement. 'Stress-induced breakdown.'

'Is that what broke up your marriage?'

I frowned. It was my turn to look surprised. I had never mentioned Gina to her. She smiled at my reaction. 'It's a small town, Glyn. I heard talk.' I used silence to keep up the pressure. 'Okay, I'm curious,' she admitted, 'but it's not prurient. I like to know what I'm getting into.'

'The relationship went down the tubes long before that.'

'And?'

'Booze. As simple as that. I was drinking too much. I was fed up with being the outsider, so I was drinking to fit in. To be like one of the guys. Kevin Fletcher had managed it and was soaring ahead of me career-wise. But I was overcompensating. I was drinking to hide the disgust that I felt about myself for wanting to be like one of the guys. I was also doing it to avoid going home and having to face up to how I was screwing things up.'

She looked at me closely for a moment before she spoke. 'I've seen you in The Fleece with a drink.'

'I've learned to control it.'

'AA?'

I shook my head. 'Sanity. I realized that I really didn't want to be one of the guys any more.'

She laughed warmly. 'That works for me.' She shifted over and patted the space on the banquette she had just vacated.

Just as I stood up there was a sharp and rapid knocking on the door. Her eyes met mine briefly. A

215

flash of regret. Then she was off to open the door.

It was one of her team. I couldn't make out the words, but there was a sense of something like panic in the delivery. Tessa reached over and grabbed a coat off of the hook. She looked briefly at me before she went out. All traces of regret had vanished.

I stripped off her sweatpants and pulled on my cold and clammy trousers, which was like climbing into two tubes of wet cardboard. I put my socks and boots on again. The tone of that voice at the door had warned me that any prospects of cosiness tonight had disappeared.

*   *   *

The snow had diminished to a few raggedy stray flakes and was melting fast by the time I got out of the caravan. I walked across towards the light that was coming from the Redshanks enclosure. Tessa emerged just as I arrived.

'What's the problem?' I asked.

She was silent for a moment. If she had been trying to control herself it hadn't worked. 'You and your fucking investigation,' she threw at me.

'What's happened?' A dark intimation surfacing.

'He's taken Redshanks.' She flung the enclosure's flap open. Inside, her assistants parted to let me see the now-empty polythene bubble.

'Now sort it out,' she snapped at me. 'I want him back.'

The ground surface was rapidly turning to meltwater. It wasn't helped by the fact that Tessa and her crew had scrabbled around and messed things up so much. Gemma, Tessa's assistant, hadn't reported seeing him carrying anything, but he could already have taken it and stashed it, ready to carry off when left alone. The bundle would have been awkward, but the weight would have been manageable.

This had to be connected. But why? Why take this risk?

Or was it another obfuscation?

I couldn't take this to Fletcher or Jack Capaldi. To them it would be the local force's baggage. To involve them in the theft of an archaeological artefact would only annoy them.

But I had to go through the motions. For Tessa's sake, if nothing else. I called it in to Emrys Hughes.

'Can you repeat that?' he asked, not hiding his amusement. I described Redshanks again. I could picture him noting it down with relish. This was the ultimate zany incomer. A 600-year-old desiccated Scottish warrior.

'It'll be one of those kids from Fron Heulog,' he proclaimed with evangelical certainty.

'Why?'

'What use would anyone round here have for something like that?'

Right, I thought to myself, every gang crib in Birmingham has got to have its own thieved archaeological trophy. 'Just put the word out, please, Emrys.'

I knocked on the caravan door before I left. Tessa opened it. She didn't invite me in, just stayed in the power position on the threshold, looking down on me.

'I'm sorry, Tessa.'

'I'm holding you responsible for getting him back.'

217

'I couldn't have prevented this.' I tried not to sound too hangdog.

She shrugged that one off. 'We were doing fine until you brought your investigation into our world. So I blame you. You make it right again and we'll take it from there.'

'I'll do my best.'

She pulled a mean face. 'No, you won't, you'll be too busy chasing after your own bloody skeletons.'

'Will you pack up here?'

She flashed me a look full of scorn, and almost didn't reply. 'The body was only the big physical manifestation. There's more to it than that. We're also working on all the peripheral stuff that will hopefully tell us who he was and why he was here.'

'I'll find him for you. I promise.'

She shut the door in my face. I took some consolation from the fact that she hadn't slammed it.

*   *   *

I got back to Unit 13 cold, wet and dispirited. The gossamer illusion of sex and romance had been briefly awakened and trailed in the air, before being transformed into the reality of a sodden pair of trousers and boots that would have made the ideal packaging for trench foot.

I changed into dry clothes and turned the gas heater on in the living area. There was no new-message light on the answering-machine display. I had hoped that Julian Revel might have got back to me by now. I checked my mobile to see if I had picked up any missed calls while driving back through limbo spots. The call log was clear.

It was getting late. But this was important. I decided to try him again.

'Julian Revel.' He gave his name a radio announcer's clarity.

'It's Detective Sergeant Capaldi, Mr Revel, I'm sorry to disturb you so late.'

'Didn't you get my message?' He sounded irked.

'I haven't had anything on my mobile.'

'I make a point of not calling mobile phones, they're too expensive. I left a message on the landline number you gave. I told you that I had nothing to do with Justin any more.'

I glanced at the answering machine again. There was no light indicating a new message.

'You're his father?'

'Yes, but you're wasting your time. He doesn't live here, and I have no contact telephone numbers or address.'

'I desperately need to talk to him about an investigation I'm working on.'

He gave a humourless chuckle. 'Good luck. And if you do manage to find the ungrateful little sod, you can tell him that I'm still feeding his mangy cat, and I would appreciate it if he could come back for it.'

'But there must be some—'

He interrupted. 'Hereford. Art college. That's all I know, and all I care.'

'He's your son, Mr Revel,' I argued, knowing that it was none of my business.

'No,' he responded sharply and with feeling, 'he's his mother's son. He's not going to be mine again until the day comes when I'm satisfied that I no longer have to worry about getting calls from the police or Social Services, or deadbeats turning up

219

at my door and asking if they've missed the party.'

I put the phone down on all that fucked-up family harmony.

Hereford Art College. The first solid lead. But I was not going to be able to do anything about it at this time on a Sunday night.

I frowned, remembering that he had said he had already left a message. Out of curiosity I tried my answering machine.

'My name is Julian Revel. I am returning the call from the policeman whose name I couldn't catch. I have no knowledge of Justin's present whereabouts, so please don't call me again.'

And a bonus call.

'Glyn. You weren't answering your mobile. I'm getting back to you on that information you asked for.' Mackay's voice was precise and to the point.

I felt uneasy. The answering machine's light had been off. I wasn't supposed to have any new messages. But I hadn't heard either of those before.

I called my landline from my mobile and left a test message. When I hung up the red light was blinking on the answering machine.

I went back to the front door and checked the lock. There was no way of telling if it had been forced. But it was hardly a serious lock, kids' lunch boxes were better secured.

I had to assume that someone had already listened to those messages. So that person now knew that I was interested in locating Justin Revel. I was also very grateful that Mackay was professional enough not to leave names on answering machines.

It wasn't exactly high-tech hacking, but it was effective. It looked like the spectre I thought I had been chasing through the snow had brought the dance back to me. I checked the phone and the room for visible bugs before I made my next call.

'Hi, Mac, I'm returning your call.'

'You okay?' He had picked up on my shaky vibe.

'Yes, it's been a weird night.' I didn't elaborate.

'Okay. The two guys you're interested in were in the Signals Regiment together. Greg Thomas made it to corporal before getting a ticket out on a medical discharge.'

'How long ago was that?'

There was a pause as he checked his notes. 'Just under fifteen years. The other one, Owen Jones, made it to sergeant. His time expired five years ago. Sources tell me that he went into specialist private security after that. I heard he was in Afghanistan.'

'He's in Nigeria now. If he was in Signals, how come he got into security?'

'He applied for and got a transfer to Military Intelligence.'

'Special Forces?'

'No, the hardware side of spook stuff. Some of the training he would have gone through for that would have made him a good prospect for private security firms.'

'What were the grounds for the medical discharge?' I asked, swinging it back to Greg Thomas.

Another pause. 'Reading between the jargon, I reckon the guy had a nervous breakdown. It was after he'd finished a tour in Northern Ireland.'

'Were you over there at that time?'

He laughed. 'That's strictly on a need-to-know basis, buddy.'

'Could you find out for me, Mac? See if there's

221

anything like a big white whale that could account for the breakdown?' I remembered then what Emrys had told me, about the fight in The Fleece after the funeral, and that this probably coincided with the accidental death of his fiancée. Grief had probably fucked the poor guy up. Still, there would be no harm in Mackay doing an extra bit of digging for me.

'Anything else, boss?' he asked sarcastically.

'Yes.' I heard him groan, he had not intended to be taken literally. 'I may need you to look after someone for me for a while.'

*   *   *

I drove to Hereford the next morning under a thin blue sky, with the only remaining traces of snow being the stubborn tonsures on the hill tops, although the quick thaw was still evident in the brooks that were running brown and full.

I had had to leave it to Alison Weir to work through official channels to clear a path for me at the art college. It meant showing my hand, but I knew from past experience that they wouldn't release personal information if I just waved my warrant card around.

Kevin Fletcher's call came through before I had even cleared the border.

'I've just had to confirm an authorization for you to access personal information off a database in Hereford.' He sounded friendly enough, which meant that the bastard was fishing.

'That's right, Kev—' I checked myself. 'That's right, boss, I've got a potential lead on a friend of Evie's.' I instructed myself to keep it vague.

'You're stepping awfully close to the demarcation line here, Glyn.'

'What line is that, boss?'

'The one that defines my particular area of interest.' By which he meant he was closely guarding his geography.

'It's just the way it's tracking.'

'How close a friend?'

'I won't know until I talk to them. It's come down from a third-hand source. So it could be a total waste of time.'

'Sure it's not an excuse to get down onto the flatlands and ogle art students?'

I recognized it as a joke and chuckled. 'Positive, boss.'

'You're going to be sure to let us know what you find there, aren't you?'

'You bet,' I chirped enthusiastically, and sublimated my gag reaction by giving the finger to a flock of sheep I was passing.

'Because if your end of things is slipping down this way, you'll need to be ready to hand over the information you've gathered.'

'How are you doing down there, boss?' I asked, heading him off at the pass, so I could swear on record that I'd never actually promised him anything.

'Not bad. Not bad at all. We've got some interesting missing-person reports we're following up on.'

'Running into the crackles this end, boss . . .'

My thumb went into atmospherics mode and created the effects of a lousy signal by switching my phone off.

Spring was further advanced in Herefordshire.

The trees were greening, the grass was losing its winter fatigue, and the lambs looked bigger. And people were dressing lighter.

A bit too light in the case of some of the students I passed as I walked into the art college. I was bustled through normal reception procedures to an administrator's office, where I went through a rigmarole to prove that I was the guy they had been told to expect.

And, they told me, in the interests of fair play and data protection they had sent Justin an email to advise him that the police were about to have access to his contact details. They had also tried phoning him to pass on the same information, without success.

I wrote down Justin's contact details that a scowling administrator read out to me in a disapproving voice off a computer monitor screen that he made sure I couldn't see. He made me feel like a born-again Stasi operative. When I asked him for directions to Justin's address, he reacted as if I had just asked him to join me in participating in some particularly messy human-rights abuse.

Outside, a student with hair that looked like it had been cut off the end of a hammock pointed me on the right track.

I just hoped that the college's email to him hadn't fucked things up, and that Justin was not now hightailing it for sanctuary. I contemplated whether I should try calling first, to soft-sell myself, but decided that it might just act as another flight-trigger.

The address was not far from the station. A quiet street of three-storey Edwardian red-brick and render semis, most of which had been converted to flats, with small front gardens and the occasional lime tree on the pavement. I parked my car at the end. I liked to arrive slowly on occasions like these, getting the feel for my destination as I approached.

As I got further along I smelled it. That unmistakeable lightning-struck primal forest smell of stale smoke and water. Recent fire damage. I flashed back on all the charred beams I had had to duck under in my time, the ash sludge on the floor, the abandoned dolls, the dead pets. The smell brought them all back.

And I just knew, as I got closer and recognized the fire-investigation unit's van parked down the street, that I had found the address.

The front garden was cordoned off with incident tape. The first-floor bay window had blown out, and the white roughcast render was blackened where the flames had reached. There was nothing smoking now. And there had been enough time since the incident to erect temporary timber buttress supports against the front wall.

A fire officer came out of the front door. He gave me the pained look the professionals use on rubbernecking ghouls. I held up my warrant card.

'Gas leak?' I asked as he approached. I had seen these things before.

His nod was noncommittal as he read my card and looked at me curiously. 'You with the team?'

'Sort of. When did this happen?'

'Late Saturday night.'

I asked the question I didn't want to have to ask. 'Anyone hurt.'

He pulled a grim face. 'The poor kid's in intensive care.'

Saturday night. I stacked it into the timeframe.

225

On Saturday night I had only just heard about the yellow-haired boy. While I had been starting to mull over his existence, it looked like someone had decided to fuel-up and ignite the rocket that would take him out of this world.

13

I don't like hospitals.

They remind me too much of my father dying. He was admitted to one as a healthy man to have a minor operation on his knee, and the place wrapped him in its embrace and killed him. Necrotizing fasciitis. They said that the bacteria must have already been present in his system, but even if it had been, why hadn't they done what they were supposed to do and fucking cure him? They weren't supposed to allow him to die.

I left my car where I had parked and walked. I wanted to use the time to think. In the interests of balance I even started out by giving some credence to the fact that it could have been a coincidental accident. Okay, I registered it as a possibility and then moved on to the real meat.

The perpetrator was taking a risk. If this could be proved to be something other than an accident, he was leaving himself wide open. People might start listening to me, and bring the investigation back home. But he must have figured that into the equation. Justin must have been deemed to be too dangerous. He couldn't afford him talking to us.

So when had he put this into operation?

It was already in the history books when he had

226

heard Justin's father's message on my answering machine. So that wasn't the trigger. But hearing it had probably reinforced his sense that he had done the right thing after all.

So it was probably a result of realizing that his master plan had developed a glitch. Putting the frame on Bruno Gilbert had had the intended effect: the main focus of the investigation had moved to the safe waters of Newport. But I had been left behind as an irritant to worry at the loose ends in Evie Salmon's short life.

And now Justin Revel was in the ICU. And Redshanks was where?

The fire-investigation officer I had talked to at the scene had not been forthcoming, but he had hinted that they were not looking beyond an accidental cause. Blinded by the light sparking off Occam's fucking razor again. And there was nothing I could give them to change that opinion apart from a hunch, which was not a valid currency in their books.

I used my warrant card to pass through the system at the hospital to the ICU unit, where I hoped to get a report on Justin's condition. I had a look in the waiting room. In one corner an elderly woman and what looked like her daughter were trying to stay as far removed as possible from the group of four or five youngsters in the opposite corner with the tribal markings of art students. Justin's friends. I marked them down to talk to after I had found a doctor.

My phone rang.

Fuck! This was the ICU, I should have turned it off outside. Two nurses appeared out of nowhere to give me admonitory looks and frantic shut-down gestures. I imagined springs and cogs flying as expensive operating and monitoring machinery went haywire.

I checked the display. Fletcher. Perhaps he was ahead of me on the gas explosion and had news for me. I held up the phone in one hand and my warrant card in the other to the nurse who was approaching and mimed that the state of the nation was reliant on me being able to return this call.

She led me out onto a roof terrace.

'Glyn, I'm just about to go into a meeting with DCS Galbraith. Where are we on Evie's boyfriend?'

He was fishing again. Looking for something to take the credit for. 'I haven't had an opportunity to talk to him yet, boss, he's been involved in a gas explosion at his flat.'

'Sounds like bad timing.'

So Fletcher hadn't heard, and didn't care too much by the sounds of it. 'He's in the intensive-care unit,' I added, trying to elicit some sympathy for Justin.

'You often seem to have that effect on people.' He chuckled. 'If I'm not mistaken, you even managed to put me in there once. Remember that?'

'No, boss,' I retorted crisply, suppressing my anger. Because he was fucking mistaken. He'd twisted the slant. Yes, I had taken him to hospital, but only after the high-speed crash he had caused that had nearly killed us both. I had held him then, tightly, blood trickling out of his left ear and from the bridge of my nose, both of us covered with the shards of the broken windscreen and the stop-motion memory of the impact, while I had

228

tried to absorb his convulsions.

I had brought him back from the edge then.

And now he was a detective chief fucking inspector with the ability to bend memory.

*　　　*　　　*

I managed to finish the call without venting my anger, knowing that the consequences of having my assignment taken away from me were not worth the short-term satisfaction of telling him that I was in total sympathy with his wife for leaving him. In the corridor I caught up with the nurse who had shown me to the roof terrace.

'What's the situation with Justin Revel?' I asked.

She looked at me strangely. 'This is the intensive-care unit.'

'I know.'

She shook her head. 'We don't have anyone called Justin here.'

'The gas-explosion victim?'

'Mary Doyle?'

'Mary Doyle?' I repeated the name as a question, not understanding yet, but starting to see a chink opening up.

'That's right. The girl who was injured in the explosion.'

That was all the news I needed. I thanked her and headed back to the waiting room, trying, out of respect for poor Mary Doyle's condition, not to be too joyful. I flashed on the art students. There had been no boy with yellow hair among them. But there had been one with a dyed-red thatch.

I opened one leaf of the double doors to the waiting room, but stayed back in the corridor.

'Justin!' I shouted.

I scored on two counts. The red-haired boy reacted with a jump, and gave a startled look in the direction my voice had come from. And the other kids had all looked at him.

I went into the room with my warrant card out, and what I hoped was my Good Cop façade in place.

'Justin Revel?' I asked, stopping in front of him.

He nodded, his expression a combination of confusion and embarrassment at being singled out. He looked to his friends for support, but they were caught up in the fascination of a new tale unfolding.

'I need to ask you some questions about the accident.'

'I've already talked to some policemen about it,' Justin protested meekly.

'Don't say anything without a lawyer, dude,' advised a gangly guy with a tuft of blond hair under his lower lip, and enough rings in his right ear to make it look like a machine.

'Too much television,' I told him, flashing him a poisoned look, before turning back to Justin. 'I really need to talk to you,' I said, trying to project strength and trust.

Justin got up reluctantly and followed me out into the corridor.

He was nervous. He wouldn't look me in the eye. His hair was dyed emergency red and had been contrived to stick up and out, as if styled to freeze the moment of jabbing his fingers into an electrical socket. His complexion was pale, the skin fine and freckled, his features still marching towards adulthood. He was wearing a green-plaid heavy flannel shirt over a lemon-yellow T-shirt, both of which clashed with his hair and complexion, which was probably the desired effect.

'Did Mary Doyle live in your house?' I asked.

He looked at me uncomprehendingly.

'How come she's the one in intensive care?'

'She borrowed my keys.' He gestured back towards the crowd in the waiting room. 'We were all out at a bar. We were going to move on to Steve's place to . . .' He cut himself off, deciding that that information was best edited out of the story. 'We weren't far from my place. Mary has a thing about going to the toilet in bars. So she went to mine. She's done it before.' He looked up at me for the first time. 'I hadn't smelled any gas,' he said plaintively.

No, you wouldn't, I thought, because there was nothing wrong with your system until someone deliberately fucked it up. 'How long had you been out?' I asked.

He thought about it. 'Probably from about eleven o'clock that morning. It was getting on for about 1 a.m. when Mary went back to pee.' He'd answered my next question before I'd asked it.

He hadn't been in the flat for over twelve hours. Plenty of time for someone to establish and consolidate the mechanics of the operation.

'Where are Mary's parents?' I asked, suddenly realizing the absence.

'On their way back from Florida. They were on holiday.' The poor guy was sick with worry and guilt.

Sadly, I wasn't going to be able to reassure him.

'It was meant for you.'

He nodded listlessly. 'I know. I should feel lucky. But I just keep thinking about Mary.'

231

He hadn't got it. 'No, Justin—' I accentuated the words very slowly, I needed him to climb on board now, to want to get in under my wing and let me take over the controls—'it was deliberate. It really was for you.'

But first, he had to adjust to the craziness. That awful things like this really did happen in this world. Even in Hereford. His look went wild. He stared at me wide-eyed. Trying to take this in. He shook his head. 'Who would . . .?'

'That's what I'm hoping you might be able to tell me.'

Panic and concern were combining to form fear in his face. For probably the first time ever his hairstyle matched his expression.

'I think this has to do with Evie Salmon's death.'

'Evie?'

'Yes, and by now, whoever did it knows he's screwed up, that he got the wrong person.' I touched him gently on the shoulder. It was important now to make physical contact, let him know he had a prop. 'I need you to trust me. He probably knows you're in here.' I saw the jolt as this news hit him.

He looked instinctively back to where his friends were sitting in the waiting room.

'No.' I shook my head. 'The less anyone else knows the better.'

*   *   *

We used the ambulance bay at the rear, beyond the public glare, where the damaged ones went in, and the dead ones left. I instructed Justin to wait with a porter I had commandeered to show me

232

the way, while I went back to fetch my car. I used a circuitous route as a precaution. But I reckoned if he was watching anything, it would be the main entrance to the hospital.

Unless there were two of them.

I bundled Justin into the rear seat-well and ordered him to stay down and not move from there until I gave him the all-clear. I had considered putting him in the boot for the additional security, but reckoned that there was a risk of him flipping. His emotional state was precarious. All this new information, followed by the grave-like darkness of the boot, and I could have ended up driving through Hereford with him screaming and kicking the shit out of my boot lid, which would not have made for an unobtrusive exit.

The porter watched me organize all this with a look of mystification.

'I've been watching too much television,' I explained as I drove off.

I took the Abergavenny road south-west out of Hereford. It was going to be a long detour, but if I had a tail I wanted them to settle in and get comfortable behind me before I slipped in the sneaky move.

The weather was holding. The sky was still blue, a sense of spring in the clarity of the light, a wonderful day to be out for a drive in the country. The traffic was light, the cars behind me were spread out and holding their positions, all bar one, who was coming up the line, overtaking at every opportunity. I let him come past me. A young guy in a hurry in an oldish Audi A3. If he was trying some fancy footwork and attempting to follow me from in front that was fine with me.

233

I came to the big roundabout at the end of the Abergavenny bypass, drove around it at speed, and doubled back on myself.

'Remember these,' I shouted back to Justin, and started listing the make and colour of the cars in the opposite stream of traffic. The cars that had been lined up behind me not so long ago. I carried on until I reached the entrance to the lane I had earmarked on the way down, and pulled into it. It was screened from the main road, and, when I turned the car around, I could watch the traffic going past.

I called out the description of the cars that went past for Justin to tell me if they were on the list I had asked him to memorize. I could remember them all myself, but I didn't want to spoil his sense of involvement. I also wanted him to start to feel that we were working as a team. I waited for half an hour. None of the cars that had been behind me drove past us.

I took to the country roads after that, up the Golden Valley, sidling over towards Kington. I was pretty certain that we weren't being followed, but as insurance I made Justin stay down.

I pulled into a lay-by on the top of the ridge near Arthur's Seat, with a spectacular view over the Wye Valley and the Radnor hills to the north. I told Justin that it was now clear for him to get out.

I stayed in the car while he walked around outside, trying to stretch the kinks out of his muscles. I wanted him to have this time to himself to let him get the sense that he wasn't a captive, and that I was a good guy. I also wanted to give him as much time as possible to clear the clog of panic and dread from his system. The sort of thing that we would have done in the old days with a quiet cigarette and manly chugs at the hip flask.

He came back over and started to open the rear door. I gestured for him to sit in the front.

'Okay?' I asked.

'Sort of.' He gave me a try-out smile.

'There's lots and lots of stuff you're going to want to ask me,' I warned him, 'but I don't have time to answer it all at the moment. Let's just start by saying that I'm taking you to a place of safety, and then please let me ask the questions.'

'Where are you taking me?'

'A good friend's.' I held my hands up at him, palms out. 'Now, remember the deal?'

'You want to talk about Evie?'

'About you and Evie.' I looked at him for a moment. 'What age are you?'

The question surprised him. 'Twenty.'

I nodded, my hunch confirmed. 'Evie was three years older than you. How come you came to be friends?'

'My sister, Camilla. She was Evie's friend at school. They let me hang around with them. When Camilla left home after sixth form, Evie and I sort of stuck together.' He saw my next question forming. 'Just as mates,' he clarified with a small laugh.

'You didn't have your own friends?'

He smiled unselfconsciously. 'Most of the kids I went to school with thought I was a bit weird. A bit too out-there for Dinas. Evie was sort of in the same boat, so, by default, we hung out.'

'Your sister left, why didn't Evie?'

He shrugged. 'Evie and I shared a problem. We both felt we were better than the place our parents

235

had dumped us in, which was another thing that kept us together, but . . .' He searched for the words.

I took a guess. 'You weren't sure you could hack it in the bigger world?'

He nodded and grinned ruefully. 'We kept trying.'

I remembered Evie's father telling me of her hitchhiking exploits. 'You persuaded Evie?'

'It was mutual support. We'd get somewhere, try to hang out where the other kids were, but we never seemed to fit in. We felt uncomfortable. We thought that we had the attitude, that we knew the jargon, the right music, but it was untried and untested. At the end of the day, we felt we were walking around with big Day-Glo hick signs on our backs.'

'But you didn't stay in Dinas, you went to art college.'

'I guess I grew up a little bit more. I realized you couldn't learn everything off the Internet, you had to get out and put your toes in the water, and keep them there. That was our problem before. We ran back to Dinas as soon as things got scary.'

'And Evie left too?'

'It was after I'd gone to Hereford.'

'Do you know where she went?'

He pulled an apologetic face. 'No, I'm sorry. Not if you're looking for an address. I only know where she used to talk about while we were still in contact.'

'Which was where?'

'Swansea, the Gower Peninsula.' He shrugged. 'It's a big area.'

'Why there?'

'It's where the guy she'd met had a place.'

I felt the focus sliding into place. 'Tell me about him.'

'She wasn't allowed to talk about him. That's exactly what she said to me. She wasn't allowed. Like he'd laid down rules. Oh, she talked about how fantastic and wonderful he was, and how well he treated her, and how confident he made her feel, but she wouldn't tell me anything real.' He thought about it for a moment. 'And I think she got a buzz out of that. Teasing me with her strong, silent lover. Like I had got my life in Hereford by that time, and she was telling me that she had found her way out too.'

'Do you know how they met?'

He shook his head. 'No.' But he was frowning.

'What's the matter?'

'I don't know whether it was actually some new guy she met. I got the impression that it could have been someone she already knew, but something had happened to change the basis of the relationship.'

'What did Evie do on her Saturdays?'

He looked at me quizzically. 'Pardon?'

'She told her father that she was working at the Barn Gallery for the Fenwicks. They deny it, but she was still coming home with a wad of cash.'

He thought about it. 'You know Gerald Evans?'

I felt a rewarding flutter in my stomach. I nodded.

'Evie used to help out with his wife's horses. She told me that he came up to her once and said not to mention this to his wife, but he and some friends had a little private gambling club they ran on the side. Just for the fun of it. They called it

237

Grass Vegas, which they seemed to think was a real hoot, which tells you what kind of losers they were. Anyway, he asked Evie if she fancied doing a bit of hostess stuff for them. Had to dress-up in a skimpy costume, pad out her tits and wear fishnet tights, while she spun the little roulette wheel, or walked around with a silver tray offering lines of coke. She hated it, but the money was good.'

'Did they come on to her?'

'A few of them tried it, but she let them know that she wasn't going to do any kind of deed with guys with turkey necks or nose hairs. None of them pushed it, she said, because they were all terrified of their wives finding out about the club.'

Gerald Evans again. Justin had just provided me with the equivalent of a big pipe wrench to dent that smug bastard's boiler-plated self-assurance.

'What about Clive Fenwick, did she ever talk about him?'

'She said the women at the Barn Gallery were total bitches. She thought one of the husband's was nice, though, but I don't remember which one.'

'What about Greg Thomas or Trevor Horne?'

He pulled a blank face. 'I don't remember those names.'

I looked out of the windscreen at the Wye Valley spread out below me. At one point I had thought that we were honing in on something, tightening the focus, but now we were back out here on panoramic view, with a whole new geographic area thrown in.

*   *   *

Poor Mary Doyle. What Justin had given me

238

couldn't come close to compensating her for being virtually flash-fried. Okay, I had Grass Vegas, and the existence of Evie's lover confirmed, and living around Swansea or the Gower two years ago. But without anything more specific, I wasn't going to allow myself to get too excited about it. And, much as I hated to admit it, Gerald Evans was looking less and less likely to be the prime mover here.

The only comforting thing was that the opposition probably weren't aware of how little Justin knew. They hadn't realized how rigidly Evie had stuck to the rules of disclosure they had laid down for her. And now that I had disappeared Justin, I was hoping that they were going to start getting twitchy.

But the spread had got too big for me. Driving around Swansea and the Gower with a photograph of Evie was not an option. Kevin Fletcher had to be told that he was going to have to widen his operations base. He wasn't going to like it. Especially coming from me.

My call caught him on a late lunch. That old familiar ripple of conversations and the steady tinkle of glass in the background. I kept the story simple—no point in mentioning gas explosions whose cause I couldn't prove at this stage.

'Swansea, he said?'

'Swansea area. Nothing ever got pinpointed.'

'And this was all before she left home? Nothing to prove that she actually went there?'

'Yes, boss.'

'And what am I supposed to do with this? Move my operation out of Newport? Dip into the coffers and set up a new team in Swansea?'

'I don't know, boss.'

'Hold on.'

That was the short phrase of doom. It meant he was about to consult with someone. And if he was deferring to that person's opinion, I didn't need more than one attempt at guessing who he was at lunch with.

'Capaldi!' I winced as Jack Galbraith's voice boomed out. 'I instructed you to investigate Evie Salmon's background, not to fucking abduct her boyfriends.'

'Sir?'

'We've had a complaint through our compadres in Hereford. I quote, "A scary-looking cop took our mate away."'

Scary? My Good Cop façade obviously hadn't had time to set properly.

'He's with me, sir. I needed to question him.'

'Why remove him?'

I closed my eyes, counted a beat, and went for it. 'I think he needs protection. There was a gas explosion at his flat. I think he might have been the target.' I kept my eyes closed.

'And who would target him?' he asked very slowly.

I saw the minefield opening up ahead of me. 'Someone who's trying to confuse the investigation, sir?' I suggested humbly.

'Did Bruno Gilbert look like a man who would inspire a following?'

'No, sir.'

'And Bruno Gilbert is dead. Right?'

'Yes, sir.'

'So drop this fucking nonsense. We'll do a fine trawl through Gilbert's background and see if there's any connection with Swansea. But if I hear another peep about you still chasing after a live perp, you are off this fucking case. And one more thing.'

'Yes, sir?' It was time to open my eyes again.

'Take that kid back to where he wants to go.'

I closed the connection and looked over at Justin. He smiled sympathetically. Jack Galbraith's voice carries. 'Where do you want to go?' I asked.

'I thought you were taking me somewhere safe?'

'Right answer.'

I drove on to Mackay's, an old farmhouse called Hen Dolmen on the English side of the Radnorshire border. It was an oak-framed house with a Victorian extension in mellow brick, which hunkered down under a moss-covered stone-tiled roof. It was a clutter of gables, dormer windows and massive stone chimneys, a collection of wonderfully restless elevations.

This, I had decided after my first visit, was the house that I wished I had been born in. Two hundred years ago. Life might have been harsher, but it would have been a hell of a sight less complicated.

I had called ahead. Mackay had been expecting me. He made me tea in the big-beamed kitchen, while Boyce, the scary ex-army buddy who helped him run his corporate-initiative-training enterprise, showed Justin to his room.

I sat at the big square limed-oak table in front of the Rayburn and squinted at the low evening sun streaming in through the window, dust motes jigging like live gnats.

'Thanks for this, Mac,' I said.

He raised his mug in salute. 'No problem.' His Scottish accent had softened from years of having

241

to slow his speech down to be understood.

'How do you reckon they worked it?' I asked.

He didn't have to ponder, which was slightly disturbing. 'Pilot light off, for starters. Then they run the cooker-ring taps full-on to get the gas–air mix up to the right proportions. After that it's just a question of keeping that balance going. A little nick in the feed supply, some compensatory ventilation, and then they rig-up a spark device that's going to be triggered by the door opening.' He clapped his hands together, then threw his arms out into wide arcs, like a physicist explaining the big-bang theory. 'Whatever they used, it's going to be blown the fuck to kingdom come when that mother goes up and become untraceable.'

'How come no one smelled it?'

He shrugged. 'Student accommodation. Rancid Central. Curries, pizzas, last year's dishes still piled in the sink. And they probably laid a light seal at the bottom of the front door. A damp tea towel? Something that's not going to look out of place in a burned-out messy flat, but not something that's going to jam the door when they try opening it.'

'Does this narrow things down for me?'

'Like?'

'Am I looking for an expert? Someone trained in sabotage techniques?'

'It sounds like whoever rigged it knew what they were doing.' He pulled a face. 'But that doesn't mean it's the guy you're looking for. These people are out there for hire.'

'So it doesn't necessarily point me at soldiers?'

He shook his head regretfully.

'Talking about soldiers, has anything more come up about Greg Thomas's breakdown?'

242

'Sorry, medical records are a bit hard to access. I've talked to some guys I worked with over there, and they're spreading the word. But those were interesting times in that part of the world.' He chuckled grimly at the memory. 'Somehow, we had a lot better things to occupy us than worrying about a guy in communications who was buying his ticket to the funny farm.'

'His fiancée died about the same time.'

'How?'

'Some kind of an accident.' It suddenly hit me. I had never asked how Rose Jones had died. It had been fifteen years ago, and I had just assumed that it had lain outside the frame of reference.

'You okay?'

I returned to the planet to see Mackay watching me with some concern. I nodded. 'Can you get back to your guys and give them another bit of information. See if the name Rose Jones does anything.'

'Okay.' He nodded carefully, but still hadn't taken his eyes off of me. 'Do you want me to come to Dinas with you and watch your back?'

It was tempting.

One way forward would be to create a crisis and send Mackay running in through the front door, guns blazing, so I could be there to net whoever came flying out through the back door.

Only two problems there. What crisis? And whose front door?

Regretfully, I declined his offer.

14

It was dark when I got back to Dinas. The fine day had left its legacy in a clear night, with stars already visible; probably a few planets up there, too, if I knew where to look. I knew enough of the lore by now to recognize that there would be a frost in the morning. Unit 13 would become the home for all the stray condensation in the neighbourhood once again.

The Audi TT and the Porsche Cayenne were parked out in front, but the lights were out in the Barn Gallery. The steps up to the house were illuminated by small bulkhead lights set in the stone treads, and a motion-activated security light came on as I approached the front door. I had already clocked the CCTV cameras on a previous visit, so I knew that my arrival was not going to be a secret.

But Gloria still played along with the game.

'Glyn!' she announced. 'What a nice surprise. Come on in.'

The hall floor was deep-blue polished slate with a red-and-yellow-ochre Persian rug, and an open-tread oak staircase leading up to a gallery with a green-tinted glass balustrade. The interior of the house had obviously been scooped out and remodelled, the original rustic Welsh replaced by architectural chic.

'I hope this is social.'

I pulled a rueful face. 'Business, I'm afraid. And I'm sorry to call so late, but I need to talk to your brother-in-law.'

She didn't drop the happy-hostess face, but a

small spark of curiosity jumped in her eyes. 'I'll put you in the study and go and see how he's fixed.'

She opened one of the matching oak doors off the hall, switched on a light, and stood aside to let me enter. 'What's your schedule for after?' she asked in a quieter voice.

I shook my head regretfully. 'Catching up on paperwork.'

'If you change your mind . . .' She brushed the back of my hand with hers, and replicated the invitation in her expression as she left.

What would I have seen in a mirror if I had looked then? What had changed in the last few days to make me desirable?

I didn't have time to look around for a mirror. Clive Fenwick emerged from the door on the opposite side of the hall, and approached carrying a heavy glass tumbler of ice-murdered whisky, to signal that this was an interruption.

He had the meticulous scrutinizing squint of a VAT inspector or a serious bridge player, and his tight and slender build proclaimed that there was more to his recreational activities than just playing golf. Squash? Tennis? Something that he would make sure that he was good at.

He was of medium height, with male-pattern baldness, the remaining hair on the side of his head close-cropped and allowing the first of the grey to show. I put him in his late forties, early fifties. An oval face, smooth features, small frameless glasses, thin lips and no smile. His clothes were restrained designer label.

'Thank you for agreeing to see me.' I started to offer my hand, but an instinct told me that he would only make a virtue out of ignoring it.

245

'Can you show me your identity, please, Sergeant?' There was a chill of superiority in the request.

I produced my warrant card. Do whatever the customer requires, I told myself.

'Thank you.' He nodded curtly. 'The women never inspect these things properly.' He stared at me impatiently, no attempt to put me at my ease.

'How well did you know Evie Salmon, Mr Fenwick?'

'She was the young woman whose body you found. She also used to pester my wife and Gloria for a job.' He smiled snidely. 'Which part of that weren't you expecting me to answer?'

'The question was how well you knew her.'

It caught him off guard for a beat. 'And why has this question been raised?'

The clever bastard had parried me. I had wanted him to deny knowing her. I had wanted to trump this cold fucker with my big card. 'We have a witness who claims that you may be the last person she was in contact with in Dinas on the day she left.'

He frowned. 'Left?'

'She left home two years ago.'

He gave me a look of astonishment. 'I'm supposed to know this? And you seriously expect me to remember what I was doing in Dinas two years ago?'

'She was seen approaching your car.'

He raised his head and spread his hands in a *give-me-strength* gesture. 'And on the basis of that, you've come round here two years later, not just interrupting me, but with a latent threat.'

'There was no threat, Mr Fenwick.'

246

He ignored me. 'Just because some young woman, who I've never met, was seen near my car, I'm hauled in as the last person to see her.' He fixed me with a cold, angry glare. 'And all because I have a distinctive car. I think that you've allowed yourself to be hijacked by the politics of envy, Sergeant.'

'You never met Evie Salmon?' I kept my own anger in check.

He dipped his head. 'That's what I've just said. She may have been seen approaching my car, but that coincidence is as far as the connection goes. Isabel and Gloria can corroborate the fact that neither my brother Derek nor I ever met her.' His eyes bored into me again from behind his glasses, and I caught a glint of hostile amusement in them. 'And if you want to ask them, it would imply that you don't believe me.'

'That won't be necessary, Mr Fenwick.' I forced myself to keep crawling. 'And once again, I apologize for the intrusion.'

I asked to say goodbye to Gloria. He made a point of ushering me out of the study and closing the door, before brusquely instructing me to wait in the hall. Gloria came out with a smile on her face that was trying hard not to upgrade to a smirk.

'Changed your mind?' she asked cockily.

I shook my head. 'Sorry, the paperwork's still waiting for me.' I inclined my head towards the door that Clive had gone through. 'What does he drink?'

She pulled a quizzical frown.

'Was that whisky?'

'I think so. Horrible stuff, I don't touch it.'

'Could you find out for me, please?' I asked

247

nicely. I was just about to leave when I remembered something else, and turned on the threshold. 'Swansea.'

She frowned, puzzled. 'What about it?'

'You don't have a holiday home down there as well, do you?'

She shook her head. 'No. But Clive and Derek keep a boat down at the Mumbles. That's near there, I think?'

'You don't go there?'

'No, Isabel and I keep well away. All that nasty, cold, wet water.'

The Mumbles. The Gower Peninsula. A geographical bull's-eye. But I hadn't been able to shake him up on the Evie front.

*　　　*　　　*

Clive Fenwick was good. He was a gold-medal Olympic eventer in stonewalling.

But was he lying? He was supremely confident that the Fenwick women would back up his claim that he didn't know Evie. But that was just common sense. If he was screwing around he wouldn't have broadcast it to his wife or his sister-in-law. And he could have met her independently. Or seen her hanging around from afar and decided that she was just the right ripe young ticket to set up in a fuck pad. To share with his brother?

Near where they kept their boat? The environs of Swansea and the Gower Peninsula, where Evie had told Justin the love of her life was located.

Because an insecure and impressionable young woman like Evie could easily have mistaken his nasty, domineering arrogance for supreme confidence and control. She didn't have the same experience of life's shits that I'd had, so where I saw self-centred boorishness, she might have read élan and urbanity.

I glanced over at the lights of the Activity Centre at Fron Heulog. They bordered Bruno's land. And Rose, Greg's fiancée's death was now nagging me. But Greg was another one who had claimed no knowledge of Evie.

I closed my eyes tightly to redirect my concentration. Because this wasn't just about Evie. I had to keep reminding myself about that. Although perhaps she hadn't just been thrown into the pot at random to confuse us. Maybe her murder had been more expedient than that. A passion gone sour? But what was the possible connection with any of these people to the other three bodies?

Where was I going to find the crisis to smoke the bastard out with?

Or could I be circling the wrong tree? Was my guy someone who wasn't even on my radar? I didn't want to consider that one. But this was getting depressing. Finding myself coming up short every time I thought I was about to get an answer.

My phone beeped at the bottom of the Barn Gallery drive to let me know I had received a text message.

When you're finished chasing married women, come and buy me a drink at The Fleece. Tx.

I smiled. From the tone it looked like I might have been forgiven. My mood tilted up the graph. If I was somehow in the middle of a desirability phase, secreting pheromones like a musk ox, then I may as well try to capitalize on it.

Tessa was sitting on her own with a tablet computer and a glass of white wine on the table in front of her. She looked up at me with a smile set for chagrin. 'I'm so, so sorry, Glyn. I shouldn't have taken it out on you.'

'It's okay, you were upset.'

'And a real bitch.' She winced theatrically. 'And to think that I had been giving you the relationship third degree.'

'As I said, it's okay.' I sat down.

'Thanks.' She leaned over and squeezed my hand briefly, then cocked her head and made a show of scrutinizing me from a number of different angles.

'What are you doing?' I asked.

'Checking for signs of exhaustion.'

'Concerned that I might be overworking?'

She grinned. 'No, shagged out.' She saw the question pop up in my face. 'We saw your car in the driveway at the Barn Gallery when we came past.'

I held up my right hand. 'Strictly business, Scouts' honour.'

'Grrr . . .' She reached out a clawed hand and made a pantomime show of raking my face. 'But seriously, what do you make of that outfit?'

'What do you mean?'

'How can they make any money?'

'I think they're in a different league from us, Dr MacLean. I don't think they have to make any money.'

She pondered that. 'How's your case coming on?'

'If I said "slowly", that would imply some sort of progress. In terms of movement, think pogo stick. I keep bouncing back to the point I've just left.'

'As bad as that?'

I nodded.

'You need a holiday,' she instructed.

I spread my arms wide. 'People come here for their holidays.'

'Wouldn't you rather be in Italy?'

A lot of people asked me that. I gave her my stock answer. 'One day, I'll spend some serious time there.'

She looked surprised. 'You don't go back?'

'We only ever went there a few times when we were kids. Travelling wasn't so easy then, and my parents couldn't afford it.' I looked at her apologetically. 'And I have to confess that I didn't really like it.'

'Shame on you.'

'The food was strange, I couldn't understand the language, and the local bad boys used to beat me up in an attempt to impress my sister.'

She laughed.

I couldn't bring myself to tell her that it got even less exotic. Summer holidays used to be a caravan at Borth. That memory took me off on a tangent. The couple of really wonderful summers we had spent with the Scottish branch of the Capaldi clan on Great Cumbrae island in the Firth of Clyde. Where someone's uncle had a boat, and I got to hang out with the wild Mackay cousins who used to be able to start the engine with a carved iced-lolly stick.

'You look happier,' she said, breaking into the memory.

'I'm sorry, I was miles away.'

She gave me a concerned look. 'You're tired.'

251

She inclined her head to the side. I followed her line of sight and saw two of her charges playing pool. 'I'd invite you back for cocoa, but I'm in Mother Hen mode again tonight.'

When I left The Fleece a little later and alone I picked up a text message from Gloria. It informed me that Clive drank Jim Beam.

Philistine.

It was only when I was nearly home that the thought came to me. It was strong enough to make me turn back. I drove past Pen Twyn and the Barn Gallery, and turned around to come back the other way. The way that Tessa would have come.

Even going slowly, with my headlights on full beam, I couldn't pick out the parking area in front of the Barn Gallery.

*   *   *

Tessa had lied to me. And why had she changed so abruptly from the Ice Queen one minute, banishing me from her kingdom, to the Sister of Mercy stroking my wearied brow the next? This had to be more than just the normal strangeness of women's ways.

Nothing was making sense. There were too many mysteries.

And it was literally freezing in Unit 13. I turned the gas fire up full, wrapped myself in a blanket, sat down on the banquette seat and stared at the map of the wind-farm site pinned to the opposite wall. This was becoming a habit.

Talk to me, I urged it.

Tessa had been right. I was tired. But underneath that, I felt a buzz. An excitement.

252

Something was taking shape. I couldn't put form to it yet, or resolve anything, I just had to be patient and wait for it to surface.

I reviewed what I had.

My hunch was still telling me that Gerald Evans probably had nothing to do with the bodies on the hill. But he had lied to me. 'Grass Vegas' meant he had got closer to Evie than he had admitted. He was a conduit to her other life, and I now had leverage on him.

Clive Fenwick claimed to have no knowledge of Evie. But he had the right geography. His boat at the Mumbles put him in the territory.

Greg Thomas was another one who denied knowing Evie. Could there be a connection between her and his dead fiancée? Although there was that huge dilemma. Something like eight years between her death and the first burial. If the killings and burials constituted a memorial dedicated to Rose, why had there been such a long delay in crafting it?

And, while I was making lists, Owen Jones had seemed more-than-naturally close to his sister. Her death would also have affected him badly. But he was in Africa.

*   *   *

It was so cold the next morning that I woke to find that my breath had turned to ice on the window. I dressed in my clothes and blanket and wiped a patch clear on the window. The frost on the grass a trapped white shimmer, but a pure-blue sky with the promise of early spring sunshine.

Nature had waited until the day of Evie's funeral

to pour its grace down on her.

I had time before Mackay delivered Justin to me. I drove over to the police house where I found Emrys Hughes watching Friel wash their car.

'We're busy, Capaldi,' Emrys greeted me fondly.

'I need to talk to you.'

'You're disturbing our concentration.'

'Emrys, Emrys . . .' I declaimed expansively. 'You should know better by now. I'm just going to hang around and pester you until you break.'

He gave up. 'Okay, whatever it takes to get rid of you,' he said crossly.

'Rose Jones, Owen's sister, Greg Thomas's fiancée.'

'She's dead and buried, Capaldi. Leave the poor girl in peace.'

'Humour me.'

'I told you before, we're going back about fifteen years there.'

'How did she die?'

'It was a tragic accident.'

'Most of them are. Can you be more specific?'

'She went to visit Greg, while he was still in the army. Where he was stationed. There was some kind of an incident. I can't remember the details. I told you, it was a long time ago.'

'Just give me the broad-brush outline.'

'She was accidentally shot.'

An internal alarm went off. 'Did he take her onto a firing range?'

'No, I told you, it was where he was stationed,' he repeated impatiently, 'Northern Ireland. During the Troubles. It was a bullet ricochet or something like that. A chance happening, wrong place, wrong time. She was a real sweet girl, and they made a

254

wonderful couple. Greg was devastated. So was Owen, but he was the rock who helped him and the rest of the family pull through.'

I turned away from him. I needed to be totally still for a moment.

I turned back. 'Where did Greg go? After he left the army? Before he and the Hornes opened the activity centre?'

He shrugged. 'Don't know. He came back on occasions, to check up on Fron Heulog. He and Rose were going to live there. He wasn't much of a conversationalist after that. You know, unapproachable.'

How did this change things? I asked myself as I drove back to Unit 13. It gave me Greg Thomas as a suspect and revenge as a motive. But revenge on whom?

Who had paid the bride price?

*   *   *

Justin had insisted on coming to Evie's funeral. I didn't try too hard to dissuade him. Funerals are strange and emotional things, and close observance can sometimes pick up useful underlying ripples of disturbance. I wanted to gauge reactions there when people saw Justin.

But I also wanted him returned to safety. So I had arranged for Mackay to bring him to Unit 13.

When they arrived I pulled Mackay to the side. 'Thanks for bringing him.'

'That's okay. He's a nice kid. Boyce and I are enjoying his company.'

'Greg Thomas.'

'What about him?'

255

'His fiancée Rose was shot in Northern Ireland. There was some sort of incident and she got caught in the crossfire. I need to know what happened, Mac, I need the details.' He turned away from me. When he turned back I saw it in his eyes. 'You already knew?'

He shook his head, but it wasn't a denial. 'Only the bare bones, there's no real substance to it yet.'

'What do you mean?' His reticence was scaring me.

'I've been warned off.'

'Officially?'

'No, informally. It turns out that I know some guys who were involved, and they're advising me to back off.'

'Is that it? Is that as far as we can go?'

He smiled. 'No. I'm just warning you, I'm going to have to make some promises. There's going to have to be total deniability.'

'Whatever you have to do.'

I got Justin into the car. I tried to suppress what Mackay had just told me. There was no point in speculating until I had more details.

'How are you feeling?' I asked Justin as we drove to St Peter's in Dinas. We were early. I wanted to be there to see everyone arrive.

'A bit creeped out,' he admitted, 'I don't know what to do at something like this.'

'Just keep looking glum,' I advised.

'Evie and I used to talk about having a green burial. They do them in the woods now in some places. Plant a tree over you. She wanted a cardboard coffin.'

Typical, I thought, she wouldn't tell him about her boyfriend, the guy who had probably killed her, but she'd chatter on about how she wanted to be packaged after she's dead. Because they were too young to believe that it could ever happen to them.

'Do you think I should tell them?'

'Pardon?' I'd missed the gist of what he'd just said.

'Her parents. Do you think I should tell them what her wishes were?'

I turned to park in front of the church. The empty hearse was stationed outside. I pictured the coffin in the nave, the flowers, the printed order of service, the rented vicar. I turned to him with as gentle a smile as I could manage. 'I wouldn't. I think the ball's rolled on a bit too far now.'

The Salmons turned up separately, each with their own contingent. They both looked gaunt and broken, and their formal outfits made them look like they had been dressed in donated clothes by institutions that had only just released them. Mr Salmon made a move towards his wife, but she turned her back on him and rested her head on a friend's shoulder. While her fate remained unknown, the absent Evie had been the tenuous glue of their marriage; now that they knew she was never coming home, the entire DNA of the thing had collapsed irretrievably.

Kevin Fletcher arrived, immaculate in a black overcoat and holding leather gloves that looked like de-boned puppies. He would have made a good undertaker. If he hadn't been secure in his conviction that we already had our guy, I would have suspected him of being there for the same reasons as me. So this must have been pure PR. He had brought a couple of uniforms along with him to dance attendance and identify him as the head

257

honcho.

He called me over. I told Justin to stay in full view of everyone and not to talk to strangers.

'Who's the strange-looking kid?' Fletcher asked.

'That's Justin Revel, Evie's friend.'

He scowled. 'I thought we told you to take him home?'

'No,' I corrected him with a smile, 'DCS Galbraith told me to take him where he wanted to go. Justin told me he wanted to attend his friend's funeral.'

He scrutinized me warily. 'I hope you're not trying to work something here?'

'Like what, boss?'

He nodded towards the Salmons. 'This is all about the fucking family, Capaldi,' he said out of the corner of his mouth, while flashing one of his trademark brown-nosing smiles at a smart-looking elderly woman. 'I don't want you hijacking the occasion for your own private agenda. It makes us look like we haven't got any feelings.'

'No one could accuse you of that, boss.'

I slipped back to Justin before he could work out whether I was being disrespectful.

A lot of townspeople came to pay their respects. A few farmers I recognized, including the Joneses from Cogfryn. Jeff and Tessa turned up with Tessa's helpers, all dressed up as best they could, given that they were living in the equivalent of a shanty town. Tessa managed to signal a small private greeting. Gloria and Isabel arrived, but no Clive. Gloria's private greeting wasn't so private. And no one from Fron Heulog.

'Recognize many people here?' I asked Justin. I was disappointed. I was only getting the usual

258

reactions of open curiosity and mild reproach I would have expected from a rural community to a slightly weird urban youth in their midst. No expressions laden with obvious guilt or anguish.

He shrugged. 'A few faces I remember. No one stands out.'

'No one that Evie ever pointed out to you?'

He shook his head.

I grabbed his arm. 'What about them?' I had just caught sight of Gerald Evans and his wife crossing the square towards the lych gate.

'I saw her a couple of times when I biked over to see Evie. And he's the one I told you about, the dude who offered her the hostess gig.'

They had to walk past us to get inside the church. Evans started to stare me out. It was pure macho bullshit, I had expected it. I raised a finger and moved it in slow-motion to close one nostril, and then gave a loud and exaggerated sniff. His face went quizzical, he hadn't understood my gesticulations. But his wife had noticed. I saw him incline his head to listen to her. He shook his head. He half turned and shot me a filthy look.

He still hadn't connected.

I air-snorted a line of coke again.

All I can think is that this was the moment when his wife told him who Justin was. Because when he turned round again his face had blanched.

The connection had hit home hard.

*　　　*　　　*

He knew that I was staring at the back of his head throughout the service. It was probably one of the rare occasions that he wished that he wasn't

259

such a big bastard. I was making him anxious. But he didn't dare turn round. It was all there in the nervous gestures, scratching his ears, the finger down the back of the collar or researching the incipient bald spot.

I got Justin out of the church fast. Most of the crowd would be dispersing, only the hard core of relatives taking the long drive to the crematorium. I wanted to get away before Evans emerged. I wanted to keep him squirming.

Because I now realized that that was the only punishment that I was going to be able to inflict on him. Because I had just had my confirmation that it couldn't have been him.

He hadn't recognized Justin.

Which meant that he couldn't have been the one who had been trying to eliminate him. Because he would have to have known what the guy he wanted vaporised looked like.

I took the call on hands-free on the way back to Unit 13 to deliver Justin to Mackay. I had been expecting it.

'Sergeant Capaldi, it's Gerald Evans.'

'How did you get this number?'

'From Emrys Hughes.'

'Have you been complaining again?'

'No,' he protested contritely. It was almost as if I had accused him of being a very naughty boy. 'I think we need to talk.'

'Which you'd rather not do in front of your wife?' I suggested.

In front of anything remotely sentient, as it turned out. He asked me to meet him at a defunct out-of-town Baptist chapel. I was deliberately ten minutes late. His Land Rover Discovery was parked on the grass verge. He was waiting for me in the small walled graveyard that was bisected by the path to the chapel's front door. He looked like he had been pacing.

That restless energy was still in evidence. He was not used to dealing with anxiety. It was fucking up his normal power-and-anger response to situations. I would have to be careful with this guy. Constraint and containment were not among his more-developed social skills.

But I was determined to get in at least one figurative punch to the nose before I had to dance off. 'Grass Vegas.'

He tried out a coy smile. 'What about it?'

'You fucked up, Gerald.'

He flared, savoured the anger for a moment, before having to deflate. 'It wasn't just me,' he whined.

'You led me down the garden path with Evie.'

'What did she tell that weird kid?'

I winged it. 'All about the drugs and the illegal gambling.'

'The gambling wasn't illegal,' he protested righteously. 'It was a private house.'

'What about the coke?'

He smiled warily. 'You can't prove anything.'

I smiled back. 'I don't have to. I just have to turn up at your house to question you about it in front of your wife. Then I leave you to do the explaining.'

'You bastard.'

'You should have used bald dwarves.'

'What the fuck are you talking about?'

'If you were aiming for elegant decadence. You should have had dwarves walking around with the lines of coke on the top of their heads. A young woman in a padded-out bustier and fishnet tights is really passé.'

'What do you want?'

'Who was involved?'

It was him and three golf-club and shooting cronies, he told me. I took down the names. The venue was the safe male sanctum of a basement play-room in the house of a recently divorced founder member.

'Why did you hire Evie Salmon?'

'Just to brighten the place up. You know, give it a touch of sparkle.'

'What happened to her?'

He pulled a face. 'She stopped coming. She just gave up.'

'Did she give you a reason?'

'She said that she'd met someone who wasn't happy about what she was doing.'

'Did she say who it was?'

He shook his head. 'No.'

'Could it have been one of the members?'

'Not one of the regulars. We would all have known.'

'When did she stop?'

He thought about it. 'Roughly six months before she went away.'

But according to her father she had never given up her Saturday work. So, if he was telling the truth, whoever she had met had being paying her to keep up the pretence. Once again I had come up against that wall. What was it about this relationship that it had to be kept so secret? She hadn't even been able to tell her best friend. Hell, I reminded myself, Justin was her only friend.

The significance of something else he had just

mentioned clicked into place. 'You said "regulars". Were there more than the four of you?'

'Occasionally we'd invite selected guests along.'

It didn't take much imagination to envisage the hypocritical self-important pricks that made up their social circle. I had a sudden spark on someone who fitted that definition.

'Was Clive Fenwick one?'

'And his brother, Derek.'

'I want a list of the names. All the ones you invited while Evie was working there.'

'This *is* going to come out like an anonymous tip-off, isn't it? You're not going to drop me in it?' The bastard was grinning at me. He thought we had fucking bonded.

I made a noncommittal grunt and pretended to be deep in thought. I was no further down the road with the identity of Evie's lover, but I was a happier man. I now had the means of putting Clive Fenwick's balls into the vice.

15

I let Evans drive away and leave me at the chapel.

I needed to force myself to reflect, and communing with a load of dead Baptists seemed as good a way as any of chopping my seething thought processes into more manageable bits.

It also kept me in check. I had had one bruising encounter with Clive Fenwick, and I needed to make sure that I was in the driving seat next time we met. Which meant not going in half cocked and riding on pure emotion, because he was the sort of tricky bastard to come out of left field and unseat me.

But first of all I needed to let Kevin Fletcher know about Grass Vegas. He would be dismissive— it was located in Dinas, therefore it didn't connect with his agenda, but if I didn't raise it I could be in real trouble if it came back to haunt us later.

As well as the four founding members, Evans had given me the names of the guests who had been invited while Evie was still in attendance. These included the Fenwick brothers, a couple of big land agents, three auctioneers, a solicitor from Shrewsbury, an accountant from Chester, and a big-time local chicken farmer. There were some pretty powerful people in there, and I needed clearance to go after them.

He heard me out. 'He definitely didn't say anything about Bruno Gilbert being a member of this club?' he asked.

'Definitely, boss.' I didn't like to tell him that the only invitation Evans and his ilk would have extended to Bruno was as a stand-in for a rugby ball.

'It is historical.' He was musing. 'And there's no way we could tie them in to dope without a live raid, and that is not going to be any kind of priority given the budget situation, and the type of citizen involved.'

'What do you want me to do, boss? We have established a relationship between Evie and these men.'

'Historical, though, as I said. And their geography's all wrong. But I suppose we could tackle them, see if there's any way we can connect Gilbert to Evie through them. They may have said something about her in front of him that set his juices running.'

He seemed to have an idea of Bruno as some kind of social gadfly, flitting around garden parties overhearing conversations. I didn't contradict him. I didn't want him to rescind my licence to go forth and harry Clive Fenwick.

*   *   *

It may sound hokey, but there is a phantom within certain ringtones that lets you know that bad news is arriving, even before you've answered it. This was one of them. My first thought was Justin.

'Sergeant Capaldi, something terrible has happened. You've got to get over here immediately.' Her voice was anguished, bordering on hysteria, and I only just made out that it was Valerie Horne.

'Can you slow down, please, Mrs Horne?' But she was gone.

With no explanation I just had my imagination to work with as I drove fast to Fron Heulog.

Was it some sort of admission from Greg Thomas? Could he finally have realized that he was running out of twists and turns and hung himself from the new climbing frame?

I drove reluctantly past the entrance to the Barn Gallery. But Clive Fenwick's reprieve was only going to be short-lived, I hoped.

The security gate was open at the activity centre so I drove straight in. There was an air of desertion about the place as I went up the entrance drive. No clusters of sulky kids suffering cold turkey due to shop-window and diesel-particulate deprivation.

Was that it? The cause of her panic? Had Emrys Hughes's ultimate nightmare come to pass? Had there been a mass breakout? Were Dinas and the surrounding countryside about to be ravaged by packs of wild gangsta youths trawling for fun and mayhem?

The place wasn't quite deserted. A young Asian boy, about thirteen years old, was standing outside the office. He looked like he had fallen into an alien space and was waiting apprehensively for something to bite him.

'You the policeman?' he asked as I got out of the car.

'Yes.'

'She told me to bring you.' He was already walking away.

I followed him down between the house and the barn. We turned a corner at the end, past an old sheep-gathering fold, and I saw the activity. Valerie Horne was surrounded by a semicircle of the younger kids.

She saw me and waved me forward. It wasn't a welcome, it was all urgency.

The kids parted to let me through. They were standing at the head of an old track that led down to the river, by the side of a steep, earth-faced bank. The top of the bank was lined by stunted hawthorns, the vestigial remains of a former hedge, and there was a run of old holes and spoil slips along its length, under the lip, probably a redundant badger sett.

Valerie pointed.

And the shock shortened my life by a measurable factor.

The bone, grey-green, was lying on the inclined

266

surface of the bank. The soil around it was damp enough to still have a metallic, freshly dug smell.

At the same time that I was trying to adjust to this, I realized that we were inhabiting an unnatural silence. Everyone was staring at me. The kids rapt, Valerie tense. All were expectant. I was supposed to do something to explain this, and bring their lives back to normal again.

'No one has touched this?' I asked.

Valerie shook her head. 'I can't promise. The boys who found it say they didn't, but . . .' She inclined her head and tailed-off.

'Is it from a real dead person, mister?' one of the braver boys called out. A voiced ripple of disgust combined with a frisson of horror went through the group.

'It's probably from a cow, isn't it, Sergeant? Or a sheep?' Valerie suggested hopefully.

I went as close as I could without disturbing anything. The loose earth was covered by kids' footprints and indentations that I realized had been made by their knees. Why had they been digging here?

And where was everyone else?

'Where are your husband and brother?' I asked Valerie.

'They're out on a trek on the moors with the older ones.'

'Can you take the children away from here, please?'

'You didn't answer the question,' she reminded me softly.

'I think it's an ulna,' I replied equally quietly.

She looked at me questioningly.

'One of the forearm bones.' Before this case

267

started I would have had a problem identifying it, but I had had cause to get reacquainted with the sharp end of skeletons.

I put in the call to Fletcher, and left it to him to call Jack Galbraith and organize a SOCO team. I put in another call to DEFRA. I drove back down to the head of the track and set up a makeshift perimeter with incident tape.

WHY?!

Why move the action from the wind-farm site to Fron Heulog? Why bring it here when he had gone to such trouble to fit up Bruno and get the investigation shifted to Newport? I took a slow look around, and felt the chill as it dawned on me. Because it didn't change anything. We were still in Bruno's immediate neighbourhood. No one but me suspected that this was the home ground.

But why bring the investigation back?

I didn't think for a minute that this was an accidental discovery. We had been meant to find that bone. The bastard had just thrown in another cryptic shift.

I used my digital camera on the bone. When I zoomed in I realized that there was something wrong with it. From the bottom of the bank it looked like the wrist-end of the bone was still partially buried. It wasn't. It just wasn't there. It looked like it had been snapped off.

Was it a coincidence that the part of the bone that should demonstrate the severance markings where the hand had been removed was missing? Was it fuck. But I knew that I was going to be the only person who would be asking that question.

Because all this was going to do was make poor old Bruno look like an even more rampant serial

268

killer than previously believed.

WHY?!

*   *   *

Emrys Hughes and a team of uniforms turned up to spell me.

He looked at the bone and turned to me with a significant set to his face. 'Your Mr Gilbert was a busy chap, wasn't he?'

I had been right. Emrys Hughes was as good a representation of the public cross-section as you get around here. And he had jumped to the immediate conclusion that this was down to Bruno Gilbert. Oh, the powers of perceptual manipulation. This fucker should be in advertising.

'It's just one bone.'

He sucked in a big noisy, dramatic breath. 'There will be more.'

'Well, you'd better get ready to roll your sleeves up, because you and your guys are going to be fucking digging for them,' I observed nastily.

I found Valerie and the younger boys in the canteen area. She had calmed them down to a degree with fizzy drinks, crisps and chocolate biscuits.

'Emergency measures,' she explained guiltily.

'Who found the bone?'

She searched the group with her forefinger raised. 'Darren, Dewayne and Rocky.' She used her finger to point them out.

'Can I talk to them?'

She looked at me doubtfully. 'What's the legal position?'

I shook my head. 'It's not an interrogation. It's

just something I need to know now, while it's still fresh in their memory.' She still looked concerned. 'You can ask it for me.'

I wrote it down. She sat the three boys down at one of the refectory benches. I squatted beside her. The remainder of the kids started to gather round, sensing drama. 'Right, no one is going to get into any trouble over this. In fact, the sergeant is very pleased with you for finding it.' She looked my way. I nodded enthusiastically on my haunches. 'But what I'd like to know is why you chose to dig there?'

The three boys looked at each other, hesitant and nervous now that the focus of attention was on them.

'Rocky?' Valerie prompted gently.

Please tell me 'a man told us to dig there', I willed them silently. A man answering the description of Clive Fenwick. Or Greg Thomas. I didn't really care which, I just wanted to end it.

'The dog was digging. We thought there might be something good underneath,' Rocky explained tremulously.

'What dog was that?' Valerie anticipated my next question.

He looked at the other two. They both shook their heads, he joined in. 'Dunno, a black-and-white one. It run away before we got close.'

A black-and-white one. In these parts that was the generic description for dog.

'You don't have a dog?' I asked Valerie when we had moved away from the kids. I hadn't bothered to infuse the question with hope, I already knew the answer.

'No. We get our fair share of farm dogs passing

270

through, though. Especially if there's a bitch in season in the neighbourhood.' She smiled wanly, she looked exhausted. 'What's going to happen now?'

'A lot of people are going to be getting very busy,' I warned her. She was a kind person. She worked too hard. And she probably loved her brother.

She was probably going to end up hating me.

*   *   *

So now the bastard had recruited fucking Lassie. The scruffy black-and-white Welsh version at least.

I pondered it while I drank my tea. Trying to figure out the modus operandi. He had probably planted the bone, scented the earth around it with some kind of *allure de chien*, found a dog from somewhere, waited until he saw that the boys were heading that way, and then released it. There had been so much scrabbling activity around that bank that the bait scent would have been dispersed. Even if I could have persuaded forensics to look for it.

Clever bastard. It was a complicated and risky operation, but at least, if my hunch was correct, he was working on his own territory. But it still brought me back to the question: why change the status quo at this juncture?

Because it widens the geography?

It doesn't shift the blame from Bruno, it just extends the zone of the operation. So why does he want to disseminate?

Because he wants to shift the focus!

He wanted to lift our attention away from the original site. He wanted it to lose its importance.

271

He wanted it to be seen as just one of a series of multiple sites. It reinforced my hunch that it could be acting as a memorial. The place had a specific personal significance, and he didn't want us trampling all over its sanctity. He wanted to shift us onto unhallowed ground.

But why wait this long? That was the question that now stabbed at me. If the spirit of the place was so important, why hadn't he diverted us away from it before now?

I instructed myself to go back to first principles. This was not the work of a classic serial killer. These bodies had been put there over time to serve as a specific memorial. A memorial to Rose? From her former fiancée?

And what did these bodies have to do with her? As far as we could tell, after the third body had been buried, the monument had been completed, because the killing had stopped.

Until Evie.

But she had been cold-bloodedly murdered to serve a purpose. To divert us. She had never been a part of the original plan.

Oh, fuck!

If he hadn't killed anyone else during his active period he wouldn't have had any more body parts at his disposal. That's what had caused the time lapse. He had had to wait until he had found some other source of suitable skeletal material. Because there was no ulna superstore.

Or was there?

The only reassuring thing was that he wouldn't have gone out there and killed a fresh victim to source the parts he needed. Not because he would have had any qualms about it, but because it wouldn't serve the purpose. It would be too fresh. He needed to find a skeleton that would match the profile of the others, both in terms of age and length of burial.

This new bone was going to fit the original pattern. I was certain of it.

And then, because he couldn't match the marks of the hands being detached, as on the originals, because he was working with something that was already a skeleton, he had snapped the bone off above the joint. And because we had swallowed his line so completely, we would find something to account for the damage. Animal dispersal, agricultural machinery, some rational explanation that would keep us on track.

What were Jack Galbraith and Kevin Fletcher's reactions going to be when I laid out this theory? It was a purely academic conjecture. Because I wasn't going to tell them. Not without something stronger than merely speculative reasoning. I didn't want to be back on the hunt for a lamb castrator.

So where did I start to look for that ulna superstore?

*   *   *

I was still stuck in that puzzle slot when the SOCO team arrived. They went to work, measuring and photographing the bone on its perch on the side of the bank, the forensic anthropologist patiently waiting her turn. Dressed in their white sterile suits they looked like a bunch of loopy acolytes paying homage to a displaced holy relic.

Trevor Horne and Greg Thomas had returned from their hike with the older kids. They had

273

been kept back from the perimeter, and I hadn't been able to study Greg Thomas's reactions. I suppressed the urge to face him. I didn't want him spooked and running at this stage.

And how involved was Trevor Horne?

Jack Galbraith and Fletcher arrived together. They strode through the farmyard, glowering like hostile bailiffs in their overcoats and Wellington boots.

'Have you seeded this, Capaldi?' Jack Galbraith asked bitterly when he saw the bone.

'Sir?'

'Is this you playing out some kind of a revenge fantasy? Bringing me down to the valley of the fucking bones again?' He looked across towards the wind farm. 'How far are we from the other site?'

'Just under a kilometre, sir.'

He groaned. 'I just hope that we don't have a procession of dead bodies stretching between here and there. Shit, this may not even be the terminus. This could be just another way-station on the fucking slaughter trail.' He glared at me. As if this was all my fault. He called the head of the SOCO team over. 'Okay, when you've finished your photography and measurements you can move the bone and start digging. I want to see what else we've got in there.'

'That's a badger sett, sir,' I said.

He flared round on me. 'So?'

'It's protected by law. Technically, we have to apply to DEFRA for a licence to dig it up.'

He stared at me, speechless. 'You're jerking my chain, Capaldi. There could be a mass burial under there, and you're telling me that I have to apply to the fucking Ministry for permission to dig it out?'

274

'I'm arranging it, sir. I've been in contact with DEFRA. I've told them that it's an emergency. I'm expecting someone to turn up at any time.'

'Fuck that. Brer Brock can give up his secrets now.'

So much for my demonstration of initiative and efficiency.

It was going to be slow. Teaspoon and toothbrush digging. Delicate excavation. At least when you were uncovering a whole body you could guess the perimeters, the rough outlines to work to. Here, all we had was one bone. The assumption was that the rest of them were somewhere deeper in the bank, and not necessarily still in the convenient shape of a body.

I had tried to suggest that one bone may be all we were going to find on this site, but no one was listening. Perceptual manipulation was still at work. No one had yet started to ask why only one bone had managed to detach itself and levitate to the surface under its own steam.

And, an hour later, we still only had our original bone. The rain had set in. A fine, soaking drizzle, wafting in on a cold westerly breeze. Because of the bank and the slope, the shelter that had been rigged was only keeping the excavators dry. Even under the golf umbrella he was making Fletcher hold up, Jack Galbraith was getting wet. And grumpier.

'There's fuck all else here,' he announced crossly, grinding out the butt of his latest cigarette.

'Perhaps we should move down the bank? Try another part of the badger sett?' Fletcher suggested. The DEFRA officer had since arrived and pronounced the sett inactive.

He shook his head. 'No, I've been thinking about

275

it. Bruno Gilbert would never have cached even one of his victims so close to an established farm.' He turned to me. 'You're the nearest thing I've got to a nature consultant. Why would a badger have just one bone in its den?'

'I thought they were vegetarians,' Fletcher commented.

I remembered the talk I had overheard from farmers about badgers taking lambs and hens. 'I think they'll eat anything. But this sett looks like it's been long-abandoned.' I looked over at the DEFRA officer standing on the sidelines, who nodded his confirmation.

'What about a fox?' Fletcher suggested, showing off his knowledge of nature red in tooth and claw. 'Maybe it found the original skeleton and has been distributing the bones around for future use.'

'I think that's what squirrels do with nuts, boss,' I offered helpfully.

Jack Galbraith moaned. 'Over what sort of a radius do these bastards roam?'

I shook my head. 'I'm not an expert, sir.'

'All available personnel tomorrow,' Jack Galbraith ordered Fletcher. 'I want an expanding-envelope search out from here.' He looked at me for confirmation. 'It shouldn't be that difficult to see, should it? If a wild animal's been digging up a human body?'

I had to try to stop this. 'It depends on how historic it is, sir. Maybe the animal died and never got back to retrieve the bone. The site may be covered up again.' I gave it a pause to charge up my credibility. 'Or there is another possibility.'

He eyed me suspiciously. 'Like what?'

'That you were right with your first hunch. That

someone has seeded this. To make it look like a burial site. Or that it came from another burial site.'

'Why would someone do that?' Fletcher snapped. 'When we already know who did it.'

Jack Galbraith made a pantomime of receiving illumination. 'No, Kevin, I think Capaldi means that the mass murderer on this side of the fucking valley is attempting a copycat operation to fit up the mass murderer on the other side.'

Fletcher laughed.

'Where are the tooth marks?' I asked, the thought swooping down out of nowhere to rescue me.

'What tooth marks?' he asked, glancing doubtfully at Jack Galbraith.

I turned the viewing screen of my camera towards them. 'If a wild animal had had that bone why didn't it chew it?'

*   *   *

They didn't buy it, though. Because Sheila Goddard, the forensic anthropologist got excited. It was only guesswork at this stage, she warned, but the bone, in terms of condition and appearance, looked like a good match with the others. She also tentatively suggested that it might have belonged to a woman, which ramped up their alpha male protector instincts.

'Before we enter the realm of the fucking minutiae, Capaldi, we have to find the rest of the body,' was the curt and succinct rebuttal Jack Galbraith used on me. Without giving me a chance to explain that whoever had deposited that bone

277

would have made certain that it would be a match with the others.

He left to oversee things from headquarters, where rain was banned. Fletcher, faced with the prospect of another night in The Fleece, used the excuse of getting the bone down to the lab to make his getaway. He claimed that he needed to pester the scientists for a quick mitochondrial DNA profile. Just in case there was a match with one of the other victims.

The blanket search for the putative carnivore-desecrated grave was scheduled for the following morning. Fletcher, with Bruno Gilbert already in the body bag, saw no glory in returning for a cold search in a damp valley, so I, as resident hayseed, was appointed coordinator.

Had the perpetrator just pillaged the ulna? Or had he taken the entire skeleton? That was the possibility that was concerning me when I got back to Unit 13 that evening. Because if it was the latter, the bastard could skip around the countryside dispensing bone after bone after bone, like some kind of macabre paper chase, every time our interest looked like flagging. And, if the perp was Greg Thomas, he could scatter the contents of his ossuary all over Fron Heulog land. Eventually it would be discovered that they were all from the same body, but by the time that happened he could have found himself another one. And so on, ad infinitum.

This time- and resource-wasting diversion bore shades of the McGuire and Tucker investigation. We had been led down some twisted routes and into some very dark places on that one, but at least the body count had been lower, and we had known

278

the identities of most of the people involved.

And I still had the problem about where he had acquired his bone. Okay, there were cemeteries across the length and breadth of the country piled full of the things. But how would he know that he would get what he wanted? A middle-aged body that had been buried about six to eight years ago, and which had turned into a skeleton. He had probably nicked Redshanks, but this guy was too slick to try to pass his old bones off as a relatively recent skeleton.

The age of the deceased and the date of the interment were easy. There were burial records for those. The skeleton was the crucial part. How would he know, when he excavated whatever grave he had chosen to rob, that the coffin wouldn't just be full of cold corpse stew? Because some of those containers were pretty damned solid, built like galleons to sail the main of eternity and repel all boarders. The body would do its best to decompose as nature intended, but most of the beasties, microbes and fungal activity that should have helped to strip it clean wouldn't be able to gain entry.

And then Evie came back to help me. Or rather, her friend Justin had done so on her behalf, by telling me what she had said to him.

A cardboard coffin and a woodland burial.

I went on the Internet and found the email addresses for all the woodland and green-burial sites within a hundred-mile radius of a point between Dinas and Swansea. I sent an email posing them all one specific question. There would be no reply until tomorrow, unless business was so brisk in the nappy-knitting community that they had to

279

run a night shift. Which I doubted.

I put a call in to Mackay. 'Sorry if this looks like pushing you, Mac, but are you any further on with the Greg Thomas thing?'

'Not yet. I told you this was a sensitive one. All I've got at the moment is that Greg Thomas was stationed over there at the time, and that Rose Jones had come over to visit.'

'Who shot her?'

'I don't know yet. Although it does look accidental. She was a civilian in the wrong place at the wrong time when some kind of firefight took off.'

'Between who?'

'Us and some bad guys. And before you ask,' he hurried on quickly, 'I'm waiting to find out who they were.'

'The bad guys shot Rose?' I prodded.

'That's not actually definite.'

'What does that mean?'

'It looks like there's no ballistics report. No one found the bullet that killed her.'

'Isn't that unusual?'

'Very.' He laughed. 'You didn't ask for straightforward.'

'Thanks, Mac. I'd appreciate it if you could get back to me as soon as you know anything else. In the meantime, can I have a quick word with Justin?'

'How are you doing?' I asked when he came on the line.

'Cool,' he enthused. 'I thought hanging out with old soldier geezers would be a pain, but these dudes know some amazing stuff.'

'Don't let them corrupt you.'

He laughed. 'They're cool, but it's not like I'm

280

going to enlist or anything.'

'I need you to think back to your talks with Evie.'

'Okay.'

'The man she met. Weren't you curious? Didn't you ever try to press for more information?'

'All the time. It was like she was teasing me. But she wouldn't give out. Said that she had had to make a solemn promise, and if she broke it she would be betraying his trust and she'd never be able to face him again.'

'Did she ever talk about boats or sailing?'

He went quiet. 'No. No, I don't think so. Something dorky like that I'd have remembered. But I have remembered something about him she used to go on about. She used to keep saying how fit he was.'

'Fit? As in attractive?'

'No, she had other words for that, like awesome and gorgeous. No, this was like buff. You know, strong?'

'Like he worked out?' I had an image of Greg Thomas when I had seen him sorting the gym equipment. Remembering that I had thought then that he could have given Mackay a run for his money.

'Yes.'

'Thanks, Justin. Get back to me if you remember anything else, however small.'

'Glyn?'

I sensed the arrival of a serious question. 'What?'

'Mackay and Boyce?' He hesitated. 'Do you think they've ever, like, really killed anyone?'

I laughed. 'No, they're full of bullshit.' He was young. Certain dark truths deserved to be kept on the private side of the barrier.

16

We assembled at Fron Heulog in the morning. Two coaches arrived filled full of curious cops, in various hill-walking costumes, staring out the window, happy, for now, at the change to their routine. Given the terrain and the weather, I wondered how long that would last.

At the same time as our coaches arrived another one left, taking the boys back to Birmingham. Our investigation had curtailed their holiday, but none of them looked too upset about it. The two kids who had finked on TB gave me the finger as the coach drove past, and fanned out the banknotes I had given them against the window.

The Hornes let us use their barn as a briefing centre, and Valerie laid on coffee. Trevor Horne and Greg Thomas volunteered to help in the search, claiming that they knew the lie of the land.

Was Greg trying to get brownie points for helping us out? While in reality using it as an opportunity to keep close to my tactics, and observe how much we were floundering?

I tried to turn his game by getting them to act as guides to two of the teams. That way I could keep tabs on where they were and get a report from the loyal troops on any misdirection they might attempt. It also kept them separated. I still wasn't quite ready to drop my hunch that there could be two perpetrators.

I kept Emrys Hughes's sidekick, Friel, behind with me to act as my contact man. I was going to be working my own agenda, and didn't want to be distracted by answering distress calls from lost or fed-up cops. Emrys wasn't happy with that; not only was I poaching a member of his tribe, but an underling was going to be cosied-up, warm and dry, with the enemy, while he was out there getting cold, wet and muddy. It wasn't personal, but Emrys was a bit too close to Inspector Morgan, and I didn't want him getting nosy about what could be regarded as extracurricular activities.

It was one of those days when the clouds had elected to come down into the valley a-courting, bearing the gift of a cold hammam. I watched the search teams file off into an atmosphere that looked like it had been created by the steam and liquid-nitrogen leaks in the kitchen of a cutting-edge chef.

I instructed Friel to keep in regular contact with the groups and to mark their shifting locations on the large-scale map that had been set up. He armed himself with map pins, and went at it with gusto, having obviously seen too many old films that featured war rooms.

I shuffled myself off to a corner, out of his gaze, and opened my laptop. I had had two replies to the email I had sent off last night.

I called the first one, a green burial ground near Swindon in Wiltshire.

'Are you conducting an investigation into satanic practices?' the man who answered asked, after I had explained who I was.

'No, just specific disturbances. As I said in my email, it's fire I'm really interested in.'

'Because we contacted the local police here, and they've been quite frankly lax in their pursuit of this.'

I tried again. 'Have you had a fire?'

'No, we've had a sacrificed rabbit.'

I cut him off and called the next number, a woodland burial site in the Forest of Dean.

'You've had a fire?' I asked, going straight for the jugular this time.

'Yes, are you following up on the visit the officer from Lydney made?' the lady asked.

'Yes,' I bluffed it, 'remind me again when the incident occurred?'

'Sometime on Saturday night or the early hours of Sunday morning. It was spotted by one of our visitors. As you can imagine, we were all very distressed. This is meant to be a place of peace and repose.'

I went back through my mental calendar. Saturday night was when Justin's flat had gone up. But, as Mackay and I had discussed, that operation was so specialized that he might have used a contractor. Even if he'd rigged it himself, the Forest of Dean wasn't far from Hereford, and he would still have had most of the night to work in.

'No one saw the flames?'

'No, we're quite remote. That's what attracts most of our clients.'

'Do you have security?'

'We have a fence.'

'No watchman or CCTV cameras?'

'We're a woodland burial ground, Sergeant, not Stalag Luft 13,' she reminded me.

'And it was definitely arson?'

'Oh, yes. It's been so damp here that there's no way anything could have burst into flames like that. Petrol, your colleague thought, and a lot of it.'

284

'The ground's been scorched?'

'The ground, the poor trees. All those markers and memorials. Why would vandals target us?' She sounded distraught. 'I've had to inform all the relatives that everything they left for their loved ones has been destroyed.'

'Could you do me a great favour,' I asked sympathetically, 'and email me a list of the graves that were affected? The names and ages of the deceased.'

As I had suspected, he had targeted a green burial site because he knew that a degradable coffin would have ensured skeletonization. And he had used the same scorched-earth tactic to cover his tracks as he had done with Evie's grave. As long as he had been reasonably careful in levelling the ground after he had exhumed his skeleton, the fire should have covered the disturbance.

And it had been put down to vandals, just as he had expected it would. Perceptual manipulation again. I was the only other person who knew that there was now an empty grave there. I had actually managed to outthink him. We had intersected at last. But how to move from here to an advantage? Even when I got the name of the body he had stolen, I knew that no one was going to put their reputation on the line to issue an exhumation order on the basis of the evidence I had.

I was on a roll, though. I was picking up answers. But not the one that I desperately needed to nail this bastard.

Where and when had he met Evie?

*   *   *

285

Anthea Joan Balmer. Aged fifty-three when she died and was buried in the Bluebell Sector of the Hornbeam Haven Natural Woodland Burial Ground. She was the only one who fitted the vectors in the list of names that came through on the email. The occupants of the other graves in the damaged area of the Bluebell Sector were either too old or too young.

I took one of the metal body probes with me. Visibility was improving, the wind had moved round to the north-east and was blowing cold, replacing the low cloud cover with a cheerless watery-blue sky.

I scrambled over the low stone wall that separated the rear lawn of Pen Twyn from the open pasture. From here I could see down to the front of the Barn Gallery. Gloria's Audi TT was gone, but in its place was another piece of expensive-looking machinery, this one a bit more discreet than her yellow monster. A blue so dark that it was almost black, four stainless-steel exhausts and a badge with a trident.

A customer?

My adolescent interest in motor racing came back to help me. That car was a Maseratti. Jesus, that thing probably cost as much as a combine harvester. I winced. I was beginning to think like a redneck. Dinas was leaching into me.

I went to work on the lawn.

'What on earth do you think you're doing?' It was Isabel, standing framed in the open French doors, in a clingy retro black outfit that paid homage to Theda Bara. Even her expression of outrage owed allegiance to the era of silent film.

And it was a stupid question. It was perfectly

obvious that I was sticking a long metal pole into their grass. 'I'm looking for a body,' I replied cheerfully.

'You can't do that here.'

'Why? Are you laying claim to the ones on your land?'

'You can't just walk onto someone else's property and start damaging things. You need a warrant or something for that.'

She was probably right, but I was prepared to take the risk. I turned my back on her and went back to work with the probe.

'Clive!' It came out like a shriek. It had worked.

He was slightly flushed from running up the steps from the barn when he crossed the lawn towards me. I heard Isabel's shrill laugh waft up from the Barn Gallery. They had swapped roles.

'Stop that at once,' he commanded, a vague tremolo in his voice from the exertion.

I jabbed the probe in again. 'What we're looking for are hollow pockets which may indicate where a body has decomposed and collapsed in on itself,' I explained helpfully.

'Do you think you're funny?' He was in control of his voice again.

'Do you?'

'You're going to be very sorry for this.'

'Clive, I'm not here for the fun of it. I know what you've been up to.'

'I play golf with the Chief Constable, who I think might be able to use a little bit of his influence on my behalf.' He leaned forward and smiled nastily. 'Boss to boss, sort of thing, just enough to earn you at least a severe fucking reprimand.'

I ignored his threat. I lowered my voice to stop

Isabel overhearing. 'I know that you lied when you told me you didn't know Evie Salmon.'

His eyes flickered, but he recovered control and tried to call my bluff. 'Get off my land before you make things even worse for yourself.' Instinctively, he had also dropped his voice level.

'You Fenwicks are a worldly and sophisticated lot. Isabel probably wouldn't give a toss about the gambling, or even the coke, but not mentioning that Evie Salmon was dancing attendance, that might raise some eyebrows. That might set her to wondering whether you weren't trying to hide something.'

I saw his face crash at the realization of what Gerald Evans had done to him. His glance twitched involuntarily to see if there was anyone else in hearing distance.

He tried to stare me down, but the hauteur spluttered out. He dropped his eyes. 'It was a hospitality thing. I was invited after a round of golf. It was totally innocuous,' he said sulkily, not yet quite able to surrender the reins of power.

'More than once.'

He shrugged morosely.

'And not something you wanted Isabel to know about?'

He sensed the possibility of a deal arriving. 'What do you want?'

'I want to know what really happened on the day Evie Salmon left Dinas.'

He looked off for a moment, weighing up his prospects. 'She arranged for me to meet her.'

'She contacted you?' I asked. I was surprised. His phrasing had put Evie in the driving seat.

He nodded glumly. 'That bastard Evans must

have given her my phone number. She asked if I had told my wife about her.' He looked at me, the mean flash in his eyes again. 'I know I shouldn't speak ill of the dead, but she was a malicious, scheming little bitch.'

'What had you been up to?'

'Nothing!' he protested indignantly. Then he remembered that this was meant to be a game of absolute truth. 'Okay, I drove her home once and we ended up having a necking session in a lay-by. Only once, and that was as far as it went. I think she must have been setting up her future options,' he observed bitterly.

'What did she want from you?'

'She wanted me to meet her in Dinas that afternoon, and then to drive her to the station in Hereford.'

'Why you, if there wasn't any relationship?' I asked.

'I asked her that,' he said, aggrieved. 'She laughed and said it was because I had the nicest car in Dinas. She told me she wanted to leave the place in style.'

'Where was she taking the train?'

'She was cagey about that. She wouldn't tell me. And she said she didn't want me hanging around the station after I'd dropped her off, trying to sneak a look. As if I fucking cared where she was going,' he snorted angrily.

'Did she say *who* she was going to see?'

He shook his head.

'Think harder,' I instructed.

'She was flaky, it was all just puff about clothes and cars and bands and how she never wanted to set eyes on Dinas again.' He paused. A memory surfacing. 'There was one thing, though.' He closed his eyes, concentrating. I didn't press. 'She said something like it was lucky that she hadn't told her boyfriend what we had got up to in my car. I asked why, and she said it was because he knew how to kill people. I asked if he was a soldier.' He paused.

'And?' I prompted.

'She didn't deny it. She just turned sideways in her seat and gave me that infuriating, simpering little grin that made you want to reach over and slap it off her face.'

The cog ratcheted round, bringing Greg Thomas another notch closer to Evie.

My phone rang when I was halfway back to Fron Heulog. It was Tessa's number.

'Hi,' I answered, conscious of the fact that she so often seemed to call when I had been at the Barn Gallery. Then I thought about the geography again. Or close to Fron Heulog?

'Hi.' She sounded chirpy. 'Are you free tonight?'

I thought about Greg Thomas. Nothing was likely to happen there in a hurry. 'Potentially,' I answered, curious.

'How about coming up here and I'll cook you a one-pot dinner on the camping hob to reinforce my apology.'

I felt my loins drop into soft focus. 'What about the crew?'

'They're going to the cinema in Shrewsbury. They'll be out till late.'

'I'll bring the wine.'

'Great.' She waited a beat. 'What are you lot doing down there? Sharon's just come back up the hill and said that the valley's full of policemen.'

'It seemed like a good day to go out looking for

bodies.'

'More?' She sounded concerned.

'I personally think it's a false alarm. I'll tell you about it later.'

'Right, but make sure you don't send all those men in this direction, otherwise my girls might be tempted to stay at home tonight.'

'What about you?'

She laughed. 'I'm not greedy. One reasonably athletic cop will do me.'

I finished the call with an involuntary grin on my face. But before I could get even flakier, another thought was arriving to fuck with my head. A confusing and disturbing one, riding in on a cold neural channel, dousing every vestige of libido. Triggered partly by the apparent coincidence behind Tessa's telephone calls. But mainly by the recall of the sign on the side of her Land Rover, and the spark of a hunch I had had when I had first visited the dig and had wondered whether there could be a Celtic connection. *Queen's University Belfast.* And her Redshanks? *They were mercenaries from the Western Isles of Scotland who hired themselves out into the service of Irish Chiefs.*

Northern Irish Chiefs?

More coincidence?

*   *   *

My head was still seething when I got back to the Fron Heulog barn.

'Friel,' I shouted over, 'go outside and have a fag.'

'That's all right, thanks, Sarge, I don't smoke,' he called back cheerily.

'Well go and look at the fucking birds then.'

He took the hint.

I took out the card Tessa had given me when I had first gone to her camp. Taking a deep breath to still the anticipatory fear, I dialled the number.

'Archaeology Department, how can we help you?' The voice was young, female and Ulster.

'Is that Queen's University Belfast?'

'Yes.'

'Can I speak to Dr Tessa MacLean, please?'

'I'm sorry, Dr MacLean's on a field trip, she's not contactable through the university switchboard at present.'

'Can you tell me where she is?'

'I'm sorry, but I can't give out specific site addresses.'

'I'm a police officer.'

'I'm still sorry, but I hope you understand that the location of an archaeological dig is very sensitive.'

'How about the wider geography?'

She laughed. 'I can probably manage that. She's in Wales.'

Then I called the real Queen's University number. The one that I got through directory enquiries. And discovered that Dr Tessa MacLean had retired two years previously. Aged sixty-three.

Why was she doing it? What was her relationship to Greg Thomas? And how the fuck were they funding this scam? All Tessa's helpers on a day rate? The fake line to the fake Queen's University staffer? I knew they were the wrong questions to be asking, but it kept me away from the personal side of things. The betrayal and the fear.

Like having to speculate on how close Tessa, or

whoever the fuck she was, had been to the actual events that had resulted in the burial of Evie Salmon and those nameless people on that cold stark hill. And the atrocity committed on Bruno Gilbert. Not to mention poor Mary Doyle and the shade of Anthea Joan Balmer.

I also had to accept that she had only been getting close to me to keep tabs on the progress of my investigation. So that she could report back to keep up the flow of obstacles coming downstream at me.

That report of the Peeping Tom at her caravan? Pure baloney. It had all been prepared to get me up there and out on a fruitless chase after Greg Thomas in the snow, so that he could get back and ream out all the available information in Unit 13. But she had allowed a sexual possibility to build. Only to have the discovery of the theft of Redshanks curtail it. The prospect of a grope had obviously been considered an acceptable sacrifice in the line of setting me up as the dupe.

So what was the disappearance of Redshanks all about? Was that supposed to send us off on another safari? Another device to divert our attention?

And what was expected from me tonight? Was I going to be stuffed, basted and roasted, with an apple stuck in my mouth?

I got Friel to call the search squads back in when the mobile catering wagon arrived to dish out lunch. I had no appetite. I sat aloof in front of my laptop trying to make sense of this new Tessa discovery.

Mackay's call blew all that out of the water. 'If I didn't feel that I owed you something for all the shit

293

I've put you through over all the years I've known you, we wouldn't be having this conversation. In fact, I'm still not sure that what I did was bad enough to warrant this sort of fucking dowry.'

I sensed a genuine reluctance in him. 'On top of everything else, you went off with my ex-wife,' I reminded him, trying to clinch the deal.

'I can't talk about this over the telephone, or commit it to an email.'

I looked over at the search teams, who all looked happier now that they were temporarily in out of the cold, with their coffee and burgers and doughnuts. I was supposed to be in charge of this operation, I reminded myself. I was meant to be their shepherd.

I came to a decision. Emrys Hughes could take charge of the afternoon session. 'Can you meet me halfway?'

*   *   *

Mackay was already at the car park at the Elan Valley Visitors' Centre when I arrived. Or rather his old Range Rover was there. I had been through enough of these meetings now to know to wait in my car until he appeared. It was an old habit he couldn't kick, he had told me, making sure that the only people who turned up for appointments were the ones with genuine invitations.

Eventually, he materialized from a direction I had not been expecting, and was already halfway across the car park before I saw him. He looked tense and preoccupied, like a man on his way to an oncologist for the results of a second round of tests. It was his way of warning me that something grim was arriving in the delivery van.

'We'll use my car,' he instructed, when he got to my open window.

'Don't you want a coffee or anything?' I asked, indicating the visitors' centre.

He shook his head brusquely. 'I don't want anyone's walls or ceiling hearing this.'

On the walk across the car park, I gestured at the huge canted face of the dam behind the visitors' centre. 'Italians did the stonework on the Claerwen Dam further up the valley,' I informed him, punching a bit of pride into the statement, expecting some Wop banter from him in return.

Instead, he just looked at it blankly. 'This is bad fucking news, Capaldi.'

I knew that he wasn't talking about the Italians.

'How's Justin?' I asked warily, after I had climbed into the Range Rover, hoping that his mood or the bad fucking news wasn't anything to do with him.

'He's good,' he replied in a tone that told me he didn't want to talk about Justin. He turned in his seat to face me, his expression pained.

He was worrying me. I was not used to him being so taciturn. 'Thanks for getting back to me so quickly,' I said, trying to draw him out.

He was silent for a moment before he nodded, accepting my thanks. 'I can't give you any details.'

'I've signed the Official Secrets Act, Mac.'

'So has the postman. It doesn't work like that. There are levels of entitlement, and from where you're standing you can't even see up to this particular window ledge.'

'Five people have been murdered.'

He shrugged regretfully. 'That's chicken shit

compared to the potential repercussions that surrounded this operation.'

'You're talking past tense?'

'These things keep on resonating.'

'You can't tell me anything?'

'All the information is already there. The art is in stitching it together.'

What was he telling me? The official version was just a mask over the truth? A distortion? A shuffled pack? 'Rose Thomas wasn't the innocent bystander she seemed to be?' I tried.

'On the contrary.'

'Her death was accidental?'

He nodded. 'You're cold. Forget her. She wasn't instrumental to anything, not even a catalyst; she was just collateral damage.'

'What about Greg Thomas?'

He shook his head. 'Only as the reason she ended up in that wrong place. He doesn't figure either.'

Not to you maybe, I thought. But he was talking about a bigger picture, not a grim set of murders in Mid Wales. He was trying to lead me forward. I put Rose back into context. He had already told me that she had accidentally been caught up in some kind of a firefight. A bystander at a run-in with Loyalist or Republican paramilitaries? 'It was an anti-terrorist operation?' I postulated.

'I can't answer a question like that.'

I spun my thought process. 'How about a pub-quiz question?'

'Try me.'

'When was the Northern Irish peace process ratified?'

He smiled craftily, seeing the direction I was

taking. 'Good Friday, 1998.'

So, when Rose was killed, all the major players, Protestant and Catholic, would have been involved behind the scenes in the negotiations for a peace settlement. By that time there was probably a general consensus for this thing to succeed. So if the army was involved in a counter-terrorist action it would probably have been against some kind of radical splinter group who were trying to fuck up the peace process.

A realization was slowly dawning.

If the terrorists had been killed in that firefight, the process that had led us here wouldn't have started. The books would automatically have been balanced. So, Rose had died, but had her killers survived?

I shivered involuntarily. The motive was starting to take shape. I forced myself to stay calm and work through the bigger picture. 'Were some people imprisoned?'

'Ask yourself why that doesn't work.'

But it did work. It would make sense of the time lag. They are put away for Rose's killing, but, with different degrees of culpability, they received different sentences, which would account for the gaps between the revenge killings—if that's what they were—after they had been released.

Then I had to face Mac's truth. It didn't work because they would have been released into a supportive community. The killer might have been able to pick one of them off, but three would have been impossible. But he had managed to kill them, and cart the bodies to a remote cwm in Wales. So they must have been living in a background where they wouldn't have been protected or missed.

I nodded to myself as the next train arrived in the station.

No one had gone to prison. A gunfight with terrorists, an innocent bystander is shot and killed, but no one pays a judicial price.

'It wasn't a military operation per se, it was an intelligence operation. Or it turned into one.' I let him hear me thinking out loud. 'No one got blamed for it. The army covered it up.'

His expression remained open.

'And it was successful.'

His nod was virtually imperceptible.

The victims had given something up in exchange for immunity from prosecution. They had opened up to Military Intelligence. They would no longer have been able to function within their own community. By talking to the enemy they had signed their own death warrants.

Unless they were reinvented.

I looked at him carefully. 'Some bad people were given new lives?'

'Maybe.'

I had to be satisfied with that. It was as far as he could direct me while remaining within the limits of disclosure he had set himself.

17

Mac had told me to forget about Rose Jones. But I had to come back to her now. This was her story. Her death was central to the smaller drama that had splintered off and left five people murdered in a tiny valley in Mid Wales.

In a way it was a love story. Except it had turned ugly when the bereaved lover had refused to stay within the conventional orbit of grief and mourning. He had exchanged sackcloth and lilies for a blood curse.

If I was correct, because the three people he held responsible for his fiancée's death had been allowed to go free, Greg Thomas had undertaken a rite of vendetta. He had brought her killers back to her childhood home, and created a memorial of dead people for her. And had then spiralled off to kill two more in an attempt to stamp out the brush fires that our investigation had caused to flare up around him.

But how had he unlocked the secret of his victims' new identities?

That was the problem that was preoccupying me as I drove back to Dinas. It was an academic exercise—the three graves told us that he had identified Rose's killers—but it kept my mind off how I was going to deal with him when I got back to Fron Heulog. With nothing more than a non-attributable testimony.

He had waited all that time before he had made his first move. Which was why Rose's death hadn't set up any bow waves when I first heard about it. It seemed to have happened too long before to have any relevance.

That was the other thing that was niggling. The time frames. Why hadn't the alarm sounded? Why, after disposing of the first victim, had he been able to come back for the other two? Either the authorities had not alerted them, or no one had realized that the first disappearance might have a wider significance.

299

And then, about two years later, he went for the other two. A male and a female. Forensic and pathology evidence couldn't be precise about the timing of the burials, but the more I thought about it the more certain I was that they had been killed at the same time, even though they had been found in separate graves.

I pictured them as a married couple. Their joint killing was accounted for by the simple economics of effort. He couldn't just top one and expect the other to wait patiently for him to return. Okay, he had the risk of transporting two bodies, but what real difference was it going to make? If he was hauled over they weren't going to make things any worse for him on the grounds that he was carrying a bulk shipment.

I was deliberately using these exercises to keep my excitement suppressed. I was on my way back to Fron Heulog. I could easily run into Greg Thomas. I didn't want anything in my demeanour to betray my new knowledge, and possibly spook him.

Because I still had to try to tie him to Evie. I was wondering whether it would be worthwhile bracing Clive Fenwick again, when that whole realm of speculation crashed as I turned into Fron Heulog and approached the reception building.

Kevin Fletcher's car was parked there.

I reversed down the drive at speed, praying that he hadn't seen me. I was thinking furiously to save myself. I had made a supposition. I knew that three people had been killed. But what if there had been more of them? It was a long shot, but I was aware that I had just run out of options.

'Mac, its Glyn,' I was parked in a lay-by near Fron Heulog, stooped down in the seat, trying to

300

make myself as inconspicuous as possible.

He picked up the edge in my voice. 'Are you okay?' he asked, concerned.

'I know you can't give me details, but it's vital that I have one piece of information.'

'What?' His voice was harsh.

'How many of them were there?'

The silence stretched out.

'Mac?'

'Sorry, Glyn.' He disconnected.

I felt an immense wave of disappointment ride in to stretch the tension that was already wound up to the limit. I cut the connection.

My phone beeped. I opened the text message: '4'.

I closed my eyes in silent thanks.

Because that was how I could bring this to the surface without jeopardising Mackay or his contacts. We had found three bodies, but four people had been given immunity. We had one unaccounted for. I could claim that he was my informant. That he had contacted me to tell me about the deal, but insisted on anonymity. I could imagine the suspicion on Jack Galbraith's face. This guy coming forward now, out of the blue, was a bit of a convenient coincidence, but who the fuck cares? It was the result I was interested in.

I reminded myself that I didn't know if he was still alive. But, apart from the murderer and Military Intelligence, no one else did either. And if Greg Thomas tried to contradict me he would be demonstrating a bit more inside knowledge than was healthy for him.

A tap on my window brought me back to my uncertain present. Emrys Hughes was staring in at me with his mouth rammed open into a great big malicious grin. I smelled *Schadenfreude*. I also, at the very moment of seeing Emrys's twisted joy, felt my newfound certainty about Greg Thomas collapse. Some instinct was screaming at me that things were not right. I lowered the window.

'Your boss wants to see you,' he announced with relish.

'How did you know where to find me?'

He cocked his head back in the direction of Fron Heulog. 'We were all watching your stunt-driving performance.'

And by 'all', I knew that he meant Kevin Fletcher especially.

But at least I now had something else to give him. Trade-goods to barter for my perceived desertion. Because my sudden and perverse loss of faith meant that I would not be giving Greg Thomas up to him. The intimation was telling me that I had to keep him to myself for the moment. It was frustrating, but on a deep and currently impenetrable level I knew I had to run with it.

I had my victims, and in Greg Thomas I had a guy with a motive to kill them. I even had the Saint Rose that they were dedicated to. So why, on a deep instinctual level, was I suddenly not sure any more? I had picked up a nagging doubt. Was there a flaw somewhere I couldn't quite see? An inconsistency? Or was the problem that it all flowed forward so perfectly?

Instead of clarity I now had more ink in the goldfish bowl. I recalled what Clive Fenwick had told me of Evie's boast. And, when I took the Greg Thomas blinkers off, I had to accept that there was more than one soldier in this valley. If I offered

302

Greg Thomas up to Fletcher it would set off an irrevocable chain of events. But that chain might just be another paper trail that had been laid out for us. Another baited trap. Just like Evie and Bruno.

Because I kept coming back to it. How would a civilian, which is what Greg Thomas had been when the deeds went down, have been able to access and act on such secret and sensitive material as the new identities and locations of the victims? The needle kept swinging back round to that obstinate point.

I felt like a recaptured escapee being brought back in under the jeering eyes of the camp guards. Fletcher had recalled the search parties. Groups of men hung around in small knots waiting for the coaches. In age and dress they were wildly different from the youths who had shared this space not that long ago, but both parties had the same sullen expression. They had obviously not enjoyed their day in the country. And, from the looks I was getting, I was the bastard to blame for that, which I had probably compounded by abandoning them.

Fletcher was standing outside the door to the reception office with Greg Thomas and Trevor Horne. Both men stared at me as Fletcher registered my arrival and strode across the car park towards me. I got out of my car and turned my head away from them, not wanting my expression to betray anything.

When I turned back, Fletcher was standing silently in front of me, making a show of looking me up and down. 'Pretend that this is a hotel, Capaldi, and that you are our guest here.'

'Why is that, boss?' I could tell that he had been rehearsing this and that something clever was arriving.

'So that as the manager of this establishment I can tell you to pack your bags and fuck off.'

'You're making a mistake, boss.'

'That's what they all say.'

'Can we talk about this in private?'

'There's nothing to talk about.'

'You'll regret it.'

His eyes lit up. 'Don't try threatening me, Capaldi. You've just been caught bang to rights in the dereliction of your duties. What were you doing anyway? Sloping off for a quick fuck? Having a couple of stiff ones with your lush-buddy in The Fleece? I promise you, the Union won't be able to help you squirm out of this one.'

'If you're not going to listen to me, Kevin, I'm going to have to go directly to DCS Galbraith with this.'

I saw the two violently opposing forces grab him at the same time. Fury at my insubordination and dread at the invocation of Jack Galbraith. He was a seriously torn man.

'It's vital that we talk in private, boss,' I whispered, my tone offering allegiance and subordination again.

It was probably the whisper that swung it. He stared at me curiously for a moment, and then swept away imperiously towards the barn. I followed him inside.

'Well?' he demanded.

I scanned to check that there was no one within earshot. 'I know the identities of the bodies.'

His face blanched, and it was his turn to check for listeners. 'How the fuck do you know that?' he asked in a low, choked voice.

'An informant.'

'Where did you find an informant?' Surprise pitched his voice higher.

'He found me.'

His look turned wary. 'This isn't another one of your wild fucking hunches, is it, disguised as a legitimate source?'

'This is on the level, boss.'

He stared me down for a moment. 'You can give me names?'

'No, not yet. He refused to be that explicit. But he gave me the information to enable us to find out for ourselves.'

'Explain.'

'Those are the bodies of former Northern Irish paramilitaries. They were involved in some security operation that resulted in them being given a change of identity. Military Intelligence will be able to provide the original identities. They can then be cross-matched with living relatives. Their mitochondrial DNA will match that of the closest ones we can find in the female line.'

'Northern Ireland!' His expression skewed from puzzlement to bewilderment.

I nodded. 'DCS Galbraith will have to open up a direct line to the high echelons of the MOD to get access to the files. They're probably not going to be very happy about it,' I added, just to warn him that this was probably not going to be a particularly warm and friendly cross-cultural experience.

'How the fuck did we end up over there?' he asked, bemused.

'Someone died over there, boss, and someone else took their revenge.'

'Don't go all fucking cryptic on me.'

I wasn't being cryptic, I was working myself back into it. Because the mental itch had suddenly stopped. I was beginning to realize how the killer could have tracked down his original victims. I had just remembered something that Mackay had told me.

I also had a motive, but what spoiled it was some seriously fucked-up geography.

*   *   *

Fletcher turned away from me to digest it. I imagined he was rehearsing his call to Jack Galbraith. And all that wasted time, effort and the cost of manpower on the Bruno Gilbert sideline was probably also running through his head.

So much so that he wasn't ready to give it up yet. 'How reliable is this informant?'

'Totally.' I gave my invented informant an impeccable character.

He frowned. His mind was racing. 'Bruno Gilbert could have met them. Realized that these were the perfect victims, because they could be disappeared without any comeback.'

'Did Gilbert have any connections with Military Intelligence?' I asked, not unkindly.

He shook his head. He closed his eyes tightly for a moment to balance his burden. 'I'd better go and put that call in to DCS Galbraith,' he said reluctantly.

'At least we'll be able to dignify the victims with names now, boss,' I called after him as he left the barn.

I called Alison Weir in Carmarthen. I needed her to check something out for me before I confronted Greg Thomas. Otherwise, I could be alerting a guilty man and giving him a chance to flee.

In the interim, I had time to act on Tessa. Try to find out what her role in this was, and, if nothing else, neutralize her.

If I knew Fletcher, he would be making the best of a bad situation and moving up into Action Man mode. He would be striding into the fray, anxious to be seen as the guy who was on top of this case. The acolyte might have delivered the raw materials, but he was going to show how flare and élan went into producing the finished results.

And I had a big headache in the shape of Tessa. He was not going to like her apparent role being introduced retrospectively. I would have to argue later that he hadn't given me the time to bring her into the story.

I had suppressed her because she had got to me. It may have been manipulated, but that small touch of near intimacy we had shared still meant something. I felt that I owed it to her to make sure she was treated with some sensitivity. I wanted to be the one to brace her, rather than some faceless plods using strong-arm hick finesse.

I sneaked off the reservation before Fletcher could assign me to some bullshit duty. I commandeered Emrys Hughes and Friel as back-up. I told them to give me a five-minute start and then to follow me up to the dig in the Land Rover. And to stop anything that was coming down the other way in a hurry.

Emrys would have protested, but he was confused. He had delivered me to Fletcher, relishing the prospect of mayhem, and was now

307

wondering why I was still wandering around with my balls swinging free.

The morning's drizzle had kept the by-way up to Tessa's camp nicely muddy, and the car felt as if it was trying to make a break for an independent existence as it slewed and bucked its way up the track.

I would have seen the approaching Land Rover earlier if I hadn't been concentrating so hard on keeping the car under control. When I did register it, it was only fifty metres away on the rutted single-lane track we were both sharing. And it was making better progress.

Was Tessa making a break for it?

I turned the wheel sharply and skidded to a slanting stop to present the widest barrier I could, and jumped out and held up my warrant card. The Land Rover stopped in turn. With the setting sun in my face I couldn't see who was driving. But it soon became apparent that the Land Rover had only stopped to change down into low-ratio four-wheel drive, as it slowly heaved itself off the track and started to make the wide, lurching curve that would take it round and past my blockade.

I ran to intersect it, my feet splashing and slipping on the sheep-shit sludge at the bottom of the puddles between the grass and heather tussocks. How was I going to stop this thing? Jumping in front of it would be great pantomime, but short on results, and potentially lethal. It was at moments like this that I regretted that they didn't issue us with huge .45 Magnum handguns.

The window slid open. 'I don't want to stop or we'll bog down.' It was one of Tessa's helpers behind the wheel, smiling at me nervously, not quite in control of the big vehicle. The other three of them were also smiling.

'She's waiting for you,' she informed me as she went past.

Was that a threat or a promise?

*   *   *

The Redshanks camp had an empty feel to it. It had the air of a place that had run out of its purpose for being there. Had I been duped? Could Tessa have been smuggled out in the Land Rover? I berated myself for not having stopped it when I had had the opportunity.

The sun was dropping and lighting up the underside of the clouds above the western horizon with a vibrant burned-orange wash. From this elevation it was a beautiful sunset, the deep shade rolling across the valleys like something tangible. Of all the fucking evenings for the sky to get romantic, I reflected bitterly.

I knocked on the caravan door and stood back so that I could keep the rear window covered as well. I was in a turmoil. She was taking too long to answer. If she was in there she must have heard my arrival.

I was about to give up when the door opened. Tessa was in a baggy grey sweatshirt and black jeans, with a large towel on her head and an evolving look of surprise on her face. 'Glyn . . . you're early . . .' She let the surprise morph into a welcoming smile. 'That's not fair.'

'What's not fair?'

'You caught me washing my hair. You weren't meant to see the build-up. I was meant to be all primped, poised and perfect by the time you turned

309

up.' She stepped back from the door. 'Come on in.'

I walked in to the smell of water vapour and shampoo. She closed the door behind me. 'Why the long face?' she asked chirpily. 'And where's the wine you promised?'

I turned to face her. 'It's over, Tessa.'

She frowned. 'That's a bit presumptuous, isn't it? When nothing's actually begun.'

She was good. Her expression read amusement over controlled irritation. She was also very lovely, I thought, as she unwound the towel from her head and let the damp hair drop. She rubbed it absently with the towel as she watched me. She wasn't wearing a bra and her breasts oscillated with the movement. I wasn't sure whether she was deliberately building that distraction into the picture.

'You're not Dr Tessa MacLean.'

She raised her eyebrows and contemplated that statement for a moment. 'So who am I?'

'I don't know. I think that you were planted here to keep an eye on the gravesite. That's why you became buddies with Jeff in the beginning. Because there was always the possibility that the construction works wouldn't disturb the bodies and everything could just return to normal. But when they were uncovered, you attached yourself to me, so that you could follow my progress and report back.' She continued to watch me, deadpan. 'You got me up here the other night with that story of the intruder.' I stopped myself mid-flow. I had been about to say that the pointless pursuit in the snow had given him time to search my caravan, but that would have been achieved anyway, just by her calling me up here. So what had been the point of

310

that?

'And I suppose I engineered the theft of my Redshanks?' she asked, her voice flat.

I nodded, trying not to let her see that this was another thing that was puzzling me.

'Am I being arrested?'

'That depends on the extent of your involvement. It's not too late to start helping us. You could begin by telling me who you're working with?'

She nodded reflectively. 'Okay, where did we go wrong?' She laced the question with an unexpected tint of mockery.

'You should have lost the Northern Ireland connection.'

She turned away and took an anorak down off a peg. It surprised me. And it disappointed me. I had been expecting more of a reaction.

'You can dry your hair first. Change into something warmer.' I was trying to be a nice guy.

She gave me a withering look. At that moment I saw an intrinsic change in her. Something hardened. 'Follow me,' she commanded.

She went out the door. I took a couple of quick steps to catch up, and then slowed down when I saw that she wasn't trying to run. She was striding over towards the enclosure that had housed Redshanks.

She held the flap open and fixed me with her eyes as I passed through. 'I had hoped for more from you,' she said regretfully, 'but when you come out to the arse-end of the universe, what else can you expect but arses?'

I was beginning to get a bad feeling about this.

The light inside the tent was brighter than outside, and it was strangely quiet without the background noise from the small generator that had been keeping Redshanks' temperature and humidity controlled inside his plastic bubble.

Tessa opened a large box, took out some kind of an instrument, and whipped the cover off. It didn't look archaeological. It looked like something that should be sitting on the bridge of a new-generation warship.

She raised a flap at the rear of the tent and located the instrument on a peg on a small metal tripod. 'Look through that,' she ordered, her voice hard and cold.

It was essentially a pair of high-intensity binoculars incorporating night-vision lenses. I adjusted the focus ring, and the door of the Barn Gallery at Pen Twyn leaped out at me. There was an eerie green tinge to the image. I turned to her for an explanation.

She nodded at the binoculars. 'That's why I've been keeping tabs on you. You keep barging into my fucking investigation.' She gestured with her head down towards the Barn Gallery. 'Continually messing around with the Fenwicks.'

I read the warrant card she handed me. She outranked me. Christine Stewart, an inspector with the Metropolitan Police Art Theft and Forgery Division. The bad feeling was now here to stay.

'You kept giving us heart attacks every time you turned up down there. Were you going to give them the willies? Scare them off? Make them wonder if this place wasn't as safe as they thought it was?'

I nodded at the binoculars. 'That's how you knew I had been there? Why you kept wanting to know what I'd been doing?'

She nodded.

'Why didn't you tell me before? Why didn't you

312

warn me off?'

'Because you're not meant to know about this, even now. Local law enforcement is never informed of an operation in their area because it could change the dynamic of their dealings with the people under surveillance. I'm only showing you now to get you off my back. For good,' she added portentously.

'What have they done?'

She thought about it, and then realized that the damage was already done. 'They're smuggling looted archaeological treasures out of Iraq. Sending them back in the containers that they ship their meat pies out in. They're using this place for distribution.' She gestured towards the wind-farm site. 'Until your little lot erupted down there they thought that this out-of-the-way corner was as safe as it gets.'

'If you know all this, why haven't you rounded them up? Why haven't you seized the shipments?'

Her smile was pained. 'We have, all the stuff has been intercepted and electronically tagged. Now we want to know who's doing the buying.'

I spread my hands out in front of Redshanks' empty bubble.

She understood the question. 'He was our cover. It makes for great surveillance. An archaeological dig. How much more non-threatening and geeky can you get? A bunch of scatty bluestockings. We even exchange waves with them when we drive past the Barn Gallery.'

'Is he real?'

'It depends what you mean by real. As an object, yes. He's a kit of parts that gets trotted around surveillance gigs. We invent a different background story to suit the particular situation.' She chuckled mirthlessly. 'I obviously chose the wrong one in this case.'

I was even more confused. 'But I was here when the forensic anthropologist inspected him. She verified his provenance.'

She nodded, with more than a hint of superiority in the gesture. 'Because she was shown a high-level Home Office directive when she was in here, instructing her to confirm that the lump of carbon fibre and nylon we were calling Redshanks was the genuine article.'

I shook my head. 'You've no idea what an awful coincidence this has been. Starting with your choice of dig site and the university you used for a front.'

'Reflect hard and verify before you jump to conclusions in future, Sergeant.'

I coloured at the rebuke. 'I'm very sorry, and I promise you this won't go any further.'

'I know it won't.'

We heard the sound of the engines at the same time. Tessa's team's Land Rover crested the rise first, closely followed by Emrys and Friel's. I winced inwardly. The girls had obviously been stopped and shepherded back up the hill. And I knew that if Tessa asked Emrys he would just look sulky and tell her that he had been following my orders.

She groaned theatrically. 'And now it gets even more fucking heavy-handed.'

'I'll get rid of them.'

She gestured down towards the Barn Gallery. 'And while you're at it, why don't you all jump up and down and wave before you go?'

'Do you want me to go and see Gloria Fenwick and make up some sort of reason for us to be up

314

here,' I suggested helpfully, but already knowing that this attempt to rehabilitate myself was hopeless.

She shook her head. 'No, Sergeant Capaldi, I just want you gone.'

I looked at her for a moment, a thought surfacing. 'Did you know my history?'

She thought about not answering, but then nodded slowly. 'When the bodies started appearing down there I asked for background details on all the officers who might be crossing my path.'

'So you knew about Kevin Fletcher and me?'

'The gist of it.'

'So why did you make a point of bringing it up the other night at The Fleece?'

'I wanted to see how you would handle the pompous son of a bitch.'

'And?' I prompted.

'Don't you remember? I took pity on you and rescued you.'

I swallowed and took a breath, and set hope into my face. 'I don't suppose we could take a memory pill, and start off with me knocking on your door again?'

She looked at me carefully for a moment. A smile almost formed. 'If it's any consolation, my interest wasn't totally confined to work.'

But no memory pill.

18

Why couldn't she have come up with some petrified Anglo Saxon axe warrior, rather than Redshanks,

I grumbled to myself as I slunk down the hill following Emrys's Land Rover. Then she could have pretended to have been employed by the University of East Anglia, or some equally neutral institution. That way I would probably now be arriving at her caravan door with a bottle of wine, a new shave, and my label as Quaintly Attractive Welsh Detective Sergeant still intact.

A missed-call message beeped when I got back into the valley. It took me a moment to recognize the number. Alison Weir. I put out a silent prayer of thanks that she had responded to the urgency of the request.

After I'd heard what she had to tell me, I sat there silently contemplating my next moves, trying to work my way through the foreseeable variables, and hoping that the unforeseeable ones would fall kindly.

It was now fully dark. Time to go calling.

'It's late, Sergeant.' Valerie Horne's voice was tetchy over the intercom.

'It's very important, Mrs Horne. Can you tell your brother that I urgently need to talk to him.'

'Is he in any kind of trouble?' her voice lowered protectively.

'Not if he's prepared to be totally straight with me.'

She buzzed the gates open. As I went down the drive I was aware that she would be reporting what I had just said to Greg Thomas. I had now shown my hand. I had to hope that it was the right one. Because I was also aware that there could still be two of them involved. But, if there were, I was at least now fairly confident that it wasn't Trevor Horne that I had to worry about any more.

316

The security lights were on outside the reception building, but without the search parties or the gang youths hanging about, the yard had an air of desertion, like a shut-down film set.

Greg came out of the house and crossed the yard. 'We'll use the office,' he announced gruffly as he passed without stopping. I followed him up the steps to the door. He unlocked it and threw a half-eaten apple out into the night.

He formalized the encounter by sitting behind the desk. I sat down opposite him. 'What's this all about?' he asked, his expression and tone hostile. I looked up at the buddy photograph above his head and silently rebuked myself for not having foreseen this possibility before now.

'By our best estimates, Evie Salmon was murdered, butchered and buried approximately six weeks ago. Can you tell me where you were then?'

He scowled. 'You're not serious?'

'I'm very serious, Mr Thomas.'

'And I've already told you that I never knew her. Are you making me out to be a liar?' he asked truculently.

'No, I'm just trying to find out what your movements were about six weeks ago.'

He considered protesting again, but thought better of it. 'Here, I suppose. Around here. I haven't been anywhere for a while.'

'So you haven't got any particular alibi?'

'What would I need an alibi for?' The question had genuinely surprised him.

'We think we know the identity of the bodies we've found up at the wind-farm site.'

'What has that got to do with me?' he asked, puzzled.

317

'They were the paramilitaries who were involved in the incident when your fiancée, Rose Jones, was accidentally shot and killed.'

He just stared at me uncomprehendingly for a long moment, his mouth open. 'Oh, Jesus!' His hands came together as if in prayer, and his head drooped over the desk. 'Oh, for fuck's sake . . . Oh, Christ . . .' His head started shaking rhythmically.

'Is there anything you want to tell me?'

He turned the head-shake into a negative.

I waited him out.

Eventually, he looked up. His expression was still etched with shock and his eyes were ghastly. 'You can't think that I had anything to do with this?' Shock had gone deep into his voice as well.

'At first, I thought it was you. Just the way I was meant to.'

'What do you mean?'

'He's set you up, Greg. He knew that once we'd started down this line we would discover that you're the one with the motive.'

He looked suddenly frightened. He shook his head in a sharp denial. But he had made the same connection. He knew exactly who I was talking about.

'What was puzzling me was how you could possibly have obtained the information about where to find the victims,' I continued. 'You were a civilian by then. And then I remembered that I'd been told that Owen Jones had transferred to Military Intelligence. It slotted together. You had the motive, but he had the same motive, and an advantage. He had the means of access to the information.'

He shook his head weakly, still trying to make

318

sense of it. 'He's my best friend.'

'I don't think Owen has friends. Not in the way that you or I would think of them. I don't know him like you do, so perhaps I can see it better, but I think that he treats people as utilities that can be brought into play whenever a particular occasion calls for it.'

But he still wasn't ready to accept it. 'If he wasn't my friend, why did he introduce me to his sister?'

'Because he needed to be in control of who she was going to marry.'

'But he didn't know I was going to marry her,' he protested.

'Then he would just have continued to bring carefully selected buddies home until, finally, she did. But, crucially, they would have been his choice. He would have done the initial screening. You may not have realized it, but you would have been vetted for suitability before you were invited to Cogfryn. That's what he was doing for his sister. As far as he was concerned, he was in charge of her life. Always had been. Those three people took that away from him, and for that they had to die.'

'He let me buy Fron Heulog,' he argued, shifting to another tack.

'Not because you were his great good friend, but because you were a part of Rose. He had already decreed that the two of you were going to live there. It was just continuity. But now that the Bruno Gilbert ruse looks like it might be about to run aground, he needs another fall guy. I'm afraid you became expendable, Greg.'

'Why?'

'Because, at the end of the day, he could apportion some of the blame to you. If you hadn't

319

done that tour in Northern Ireland, Rose wouldn't have come over to see you, and she wouldn't have been killed.'

Another cog creaked round. 'Do you drink whisky?' I asked, while he was still digesting that.

He frowned at the randomness of the question. 'Yes.'

'Bunnahabhain?'

'Amongst others; I've got a thing for Islay malts.'

'Can you show me?'

He got up. By now he knew better than to question me. I followed him across the yard to a single-storey extension on the side of the main farmhouse.

'This is my apartment,' he informed me as he unlocked the door. 'Val and Trev use the main house.'

He led me into an open-plan living room and kitchen with a vaulted ceiling. It was bachelor red-and-cream, with a wood-laminate floor, black leather three-piece suite, and blond-wood furniture. The room was clean and tidy apart from the remains of his dinner, which were still sitting on a glass coffee table opposite the television set.

He opened a cabinet. I saw bottles stacked in rows, more than I could count at a glance. I made out Ardbeg, Bowmore and Lagavulin before his back blocked the view.

He turned round frowning. 'I was sure I had a bottle.'

'It's gone?'

He nodded, puzzled by the absence.

'And Owen was round here recently?'

'Yes.' He frowned again. 'What's the significance?'

'Bruno Gilbert was forced to drink most of it.'

He took that in and his expression blanched. 'That couldn't come back to me?' It was more plea than question.

'On its own it's only circumstantial. But it's all part of the Gestalt.'

'What does that mean?'

'The bigger picture adds up to more than all the little parts taken individually.'

'Is there more?' he asked anxiously.

I looked round the room. I felt a twinge. It was almost spectral, as if I was picking up a trace of the same intruder who had been in Unit 13. I just knew then that the place had been seeded. Probably the bedroom. If I hadn't stalled in my original purpose and had taken Greg Thomas to Fletcher after all, I was convinced that a search warrant would uncover at least trace evidence of Evie and Bruno here. Enough to keep the finger pointed.

'Where does Owen stay in the UK when he's not at Cogfryn?'

'He's got a cottage in Port Eynon on the Gower Peninsula.'

The gears whirred, meshed, and locked home.

'Have you been there?'

'Yes. It's an annual event. A long weekend. Sea fishing and surfing.'

'Did you ever make any impromptu visits? Just turn up?'

He shook his head. 'No, you don't do that to Owen. He likes everything organized.'

'When you were there, were there any signs of a woman living there?'

'There were always girls' things around, wherever Owen lived.'

'But you never met any of them?'

'Not there.'

Where would he have shipped Evie off to, I wondered. I was distracted from this speculation by the sight of Greg frowning and shaking his head.

'What's the matter?' I asked.

'This doesn't work.'

'Why not?'

'Owen's in Nigeria. I drove him to Birmingham Airport myself.'

'That's right, you saw him onto one plane. And I'd already checked that he'd got on the flight in London. He was out of the picture. Africa makes great cover. Or so I thought. That's why you eventually became my target. But I've had one of my colleagues check again. He left that flight in Paris. Which gave him plenty of time to get back.'

'He came back here?' He knew it was a pointless question, but it gave him time to adjust. He shook his head, still confused. 'Where's he been staying?'

'That's been bothering me too. But he was brought up here, he knows the area like the back of his hand. So where could he find total concealment?'

'One of the Cogfryn barns?'

'Too close to home. The farm dogs would sense him. No, I think that he might have literally gone to ground.'

*   *   *

I drove up the approach track to the gold mine with my headlights full on. If Owen was watching, I wanted him to realize that this was the only car, and that I wasn't sneaking up.

322

I stopped in front of the gates and put the call in.

'Where the fuck are you, Capaldi?' Fletcher demanded.

'I can't say, boss. I'm calling to tell you that the man we're after is Owen Jones, the brother of Rose Jones, who was killed in Northern Ireland. He's got a house on the Gower Peninsula. You'll get the address from Greg Thomas at Fron Heulog. I think we'll find that that's where Evie was living.'

'Are we going to find him there too?'

'I don't think so. He's going to be going on the run. We need to get a bulletin out to airports, stations, ports and all mobile units.'

'*Going to be . . .?* Are you adding fortune-telling to your fucking skill set?' he asked angrily.

'This is more than a hunch.'

'I want you back at The Fleece.'

'Later, boss.'

I disconnected, cutting him off in mid-protest. I had a bloodbath to try to avert.

I had to climb over the gates, which had been secured with a new padlock. I walked down the line of the static cortege of ruined and bramble-choked cars and past Bruno's shack, which seemed to have taken on even more of a list. That same sense of attenuation was in the air, as if we were working to different natural rules on this side of the fence.

At the sluices the cover of the mineshaft was closed. But I had already decided that he had to have a way of opening it from the inside.

Because I had figured out that Owen had set the mine up as home base. An intuition that I desperately wished I had never received. Because now, in all conscience, I was going to have to act on it.

323

After he had murdered and buried Evie, when the situation with the burial site was still in flux, he could have remained at a safe remove, monitoring things from a distance. But once the bodies had been discovered he had to move back in. First, to kill and set up Bruno. Then, when I looked like fucking up his diversionary plan, to keep close to what I was getting up to.

But everyone had to believe that he had returned to Nigeria. He had to stay hidden. Once we had cleared it of its crime-scene status, what better place to go to earth than a creepy mine tunnel?

This was his old stomping ground. He was probably using a motorbike or a quad bike to get around. With his intimate knowledge of the country he didn't even have to stick to the roads. This was where he and Rose used to play as children. He had demonstrated that he knew his way around the mine when he had sneaked Evie's dress into Bruno's substitute-mother's boudoir.

He was either already in there, or he was soon going to return. Either way I had to set the meeting in motion. I wasn't looking forward to it, but I owed this to a lot of dead people. And to people who were alive at the moment who I didn't want to see dead.

I had prepared Fletcher for the possibility of Owen going on the run. I could be prescient about it because I was going to grant him that option. Not as any kind of favour, but because the vital thing was to get him out into the open. He would be armed and he could take people out as they approached down the tunnel. He could do too much damage in that confined space.

How much of a surprise would my arrival be to

him? I wondered. Did he still think that he was in control? Or was desperation starting to set in?

The important thing was not to surprise him.

I stood at the top of the shaft. 'This is DS Capaldi. I am alone and unarmed, and I am coming in,' I declaimed into the evening air, hearing my voice drift onto the hillside, sounding like a prat.

I opened the hatch and climbed down to the bottom and repeated the announcement. I felt the terror close in as I got down on my hands and knees and started to crawl along the first tunnel. Even with the beam of my torch filling the space ahead, the light seemed to have a sinister quality, an absence of anything warm or spiritual, the tunnel walls striated and facetted, as if they had been gouged-out by a huge and desperate burrowing thing. Claustrophobia manifested itself in a sense that the tunnel was actually contracting behind me. Collapsing like a rotten artery, cutting off my escape route.

I was hyperventilating and sweating. I had to convince myself that these were all sneaky tricks created by my mind in an attempt to make me abandon what it considered to be a fucking crazy notion and not conducive to the survival of the body that it was conditioned to preserve.

I stopped and forced myself to repeat my arrival announcement. 'This is DS Capaldi. I am alone and unarmed.'

It was strangely comforting to hear my voice rolling on down the tunnel. It broke the isolation. Even the torchlight took on a new vibrancy. I was my own good company. I felt the tension ease slightly.

I continued to repeat the announcement until I

reached the chamber Bruno had dedicated to his mother.

Inside, all the former smells of spinsterhood and latex had disappeared and been replaced by the same mineral dampness that pervaded the rest of the mine. I swung the torch beam round slowly. The furniture had been removed by Forensics. I played the light over the *trompe l'œil* painting of the window, which seemed even more sad and primitive now that it had lost the context of the pretend room.

I shifted the beam to the next quadrant, and illuminated the sleeping bag and inflatable mattress on the ground. But it wasn't those that made me catch my breath. It was the shapes behind them that seemed to have no logic in this place. And then all too much of logic, as their form and intent combined.

Gas cylinders.

So had Owen prepared a treat for our arrival?

I moved the torch beam again and a terror archetype overwhelmed me. The two dead things had been arranged on the floor in a simulation of sodomy. I forced myself to do a double take. Only one dead thing, I reminded myself, the realization diluting some of my fear. Redshanks was synthetic. And so, by elimination, the skeleton that he appeared to be humping, his sightless eye sockets and rictus grin adding demonic intensity to the performance, had to be the mortal remains of poor Anthea Joan Balmer.

I invoked a silent imprecation on the sick bastard, and then I was visited by blindness.

* * *

I had instinctively shut my eyes against the sudden incandescent flare of light that seemed to explode right in front of my face, but I still held the afterimage on my retina like a popped flashbulb.

I felt a tug on my torch. I resisted the reflexive instinct to clutch harder, and loosened my grip and let him remove it. I told myself to stay absolutely still.

'There's a shotgun pointed at you,' he warned.

I nodded carefully, acknowledging it.

'Turn away from me slowly, sit down and put your head between your knees, and put your hands out behind your back.'

I sank to the ground and did as I was told, trying not to remind myself that this was a classic execution arrangement. He slipped the loop of a cable clip over my hands and onto my wrists, and pulled tightly, the thin plastic cutting in painfully as the ratchets caught and held.

I opened my eyes experimentally. He had a huge flashlight trained on me. I could see nothing past it. I kept my head to the side, my eyes averted from the beam. I didn't want to look down; that would make me appear too much like a victim.

'What the fuck are you doing here?' There was a taint of tension in his tone, although he had obviously been aware of my presence for long enough for it not to have come as a surprise.

'I came here to head off the carnage.'

'Are there more of you outside?'

'No, I'm alone. No one else in the force knows I'm here. I promise you that.'

'That's a bit fucking stupid.'

'Listen to me.' I put command into my voice. It

was vital that he saw me as an equal. 'I worked it out, Owen. I knew you'd be holed up in here. And I knew you'd have guns. Probably more than that shotgun. I came here on my own to stop you killing other people, and then probably getting killed yourself.'

'Are you offering yourself as a sacrifice?' I heard the puzzlement in his voice.

'You won't shoot me.'

'No?'

'There's no advantage to you. Work it out.'

'You tell me.'

'You haven't been doing this at random. Every time you've killed someone you've gained something from it. It was justice with the ones you killed for Rose. Insurance from Evie. A diversion from Bruno. There's no gain from killing me. I'm a policeman. You'll just be hiking up the wrath-storm.'

'I would be gaining time.'

'That's what I'm offering you. You don't need to kill me for that.'

'What are you talking about?'

'It's over, Owen. I know what went down. Greg has realized too. Soon everyone else will. I'm giving you a head start.'

'Greg won't turn me in.'

'He doesn't have to. They know about your place in Port Eynon. No matter how carefully you think you've cleaned it up, we're going to find traces of Evie.'

He was silent, absorbing the logic of that. 'Why are you here? Why are you telling me this?'

'I've already explained. I want you out of here. Sooner or later, someone's going to put things

328

together the way I did. I don't want you here when they do, because they'll come in force and they'll come armed.'

'Since when have you cared what happens to me?'

'If we're being brutally honest here, Owen, I don't give a fuck what happens to you. But I do care about my colleagues. I don't want a load of twitchy cops facing up to an armed gunman in a mineshaft. You're going to end up dead, and the chances are that some other people are too, and I'm trying to prevent that. That's why I've come here to warn you. It's over now. But you still have some time left to act. If you stay here we'll find you. I'm not promising you anything. If you run we'll probably still catch you, but at least that way there's options open for you, and who knows, you might even get away.'

Without eye contact I had to imagine him weighing it up.

'I've got this place wired.'

'Why?' I had already figured that out, but it was important to let him hear my surprise. I needed to persuade him that this was out of character. An act of desperation.

'In case it comes to negotiations.'

'You're holed up in a rat trap, Owen. That's not the way you play it.'

'What are you talking about?'

'You're a planner and an enactor. A soldier. You work through the contingencies, calculate strategies, move yourself forward. But most importantly you give yourself space for manoeuvring. You're not the kind of guy to dig yourself into a hole and threaten to blow yourself up. That's for losers.'

'How the fuck do you know so much about me?'

'I recognized your gift to your sister.'

'Are you trying to shit me?'

I looked at him as directly as I could without scorching my eyes on his flashlight. 'Why did you bury them where you did?' I asked quietly. 'No matter how hard I looked at it, I couldn't see any significance in that place.'

The silence extended for so long that I thought he wasn't going to answer.

'When we were kids, Rose and I found a dead buzzard up there. Not a mark on it. We each held an outstretched wing and it was as big as us. Looking back, it had probably been poisoned. But to us it was perfect. It was as close as we had ever been to something wonderful. Something so powerful. So we buried it. And that became our special place.'

'You were very close to her?'

'She was my sister. She trusted me to do things for her. She relied on me. I found her future husband for her. When they had children I was going to be the best fucking uncle in the world.' He was quiet again for a moment. 'And then those bastards killed her!' he spat out.

'I heard that it wasn't deliberate,' I suggested carefully, 'that it might even have been our guys.'

'It doesn't matter. They were the cause of it. They killed Rose. They didn't deserve to just pick up a new life and go on as if nothing had happened. They had to pay.'

'We only found three bodies. What happened to the fourth?'

'He died before I could get to him.'

'His former compadres catch up with him?'

'No, thank Christ. If those pricks had got there first the others would have scattered. No, just to prove that there is a God in His Heaven, leukaemia got the bastard.'

'Did you use your MI contacts to find them?'

'I asked around. I had to be patient. I had to work fucking hard to find the right source.'

'That's why it took so long?'

'Yes.'

'You waited about two years after the first one. Why didn't the other two get spooked and cut and run?'

'Because I kept him alive.' I heard the pleasure in his tone.

'You imprisoned him for all that time?'

'No. Not literally alive. Only on paper. I kept paying all his bills.' He laughed. 'And spending his Social Security payments.'

'The other two were married?'

'The other two were bastards who gave up any shred of human dignity when I came for them,' he spat at me angrily.

I veered away from the danger topic and let him see me gesture towards the dead-sex tableau. 'I understand why you stole the skeleton, but why did you take Redshanks?'

'The what?'

'The body at the archaeological dig.'

'That thing's a pile of plastic.'

'I know.'

'The Northern Ireland connection spooked me. Then you and the so-called professor looked like you were getting chummy. I had to make sure that MI hadn't rumbled who the bodies were, and that you weren't pooling information with them. When I saw what they had in that tent, I realized it was a surveillance gig and had nothing to do with me.'

'You still took the body.'

'An exercise in disinformation.' I heard the cocky smirk in his voice.

'How did you meet Evie?' I asked it quickly, trying to fit it in as part of the seamless flow of the conversation.

He was silent. I didn't push it. I had heard the pride in his voice. He was enjoying the recounting. It went hand in hand with the power he felt he had over me.

'I was in the UK between jobs. I had just finished a tour in Afghanistan and was waiting for the security clearances to go through for the job in the Nigerian oilfields. I was having some renovation work done at home, so I was staying at Cogfryn. I saw her a couple of times standing by the road.'

'Near Pen Twyn?'

'A lay-by just down from there. The next time I saw her I stopped and asked if she wanted a lift. She said no, she was waiting for someone. But the look she gave me, I got the impression she was sorry about that. So, I went and parked down the road, just out of sight. I was curious.'

'Gerald Evans picked her up?' I asked.

'Yes. I was leaning against my car. I was looking buff, if I say so myself. I made a point of giving her the look as they went by.'

'You had a nice car?'

'BMW M3. How did you know?'

'Evie liked nice cars.'

'I went back there the next week. I could tell that she was attracted. She told me about the Evans gig, how it creeped her out, but she needed the money.'

'You offered to pay her?'

'That's how it started. It wasn't sex at first, it was just a bit of fun. I could afford it. And it stuffed Gerald Fucking Evans.'

'But you told her not to tell anyone about you?'

'That began as a bit of a joke. I was playing the man of mystery.' He went silent. 'Funny that, isn't it? Do you think these things are meant to happen? That somehow, even right at the beginning, subconsciously, I knew what I was going to have to do to her?'

I didn't want to get into a cosy speculation about predestination with him. I also didn't want to tell him that I knew why he had made Evie promise not to tell anyone about him. That he hadn't wanted his mother to know that he was hanging out with someone she would have regarded as inappropriate. 'She moved in with you?' I asked instead.

'She kept harping on about how much she hated Dinas. How she felt protected by me. How much she loved me and couldn't do without me. By that time, I was driving her up and down to the Gower on Saturdays. She was getting a feel for the place. I thought, Fuck it, she's attractive, not bad company, all right in bed, and with my job I didn't have to be around her all the time. Let her look after the place when I'm away.'

'What went wrong?'

'She lost her fear of the big wide world, and got to be a bit too fucking free. Started hanging around with the third-rate wannabe surfers down there. The dope-and-cider brigade and their mash-up barbecues on the beach. I was thinking of turfing her out the next leave I got, and then Mum sent me a cutting from the paper.'

'The wind farm?'

'Of all the fucking hills in Wales!' he declaimed bitterly. 'I panicked at first. Thought I could never go home again. Then I thought about Mum and Dad, what they would think when they heard. After that I started thinking a bit more carefully. That there was still a chance their excavations might miss the bit that was dedicated to Rose.'

'Or, even if they did, there was a way round it that wouldn't lead to you?' I ventured.

'It took some fucking working out,' he said, sounding pleased with himself. 'As I said, it's strange the way things fall into place. Because Christ knows how I would have managed it if Evie hadn't turned herself into a slut.'

'Or if Bruno Gilbert had been normal?'

'No one was going to miss him. It was a kindness, in a way. What kind of a life did the crazy old bastard have?'

I wanted to tell him that this place would miss Bruno, that his loss diminished the natural balance, but I forced myself to keep quiet. He had reached the end of his narrative. He knew that he had decisions to make.

*   *   *

I could tell by the movement of the torch beam that he had just checked his watch. I felt my heart rate surge. It was the gesture of a man who was preparing for action.

'Where's your car?' he demanded.

'At the gate.'

'Keys?'

'Left-hand pocket.'

'Turn round, face away from me.'

The torch beam jiggled. I heard the faint sound of metal against rock, and then felt his hand in my jacket pocket rooting for the car keys. He had had to put the gun down to release a free hand. Was there an opening? I flashed through the permutations, and realized that, with my hands tied and my back to him, I didn't even have surprise on my side.

And I didn't want to jeopardize his momentum.

He took his hand out of my pocket with the keys. I was conscious of him rearranging himself. He would have the gun under control again. This was the point, I recognized, where my forward planning had stopped. From here I had left it deliberately vague and fluffy.

'Let's move,' he ordered.

He went down the tunnel backwards in front of me, keeping the torch pointed in my face. I had to shuffle along like a penitent on my knees, my hands still tied behind my back causing me to sway painfully against the walls.

He stopped before we reached the entrance. I saw the shotgun for the first time as he poked it into the torch beam. The barrel had been cut down. It was a vicious short-range weapon. 'From now on you are going to be totally silent,' he instructed. He pushed the gun forward. 'Put your forehead against this.' I hesitated, hearing the tension in his voice. He jabbed the barrel at me, barely missing my right eye. I leaned forward until I felt the metal pressing on my forehead. He lowered his voice. 'I'm turning the torch off now. We're going to continue in the

335

dark, without a sound. If I stop feeling that pressure against this fucking gun, I'm just going to fire both barrels into the dark and leave what's left of you here. Understand?'

'Yes.' I wasn't going to argue. He had gone through a mood change. Now that we were moving, he had revved-up to righteous anger. He was cranking himself up for flight. Becoming more dangerous.

'Your life is now in your hands. Just keep your head pressed to the metal.'

The light went out. The centre of my universe was now a painful pair of third eyes that felt as sharp as pastry cutters against my forehead, and I made them the focus of my entire being as we commenced our shuffle down the tunnel again, him in front of me, moving backwards, as before.

We emerged into the shaft. He removed the gun barrel from my forehead, and grabbed my bound wrists and pulled me upright. It took me a moment to realize that we were no longer in total darkness. I looked up. Above me it was more deep dark blue than black. As I adjusted I started to make out stars. The hatch on the sluice deck above was open as I had left it.

'Turn round,' he hissed quietly.

I complied. This was where he was going to hit me over the head and leave me. I clenched my eyes shut and tensed myself, preparing for the violence.

The sudden sense of a cord tightening around my neck was even more of a shock because of its unexpectedness. I started to throw my head around to stop him getting a strangulation hold, but stopped when I felt the now familiar gun barrel tighten itself painfully against the hollow in the back of my head at the top of my spinal column.

'I'd stop struggling, if I were you,' he advised with a chuckle, sounding pleased with himself, 'the gun's strapped to the back of your head, so you'll either choke yourself to death, or you'll cause my finger to jerk on the trigger.'

'This is crazy, Owen,' I whispered, trying to fight down the hysteria that a sawn-off shotgun welded to the top of my spinal column was creating, 'I'm only going to slow you down.'

'Shut the fuck up, and start climbing,' he hissed, steering me over and pushing me against the metal rungs on the side of the shaft. He straddled me and pushed against my back in a tight creepy intimacy as we climbed up like a pair of conjoined and clumsy toads.

He stopped us just before the lip of the shaft, and, using the shotgun to control me like the stick on a Balinese puppet, he forced me to raise my head up over the rim. I was a human white flag. He was using me as a sounding board for either a searchlight or a shot.

But the night stayed still and dark.

'Okay,' he whispered when he was satisfied that the night was not going to break apart, and we continued the awkward stumble out of the shaft.

We stood there at the top of the shaft in silence as he took his bearings. The skewed geometry of the climb had caused the cord around my neck to nearly choke me, and I used the respite to haul in big reserves of air.

I was the only sound. I became aware of it. My heavy breathing was the only thing that was disturbing an otherwise total silence.

It was unnatural. The night seemed to be holding

itself in an expectant suspension.

He pushed me forward, using the shotgun like a goad to the back of my head. There was no moon, but the cloud cover was light enough to navigate by silhouette, the track showing up as a lighter entity between the darker masses of Bruno's twisted shack and the trees and matted undergrowth.

What was he going to do at the locked gate? I had mixed feelings about the problem that that was going to present to him. He was either going to have to take the risk of untying me to get me over, or he was going to have to abandon me on this side. But if he did that, what sort of a state was he going to leave me in?

We turned the corner on the track that led to the final approach to the gate. I did a double take. Was it a trick of the dim light?

The gate was open.

I tensed.

'What's the matter?' Owen whispered angrily, picking up on my reaction.

I shook my head. I could make out the darker outline of a car on the far side of the gate.

'Is that your car?' he whispered tensely.

'Yes,' I lied.

We shuffled forward. The night broke apart. The car's headlights erupted on main beam, pinning the two of us in the middle of the gate opening. The blue strobe light on top started flashing to reinforce the message. I turned my eyes away from the light onslaught and gagged as the cord tightened on my neck and the gun barrel gouged even harder into the back of my head.

'You bastard,' Owen hissed into my ear as he socketed himself against my back.

'I didn't—' I started trying to tell him that I was as surprised as he was, but he cut me off with a twist of the gun barrel that tightened the cord like a garrotte.

'There's a gun tied to the back of his head,' he yelled out.

The voice came out of the light. 'You're making things even worse for yourself, Owen.'

Kevin Fletcher. Of all the possible fucking saviours! What a bittersweet irony.

'You are covered by armed police officers,' he continued

'And I told you, this gun's tied to the back of his head. You can't take the risk. I'm a trained fucking soldier,' he shouted defiantly, 'and I promise you, if you force it, my last reaction will be to squeeze the trigger.' He twisted the barrel again. 'Tell them, Capaldi.'

'I'm strapped in pretty tight here, boss,' I managed to wheeze, the cord cutting in savagely above my Adam's apple.

Fletcher stepped out into the light, as if he had just walked into a photo opportunity.

This was going to be reported later as an incredibly heroic action on his part. But he had never been in any danger. I know because I was the dead meat between him and oblivion. The shotgun was secured so tightly to the back of my head that Owen had no field of shot. He had restricted his options. If he did shoot he wouldn't be given the opportunity to get the gun clear and load again. Whichever way it went, I would be the only victim on the side of the angels.

Fletcher walked towards us slowly. He was wearing the same overcoat that he had worn at

Evie's funeral. I hoped that that wasn't prophetic.

'That's far enough,' Owen warned.

Fletcher spread his arms to show that his hands were empty, and kept on coming. He had a strangely satisfied smile on his face.

He stopped immediately in front of me and leaned forward slightly so that only Owen and I would catch his whisper. 'We don't care.'

'What?' Owen asked, puzzled.

'We don't care,' Fletcher whispered again. 'In fact, you'd be doing us a favour.'

'He's one of yours,' Owen protested, not hiding his shock at the realization that Fletcher was talking about me.

Fletcher made a point of smiling at me. It felt like the equivalent of a final pat on the head. He turned to Owen and shook his head. 'Only on paper. In real life he's just fucking trouble.' He contemplated it for a moment. 'So there you have it. Your choice.'

He started backing away.

'Is he serious?' Owen whispered. I could hear the alarm in his voice.

'Probably,' I whispered back.

Fletcher started to raise his arm.

'Okay,' Owen yelled, 'I'm backing off.' I felt a painful whack on my back as the gun dropped free of his hand, and a sharp pain as if a long bamboo splinter had just been thrust down the length of my ribcage.

I caught Fletcher's smile flash triumphant, and, out of the corner of my eye, to make my humiliation complete, saw Emrys Hughes and his sidekick, Friel, move in to take charge of Owen. Fletcher had been bluffing. There had been no armed-response unit.

It wasn't in any training manual that had ever been devised. There was no such move as the deliberate place-your-colleague-in-jeopardy gambit. It was the sort of trick that, if I had attempted it, would have been condemned as irresponsible, dangerous and foolhardy. But he had the rank, the grooming and the PR nous, and I just knew that he'd be credited for a brilliant tactical move. Even if no one had bothered to consult the tethered goat.

But at least I had the consolation of knowing that it had worked. I had got Owen out of that mine, where he could have fucked up so many of us. And, as a reward, I was now left standing there with the gun still hanging from the cord around my neck with all the weight and psychological heft of a fucking anvil.

But what was perhaps even more disturbing was the expression that I saw on Fletcher's face as he directed a glance towards me.

Regret?

Or was I only imagining it?

SORTING THROUGH THE TAILINGS

And of course, Kevin Fletcher was the hero of the hour, while I came across as the dumbfuck patsy plod who had allowed himself to get caught up in the situation.

But even all that glory didn't stop him getting carried away with his metaphors and accusing me of being a fucking-vigilante-maverick-loose-cannon liability. Luckily, I was in the hospital at the time, getting checked out for various contusions and suspected cracked ribs, so I was able to work the sympathy vote. And even he had to grudgingly admit that I had produced the results. If I hadn't prodded Greg Thomas with the shock of enlightenment, Fletcher wouldn't have been able to sweat Owen's hideout in the gold mine out of him. So, in the end, my merit badges balanced out my misdemeanours, and I found myself right back where I had started.

The second time round that is. Dinas, not Cardiff.

Big deal.

I never did get round to asking Owen Jones how he had killed. Something warned me off. He was okay handling what he had done in the abstract, where he could convince himself that he had acted nobly for his sister's memory, and had been inventive in diverting our attention. But I had got the impression that if, while he had a gun to my head, I had brought it round to the practicalities of blood and butchery, his state of denial could have turned demonstrative.

342

We never found any of the heads or the hands. Portable and easily disposable, I suppose. We had had to satisfy ourselves with the theory that he would have used a shot to the head. It was a good one to adopt. It salved something. Death would have been quick.

The house at Port Eynon turned out to be Evie Central. He had been too cocky; he had assumed that we would never be knocking on that particular door. He hadn't cleared anything. The broad outline and the minutia of her life were still there. He was linked to her on every level, from the macroscopic down to fibres and mingled fluid stains on his mattress. And then we got really lucky. His cottage wasn't on mains drainage. We found blood, bone and soft-tissue residues that matched Evie's in both the pipe work and the septic tank.

Forensics revisited Bruno's treasure chest and started to find cross matches with fibres in the Port Eynon cottage.

He wasn't talking. But we had the victims and the motives and were building up evidence to place and fix him at the scenes where both Evie and Bruno had been murdered. The CPS was going to let us run with it. And I was going to be the star witness. Tidied up and popped into a suit, I was going to be the unfortunate hostage who had been held at gunpoint while Owen spilled his guts out to me.

I asked Jack Galbraith if I had a choice in the matter. This was too reminiscent of the PR fiasco they had woven around my fall from grace in Cardiff. That memory was still a raw wound. He had looked hurt, and then mean, and told me that my presence was so vitally important that unless

I went forward voluntarily, he was prepared to personally upgrade the damage that Owen Jones had inflicted, to improve my credibility on the stand.

Because we were only going after him for Evie and Bruno.

Jack Galbraith and the Chief Constable had been summoned up to the MOD. The other three bodies were going to remain a closed book. Stormont was going through one of its periods of seismic activity, and it was deemed politic to keep old wounds firmly sutured. It was assumed that Owen Jones would not be loudly confessing to the additional murders.

I made a point of keeping away from the Barn Gallery. I was too keenly aware of the focus on the place, and would have felt like a rabbit in the cross hairs. Not that I would have been welcome. The few times I saw Gloria after that in Dinas, she was polite, but distinctly standoffish. Either I had outlived whatever usefulness she had seen in me, or Clive had put in a good word for me.

David Williams got his wind-farm workers back in The Fleece. Although he confided in me that he was surprised that Tessa and the Redshanks crew had moved to another pub. I said nothing. That one still hurt. And then I heard that the Redshanks carnival had upped sticks and left town. Shortly after that, unmarked furniture vans were seen at the Barn Gallery, stripping the place, and the Fenwicks disappeared into folklore.

Tessa never did get round to taking the memory pill. Or if she did it was some other lucky bastard that she forgave.

I went round to Fron Heulog to try to make my

344

peace. They never raised the barrier for me. Their loss. It means the local weed will continue to arrive on the shithouse windowsill on Tuesday mornings.

The one piece of bright news that finally made spring blossom for me was that Justin brought Mary Doyle up to visit. She had made a complete recovery, apart from a small burn scar on her left temple, which she was happy to describe as 'funky'. And she and Justin had turned from casual friends into an item, and were now sharing a flat in Hereford, which had had the mains gas disconnected.

Justin still hadn't gone back to see his mother or his father. Although he did get me to go round to his father's to pick up his cat and to deliver it to the home that he and Mary were now able to offer it. And he was a regular visitor at Mackay's farmhouse, where he and Mary had been commissioned to paint a mural on the wall of the barn that was used to put corporate executives through their paces.

I stood at the back of a pleasingly large congregation of well-wishers and relatives when Anthea Joan Balmer was reinterred in the Bluebell Sector on a beautiful late-spring morning. I wished her a peaceful and undisturbed eternity.

And Gerald Evans?

Well, Gerald Evans was a case of slowly maturing vengeance that I was working on.

The big consolation I had on returning to normal cowboy duty was that my sheep molester had turned himself in. It transpired that he felt that his work was now done. He had been a breed fanatic who had been on a crusade to preserve the genetic purity of Badger Face Welsh mountain sheep.

345

And I had just taken a call from Emrys Hughes and agreed to help make up the numbers on a nocturnal stakeout that Inspector Morgan had organized. Normally, I would have told him where to stick his stakeout, but I was feeling the need to rehabilitate myself with the local force.

How was I to know that this was going to be the start of another terrible chain of events?